Marsali grew up near Edinburgh, Scotland. Her family holidays were spent in a remote cottage in the West Highlands, the region where her detective Gavin Macrae lives. Like her sailing heroine, Cass, she has always been used to boats, and spent her gap-year earnings on her first sailing dinghy, *Lady Blue*. She studied English at Dundee University, did a year of teacher training and took up her first post, teaching English and French to secondary-school children in Aith, Shetland. Gradually her role expanded to doing drama too, and both primary- and secondary-school pupils have won prizes performing her plays at the local Drama Festival. Some of these plays were in Shetlandic, the local dialect.

Death in a Shetland Lane is the eleventh novel in her much-loved Shetland Mysteries series.

MARSALI
TAYLOR

DEATH IN A SHETLAND LANE

ACCENT

First published in 2023 by Headline Accent
An imprint of HEADLINE PUBLISHING GROUP

1

Cataloguing in Publication Data is available from the British Library

ISBN 978 1 0354 0062 1

Typeset in 11/13.5pt Bembo Std by Jouve (UK), Milton Keynes

Printed and bound in Great Britain by Clays Ltd, Elcograf S.p.A.

Headline's policy is to use papers that are natural, renewable and recyclable
products and made from wood grown in well-managed forests and other
controlled sources. The logging and manufacturing processes are expected
to conform to the environmental regulations of the country of origin.

HEADLINE PUBLISHING GROUP
An Hachette UK Company
Carmelite House
50 Victoria Embankment
London
EC4Y 0DZ

www.headline.co.uk
www.hachette.co.uk

Contents

To the Westside Readers:
Catherine, Christine, Grizel, Gundel, Janet and Mary.
Thank you all for the amazing books I'd never have read
otherwise, the comradeship and, of course, the cake!

I

Dinna meddle wi' da Deil or da Laird's bairns.
(Don't meddle with the Devil or the Laird's children.)
Both will bring trouble.

All the section and chapter headings are taken from
Shetland Proverbs & Sayings
edited by Bertie Deyell, published by the Shetland
Folk Society, 1993,
by kind permission of his daughter Mona.
The English translation in brackets is mine.

Prologue

Da stane at lies no i your gaet, braks no your taes.
(The stone that doesn't lie in your path doesn't break your toes.)
Avoid getting into matters which are not your concern.

It was the night of the black moon. Yesterday there had been just the thinnest sliver of silver outlining one side of the dark circle, and tonight there was nothing, just blackness, so that Lizzie Doull stumbled into the chair in her attic room as she made her way to her bed. She'd taken off her frilled apron and barely started to unbutton her blouse when she heard the gate latch click. Outside there was a circle of light, a lantern moving up the path towards the front door.

It was her work to answer the door. She flung her apron back over her skirts, tied it at her back waist and began to hurry down the stairs, fumbling her blouse closed again as she went. The knocker sounded as she was halfway down, a tentative knock, as if the caller had seen the house was in darkness, then a second one, a loud rapping as if the business, whatever it was, wouldn't wait until morning. She reached the ground floor, smoothed her long skirts and went forward to undo the chain and bolts, and open the heavy door.

It was Joanie Williamson from the Haa o' Midbrake standing there. She'd kent him all her life. He was her father's age, and she remembered him from when she was a peerie thing. He'd

3

had a croft, but the speed o' him was like the sun upon the wall. His tatties were planted later than anyone else's, his sheep sheared last, his peats left on the hill to bring home as he needed them, so that he was taking the last of them off as the rest of the village was sharpening their tuskers for the spring casting. He went into Lerwick more often than they did, and sat in the pub yarning, and her father shook his head over him, and said he'd never come to any good. Well, Faither had been wrong, for two years ago last hairst he'd seemed to take a notion to himself, and smartened himself up. He'd courted a wife from Nesting, and all of a sudden he was like the man in the story, everything he touched turned to gold. A man from south took a fancy to his sheep and bought the lot at a ridiculous price, and with the money Joanie'd taken over the shop. His wife served at the counter, and he delivered the messages to the gentry, local goods along with fancy goods which nobody but gentry could afford to buy. Now he had two girls in service with him, one in the house and one in the shop, and a nursery-maid for the baby, and they all came along to the kirk on Sunday and sat in a pew to themselves just behind the minister's household.

Lizzie'd been watching his face in the kirk. At first he'd come in and plonked himself down with a defiant air, as if he kent fine he was pushing forward to make a silk purse of himself when he was nothing but a sow's ear; then gradually she'd seen new lines on his brow and a haunted look in his eyes. When he came in with his grand wife and two servant lasses coming before him, he'd give an uneasy look behind him before he pulled the door to, and as he left he'd look all around and pull his coat close to him for a moment, before he remembered who he was now, and straightened up again, ready to shake the minister's hand and greet him with a voice that was just too cheery.

Now his face was white as a sheet and his voice trembled as he asked if the minister would see him. He was sorry it was so late at night, he said, but his business was urgent. He made a

4

half-gesture towards the bulky parcel under his arm, then stopped, and clutched it to him.

'Aye, sir,' Lizzie said, as she'd been taught. The parcel was rectangular, the size of one of the tin deed-boxes she'd seen Mr Duncan the lawyer bring to the minister from time to time, and wrapped up in a blanket. She heard the minister's step on the stair behind her, and turned to him. 'Mr Williamson on urgent business, sir.'

'It must be urgent indeed to bring you out at this hour,' Mr Macraisey said. 'Give Lizzie your coat and come into my study, Mr Williamson.'

Lizzie reached for the parcel, to lay it on the table while he took his coat off, but he snatched it away from her hands with a growl of alarm, and held it firmly while she pulled first one sleeve then the other down and took his coat to hang.

'Mr Williamson's hat too, Lizzie,' Mr Macraisey said, 'and bring us a tray with two glasses.'

When she came in with the tray, they were sitting with serious faces, and the parcel was on the table, the blanket lying beside it. It was indeed a deed box, and it had been open, but as she pushed the door Mr Macraisey had leaned forward to close it, so that she didn't see what was inside. 'Leave the tray here,' Mr Macraisey said, 'and go back to bed. I'll show Mr Williamson out.'

He'd never said such a thing before, for he was one to stand on his dignity, the minister, but Lizzie wasn't going to complain about not having to wait up, except that she was curious. She couldn't wait by the door to listen, for the minister would be expecting to hear her steps go up the stairs, but she undressed slowly, listening for the front door, and when she went to bed she lay awake for a while. It seemed a long time later that there were steps in the hall, then the creak of the door and the glint of the lantern on her ceiling. She rose at that, keeping her face well back from the window so that nobody would see her spying. Both men were coming out of the house, Joanie Williamson still

5

with his parcel under his arm, and something long that she couldn't make out in his other hand, Mr Macraisey carrying the lantern. She watched as they went to the gate, across the track and into the kirkyard. The lantern shone on Joanie for a moment as he passed through the kirkyard gate, and she saw the long thing was a spade. They went to a corner of the graveyard where nobody was buried. Joanie and Mr Macraisey stood facing each other for a moment, formal-way, and then Mr Macraisey held a silver sixpence up in the light of the lantern, and Joanie took it, and gave him the parcel. She heard the crunch of a spade, and saw the blade flash in the pale circle of lantern light. Joanie was digging. She waited, and waited. At last the noises stopped. There was a long pause. She saw Mr Macraisey bend down and place the parcel in the hole, then hold the lantern while Mr Williamson covered it up, shovelling the earth as if he was afraid the box would come back up out of its grave by itself if he didn't get it covered quick enough. When all the earth was in, he stamped hard on the ground, then replaced the turf and pulled a piece of broken gravestone over to lay on top of it.

She saw their faces as Joanie lit Mr Macraisey back to the door. Joanie's was filled with relief; Mr Macraisey was grave and uneasy. He came into the house and Joanie bobbed away across the dark moor, his circle of light diminishing until he went over the rise and the darkness flowed in once more.

The next morning Mr Macraisey reminded her that she wasn't to mention people who came to the Manse; she was to forget she'd seen them. 'Are you remembering that, Lizzie?'

'Yes, sir,' she said, and curtsied. But she didn't forget Joanie Williamson's visit.

North Yell, five years ago

Her nan couldn't be left alone for long now. Lizbet didn't mind sitting with her, the last of these dark evenings before spring brought the bonny light nights. If Nan was sleeping, well, she could watch the music channel on the telly and dream of someday making videos like that: walking slim and athletic along Breckon beach at sunset, singing her heart out to the waves, or meeting a handsome lover in soft focus, or the 'in concert' ones with the cheering crowds, the lights dazzling the stage, and her in the middle of it, holding them spellbound. Sometimes, when Nan's head was clear, she'd chat away, just as she used to, asking Lizbet how her Saturday job in the shop was going, and what kitchen gadgets folk were spending money on nowadays: 'My mercy, did you ever hear the like? They must have more money as sense.' When her head was clouded, she'd tell stories, mostly ones Lizbet had heard over and over, tales of her time in service at Busta House as a girl between the wars, or of working at the camps when oil came to Shetland. Her husband, Lizbet's great-grandfather, had been killed in the Second World War, in the east, and Nan had met an American in the camps, and nearly gone off with him to Texas. 'Imagine that! You could all have come and visited me on a ranch, just like in the Westerns.' Sometimes she reached further back into her memory and told some of her own grandmother's tales, the tale of the Trow o' Hakkrigarth, and the night she saw a ghost walking home from a wedding dance, and the one she was starting on now, the story of how when her grandmother had been in service at the old manse, she'd seen the minister bury something in the kirkyard one night at dark of moon; the tale her own grandmother had told her when she was dying. 'I'd never heard it from her before,' Nan said. 'She said someone ought to ken what was buried there.' Nan's faded blue eyes looked uncertainly around the room. 'I think I should maybe tell someen now. It mustn't be dug up again, never. But then, you're a young lass, and it maybe shouldna be you I tell.'

Lizbet was intrigued. 'Mam's no' home, so if you need to tell someone it'll have to be me. So what was in the box? I thought she didn't see inside it.'

7

'That she didna. It was later that she put twartree rumours together and worked out what she'd seen. The way Joanie had prospered, after being the most pushionless creature, and the minister giving Joanie the silver sixpence, and taking the box, and burying it.' Her Nan paused for a moment, struggling for breath. 'The thing that the minister bought and buried in that kirkyard was the Book o' the Black Arts.'

Chapter One

Tide times, Brae:
LW 00.32 (0.98m);
HW 06.30 (1.66m);
LW 13.03 (0.75m);
HW 19.15 (1.66m)

Moonset 06.30; sunrise 07.23; moonrise 12.18;
sunset 19.04. Moon waxing gibbous.

Der had a craa's court apon him.
(They've held a crow's court on him.)
He has been judged and sentenced by a clique with no defence allowed.

The girl in the dark coat was huddled up at the far end of the beach, head bent, knees up against her chest, back pressed against the last corner of the low bank running around the beach edge, as if she had run as far as she could and pressed herself against the earth in the hope it would hide her. I glanced up at the road above the beach. There was a car there, parked where the track ended in moorland, wheels only just on the gravel, bonnet sticking out over the heather.

I ran the motorboat onto the beach halfway along, pulled her up enough to hold her and scrunched towards the dark hunched shape at a steady pace, not quite making as much noise as I

9

could, but scuffing enough so that she would hear me coming. The brown head turned further seawards, the body made a little turn so that her back was square on to me. The feeling I should respect her privacy struggled with knowing something was badly wrong here. She was young, I could see that, a lass in her late teens or early twenties, and I was an adult who spent her days in charge of teenage trainees on board a tall ship. I couldn't walk by. I took a deep breath and went almost up to her, stopping ten metres short and sitting down on a handy rock. 'Fine day for a walk,' I said.

She hunched one shoulder towards me. 'Aaright,' she agreed. *Now leave me alone* was unspoken. I stayed put and waited. 'No' as cold as it might ha' been in March,' she added. She had a singer's voice and a Yell accent; that aa sound was unmistakeable. Only Yell folk could pronounce the Norwegian town Å properly.

I'd heard that voice before. I tried to place it and visualised coloured lights, the boating club, this same voice joking, 'No' as cold as it might ha' been in June.' Outside. Some sort of doo, Regatta day maybe, and they'd set up a stage in front of the club, beside the barbeque queue. Local bairns with fiddles and accordians, and several fledgling groups, and this girl had been the singer in a group . . . *No' as cold as it might ha' been in June*, and then she'd launched straight into one of those fifties show songs. 'June is Busting Out All Over', the sort of title to bring out the worst jokes from sailors who'd had a dram. She had a beauty of a voice, rich and full, lower than you'd expect from a young lass – and with that I got her pedigree. She was one of my friend Magnie's Yell cousins.

I said that first, by way of reassurance. 'You're Magnie's cousin, are you no'?' My memory was fighting for her name. Elizabeth, no, Liz. Lizzie . . . Lisbeth. I said it. 'Lisbeth.' It didn't sound quite right. 'No, Lizbet, isn't it? You're the one with the amazing voice.'

I'd meant to be complimentary, but I'd hit the wrong nerve. She gave a wail and buried her head in her knees. Her shoulders shook with sobs. She poured out an incoherent sentence which ended with an impassioned *no good* and lifted a tearstained face to glare at the waves.

I gave the boat a quick glance, noted that the cats had jumped out and were investigating the tideline, yellow and pink life-jackets bright against the brown seaweed, and shifted to a closer rock. 'If someone's saying your voice is no good,' I said firmly, 'they're talking nonsense. Your voice is very good. I heard you only once, it must have been two regattas ago, nearly two years, and I remembered you.'

She shook her head and sniffed, then drew her hand across her eyes and stared bleakly across the tumbled waves of the Røna to the hills of Vementry behind. Then she turned her head to look at me, half-shy, half-shamefaced. 'It's no' my voice. It's me that's no' good enough. I'm no' pretty enough.' Her voice cracked. 'It doesna matter how good I am, how much work I put in, if I'm no' sexy as well.' She put her head back on her knees for a moment, then lifted it again, resolutely blinking the tears away. 'You're Cass, aren't you? You're that brown I took you for a tourist.'

'My ship's been in Africa,' I said. It had been stickily, blazingly hot, and in spite of all the high-factor suntan lotion I'd slathered on, the scar on my right cheek ran white across my tan.

Lizbet wasn't worrying about my scar, though that was probably what had reminded her who I was. 'You ran away to sea, because that was all you wanted to do. You were sixteen, and got on a tall ship in France and never came back to Shetland till two years ago.'

I shouldn't have been surprised that she knew all about me. Magnie knew everything about everyone.

'But suppose,' Lizbet said, 'suppose the ship wouldn't take

you? Suppose you'd turned up and they said *You're too small* or *We don't want girls*. What would you have done then?'

'She was a sail training ship, and I'd booked my passage, so I knew she'd take me.' I stuck my chin out. 'But I'd have found another ship. I worked, I did waitressing and dish-washing, just to get to sea, because it was what I wanted.' I looked at her flushed face. 'Not just wanted. Needed. I needed it more than anything in the world, more than exam results or boyfriends.' I let that thought linger for a moment, then said, 'But don't tell me you're not getting gigs locally.'

She nodded, and shuffled round towards me, uncurling her legs a little.

'Have a rock,' I suggested. 'It's less damp on the bum.'

She nodded again, and came stiffly upwards, then sat down, facing me, and with her back to the chilling wind. 'It's never been a problem here in Shetland. We've done loads of gigs, me, Tom, he's the guitarist, and Chloe.' Her voice snagged, like a kinked rope hitting a block, then continued. 'She's my pal, she does backing vocals. We do pubs, and clubs, and this year we've been asked to do a set at the Folk Festival. Only, today, well,' she gestured back towards Brae. *'You're the Stars!* You ken, the TV talent show. The auditions, in the Hall here, and in Lerwick tomorrow.'

Ah. Her ambitions and dreams and talent had hit the commercial world head on. When there were dozens of good singers about, the ones who got further all happened to be slim, tall and pretty.

'We applied,' Lizbet said. 'Ages ago, as soon as we heard about it, and they gave us a slot. It wasn't televised or anything, like, just the heats to possibly be in the regional heats next month. I was so nervous, because to get that kind of exposure, it's everyone's dream. I thought it went well.' She paused, then repeated, firmly, 'It did go well. We sang a couple of crowd-pleasers, you know, 'Love is Like a Butterfly' and 'My Heart Will Go On',

12

with me doing the leads and Chloe harmonising, and they seemed to like us. Then the presenters asked us to swap round, Chloe singing lead, just for one song.' Her mouth twitched. 'Well, it was okay, but . . .'

I nodded. 'I ken. There's more to singing than knowing the tune.'

She was silent for a moment. Her eyes looked as if she'd suddenly grown up. 'So they paid us a few compliments, and thanked us, and we listened to the rest of the acts. I thought we had a chance. We'd done as well as anyone else and better than some, I knew we had. At the end we all filed out, and then once we got into the car park I realised I'd dropped one of my gloves somewhere, so I went back in to look for it.' She stopped, swallowed. 'I heard them. Backstage.' Her cheeks crimsoned. 'They, the presenters, they were talking about us. About me. *The other one has a better voice though*, one of them said, and the tall woman said right back, *Plain as a pudding and two stone overweight once the cameras get on her. The blonde's sexy, and she can be taught to sing.*'

Her hands were trembling. She slid them between her knees and fought the tears back. 'They didn't know I was there. I left the glove and got out into the car park. Chloe was high as a kite and talking about going out to celebrate, and I couldna, I just couldna, so I said something about going to see Magnie, and I just drove away from there as fast as I could and kept going to the end of the road. I didn't want to see anyone or try to talk to them. I just wanted to go somewhere I could howl like an animal, let it all out before I had to go back and face them. Chloe and I share a flat here in Brae, you see, and Tom still lives with his folk, but he's always in and out, and they'd both be wanting to talk over every note and every little thing the producers said to us, and I just . . . I just couldn't bear it.' She sat in silence for a moment, then said bleakly, 'So that's Chloe in. She'll get the invitation for the regional heats, and even if she says she's my pal and doesn't want to do it without me, I'll have to tell her to

13

take it. I'll stay here being plain as a pudding and singing in pubs.'

There was nothing I could say to comfort her. She wasn't as plain as a pudding, nor horribly overweight, not even in the clingy velour dress she wore under her black coat, but she wasn't pretty either. She had wispy brown hair, with a fringe over her low forehead, sparse lashes over her brown eyes, plump cheeks, full red lips over a pudgy chin; the sort of face you might see every day behind a shop counter and fail to recognise on the bus home. She was pleasant girl-next-door, just like her fifties musical songs. She was the plain sidekick who got the comedy boy in the end, and went off with him to make apple pies for the church fete. The special thing about her was her voice, and it hadn't been special enough.

Lizbet sighed, and rose. 'I'd better go back and face them.' She braced her shoulders and squared her chin. 'Thanks.'

'I wish I could help,' I said. 'I wish there was a magic wand I could wave to make the next few days better for you. But it's like being at sea in a serious storm. There are times even I wish I was, well, maybe not onshore, but somewhere else. But there's no magic wand. You just have to tough it out and believe it'll get better.'

Something changed in her face the second time I said 'magic wand'. She closed in on herself, her eyes moving quickly across the beach, the water, as if her thoughts were racing. Her carefully painted lips tightened, then she turned back to me. Her smile was mechanical. 'Thanks, Cass. See you around.'

She strode up the beach to her car, did a several-points turn and drove away.

Chapter Two

Dem at has muckle wid aye laek mair.
(Them that have much would always like more.)
Riches breed love of more riches.

It was a day atween weathers, as the old folk would say, a bonny, bright mid-March day with one gale just past and no doubt another few expected before March wore out. After the greys and blues of sea and sky as we'd crossed from Boston, the brightness and bustle of West African markets, the striplights of airports, it was good to be in the clear colours of home: a path of blue sea between low green hills, a great expanse of sky. It had been half-dark as we'd landed last night, but as the plane had come low in to the runway I'd glimpsed the sea pounding on rocks, and an old crofthouse with a sweep of hill behind it. My heart had lifted at the familiar sight. Home.

I'd seen gardens yellow with daffodils on the mainland, but Shetland was still poised on the transition from winter to spring. The sun danced on the water in the morning light, turning these northern seas back to spring blue, but the hills still wore their winter fur of weathered long grass, and there was no sign yet of the dark green heather shoots thrusting their way through last year's brittle stems. The ghost of a half-moon hung in the sky.

I was on my way to check on my yacht, *Khalida*, sitting ashore at Brae. I called the cats from their investigation of the tideline, and put my shoulder to *Herald Deuk*, Gavin's sixteen-foot motorboat, to shove her back into the water. My handsome

15

grey Cat stayed up in the cockpit while I got the motor going, but tortoiseshell Kitten headed below to sit in her box and wash the sand from her white paws. I glanced down at her, lifevest glowing pink against her ginger-allspice-cinnamon fur. Her little face was pleased as she looked from Cat to me, then up at the moving sky. Cat sat upright in his corner, enjoying being at sea. He'd grown up as a ship's cat, and I missed him on board *Sørlandet*, but my full-time live-aboard life had changed when our beautiful three-master had become an A+ Academy. Now we had sixty teenagers aboard for the school year, along with a set of teachers for academic lessons between watches. The ship's crew worked eight weeks on, then flew home for eight off, which made it too awkward to take Cat back and forward; and besides, he'd miss his girlfriend, the Kitten, more than he missed me. Even as I thought that, he jumped down from the cockpit seat and went below to join her in the box. He bent his head to give her a lick on the forehead, and she sat up to sniff his whiskers and return the lick.

The eight weeks on, eight off, routine made things easier for Gavin and me too. DI Gavin Macrae, of Police Scotland. We'd met nearly two years ago, when I'd been his chief suspect in the Longship case, and, well, we'd liked each other then. I smiled, remembering the cautious way we'd moved around each other until spring last year, when we'd become lovers. We'd moved in together in October, when Gavin had accepted an Inspector post in Shetland on condition that life here included me. We'd had the last of my leave then, and another fortnight together over Christmas. This would be my first full leave at our cottage, and the longest I'd lived ashore since I was sixteen. I hoped it would all be okay, and that Gavin wouldn't be so established in his own routines that I felt like an intruder – my fellow sailors had warned me about that one. I planned to spend his working days getting my own boat ready for mast-up, in April, as well as doing the partner stuff: cleaning, cooking, evenings together. I took a deep breath, gave one last look at the open road to the Atlantic shining behind me, and set my face landwards.

Gavin's flash electric outboard took less than ten minutes to get us level with the bridge over to Muckle Roe. Five minutes more and I was bobbing gently in the marina. I'd meant to tie up at the dinghy pontoon sticking out into the circle of marina shorewards of the lines of larger boats, but this side of it was taken by a sizeable fishing boat bristling with those orange spools for unwinding baited longlines.

'Hey!' a voice called. A blonde girl in a black coat was stip-stepping along the wooden planking. 'You can come behind us!' she called out, and made a circular gesture. I eyed up the space between the high-tech fishing boat and the sticking-out tube, putted round in a circle and glided alongside. The girl leaned forward to take my line.

'Thanks,' I said.

She was a most improbable apparition to find on a pontoon on a March day. She had long blonde hair curving down over her face to hide one eye, and tumbling in carefully-crafted waves over her shoulders. Her skin was painted to porcelein smooth, the visible brow was gelled into a spiky shape, and her lashes were black as a ship's funnel. Her lips were fashionably pale. She wore a painted-on red spangled dress under the open coat and heels which were completely out of place on a wood planks walkway.

She was, without question, Chloe, whose looks had taken Lizbet's chances of stardom.

'Thanks,' I said again, and she gave a *you're welcome* flip of her hand and sashayed back towards the flash fishing boat. A boy-friend? I was intrigued enough by the combination of her general looks and her obvious ease with boats to keep watching as I tied the *Deuk* up. She called 'Aye aye' into the boat, and a young man appeared.

He was no more likely than she was to be hanging around a

fishing boat: a smooth-looking, polished man in his early thirties, ten years older than Chloe. His hair was cut smoothly to just above ear-length, and moussed in some way so that it curved out around his head from a centre parting. It gleamed in the light. Below it, he had dark brows and eyes, a thin line of moustache over full lips and a triangle of beard below them which ran down in a line to a curve around his chin. He was just taking off his oilskins – new, matching and an expensive brand – to show a white shirt and tailored trousers. He looked like a sooth-moother, and I was sure I'd never seen him before. Chloe draped herself over him and they kissed. I passed them with an 'Aye aye', the cats at my heels, and headed around the dinghy slip to the hard standing.

Out of water like this my little *Khalida* towered over me. She sat on her bulbed iron keel in a cradle cage, supported by six pads. Having been away from her made me see over again all that was needing done to her: antifouling, a good scrub of her white hull, new varnish on all the wood, repainting the decks, rewiring the guard rails.

Cat knew his own boat, even from this unfamiliar angle. He stretched his front paws up one of the supports and gave me his silent miaow. I propped a handy plank against *Khalida*'s stern and he shimmied aboard. Kitten put her paws on it, hesitated, then followed slowly. She'd put on weight, I noticed. 'Too much fish,' I told her as I steadied it for her. The pair of them watched from above as I fetched one of the ladders from the shed and followed them. My boat felt strange on land like this, dead, without the constant movement of the water under her, but a rush of love for her filled me, back in my familiar cockpit with the helm ready to my hand. I paused for a moment, smiling round, then flung the cabin hatch open, and screwed up my nose at the smell of damp. A good wash inside and out, that was what she needed. I was about to go below when I heard a vehicle approaching: Magnie, come to catch up on the news.

Magnie had been my sailing teacher here at Brae when I was a bairn. He'd started his working life as a teenager in the South Georgia whaling, then risen to fishing skipper before retiring, in so far as any Shetland fisherman retired. He was dressed for helping in his boiler suit and yellow rubber boots, with a knitted toorie cap on his red-fair curls. 'Aye aye, Cass,' he greeted me. 'I thought when I saw you out on the water that you'd be coming to check on your boat, and here you are.'

'Checking on my boat,' I agreed. 'Seeing all I need to do. Have you time for a cup of something?'

'Always time for that,' Magnie said. *Khalida* shuddered as he clambered up the ladder and sat down in the cockpit. Cat came up from his inspection of below, raised his tail at Magnie in greeting and headed off along the pontoon towards his favourite bit of beach. Kitten inched her way down the gangplank, then bounded after him. I got the kettle on and surveyed the stocks of biscuits aboard. It was Lent, when I pared food-eating to meals only, with no frills like biscuits in between, so I wouldn't be having one, but in Shetland no cup of tea went unaccompanied. The KitKats had only gone out of date last December. 'Tea without milk or white drinking chocolate?'

'Na, na, I can't be doing with black tay. There'll be milk in the boating club.'

Tea made, and Magnie given a KitKat, with due warning, we settled ourselves one each side of the cockpit in the warmth of the sun.

'So,' I said, 'tell me all the news.' I glanced down at the flash fishing boat. Chloe and her boyfriend had disappeared inside. 'Who's that parked at the dinghy pontoon?'

'Ah,' Magnie said. 'Our latest problem.'

'Pedigree,' I said. That was where you always started in Shetland: who you were related to.

Magnie shook his head. 'Down south of London somewhere. Antony Leighton. His wife, well, his ex-wife, whatever, they're split up, but I couldna tell you the exact state o' divorce, she'd likely a' been a classmate o' yours. Her folk bide up in North-mavine. Andersons.' He frowned. 'I canna just mind the lass's name. It'll come to me. There was a family o' them, wi' several lasses. An old-fashioned name. Ruby, maybe, or Laura.'

It didn't ring any bells, but there were dozens of Andersons in Shetland. I got back to the important bit. 'What problems is he causing?'

'He came here, oh, maybe six months back, and he talked Kenny o' the Banks into sub-letting him his berth, while Kenny was between boats. Well, that annoyed a couple o' the folk on the waiting list. Then . . .' He paused for emphasis. 'Dear knows how, likely a back-hander to the right person, but he got himself a regulating order, and that really got folk ramping mad.'

'What's a regulating order?'

Magnie scratched his jaw. 'Well, there's this body, SSMO, that regulates fishing in inshore waters. They were set up in the eighties to keep big trawlers outwith six miles o' the Shetland coasts. This SSMO gives out licences to fish for shellfish, you ken, scallops and buckies and lobsters and crabs, all that, and you can't fish for them without one.'

'Oh, yeah?' I said sceptically, thinking of the numbers of pot buoys that I dodged every time I sailed.

'These licences are like gold dust. There're folk like, well, Ewan Pearson for one, he applied when he bought the *Day Dawn*, two year ago. He can catch prawns and line fish, but no' lobsters or crabs, where the real money lies, so to see a new-comer just walking into a licence like that, well, you can see it makes folk spitting mad.'

I managed to envisage a face to go with *Day Dawn*, which was a most beautiful old-fashioned wooden fishing boat with the elegant stern of a thirties Norwegian vessel. Ewan Pearson. Medium tall, with a long, sallow face and intense dark eyes. You never saw him without his toorie cap, but I suspected his dark hair was thinning already. He was in his mid-twenties, and worked part-time on a larger pelagic boat, but when he wasn't at sea he pottered round the westside in *Day Dawn*, letting out lines for mackerel and catching huge skate with a rod.

Magnie nodded over towards the new fishing boat. 'The licence allows this Antony six hundred creels, but Ewan's been watching him, and he reckons he's set far more as that, just not put his boat's name on the marker buoys. And Ewan was down working on *Day Dawn* one evening, and he was certain he saw this Antony setting up a French dredge. That's forbidden in the rules, because it makes a right mess o' the seabed as well as taking smaller scallops. He's overfishing this area, just here to make a quick buck and go. So we had a word wi' Kenny and suggested he'd maybe give the berth up altogether, and then we could assign it to the first on the waiting list, and move this man out. Kenny was agreeable, so we gave this Antony notice to quit, but he's just shifted onto this pontoon and he's flatly refusing to move. He says it's a public slip, and he's as much right to use it as anyone else.'

'I suppose that's true enough.'

'We thought about pulling the pontoon ashore for maintenance, but it'd be a huge job, and then he'll likely move to the marina pontoon hammerhead and refuse to budge. Well, what can you do? We canna cut his boat loose.'

'No,' I agreed.

Magnie shook his head. 'Rules are made for reasonable people,' he said. 'If folk are determined not to follow them, well, that's when folk who'd normally be reasonable start taking the law into their own hands.' He sighed. 'And then, to make it all worse, this Antony took up wi' Chloe, that's the young lass that sings wi' our Lizbet, and her folk aren't best pleased, between him being married and ten years older as her. Ewan's a cousin o' hers, well, his mother and hers are first cousins, but the kind that are more like sisters, aye in and out o' each other's houses. His mother will have it that Ewan and Chloe'll make a match o' it, but I doubt no. I think he'd be keen enough, but she's got her sights set higher than the boy she grew up with.'

As if they'd heard us, Antony and Chloe came out of the boat's cabin into the cockpit. Magnie fell silent. I looked at Antony's moussed hair and ironed shirt. Ewan's usual marina wear was oilskin breeks in olive-green plastic, and a neon-yellow jacket with FERRY CREW in black on the back of it (he'd bought it, he'd told me proudly, for a tenner at the Whalsay charity shop, and it was practically new, because the boys on the ferry were issued with a new set every six months). I suspected his 'best' was suit breeks and a knitted gansey. However fond she was of her cousin Ewan, I didn't think Chloe would even consider clubbing with him.

'And now,' Magnie said heavily, 'there's this.' He nodded beyond the blonde head and the conker-shiny one towards the far pontoon. There were two thick green ropes stretching out across the water, one to the pontoon and the other up the rock side to a lamp post. I frowned and followed them with my eyes back to the empty berth.

It took me a moment to register what I was seeing. The green ropes disappeared underwater at the entrance to one of the berths, and in the berth there was a metre-high white wooden pole sticking up from the water. Then my brain made sense of it, and I felt my heart jolt. *Day Dawn* had sunk in her berth, leaving only the top of her mast visible. I imagined how I'd feel if it was my own *Khalida* there on the bottom, with seawater destroying her electrics, her engine, her varnished wood, and grieved for Ewan.

'Sunk,' Magnie said. 'Last night, during the night.'

'What happened?'

Magnie shook his head. 'We'll no' ken that till we get her up. A rotten plank, maybe, in spite of all Ewan's care, or a stopcock that suddenly went. The Ocean Kinetics boys are coming tomorrow. Well, actually, it's handy you came by, because you could be a help to us wi' that.'

'Anything I can do, of course,' I said. 'Though I don't know anything about airbags or the like.'

'Na, na, the Kinetics boys'll do all that. They ken exactly what to do. It'll take most of the day to get her up, they reckon, and get her to the slip, but of course it's the Up Helly Aa on Friday, so we need her off the slip for then.'

I'd forgotten about the Delting Up Helly Aa, the last of the Shetland fire festivals, and the biggest, after Lerwick, with six hundred guizers parading with lit torches from Brae Hall to the boating club, where the galley was burned. The tradition had come from the Norsemen, who'd lit a bonfire to celebrate Yule, then modified into pulling a burning tar barrel round the streets, except that the Victorian burghers had taken exception to a rowdy mob who left the blazing barrel for longer in front of shops whose owners they didn't like. They invented a mock Viking funeral where a galley carrying the Jarl, or chief Viking, was drawn through the streets by Viking guizers carrying flaming torches, and burned in a space well away from houses. Shetland's blind poet, J. J. Haldane Burgess, wrote the words for their march, and it was still sung during the parade. Each country area had its own Up Helly Aa, and Brae was one of the ones where the galley was burned on the water, in true Norse fashion. The guizers threw the torches into her on the slip, then pushed her out into the water. Given the heat of a blazing galley, I didn't want my fibreglass boat anywhere near any of it.

'We can't get a crane for tomorrow,' Magnie said, 'they're all up building the windfarm, but Tulloch's said since it was an emergency they'd get their big one down on Thursday. Well, yours is the boat nearest the water, and the smallest hull too, so if you haven't much to do, and you could do it all in the day and the morn, the crane could pop your *Khalida* back in and use the cradle for Ewan's boat.'

Tomorrow! I began to think of all I'd need to sort before then, and felt a curl of excitement rising within me. 'Sanding and antifouling. I can sand now, then wash the hull, hose her again, then get the first coat of primer on the rust, maybe two coats if it dries enough while I go along to the Building Centre for antifouling. Do they have anodes?'

'I doubt no'. You'd need the Malakoff for that.'

'Lerwick.' I tried to think that into the equation. 'I could get a lift in with Gavin in the morning, then get the first bus back out to Brae. I have cleaning stuff for the hull.'

A bicycle crunched down the gravel, and Magnie's mouth twisted. I turned and saw a racing bike stopping at the slip. Ewan Pearson got off. His face was black with anger. Magnie shifted uneasily and gave me his cup, as if he would need to go and smooth things down. Ewan marched towards the flash fishing boat and halted on the pontoon, glaring down into the cockpit. It was Chloe he spoke to first, his voice restrained. 'Your mother's alongside my mother, checking her phone every two minutes. Waiting to hear how you got on wi' your singing.'

Her face turned sulky, and lost most of its prettiness. 'I'm just going,' she glumped, her voice dropping back to teenage.

'Spending time wi' this waster here,' Ewan growled. If looks could kill, Antony would have dropped dead on the spot. 'Now you see what he's capable o' – sinking my boat because he kens I'm on to him.'

Antony flushed and squared up to him. 'I never touched your bloody boat.'

Ewan's jaw thrust out, and he took a step forwards. Chloe moved swiftly between the men. She turned back to Antony and became pretty again. 'Tomorrow, then, quarter to one at The Dowry?'

'Tomorrow,' he agreed, and leaned forward to kiss her again.

The clinch lasted rather longer than was necessary. I saw Ewan's right fist clench, and wondered if Antony was hanging on to Chloe to protect himself. He let her go at last and handed her up onto the pontoon. She tripped along the walkway, gave a look back and waved, then headed for a little red car by the clubhouse door.

Ewan watched her go with that same brooding look, only turning to face Antony again once the car had climbed the slope and disappeared towards town; once the noise of it had died away, and the only sound was the soft hush of waves nibbling the slip. He looked across at *Day Dawn*'s mast above the surface, a long, bleak look, then turned his eyes back to Antony. 'I hear you're been saying that this was only to be expected.' His voice mimicked Antony's English accent. 'An old boat, not properly maintained. The main wonder is she didn't sink years ago.' He thrust his face forward so that it was inches from Antony's. 'That hull was sound, and I'd checked the seacocks myself. I won't set foot aboard her when they get her up until the Ocean Kinetics boys have checked every inch of her for sabotage.' He stepped back, and looked Antony down and up again. 'And I ken who I'll be pointing the police towards if they find anything.'

'Check away,' Antony said.

'I will,' Ewan retorted. 'And I'll be having a look at the CCTV footage from last night. See who was snooping around the marina.'

'I think you'll find I have an alibi for last night.' Ewan's fist clenched again as Antony glanced in the direction Chloe had gone. 'How would your mother and her mother feel if she was dragged into your accusations?'

Ewan spat at his feet. 'Bloody waster,' he snarled. 'If you were here, you'll be on the cameras. As for Chloe, you keep away from her. She has the chance of a good career wi' her singing, and she's no need to be taking up wi' the likes o' you.' He paused, and Antony's mouth opened. Ewan spoke over him, his voice rough with anger. 'Especially as you've got a wife and bairns o' your own. You take a telling, or you'll regret it.' He gave a last glare then turned on his heel and marched down the pontoon, his heavy tread making it shake in the water.

Antony watched him go, arms folded, jaw set. He waited there on the pontoon until Ewan's bike turned with a bad-tempered spurt of gravel and headed around the marina, then he came ashore himself. He got into a shiny-paint van with a 'Westside Shellfish Co. Ltd' decal on the side and drove off.

Magnie sighed. 'Well, maybe the lasses'll get this *You're the Stars!* thing they're so keen on, and that'll take her out o' this Antony's orbit.'

'Maybe,' I agreed. I'd leave Lizbet to talk to him herself, if she wanted to. I took his mug and paused a moment, looking out over the water. 'Magnie, when did folk start wanting so much? Wanting to be rich, or famous, or have a glamorous life-style? Have folk always wanted more, or is it a new thing, with the TV constantly showing people the kind of life they might lead?'

Magnie scratched his chin and thought about it. 'I dinna ken, lass. That's a right Sunday question for a Tuesday afternoon. I doubt folk have always had get-rich-quick schemes. My grand-mother's postcard album had pictures of the Jersey Lily in it, dressed to the nines, and one of her brothes went off to the Yukon in the goldrush. I'm no' sure though . . .' He paused and resettled his toorie. 'Well, me sisters, they liked looking at the fashion pictures, but they never expected to own a Dior dress or meet Prince Charming. They kent that for them it'd be Smith's of Lerwick and the boy next door. Realistic expectations, that was it. They learned to want what was within their reach.' He glanced around and nodded over at the caravan parked in one of the spaces overlooking the marina. 'Take those folk now. Merran and Davie. That's the most contented couple I ken. They just come here for a day or two, and he sits in the sun, if any, and watches the football on one of those little tellies, and she visits her daughters and plays with her grandchildren, and then they buy treat food at the Co-op and go back to Yell happy as anything. They want what's around them.'

'But it's amazing what you can reach, if you want it enough.' I gave him a sideways glance, half-shy, and told him what I hadn't admitted to Gavin yet. 'This runaway teenager's been halfway round the world, and now she's Acting First Officer of the tall ship *Sørlandet*.'

'Boys a boys, are you now? Are you standing in for your friend who's having the baby?'

'Agnetha.' I nodded. 'Due next month, and she's gone off on her maternity leave.' I rose and stretched. 'Well, I'd better get to work if this boat's to be ready to go back in the water the day after tomorrow.'

'Right enough.' Magnie stood up too, and gave the flash fishing boat, the green lines leading to *Day Dawn*'s mast, a last look, a shake of the head. 'There'll be more trouble come of this yet.'

Chapter Three

What's weel cairdet is aesy spun.
([Wool] that's well carded is easily spun.)
Careful preparation makes a task easy.

I was pleasantly weary by the time I set off back to our cottage at the Ladie. Magnie and I had been hard at work. We'd slathered intensive hull cleaner around the waterline and began sanding the old antifouling while it got to work, then I'd knelt on the deck and leaned precariously over the side of the hull to give the wooden rubbing strake a quick sand and wash the upper hull, while Magnie kept sanding away below. Both of us were blue with highly poisonous paint dust once we'd finished, but a good hose turned the upper hull gleamingly white, with only a couple of areas needing a second shot of cleaner. I felt that bubbling of excitement within me: soon she'd be back on the water. I'd start working on her interior, and then come April she'd have her mast back, her white wings. We'd be sailing again.

Furthermore, I'd ordered new sails for her, on the strength of my *Sørlandet* pay, and they were waiting in three boxes in the sail loft in Brae: strong, crackling-white canvas that would make all the difference to the way she went. Her current suit were over ten years old now, and had all the aerodynamic qualities of a flattened-out sugar bag.

Magnie bunged our boiler suits into the club washing machine while I washed the blue off my face and hands, then headed for the Brae building centre for antifouling and, while I was at it, the Co-op for a pair of those iced German biscuits with the sweetie on the top to encourage Magnie. By the time I got back he'd got the first coat of primer on, and we had a breather before applying the second, and a coat of woodskin to the rubbing strake.

By five, the sun began sinking behind the Clousta hills. I straightened my back and inspected our work. 'One more coat of primer, then she'll be all set for antifouling tomorrow.'

'I'll do that,' Magnie said. 'You get home to make your man's tea.'

'He's bringing us a takeaway.'

'It'll taste better if you're there to eat it while it's hot.'

I conceded that one with a flip of the hand, called the cats and headed back to *Herald Deuk*. She skimmed swiftly over the gold-tinted water, startling an otter which was sculling round the mussel rafts below Cole Deep. We arrived at the jetty just as the lights of Gavin's Land Rover flashed above the hill. I clipped the *Deuk* to her mooring lines and headed upwards to welcome him. A flurry of hooves from the field by our gravel track was the two Shetland ponies beating me to it – a red-and-white and a black-and-white, both small and bolshie, and, it seemed, expecting conversation or preferably food from a home-coming police inspector.

It had obviously been a quiet day at the Northern Constabulary's most northerly station. Gavin was smiling as he got out of the Land Rover, and his movements were brisk and sure as he reached into the other side for the white carrier bags of food. He paused for a moment, looking at me. His hair was the colour of a stag's ruff in autumn, cut short enough to suppress its natural curl, his eyes sea-grey. He wasn't quite handsome but he had a face I loved to look at: someone who was as real, as uncompromising as his own Highland hills. He was wearing his work-a-day kilt, green tartan with a leather sporran, and his grey-green tweed jacket. He held his free hand out to me. 'I wasn't sure if you'd be back. Visiting your boat, well, that could take some hours.'

'Magnie chased me home,' I admitted. 'He's wanting to get her back in.'

'The sunken boat. I ken. We came out to look at it yesterday, and no doubt we'll need to make a token gesture appearance tomorrow, but it's no good us looking for signs of sabotage. That's the salvage workers' job. We'll go by what they tell us.' He turned to the ponies, who were showing signs of impatience, and admonished them in Gaelic, then turned back to the Land Rover for a lidless ice-cream tub with sandwich crusts and apple cores in it. The black-and-white pony stamped impatiently. Gavin tipped the box into their field, in two piles, and the noses went down.

'The owner was speaking about CCTV footage,' I said.

'We've secured it, but I think I'll wait for the report before giving some poor PC the excitement of watching a complete nine hours of Delting Marina in the dark.'

'It might be motion sensitive.'

'We can hope,' Gavin agreed, and gave me the carrier bag. It was warm, and smelled delicious. 'Post. The postie and I have agreed I'll pick up the post at Bixter on my way past, save him this track.' He reached into the Land Rover again and came out with a bundle of letters in one hand. 'There's a brown envelope from the DVSA for you. Maybe a cancellation slot for your theory test.'

I wrinkled my nose. I'd been driving illegally since a summer stint at a holiday resort with children's sailing on a Greek island and I'd worked on the theory during quiet night watches this last voyage, but I suspected taking driving lessons and actually sitting the test might be more traumatic than being caught in a sudden summer gale with full sails.

'Look and see,' Gavin said encouragingly. 'I'll shut the hens in, then we can eat.'

I opened the DVSA envelope on the doorstep while he poured Layers' Mash into the hens' trough and closed their mesh door on them. I read the official missive, my mouth slowly dropping open, then read it again. 'Yell?' I said disbelievingly. 'I have to go to Mid Yell for my driving theory test? What happened to the centre in Lerwick?'

'They closed it,' Gavin said. 'They wanted to make the test more accessible for everyone, with nobody having to drive more than forty miles for the test.'

I made the sort of sound that cartoons would write as *???!!!*

'So,' Gavin said, 'in pursuance of this noble aim, they moved the theory test to the isles, to Mid Yell and Whalsay, and the HGV and motorbike tests to the old Scatsta airport up north by Sullom Voe. Are you going to stay on the doorstep forever, or shall we eat indoors?'

I moved into the kitchen and set the carrier bags of food on the table. 'So I have to sail to Yell to sit my theory test. A day's sail, stay overnight, another day's sail back, for a test lasting an hour and twenty minutes?' My indignation subsided as I realised it was a chance to get my mast back. I looked at the letter again. 'Monday 20th March. That's Monday!' I'd have a lot to do: I'd need to check the mast over, and get the halyards back on, and the sails.

'A frightful hardship, sailing to Yell,' Gavin agreed. His grey eyes laughed at me. He brought plates over to the table and slipped his arm around my waist. 'You should see yourself. Your eyes have lit up like searchlights at the very thought.'

'Antifouling tomorrow,' I said. 'That doesn't take long, with a roller. I need to get an anode for the prop, from Lerwick.' I could feel my heart beating faster. 'Back in the water on Thursday. I'll need to get the mast all sorted after the antifouling, that won't take long either. Sails on.' My spirits rose even higher. 'A shakedown sail on Saturday . . . I'll need to check the weather forecast, and I have a feeling that the Mid Yell marina may be too shallow for *Khalida* at the lowest tide. My marina guide's up in the spare room, and my charts.'

'Or you could just get the bus from Voe.' The laugh had reached his mouth now. 'There are several which go from Lerwick and all the way to the Unst ferry, maybe even on to Baltasound, to save isles folk having to pay for their cars.'

'Bus,' I said, 'instead of sailing?'

'No,' Gavin agreed, gravely. 'I can see there's no comparison.'

I looked at the letter again. 'New centres in Yell and Whalsay I can see,' I said. 'It'll make life much easier for the isles folk. But to close the one in Lerwick is just plain daft. And what about folk in Sandness, or on Papa? It's well over forty miles for them just to get to the ferry.'

'Our MP commented that he didn't know what substance the person who dreamed that one up was on. There was such an outcry that they re-opened the Lerwick one two weeks later, but as a near-Brae resident you obviously qualify for Yell.'

'Drive up to Toft. Twenty minutes from here, an hour and a half from Sumburgh, easy. A twenty-minute ferry, then another fifteen-minute drive.' I scowled at the letter. 'Why can't they do it online?'

'Probably because the candidates would look up the answers on their phones.' Gavin smiled at me. 'Dear Cass. You can spend the evening with your charts, planning your passage. Meanwhile, shall we eat this Chinese before it gets cold?'

I found serving spoons and eating irons. Gavin sat down in a swirl of kilt pleats and patted his lap for Kitten, then reached over for the prawn crackers. He broke one in half and gave it to her, and she crunched it noisily, purring. Cat looked up with interest, then came over, whiskers twitching, and gave his silent mew.

'I don't remember the cats recognising prawn crackers last time I was home,' I said.

'I've got into bad habits,' Gavin said. 'Pick up a takeaway on the way home. Apart from fish at the weekend, when it's been about to catch, I've barely cooked since you left for your last spell of duty. Shocking extravagance.'

'It's ages since I've had a takeaway of any sort.' I helped myself to a generous spoonful of rice and another of king prawn and Chinese mushroom. 'I've been eating norsk food. Porridge with raisins, herring, *pankaker* with syrup, *brunost*, you know, that brown cheese that tastes like caramel. That's just breakfast.'

'And *fisk* for tea,' Gavin said. 'I ken.'

The takeaway portions were generous, and by the time we'd emptied the little foil trays I was stuffed. We took our tea through to the sitting room, where Gavin had pre-laid a fire, and sat together on the couch, hands clasped. His fingers were warm between mine. Cat jumped up onto my lap. I leaned my shoulder against Gavin's, stroked the white fluff behind Cat's ears, and gave a long sigh. It was good to be home. It felt like coming home too, though I'd never expected to say that of a house.

Gavin had been busy while I'd been away. I'd noticed a holder for his rods had appeared in the porch, a shelf with a length of tube on it for each rod to stand in, and a coat-rack opposite for dripping jackets. In this room there was a new shelf on brackets; the books on it were at least fifty years old, either cloth-bound or with faded paper covers, and had titles like *Pike and Perch* and *The Roving Angler*. A pair of wally dugs had appeared on the mantelpiece, and the south-facing deep window shelf had a green cushion on it, with a two-cat-shaped dent in the middle.

'I've been doing a bit of refurbishing,' he said, following my gaze. 'The cats like their cushion, though Cat misses having you around all day.'

'You can come with me to Yell, boy,' I promised him.

'Though how the Kitten'll take to life in a small boat, when she's got used to charging all round the croft . . .'

'She'll be fine,' Gavin said. He was just starting to add something else when the phone rang. He pulled his mouth down and reached for it. 'Gavin Macrae . . .' His voice warmed to friendliness. 'Fine, thanks. Yes, she is – she's right here, I'll pass you over.' He gave me the phone. 'It's Father David.'

'Hello, Father. Cass here.'

Father David's Scottish voice came as clearly over the phone as if he was in the next room. 'Now then, Cass. How are you?'

'Glad to be home,' I said.

'Good, good. I'll tell you why I'm phoning. I have a favour to ask. One of our parishioners, an older man, he's not great. He's in the hospital, and I want to keep tomorrow free to be with him. Could I possibly get you to take my turn volunteering at the foodbank? Nothing difficult, just packing the food into bags. It's from two to four.'

I thought of the day I'd planned, getting my boat ready. I'd just have to work faster in the morning. 'Sure. Where is it?'

'Market Street, down at the main road end. I think the address is 20A, but there's a notice on the door, you can't miss it.'

'I'll find it. Two till four. No problem.'

'Thanks, Cass. God bless, and see you on Sunday.'

He rang off, and I sat for a moment, working this into my schedule for tomorrow. It had been light by half past six this morning. If I headed out at half past seven then I'd be in Brae by ten to eight . . . get the antifouling on, and another coat of woodskin on the rubbing strake if I had time. Get the halyards on the mast. There was a bus into town at one, arriving quarter to two. I could get that. I'd needed to go into town anyway, for the anode. I'd have to leave the cats at home, rather than have them pottering round Brae on their own all afternoon. Cat wouldn't like that; he'd been so pleased to come out in the boat today. Two till four. I'd be stuck in town until the workers' bus, just after five. That would give me time to get what I needed from Malakoff.

'I can feel your brain working overtime,' Gavin said. 'What are you trying to fit into your already busy day of boat work?'

'A trip into town in the afternoon. I'm covering for Father David at the foodbank.' I reflected on that for a moment. 'I didn't realise Shetland had a foodbank. That we needed one.' I swept my hand round in the direction of the neat houses in Brae, set among their bonny gardens and green lawns. 'We're so prosperous here. And there's plenty of work, between the Council, and services, and what folk create for themselves, like B&Bs and tearooms.'

'Poverty's not what it used to be,' Gavin said seriously. 'When folk talk about poverty they think of Victorian photos of children dressed in ragged breeks and adult-size jackets. Poverty now is haunting the charity shop on the day it puts its new stock out, so that you can grab something for the bairns to wear to school that they won't get teased about. It's living in one room of a three-bedroom council house because that's all you can afford to heat after you've paid the rent. It's working three part-time jobs and still only managing to scrape by.' His arm tightened around me. 'You ken about that.'

'Never actually going hungry,' I agreed, 'but knowing to the last penny what's in your purse, all the time.'

'And hoping nothing breaks,' Gavin agreed.

'Are there many folk in Shetland like that?'

'The number's rising all the time by whatever way you count it. More folk on income support or whatever it's called now, more bairns on free school meals. It'll get worse too, because there's a rumour going that come the Budget the Chancellor's going to announce that the system's to get tightened up, to make efficiency savings.' His voice filled with passion. 'And what that really means, what it always means, is that the poor get poorer. And with poverty often comes abuse, the man who can't work

35

taking his frustration out on his wife and bairns, and then she leaves him and finds herself better off emotionally, once she's recovered, but worse off financially.'

I thought of the flash fisherman, Antony, whose wife and bairns were somewhere here in Shetland, and wondered how much they were getting of his lobster catch money, or whether it all went back to the bank to pay off the loan on his fancy boat.

Gavin hugged me again, then withdrew his arm. 'You'd better get on with that passage planning if you're sailing to Yell on Sunday.'

I was happily occupied for the rest of the evening. I'd sailed to Yell before, so I had the key waypoints logged in my rather primitive GPS, but the timing was crucial, because Bluemull Sound, between Yell and Unst, had an interesting tide race, though not so bad as Yell Sound, which was so serious that it got an inset diagram to itself in the Tidal Atlas. I flipped through the pages. I wanted the tide with me as much as possible, going east along the top of Shetland, but most crucially going south down into Mid Yell. The atlas showed the tidal arrows turning my way from four hours before high water Dover and slack water at HW+1. If I timed it right, I'd get the tide with me going along the top, then I'd cut into Bluemull Sound at slack and get into Mid Yell before the arrows on the map turned against me.

'We are still in Greenwich Mean Time in the UK, aren't we?'

Gavin nodded without raising his eyes from the fly he was tying, a red and green monstrosity that I'd have thought would be guaranteed to terrify every fish who saw it. 'It changes on Saturday night. Spring forward, fall back.'

I got my chart out and swirled my dividers round the coast. It was thirteen hours' sailing from Brae to Mid Yell, and the Bluemull sound bit into Mid Yell was three and a half hours' worth, so I needed to be entering Bluemull sound at bang on half an hour before that HW+1 slack water. High water Lerwick on Sunday was 20.02. It would be dark by then. Though the forecast was for a clear day, and there would be a moon, I couldn't rely on that to light me into Mid Yell. The evening tide wouldn't do. I'd have to go earlier, and arrive there on the morning tide, 07.34, plus one, 08.34, less half an hour, 08.04, arriving in Mid Yell at 11.04, which meant leaving here at 11.04 minus thirteen, 22.04, and sailing all night.

I made a disgruntled sound, and Gavin looked up. 'Problem?'

'The tides are all wrong. Mornings and evenings. To get there at a sensible time I have to leave at ten o'clock on Saturday evening and sail all night.' I checked Windguru, and felt my spirits rise. 'The forecast's for a steady northerly three to four, cold but great for direction, and clear skies.' My heart began dancing. I'd be sailing my *Khalida* again, with Cat as crew and my familiar northern stars above me. 'I'll need to get busy tomorrow.'

'I can give you a hand on Saturday too,' Gavin said. 'And how about I drive up and visit you on the Sunday? It's a Cullivoe Mass day, at three, so we can go together, explore Yell a bit and have dinner somewhere, then I can get an early ferry back on Monday.'

I hadn't thought of that. I'd only thought of having my *Khalida* to myself, and the sea in peace, with no teenagers. I sat back on my heels and stared at him.

He added, diffidently, 'You've only just got home. It's good being together again, and I've no' had a chance to explore Yell yet. If I let Rainbow know, she could come up and feed the ponies, and shut the hens in.'

I was being too slow to reply. I saw his face change, close against me, and rushed into speech. 'That would be great. Yes, do come!'

He smiled now, but there was a sadness in the smile that gave me a pang. I rose and went to sit on the arm of his chair. 'I just didn't think of you driving all that way.' I leaned my shoulder against his. 'Do come.'

His arm came up around my waist. 'Then I will. In the meantime, is it maybe bedtime?'

It maybe was.

Chapter Four

Wednesday 15th March

Tide times, Brae:
LW 01.14 (0.87m);
HW 07.15 (1.78m);
LW 13.39 (0.63m);
HW 19.51 (1.78m)

Moonset 06.40; sunrise 07.20; moonrise 13.49;
sunset 19.06. Moon waxing gibbous.

What's forborne sood aye be forsworn.
Something that's been warned against should be left alone.

The next day was surprisingly bonny for the middle of March: we woke to a clear blue sky with only a light fret of wind on the water, and the early sun making sharp shadows on the banks above the beaches. I went out to sniff the air and was met by an outrage of cheeping from within the flowering currant bushes – and they almost were flowering too, with the first unfurling green leaves, and pink on the hanging buds. Below them were bright pools of yellow and purple crocus, and bunches of little daffodils by the gate. The air smelt of earth and growth and warmth to come, and the forecast was good for *Khalida* to lie at the pier for several days. I got Gavin to keep the cats in while I hurried down to the *Deuk* and got her underway.

I headed straight for Brae, and was there on the dot of quarter to eight. I glanced over my shoulder at the green ropes leading to where the *Day Dawn*'s mast stuck forlornly from the water, and shuddered. Ewan was at work already, clearing the pontoon of as many ropes as possible. I waved, then tied the *Deuk* up and headed over to my *Khalida*. There was plenty to do before I got on with painting: the now-pristine hull needed a line of masking tape to protect it from splashes of blue antifouling, and I had to get out the roller, brushes, tray and my protective gear.

Magnie's Fiat rolled down the boating club slope and stopped a safe distance behind *Khalida* just as I was smoothing the last foot of masking tape across her stern. He got out and looked around the hard standing. 'No cats the day?'

'I have to go into town in the afternoon. Lunchtime bus. Besides, we don't need them underfoot for the rescue operation.' I gave him a sideways look. 'How d'you think the committee would feel about me putting the mast up tomorrow?'

Magnie pulled a face. 'You ken how it is. They wouldn't mind, but there's the insurance thing, and if you let one body do it then you'll have three more asking. Why can't you wait?'

'I have to go to Yell for my theory driving test. On Monday. If I can get the mast up tomorrow, I can sail there. After that, well, if the dinghy pontoon isn't under marina rules – ' I nodded at the ultra-flash fishing boat – 'maybe I could lie the other side of it until the end of March.'

'I'll get you sorted somehow. You could even be a visitor until April starts, I'm no' sure if they come under the ban.' He reached into his car for his boiler suit. 'Well, if you're doing masts as well, we'd better get painting.'

I'd already changed and tied a headscarf over my hair, knotted at the back, peasant-style. Now I donned my goggles, mask and gloves before prising the antifouling lid off with a screwdriver, stirring it and pouring it into the tray. 'Which d'you prefer, brush or roller?'

'My rheumatics would prefer the hull. You're young and spry, I'll let you go down on your knees.'

'My boat,' I agreed. I borrowed the roller for a minute to give the flat part of the keel a quick covering, then had a look round for a couple of bits of wood to kneel on. Magnie headed for the bow and began rolling away, and I knelt down under the curve of her hull and began slathering paint around on the curved keel-front and heavy iron bulb that she was sitting on. It was the sort of job that made me grateful for my little boat, especially looking from this angle at the vast underwater expanses of the thirty-five-footers beside us. I was under there for only half an hour, but by the time I uncurled myself and eased backwards to where I could straighten up, I felt like I had the rheumatics myself, and my boiler suit, scarf, goggles and gloves, and no doubt the visible bits of my face too, were spattered with blue drops from Magnie painting above me. I stood back to admire. She was looking good: the paint had covered the silver primer a uniform seamanlike blue. I dodged around Magnie and began working on her stern and rudder.

Magnie glanced at his watch as we finished that side. 'Five past nine. Now there's a difference in an hour.'

'Isn't it,' I agreed. It was amazing the difference a coat of paint made. My boat was starting to look as she should. 'Other side?'

Magnie nodded, and we were just about to head around when a rattle of white vans came down the marina slope, followed by Ewan in a black pick-up. The salvage party had arrived. I paused, brush poised. 'Do you need to go and liaise?'

'Na, na, lass, they ken what they're doing. I'll just go and tell them I'm here, in case they need to ken anything, or want access to the club.'

He laid the roller in the tray and headed around, raising a hand. I began on the other side of the keel, keeping an eye on what was going on while I was at it.

41

They obviously knew exactly what they were doing. Two of them got a compressor set up and began uncoiling festoons of yellow air lines, while another pair carried air bags along the pontoon and flaked broad green webbing on the arm. The final three got busy unpacking their diving unit, a small walk-in trailer with the multi-coloured air hoses coiled in a figure of eight along its side. There was a lot of to-ing and fro-ing between pontoon and machines before the diver shrugged on his air cylinders, screwed up his helmet, slipped off the pontoon and began to fix the slings under the sunken boat.

'The idea,' Magnie said, pausing in his rolling to watch, 'is to get an airbag on each side of her, bow and stern, then raise her slowly by inflating them. They'll add an extra pair in the middle if they're needed.'

We both kept looking as the diver went down, trailing bubbles behind him, and came up again. The men on the pontoon wrestled a large red airbag over the side and he ducked down and hauled it under. Second airbag. He began to work at the bow. Third airbag. Fourth airbag. By then Magnie had done all the hull, I'd finished the keel, and there was just enough paint left to double-do the waterline and rudder and still have some to touch up where the supports were once she was lifted up. I used all but the last brushful, stamped the tin shut and wrapped the brush in cling film with a sloosh of turps added, then took a deep breath and fumbled a hold on the sticking-out end of masking tape. Conjuring trick time. I stepped back, pulling it off in festoons as I went, crumpling the painty tape in my gloved hands, and hey presto, the messy edge became beautifully sharp.

'Very bonny,' Magnie agreed.

I peeled my gloves, boiler suit and scarf off and laid them aside to dry. 'Cuppa time?'

'I'll nip up into the club,' Magnie said. 'Tea with milk?'

'Thanks.'

I watched while I waited. Word had got round that something interesting was going on at the marina, for there was a constant stream of cars and flashing of phones. Magnie came back, and we sat on the edge of the pier, legs dangling over the water, steaming mugs of mahogany-brown tea clasped in our cold hands. There was something irresistible about other people messing about with boats, about that mast sticking out of the water, the boat below waiting to rise from the depths. The diver came up and gave a thumbs-up; the compressor changed gear.

'Interesting, isn't it?' said a familiar voice from behind me. It was DS Freya Peterson, Gavin's sidekick – in so far as he had one in his new exalted desk role – his eyes and ears out in the world, come to see what was going on. She was dressed in black as usual: boots, trousers, a padded police jacket. Her shining blonde hair was uncovered, and held back with a clip at the nape of her neck, and her green eyes were alight with interest. She nodded at the ground beside me. 'May I?'

I made a vaguely welcoming gesture and shuffled over.

'Grandstand view,' she said, sitting down.

'I'll make another cup o' tay,' Magnie said, and rose.

'Thanks.' She watched for a moment. The compressor chugged steadily on. There was an impression of red below the surface: the bags filling. 'What d'you reckon sunk the boat?'

I shrugged. 'A failed stopcock's the most likely.'

A wintry smile twitched her lips. 'Explain that to me in layman's language.'

I rose and turned towards *Khalida*. 'Easier to show you. See those two holes in *Khalida*, this side? An inch in diameter, with a rim around them?'

She nodded.

'Those are to pump water out the heads, the toilet, and draw seawater back in.' I'd been meaning to inspect them anyway. I gestured her over to *Khalida*, and we climbed aboard. She followed me into the cabin. I crouched down beside the toilet, and laid a hand on one tube coming out of the inlet seacock. 'These two things are seacocks, just like stopcocks in houses. You turn the handle, the water shuts off.' I demonstrated with one handle. It was moving freely, though a skoosh of WD40 wouldn't hurt. 'Turn it again, the water flows.' I used the other handle. 'A simple gate valve. If for some reason the seacock inside the boat fails, you have an inch hole in the bottom. Enough to sink a boat in minutes.'

Her immaculate brows rose. 'Minutes?'

'Minutes,' I said firmly. 'Five, ten. A one-inch hole with the pressure of the sea behind it. It's frightening how fast the water comes in.'

'And what might cause a seacock to fail?' She gave one a knock. 'These look pretty solid.'

'They go brittle. It depends on what quality of brass was used in the first place. The brass gradually loses its strength, and it does it from the inside out, so there's nothing to see. Then one day it just collapses.' I rose, thinking that it wouldn't take long to dismantle these. Hoses off, a quick check inside. I'd have time to do that once the mast was ready. 'Or more simply, if one day you forget to turn it off, and the hose isn't properly fastened to the stopcock, well, the water'll come in.'

Ewan's hoses would have been fastened. He'd have closed the stopcocks each time he left the boat.

DS Peterson's head was turned towards the marina. 'Something's happening.'

She led the way off *Khalida* and we returned to our seat. Now the inflated air bags were clearly visible under the surface. A shudder ran through the mast and it became more upright then, slowly, it began to move. A square glimmer of white below the water formed itself into the cabin roof, breaking the surface, rising up, then the wheelhouse itself, the pulpit rails . . . then, suddenly, with a judder, the airbag on the far side bounced around her prow, the mast lurched and she slewed across. The pontoon dipped. One worker leapt for his van, took a turn of the green ropes around his towbar and pulled forward a metre, taking the weight off the pontoon.

'Not good,' Magnie said from above us. 'They'll likely have to start again.' He leaned down to give DS Peterson her mug, and returned to his seat on the other side of me.

Over on the pontoon, Ewan looked around, spotted DS Peterson and came over to us. 'Now then.'

'Now,' I replied. I nodded towards the boat. 'I'm vexed to see this.'

He flushed scarlet. His voice sharpened. 'I dinna ken what caused it yet. An opened stopcock, maybe.' He glared at DS Peterson. 'But it's no' hard to guess who. I hope you'll be looking at the CCTV recordings.'

'We will,' she assured him.

'And dusting the cabin for prints,' Magnie suggested, 'if they can bide once the boat's been underwater.'

'We'll do everything necessary,' DS Peterson said. 'But I'd be grateful, sir, if you'd keep from making accusations against anyone in particular until we've had a chance to gather evidence.'

'I'll make no accusations, then,' Ewan said. 'But I'll tell you this. The hoses on every one of my cocks were tight on the pipe to begin with. I heated them to get them on, and double-clipped every one, and besides that, I close every stopcock on the boat when I'm not aboard. If it's a stopcock gone, it might have been meant to look like an accident, but it was deliberate sabotage and I'm wanting it investigated. As for who –'

She cut smoothly over him. 'Accusations, sir, could impact on our ability to make an arrest. I'm hoping the CCTV will show us more.'

Ewan snorted, then gave a curt nod and strode off in the direction of the activity on the pontoon. Magnie took my mug and stood up. 'What next, Cass?'

'Mast,' I said. 'I've got the bags of ropes in the *Deuk*. One bag now, one for once the mast's up. We could get the sails aboard too.' I glanced at my watch. 'Quarter past ten. We're doing well. I want to check my stopcocks as well.'

'Better safe as sorry,' Magnie agreed.

'What do you think sank this boat?' DS Peterson asked him.

Magnie gave her a sideways look. 'The salvage boys'll ken that better as me.'

'D'you think sabotage is likely? It's an old boat.'

'He kept her well maintained, though,' Magnie said.

The diver had gone down again. We followed his bubble-trail to the pontoon; the third green strap inched from the walkway, and the workers passed down two more airbags for amidships, then, once they were in place, the diver hauled his body over the rogue airbag. We heard the hiss as it deflated, then he wrestled it back into position. The compressor took up its higher note again.

DS Peterson glanced at her phone and rose. 'I'd better go. I've a ferry to catch.' She gave Magnie back his mug. 'There was an odd thing happened in Yell during the night.'

I refused to show interest. She'd tell us or she wouldn't. She gave me a sideways glance and continued. 'Someone dug some-thing up in an old graveyard.'

If she was being forthcoming, I'd cooperate too. 'What?'

'Unknown. It was a neat rectangular hole, about this size.' She made a rectangle with her hands, the size of a large paper-back. 'Two feet deep. Too small for a baby's grave, and anyway there wasn't a grave there, according to the man who maintains the kirkyard, and never was.'

'Neat how?'

'A packed-earth rectangle at the bottom of the hole, like there had been a box there. My guess is that that's what it was, a metal box, like one of those deed boxes lawyers used to have. Someone had found the exact place using a metal detector, then dug it up. As to what was in it, though . . .'

Magnie was frowning. 'The Cullivoe kirkyard?'

Her green eyes narrowed. 'Yes.' I felt Magnie stiffen. DS Peterson waited for a moment, watching him, brows raised, but he turned away and strode off towards the club, the three mugs dangling from his hand. We watched him go.

'If he talks to you,' DS Peterson said, 'you can always tell Gavin. It'd be interesting to hear what the local grapevine thinks. See you.'

Magnie said no more until after we'd disentangled the mast stays, washed and checked each one and had begun re-threading each halyard through its pulley. Below us, the compressor churned, and the new airbags filled. Now the *Day Dawn* was visibly rising, inch by inch, until her gunwale was above water.

'They'll get a pump aboard now,' Magnie said.

We kept threading while they wheeled it along the pontoon and got the nozzle in place. 'Man, this boat has a tangle of ropes.'

'They settle into place once it's upright.' I made the genoa halyard fast at the mast foot and tucked the rope tail in. 'Come on, then, what do you reckon was dug up in Yell?'

'Nothing for you to meddle wi', lass, particularly as you're going up there.' He gave me a serious look. 'I mean it. I want you to promise me that you'll have nothing to do wi' it. Not look, not investigate, nothing.'

I could see he absolutely meant it. 'Okay,' I said. I held up one hand, as if I was taking an oath. 'I promise. No meddling, no investigating.'

'What someone's dug up,' Magnie said slowly, 'is the Book o' the Black Arts.' Behind him, the *Day Dawn* was still rising; I could see her red antifouling now. A sheen of diesel floated on the water around her.

'The Book o' the Black Arts,' Magnie repeated. 'It was a book o' spells, supposedly stolen from Auld Clootie himself during one o' his visits to Orkney. It was white writing on black paper, bound all bonny in leather. It could be most awful useful – it would help you do boring work like shifting stones from a field without having to do a scrap o' work. There were more sinister spells too, like cursing a neighbour who'd annoyed you, and it was used for that too.'

'But . . .?' I said.

'Yea, there's aye a but wi' these magical things. You had to get rid of it afore you died, or the Devil would take your soul. That's how it passed from hand to hand, and ended up in Shetland.' He leaned against the mast, and settled into yarning mode. 'You couldn't just throw it away either. The Book wouldn't let you. There was ee man in Cullivoe tried that, he took it to the banks one stormy night and balled it into the sea, but when he got home, there it was sitting on his mantelpiece. Another man in the Herra, he tried to lend it to a pal. That way neither o' them would own it, you see.' He paused, and lowered his voice. 'On his way home from the pal's house, he met a dark shape wi' glowing red eyes, holding the book out to him. Naebody kent what happened that night, but he made it home and stumbled over his briggistane wi' the book in his hands, and he died the day after – o' fright, they said, and that's what's written on his death certificate. His wife selt it to another man that didn't believe a word o' it, and he prospered, became a merchant, but they said he got more and more uneasy about it. They said he went to the kirk, and when he came out, though nobody else could see it, he saw the Devil waiting at the kirk gate for him. So he went to the minister and made a bargain wi' him. The minister gave him a silver sixpence for it, and took the book without opening it – that way, the curse wouldn't lie on him – and he took and buried the book in the graveyard, with a Bible on the top of it, and there it's been ever since.'

'Until now,' I said.

II

What's gotten owre da Deil's back'll geng owre his belly
(*What's got over the Devil's back will go over his belly.*)
Ill-gotten gains often make an equally bad end.

Chapter Five

Skaed never made a man rich, but hit sood mak him wise.
(Things that have happened to him never made a man rich,
but it should make him wise.)
Experience can be dearly bought, but brings wisdom.

I thought about Magnie's story as the bus ran round the brow of the hill to Voe and came onto the broad motorway leading due south to Lerwick. I was certain I believed in God, and so that meant believing in the Devil too, but I couldn't swallow a Devil who carried a book of spells about with him, and carelessly left it behind in Orkney. Human malevolence was different. Could a book that had been handed down from one twisted, unhappy person to another absorb some of their spite against the world, so that it cast a dark spell over each subsequent owner? I couldn't answer that one, but I didn't feel any inclination to meddle with it.

Meanwhile, I'd got most of the paint off my hands, I'd tidied my hair and I was ready to help at the foodbank. I got off at the Esplanade, bought myself a sandwich at the little cafe in the square and paused to take a bite from it, debating within myself whether it was quicker to go along the curve of the seafront or take one of the lanes onto the Street, go up Harbour Street then down on Market Street itself. The latter, I thought, and headed for the nearest lane.

The lanes, or *closses*, were a feature of Lerwick. There were a dozen of them leading down from the Hillhead to the sea. Most of them ended with a flight of steps, because where I stood had once been a beach, and there would have been a steep bank above it. The closs I'd turned into, Campbell's Closs, was one of the narrower ones, with a particularly precipitous stairway, and there was a group of people at the top, so I stepped back to let them come down.

They were younger folk, brightly dressed, as if they'd been out for lunch. I noticed that, and then everything seemed to happen both fast and in slow motion. There was laughter, and then a scrick of a high heel stumbling on a stone step, and warning shouts, and one of them was falling, a girl whose blonde hair fanned out around her head as it came forward.

She fell towards me, hands swinging forwards. There was a horrid thud as her head hit one step, then she tumbled heels over head down to the bottom of the stairs and lay in a crumpled heap on the flagged ground. The others were still at the top, frozen with their hands stretching out towards her. For a moment we were all suspended in time, then one man began to come down the steps and the others followed.

'Don't try to lift her,' I said, as he bent over her, hands going down. I went swiftly to the foot of the steps, and knelt beside her. 'Don't move,' I told her, but there was a sick feeling in my throat. She wasn't trying to move; she lay in a limp heap. 'I'm Cass. I'm a First Responder. You took a nasty fall. I'm just going to take your pulse.' I slid my hand under her wrist without moving the arm. Nothing. I shifted my fingers, but there was no beat of blood. 'Call an ambulance,' I said to the man above me, without looking up. I moved my fingers to her neck, then laid them on her lips. Nothing. BBC. Breathing, bleeding, consciousness. Beside me, a woman crouched down, watching me. 'Tell them first that she's not breathing, that I'll start CPR. Then say where we are.' I looked up now and saw Lizbet's horrified face. 'Lizbet, support her head while I turn her over. Keep it straight, turning as I turn. Don't let it touch the ground.'

'I'll do it,' the woman said. 'I'm a nurse,' she added. She nodded up to the man with the phone, and he began dialling, then she knelt beside me and stretched her hands out to the girl's head.

Carefully, carefully, we turned the girl over onto her back, and it was while we were doing that that I recognised her, with a shocked jolt that took my breath for a moment. It was Chloe we were laying down, the blonde bombshell who'd been so full of life on the boating club pontoon yesterday. Her foundation lay like paint over her colourless skin, her jaw sagged loose.

'Here's my jacket,' one of the others said, hauling it off and bundling it into a pillow. I hesitated for a second, looking at the nurse. 'You can do CPR?' she asked. I nodded. 'Go ahead then, and I'll talk to the ambulance.' She watched me as I tilted Chloe's head back, checked her mouth, pinched her nose and began breathing into her, then she stood to take the phone from the man calling 999. I focused on Chloe. Five breaths to start, then heart compressions, two breaths. Her chest was rising and falling with my breath, but there was no sign of life otherwise. I paused to check her pulse again, then continued. A crowd was beginning to gather now.

Two breaths, thirty compressions. Two breaths, thirty. The children's jingle *We're all going to the zoo tomorrow* rang in my head. One verse was thirty compressions at the right speed. Two breaths, thirty. The nurse crouched to feel her pulse, and shook her head. Two, thirty. Two, thirty. I'd been going for five minutes now.

'I'll spell you,' the nurse said. I nodded and slid backwards, heart thudding as if I'd just done a two-hour race. Surely the ambulance would be here soon.

Lizbet had stayed crouching by Chloe's head, eyes enormous with fright. The man standing behind her might be the guitarist she'd mentioned, Tom. Antony was on my other side. The other man had his phone in his hand still, as if he was waiting for the ambulance to call back. I didn't recognise him; he wasn't a Brae man, or a sailor. The nurse had been part of their group too.

53

Five minutes. We swapped places again. Two breaths, thirty. There was still no flicker of life. I focused on breathing, compressing to the song in my head, and pushed away speculation.

There was a stir among the crowd, flashing blue lights and the noise of a siren echoing between the closs walls. Our task was to keep going until the paramedics told us to stop. I was conscious of the green trouser legs bustling around me. A man's hand came down to lift Chloe's hand. 'Pause a moment.' He clipped a peg on her index finger and looked at the attached read-out, then unclipped the device. 'Okay, keep going.'

I kept going, ignoring the noise above me. There was another stir, and an authorative voice asking people to 'Clear back there please' announced the police arriving. The air lightened as the crowd thinned, and there was a murmur of questioning. What had happened? Had she tripped? Her friends were too shocked to give more than vague answers. She'd just seemed to fall. I revisualised what I'd seen: the group coming down the steps, and Chloe cartwheeling forward.

My arms were aching. The green trouser legs came back to stand by me. 'Okay, come away.' An oxygen mask came down as I sat back, and was pressed over Chloe's nose; the stretcher was set where I'd been kneeling. I stood up and looked around. A couple of uniformed officers had Chloe's friends in a huddle where the lane opened out. There was no sign of DS Peterson yet, and I wasn't sure who was in charge, to give my name to – but Lizbet could tell them who I was if they needed to speak to me, and besides, I was just a passer-by, and late already. I hurried off.

As I climbed the steep steps, that moment where Chloe had fallen seemed to replay in front of my eyes. She'd come tumbling over like a sleepwalker. I tried to search my memory for any attempt to hold on to something, or hands flung out to break her fall, and didn't see one. She'd just fallen as if she was already dead.

I couldn't help wondering if a sudden sharp push would have had that same effect. They'd been all in a group together at the top of the stairs. Any one of them could have shoved her. I wasn't convinced though. However sudden, surely your instinct would be to save yourself, the reflexes overriding conscious thought.

Thinking about how was just my mind shying away from what I knew in my heart: that Chloe was dead. The horrid thud of her head striking the stone step still echoed in my brain. She'd already been dead when I'd knelt down beside her.

I'd reached Market Street now. I paused for a moment, chest heaving, and looked around, but there was no problem in finding the foodbank: a rectangular building like the warehouse of a former shop boasted a prominent blue and white notice. The door was open. I called out 'Aye aye' country-style, and went in.

There was a small entrance hall. A table by the door had an 'Out of date, help yourself' box on it, filled with ready-meal containers from the Co-op. The first door was being opened by a tall, thin man whose face was familiar from inter-church services. 'You'll be Cass?' he said. 'Father David phoned me to say you were taking his place. It's good of you to come and give us a hand.' He indicated a woman of my own age. 'I'm David too, and this is Jesma.'

Jesma nodded, smiling. 'I'd a kent you,' she said. 'You're no changed much fae we were at the school together.'

Her voice placed her for me. It had a soft, breathless sound, as if she was permanently nervous, with the gaps between the words unevenly spaced. Otherwise, I wouldn't have been able to link her up with the Jesma Anderson I remembered, a quiet, shy girl who struggled with maths but was a whiz with any kind of craft work, and whose onions never burned in Home Ec. She'd been a slim lass, with wavy hair of that indeterminate brown-fair, and about my own height. Now she was strongly built and several inches above me, not that that was hard, as I'd stayed knee-high to a Mirror mast. Her hair was straightened and lightened to glossy blonde. She was dressed for working in a practical nylon overall over a dark pink jumper, jeans and trainers. There were tired lines around her eyes, and when she stopped smiling there was a worried droop to her mouth.

'I mind you fine,' I replied. 'You saved my onions in Home Ec.'

'You saved my maths homework. You explained it much better than the teacher.'

'I'm sorry I'm late.' I swallowed. 'There was an accident.' They both stilled. 'A girl fell down the steps just by the Peerie Shop Cafe.' I stopped, and Jesma gave me a concerned look. *Cool Cass*, I'd been nicknamed at school, because nothing bothered me, but my coolness was shaken out of me now. I could see Chloe in front of my eyes, cartwheeling down.

'Was she hurt?' David asked.

I nodded. 'She hit her head on the way down. She wasn't breathing. I think – I'm afraid – ' I stopped and linked my hands together to stop them from shaking. 'We had to do CPR.'

Jesma's mouth fell open. Her lips formed the word 'Dead', and her eyes went blank for a moment, as if she was visualising the accident. Then she rallied. 'Sit down for a moment, and I'll make you a cup of tea.' She bustled off, and David moved tactfully away. I sat and let the trembling wash over me. My head was filled with the dark lane, and the heads silhouetted against the shop window at the top, and Chloe's blonde hair swirling as she fell.

'There,' Jesma said, plonking a mug of tea in front of me. 'I ken you never used to take sugar, but I've put some in, for the shock. You just sit there and catch your breath.'

I took a sip of the tea, another, and the taste steadied me. Jesma had been generous with the sugar. I managed to keep my face straight as I drank it.

'That's better,' Jesma said. 'There's a bit of colour back in your face now.' She tried for a lighter tone. 'You didn't get that tan here, that's for sure. Where've you come back from?'

'Boston, then West Africa.' I struggled to my feet, and tried to think more positively. 'The ambulance came and took her. They came straight away. She's where they can help her.' I took a deep breath and glanced around the shelves. 'What shall I do?'

Jesma nodded, as if she was agreeing that work was the cure for a shock. 'We usually make up bags first.' She lifted a green plastic crate from a pile in the corner and unfolded it onto the table, then indicated a whiteboard on the wall. 'That's what's to go in each parcel. These shelves here −' she laid a hand on them − 'the food on them's in the order of the list, so cereals here, then tinned custard, fruit, rice, tinned meat, and so on.' Her hand danced down the shelves. 'You'll soon get the hang of it. Put it all into the tray, then bag it in two bags. Here, you fetch this first one for me.'

I began working through the list. Breakfast cereal, a tin of fruit, a tin of custard, a tin of rice pudding. A jar of jam. A tin each of peas, carrots, sweetcorn, tomatoes, potatoes and two tins of meat meals. Chloe's blonde hair fanned in front of my eyes once more, and I pushed the picture away. Cold meat, tuna, a jar of pasta sauce and a packet of pasta. A bag of rice. Two tins of soup, two of baked beans, one of spaghetti, two cartons of milk, little bags of coffee and tea bags, two packets of biscuits. The movement steadied my fingers.

'And from over there,' Jesma said, 'two toilet rolls and two washing tablets.'

'But this is a lot of food,' I said, looking at the crate. 'It's not what I'd choose to eat, but I'd live for a week on this, no bother, with some bread added.' I took two carrier bags from the drawers and began packing my crateful. She had fallen, just like that − she was in hospital now, where they'd help her. I focused on packing the tins neatly.

'Three meals for a single person,' Jesma said. 'At the moment, the families are helped differently, through Social Work, but we're expecting more here in a couple of months.' She made a face, then echoed Gavin: 'The Government's announced that it's going to make the welfare system more efficient.'

'Less money for those at the sharp end?'

'That's what it usually means.' Her tone was disillusioned. I wondered if she'd been caught in the system herself. She put the carrier bags back in the crate and stashed it under the work surface by the door. 'First customer served. You all set to get on with it, then?'

I nodded, and collected another crate. Cereal. Fruit, custard, rice pud, jam. 'The veg tins are all different sizes. Do I balance them out?'

'Yes, compensate with a larger one of something else if you've given a small one.'

I collected away. The memory of Chloe falling kept coming back, shortening my breathing and making my fingers tremble again, but each time I gripped the container I was holding tighter, said a prayer for her in hospital and forced other thoughts in. Tinned food. I had a prejudice against tinned food, in part because Maman would never have allowed British tinned food in the house, in part because it was the most expensive way of eating. I saw Jesma glance at me, concerned, and set my jaw. Expensive eating. I could make a pot of soup to last several days for the price of one tin. On the other hand, maybe people in temporary accommodation didn't have even as good cooking facilities as my *Khalida*, with two gas rings and a grill.

The bell rang. David reappeared from the back store, slipped out of the door, returned for the bags I'd just packed. There was the murmur of voices in the entrance.

'It is just a short while, for most folk,' Jesma said. 'A stopgap, in an emergency situation.' She gave my shabby black jacket an appraising look. 'You maybe ken about this yourself. You're managing fine, just, to keep everything going, but you don't have anything spare. No safety net. Then one day something goes wrong. Your pay gets delayed by some muddle in the office, or the taxman decides to take more than he usually does, or the car breaks down, or there's a particularly cold spell, like those snowy days at Christmas, and you have to use more heating, but then the hydro bill comes in, and you have to pay it, but that leaves you with nothing to live on for the rest of the month.'

The bell rang again. David picked up Jesma's bags and went out with them. I finished mine off quickly and set them ready, collected another crate and began again with the cereal. Custard, fruit, rice. Tinned meat.

The two hours dragged by. I wasn't able to absorb myself into the work. Chloe's death had been too sudden. She'd been there, and then she was gone. I didn't know she was dead, I reminded myself. The ambulance had taken her. Jesma kept glancing at me, and halfway through she put another sugared mug of tea by my hand. Once we'd got a good stack of waiting bags, we went into the back warehouse, a cold, cavernous place like a ship's store, with racks of roughly made shelving stacked with boxes, and bins at the back filled with tins. 'Stuff comes in from all over,' she said. 'The supermarkets are regular donors, and there are containers in all the local shops and churches, with a list of what's needed, so that folk can just buy an extra couple of items and drop them in the basket.' Her voice came faintly, as if she was far away. I forced myself to listen. 'We get donations of money too, so we can buy stuff we're short of, or sometimes people specify that it's a donation to help someone with their electricity in winter.' Her face clouded. 'The way prices are rising, even well-off folk may not be able to afford to help others this year.' She was silent for a moment, lips drawn together, then she squared her shoulders. 'But the worst o' the winter's by with now.' She gestured at a stack of tins and boxes and became practical again. 'All this needs shelved. Here.' She handed me a black marker pen. 'Check the sell-by date, write it nice and big on the item, and then when you shelve it, make sure the shortest dates are forward.'

We worked away at that until the pile was cleared, then Jesma headed back into the office to put the kettle on, and I returned gratefully to the warmth of the two-bar wall heater and notched up another couple of deliveries while I was waiting. The doorbell had pinged at intervals while we'd been through, and there were only two of the trays we'd done remaining.

We all sat down around the table. I was feeling steadier now, and as if I'd had enough tea, but I lifted the mug to my lips all the same. The biscuits that came with it were obviously broken ones from a packet that was too bashed to be given out. I shook my head at them.

'How're you doing?' Jesma asked.

'Steadier,' I said. 'Thanks. It was awful. It was worse because I kent her – well, not really, but I was speaking to her just yesterday at the boating club.' The Shetland tradition that you didn't say the name of a person who'd died was clamping my tongue. I reminded myself that she'd gone to the hospital, that she could be in a bed now, wired up to monitors with doctors hovering round her. I didn't believe it, much as I wanted to. Jesma watched me, and didn't ask.

There was a long silence, then David stretched and looked around. 'I think we're just about done for the day. If you could do me another few bags, lasses, then you could head off, and I'll stay to hand out.'

'I can keep working,' I said. 'My bus isn't till five.'

'I'm heading home to Brae,' Jesma said. 'I can easy run you.' She smiled at David. 'David kens I don't like to leave the bairns with their pals' folk for longer than I have to. Thanks, David.' She looked back at me. 'It's Voe you live at, isn't it?'

'I'm going to Brae, though. I'm working on the boat there.'

Her face brightened. 'Oh, in that case, it's easy. No detouring at all.'

'Only I do need to go to the Malakoff, for an anode for the boat. I won't be more than five minutes.'

'Head off there now,' Jesma said. 'I'll do these last bags.'

I could see she was anxious to get home, so I ran down the hill to my favourite chandlery, grabbed the right size of anode and returned at a smart walk. When I got back there were three more pairs of bags standing ready at the door, and Jesma had her coat on. She turned as we left, and picked up the next lot of carrier bags, her cheeks reddening, and paused in the porch to take several packets from the 'out of date' box.

'Here,' I said, 'let me carry those.' I was going red myself at her embarrassment, and tried to make a joke of it. 'I didn't realise you were a customer too.'

She managed a smile. 'Temporary,' she said.

Her car was parked right outside the door, a small white hatchback with a jumble of child-bright jackets and bags in the back seat. We squeezed her food bags in and climbed into the front seats. The car started with a sullen-sounding series of thuds. If it had been *Khalida*'s Volvo Penta I'd have been worrying about serious money needing to be spent on it.

'I don't know if I'll be able to keep it running much longer,' Jesma said, echoing my thoughts. 'But you need a car here in Shetland, especially with bairns. Sabina's keen on her gymnastics, well, that's Lerwick, she's ten, and Gerry's only seven, but you ken what these boys are like with their football. And Inga's really good about the gymnastics, because her Dawn does it too, but you canna aye be asking other parents to run them, you have to do your fair share. On the other hand, it's money I just don't have.' She shrugged. 'You canna bring but what's no' ben, as my gran used to say.'

She broke off to negotiate the final roundabout then

61

accelerated up the hill. The car wasn't willing, and several cars passed us as it laboured upwards.

'Potted catch-up,' Jesma said. 'I went off south, and married a south man. Far too young. When that broke up I came home to be nearer my folk, and I was lucky, I got a council house in Brae nearly straight away. I work in the care home, that's twenty-five hours, minimum wage, and I do supply cleaning at the school a few hours a week, minimum again, with increments, so it's not much, but at least both of them are permanent jobs, and they fit the bairns' school hours, mostly, and I get my holidays paid too. It's not like these zero hours contracts you hear about south, they really are skin-of-the-teeth survival. But we wouldn't get by without the foodbank.' She indicated the bags in the back seat with a jerk of the chin. 'You'd be amazed how far I can make this go.'

Twenty-five plus odd hours of a minimum wage. I did the arithmetic. It didn't sound a lot to pay rent and heating and keep two growing children.

'And clothes,' she added. 'The Eid charity shop's a godsend. £1 an item for children's clothes. My folk got them jeans and shoes for their Christmas. I wouldn't want my bairns teased at the school about not being as smart as everyone else.' She changed gear for the long, slow climb over the rise to Girlsta.

The bairns' father was conspicuous by his absence. I didn't like to ask.

'Their father,' Jesma said abruptly. 'He doesn't have a regular income, but he slips me money when he can. Only –'

There was another pause, then Jesma said jerkily, as if the words were being shaken out of her, 'Only I'm no' sure how long he'll still do that. He's got a girlfriend. Young and slim and bonny, and for all she looks like a blonde bombshell I think she's the sort whose biggest ambition is a wedding ring and two point five perfectly turned-out designer kids.' Her voice was bitter. 'I don't ken how keen he is really, but now she's got her claws in she won't let go. If I get the car repairs off him, that might be his swan-song.' She was silent as we passed Sandwater Loch, with the little house dominated by the windfarm workings, Petta Loch with the bulldozers busy on the hill above. Then she sighed. 'It's that strange. He was the bairns' father. He was there to see them being born. He changed their nappies and filmed their first steps. He took the day off to come to the nursery nativity performance. Then when my day was over, somehow so was theirs. Oh, he loves them, he says, and he came up here just so he could still be near them, but if he has another family they'll join me out in the cold.'

There was nothing I could reply. Then my brain began to compute what she was saying: a south man with a young, slim, bonny, blonde-bombshell girlfriend.

'Is your husband Antony,' I asked, 'who has the new fishing boat in Brae?'

Jesma snorted. 'He managed the money for that. And he's done some kind of paperwork that means he makes no money from her. He's a director and gets paid in shares in the boat, or some such chicanery. Meaning the social work can't order him to make me an allowance.' She glanced sideways at me. 'Have you seen the girlfriend?'

I thought of Chloe lying at the bottom of the steps, her blonde hair fanned out across the cold stone slabs, and nodded. I was glad now that I hadn't spoken her name.

'I was as pretty as that once,' Jesma said. She kept her face forwards, eyes looking blindly at the road. A tear ran down the cheek nearest me. Her hands gripped the steering wheel. 'Now I'm old and fat, and she's walking in to take everything.'

She drove on for another mile, then said abruptly, 'You're living with a policeman, aren't you? And you're away at sea a lot. If you're keen on him, maybe you should think – well, men . . .' She sighed. 'They're not good at living alone.'

'But I'm not good at living ashore.' I gave her a sideways

glance and wondered if there was something she wasn't telling me. 'And I trust Gavin.'

She gave a half-laugh at that. 'If you find there's someone else while you're away, well, you decide if you want to keep him. Don't let hurt and betrayed trust and pride take over.' She gave me a quick look, smiling. 'You aye were proud as the Devil.'

I reddened and made a protesting sound.

'I didn't mean stuck up,' Jesma said quickly. 'Just that if you were going to do something at all you'd make sure you did it best. I didn't mean to be cheeky. I was thinking . . . well, when Antony came up here, saying he was sorry and talking about trying again, I was still mad at him, and I turned him down flat. I wish now I'd bitten my tongue and kept my man.'

We'd reached the outskirts of Brae. Jesma sniffed and ran one hand over her cheek. 'Ignore me talking so stupid. I live in the houses here, but I'll just take you along to the marina and turn there – no, it's no bother. Save you a walk.'

She dropped me off and gave me another long look. 'Sure you're okay now?'

I nodded.

'Take care, then.' She turned the car around in a large circle, waved and accelerated into the road. The car sounded even worse from the outside. I hoped Antony would pay for getting it fixed.

Jesma's car had been parked outside the foodbank, but she could have nipped down to the Street for something. There had been a new Boots bag by my feet, and the Boots in Lerwick was fifty yards from Campbell's Closs. She'd been concerned about the shock I'd had, considerate about not asking questions . . . too considerate? Wasn't it strange that she hadn't asked who?

I felt bad even thinking it, but I wondered where exactly Jesma had been when Chloe had fallen down those steps.

Chapter Six

Dey hae a reffled hesp ta redd.
(They have a tangled skein of wool to straighten.)
They have a complicated situation to deal with.

I spotted the *Day Dawn* as soon as I came around the corner. She was floating again, with one of the oversized red balloons at each corner, and the Ocean Kinetics boys were manoeuvring her towards the pier. Magnie was on the dinghy slip, watching. He glanced over his shoulder as I came down, and lifted a hand, but kept his attention focused on the boat as she inched across the gap between the pontoon and the pier. There was no sign of Ewan, unless he was aboard.

A work-squad had been busy in the afternoon too, getting ready for the Up Helly Aa. A line of pick-ups stood along the marina side, with the occasional Berlingo among them. The slip had been cleared of seaweed and there was the chemical smell of algae killer. The trailers that had congregated in front of the club over the winter had all been shifted over to the big shed doors, which were standing open. Banging noises issued from inside, as if people were shifting dinghies.

One of the workers came out, went to a black pick-up, rummaged in his toolkit, spotted me and came over, substantial wrench in hand. I diagnosed a stuck trolley wheel. 'Aye aye, Cass, you're won home then,' he said. With a bit of effort I identified him as a regular crew on one of the other racing yachts. 'I can see you're been in warmer parts. You didn't get that tan here.'

'Africa,' I said.

'When did you win home?'

'Three days ago.'

'You'd just a been in time for the big concert in the Hall – *You're the Stars!* Did you go?'

I shook my head. 'I didn't even ken it was on.'

'Man, that's a pity. It was a real treat.' I spotted the signs of a proud parent and braced myself. 'All the acts were good, but though I say it as shouldn't, Magnie's young lass Lizbet and my boy Tom were the ones that stood out. Several other folk said the same. Lizbet sang like a lintie, and you could hardly see Tom's fingers on the guitar, they moved that fast. They got the other lass to sing too, Chloe, but she wasn't a patch on Lizbet. Real talent there. That's what the presenters said, afterwards. It's a pity you missed it.' He was all set to say more, but a shout from inside the shed took him back there, rather to my relief. The presenters had obviously said the right things in public, whatever they'd said in private. There was no need for me to spoil his moment with a doubtful face.

Jesma's lift had given me an extra hour. I got back into my boiler suit and screwed the anode on around the prop shaft, then went inside to coax the hoses off the stopcocks and check the inner workings. All seemed fine. I reassembled them, made sure that the mast-on tub and tools were to hand on the table, then went to see what was going on.

Day Dawn was alongside the pier now, run as far up the slip as possible. Inside her, the pump churned away. The water poured in a splashing stream over her side. Magnie was waiting at the pier end, hand extended to catch a rope from *Day Dawn*'s stern. It was a diver who was aboard, one hand on the wheel, the other with the rope ready to throw. I watched as they got her neatly settled in place, with room for *Khalida* to go aft of her.

66

There was something not right about *Day Dawn*. It had been niggling me as she came up. Now I could see her properly, I realised her cabin roof was bare: no aerials, no round radar unit. Ewan must have been redoing the electrics over the winter, and taken everything out. It was just as well. If all his instruments had been sunk, that would cost a pretty penny to replace.

Mast. I left them to it and double-checked that every one of the festoon of wires and ropes around the mast was free. I dunked each of the stay-end bottlescrews in a bucket of hot soapy water and unscrewed it as far as it would go, then added a skoosh of WD40. As I worked there were thumping noises from *Day Dawn* to go with the shed clanging, and the occasional shout. I took a walk around *Khalida* just to check we really had covered every last inch with paint, and paused to look over the edge of the pier. They'd shored the *Day Dawn* up with tyres and props of wood wedged with the weights we tethered the dinghies to when wind was expected. The pump had fallen silent, and the Ocean Kinetics boys were busy stowing all their gear back into their vans.

Well, I conceded, it was time to go back to the Ladie. Gavin and the cats would be waiting for me. I gave *Khalida* a pat on the gleaming white of her topsides. 'Tomorrow,' I promised her. 'Mast too.'

Magnie was waiting for me as I walked towards the clubhouse.

'All ready for tomorrow,' I said. 'When's the crane coming?'

'Mid tide. Half past ten.' He was looking sombre. 'Have you heard the news about Lizbet's pal, the blonde lass that sings wi' her? She took a tumble on the steps in one o' the lanes, and hit her head.' He paused, looking out over the water. 'She's dead.'

I'd feared it, expected it, but it was still a shock. I felt my heart stop for a moment, then begin thumping irregularly. My breath caught in my throat. 'I was there,' I said, when I was able to speak again. 'I was just coming off the bus and I saw her fall. I hoped – the ambulance came very quickly.'

Magnie shook his head. 'The hospital contacted her folk. She was dead from when she fell. She hit her head and never wakened more.' He sighed. 'Such a bonny lass, and talented wi' it. Her mother's devastated – she was the only child.' He nodded at the *Day Dawn*. 'That's why Ewan's no' here. He asked if I'd see it was all set up for tomorrow. He'll be here then, if he can.' He turned away from me and gave the darkening sky a quick glance. 'You'd best be heading home, lass, if you're not wanting to be benighted among all those lobster pots at the far side of Linga.'

'I'm going,' I agreed. I hesitated. 'Are they cancelling the Up Helly Aa for the lass?'

Magnie shook his head. 'We all spoke about it, but her father rang Drew, he's the Jarl, specially to say they weren't to think o' it. He wouldn't be there, but he wanted it to go ahead.'

'That's good o' him. I'll head off, then. See you tomorrow.' I re-donned all the jerseys I'd taken off, zipped up my sailing jacket on top, pressed the button to start the *Deuk*'s engine, and turned her nose homewards. I'd be glad to be there with Gavin and the cats. I felt like I'd had enough of today.

Gavin had a pot of mince bubbling gently on the stove. 'I didn't want to put the tatties on till I saw the whites of your eyes.'

'Like living with a policeman,' I agreed. It was blissfully peaceful in the kitchen. Kitten stretched and came out of the basket to say hello; Cat turned his back without looking in my direction. 'I'm not popular.'

'He was furious at you leaving him behind this morning.' Gavin gave the mince a stir and set the tatties on to boil. 'I got a growl and a hiss when I shut the door on him, then he sat in the sit-ootery window and watched you go, still growling to himself. All the same, it was better the Kitten didn't go. Not in her condition. Glass of wine?'

My head jerked up. I stared at Kitten, sitting in the middle of the kitchen floor, washing her white paws. Now Gavin came to mention it, I'd thought she was rounder about the belly than she had been. 'She's having kittens?'

'I thought I'd wait till you were home to break it to you. The patter of tiny paws.'

'But she's only a kitten herself!'

Gavin sat down opposite me and patted his lap for her to jump into. 'You got her in mid-August, and she was maybe eight, ten weeks old then. Weaned, anyway.'

I worked it out. 'So she's nine months old. Is that old enough? And she's so little. Suppose they get stuck coming out?'

Gavin smiled at me. 'Dear Cass, relax. Cats have kittens all the time. She'll be fine.'

'Well,' I said doubtfully.

'Trust me.'

I looked across at Cat, curled tight in his basket, with that 'I don't see any humans' speech bubble above his head. 'Cat's kittens?'

'As far as you can tell with cats. He's certainly letting her eat even more of his food.'

I shook my head. 'Well, if you're sure it'll be all okay . . .'

He stretched out his hand across the table. 'Sure's too definite a word. God willing, it'll be fine.'

Another thought struck me. 'I can't possibly take her to Yell if she's going to kettle on the way.'

'To kettle?' Gavin said, interested.

'Shetland verb, to kettle, to have ketlings. She can't give birth on *Khalida* halfway to Yell.'

'She won't,' Gavin assured me. 'She came into heat in the second week of February. No kittens until the second week of April. She'd be perfectly safe aboard *Khalida*, if you want to take her. If she wants to go.'

I sat watching the Kitten. Now I was looking for it, the

round bulge at her midrift was obvious. 'She's so little,' I said again.

Gavin's hand tightened on mine. 'You leave her to get on with it. Have some dinner. I don't know about you, but I'm starving.'

We ate in silence for the first half-plateful. Now I came to think about it, I was ravenous.

'How was your day?' I asked, once we'd got to the bread-mopping stage.

'You ken all about it already.' His face was sombre. 'A young lass who fell down the steps above the Peerie Shop Cafe and was killed. When she talked to the folk afterwards, Freya had no difficulty identifying the woman with the black plait who helped do the CPR.'

'No,' I agreed. 'And I didn't know then, of course, or at least I was hoping I was wrong, but Magnie told me that she had died.'

'Yes.' He gave me a swift glance. 'I won't ask you about it. Freya said she'd call in later, to get your impressions.'

I frowned. 'Why does she need mine?'

'A report has to go to the Fiscal, to see if further action needs to be taken. You're an uninvolved witness, and you were below them when she fell.'

I remembered the way she'd tumbled down. 'Is she being sent south for an autopsy?'

Gavin nodded.

'When's DS Peterson coming?' She was Gavin's colleague; I made an effort. 'Freya. Will I light the in-by fire?'

'I've done that. She said she'd be here around seven, to give us time to eat our tea in peace.' He cocked his head, listening. 'That'll be her.'

I stacked the plates and shoved them under hot water in the basin. 'I'll put the kettle on.'

I washed the dishes as the car outside came over the hill and parked. DS Peterson's footsteps crunched down the gravel and along the garden path. She brought a wave of cold air in with her.

'Hi, Cass. Sorry to disturb you in the evening. You're my last witness, then I can get this report off for forensics in Aberdeen to read in the morning.' When the body arrived with them, she meant. It would be on tonight's boat.

She took off her scarf and laid it down over the back of Gavin's chair, entirely at home, as if she was a regular visitor. I suddenly wondered how often she dropped in like this. I had complete faith in Gavin, of course I did, and there was nothing wrong with one of his workmates calling in of an evening to discuss a case, but I didn't like it. Jesma's voice echoed in my head: *If you find there's someone else while you're away, well, just you decide if you want to keep him . . . I wish now I'd bitten my tongue and kept my man.*

I was on a tall ship surrounded by workmates, mostly male. I didn't have a leg to stand on if Freya Peterson chose to visit Gavin of an evening. 'Coffee?' I asked.

'Please.'

I gestured her through to the sitting room. 'The fire's on inby. Go through.'

'I'll leave you to it,' Gavin said, and sat down at the kitchen table again. Cat yawned, stretched in his box, then got out of it, stretched again and followed DS Peterson.

I filled up the percolater, added mugs and milk and took it through. She'd installed herself on the fire end of the couch, as if she knew the armchair opposite was Gavin's. I sorted the coffee then sat down facing her. Cat came up on my lap, and I tickled the soft white fluff behind his ears. 'How can I help?'

'I take it Gavin's explained? I did try to ring you, but your phone seemed to be switched off.' Her laptop pinged as she opened it. 'Now, background. Chloe's band had taken part in the *You're the Stars!* heat yesterday, up here in Brae, and they felt they'd done pretty well, so they went out to lunch to celebrate:

71

Chloe, the other singer, Lizbet, and the guitarist, Tom, along with Chloe's boyfriend, Antony.'

I thought of Lizbet, trying to be cheerful about the defeat of her hopes. I didn't think she'd have woken up this morning feeling better, but equally, I didn't think she'd have shared what she heard with the other two. If the letter was going to come to Chloe, well, she'd face that when she had to.

DS Peterson gave me a sharp look. 'Something you know about that?'

I shook my head. She waited a moment, then resumed.

'They were at The Dowry. Once they got to their table it turned out they knew the people next to them: Irvine Robertson, who was apparently an old boyfriend of Chloe's, and his new girlfriend, Amy White – she was the nurse who spelled you at the CPR. They chatted during the meal, and they all left at the same time.'

I nodded.

'They turned down that flight of steps just above the Peerie Shop Café. I gather you were below the steps when she fell, and came forward to help. What were you doing there? Just take me through it.'

'I'd got off the bus,' I said. 'At the Esplanade. I was headed for Market Street, and I was just passing the café to go up the lane when their party came around to the top, and they were obviously coming down, so I stopped to let them get down to ground level.'

'Okay. Try and visualise them.'

I tried. 'It's hard. I wasn't staring at them. I noticed them, and stood to the side, then Chloe fell. I didn't know who it was then. I just saw her falling.'

'Try to describe that for me.'

I spread my hands. 'She just fell. She pitched forward. The odd thing was, she didn't try to grab on to anything. Her arms

72

spread out because she was falling. She went down and heels over head, and ended up on her back.'

DS Peterson leaned forward. 'Just fell,' she repeated. 'She didn't trip on those ridiculous strappy heels?'

I shook my head. 'I don't think she stumbled. She just went forward in one smooth movement.' I remembered the horrid smack as her head had hit the hard steps. 'Her head went down and she landed on it, and then tumbled right over.'

'I don't want to put ideas in your head, but are you sure she wasn't pushed?'

I thought about that. 'She didn't fall as if she'd been pushed,' I said at last. 'It wasn't like she was propelled forwards. She just tipped.' I saw her again in my mind's eye, and made an effort. 'As if she'd leaned forward and overbalanced. Or like she'd fallen asleep. Had she drunk much at the meal? Enough to make her just blank out?'

'They'd none of them drunk anything, because of either driving or work. Amy thought Chloe was stumbling as they walked along, but she blamed it on the high heels. Irvine thought she was walking as if she was drunk, wavering-like, he said, but she didn't drink in The Dowry, unless she had a hefty swig of something in the toilet. The post-mortem'll pick it up if she did. And then once she was down?'

'I felt her pulse. Wrist then neck. There wasn't anything, so I started CPR.'

'What did the others do while you were doing that?'

'They came down. I think one of the men looked as if he wanted to raise her, and I told him not to. I wasn't watching them. I was focused on what I could do for Chloe. Then the nurse – Amy? – she checked her pulse, and told me to carry on, and she talked to the ambulance.'

'Do you have any idea of how they were standing when you first saw them at the top of the steps? Think of where you were standing, and what you saw, looking upwards. Were they outlined against the sky?'

I shook my head. 'No, against the baker's shop on the other side of the street.'

'A lit window? Posters in it?'

I nodded. 'Lit, though it wasn't very bright, because it was daylight. There was a poster with an offer – coffee and a doughnut, something like that. Chloe was in the middle of the group, in front of the writing. They were bunched together.' I tried to see the heads against the bright poster. 'There was someone as tall as her beside her, half covering up the picture of the coffee. Male. It might have been Antony – no, I think he was behind her. Maybe it was the other bloke, what did you call him, Irvine?'

'Irvine's dark, and below-average height.'

I shook my head. 'I'd expect someone to look dark against the window, and I couldn't judge heights from down below. He looked to me slightly taller than Chloe.'

DS Peterson's fingers rattled over the keyboard. 'Okay. Who else?'

'Amy. I'm not sure where she was. The band guitarist, Tom, he was on Chloe's other side, but he was letting Lizbet go in front of him.' I shook my head, and repeated, 'They were bunched together. You can only get two going down those steps at once.'

'Who was going to come down first?'

'Chloe and Lizbet, I think. Chloe on the right, Lizbet on the left.'

'Their right and left, or yours?'

'Mine. Chloe to starboard.'

DS Peterson brought her notebook out of her jacket pocket and drew a quick sketch: the two walls of the houses each side of the steps, the shop behind, and the heads between the walls. Lizbet with Tom behind her, Antony, Chloe, Irvine, Amy. 'Is that right?'

There was something about her voice. 'Are you happy about it being an accident?' I asked abruptly.

Her face stilled. She gave me a long, thoughtful look. 'No,' she conceded. She closed her notebook again, and turned it over in her hands. 'But I've no reason for suspicion. Just my police instincts. I talked to them all, and each of them was understandably shocked and upset. Only somehow . . .' She gestured with her hands, the slim fingers closing on air. 'Somehow, nobody was sorry enough. Each of them, her old friends Lizbet and Tom, and her boyfriend Antony, and her old flame Irvine and his new girlfriend Amy – each of them, I felt this relief that they were ashamed of, and either were trying to hide or hadn't quite articulated to themselves. I sensed it. She'd been a problem, and now she was gone.'

She put the notebook back in her pocket, and closed her laptop. 'So what were you thinking just now? About the talent contest?'

I wasn't sure what I was thinking. *Relief* . . . Lizbet couldn't have pushed Chloe, if she had been pushed; she was beside her, slightly in front if anything. I'd need to know more before I gave DS Peterson what I'd learned from an upset youngster shaken out of her usual self-control on a lonely beach. 'Nothing to share,' I said.

DS Peterson was silent for a moment, eyes narrowed, then she shrugged, put her laptop away, and rose. 'Thanks for your time, Cass. You'll hear if this needs to be taken any further.'

Chapter Seven

Thursday 16th March

Tide times, Brae:
LW 01.47 (0.76m);
HW 07.53 (1.91m);
LW 14.11 (0.52m);
HW 20.24 (1.88m)

Moonset 06.46; sunrise 07.16; sunset 19.09;
moonrise 23.19. Moon waxing gibbous.

Der aetin der ain ten fingers.
(They're eating their own ten fingers.)
They are showing remorse over some action or lack of foresight.

Cat was determined not to be left behind today. He hurried his breakfast with the air of a cat who had important things to do and headed out of the catflap at a purposeful trot, the Kitten behind him. When I got down to the *Deuk* they were already sitting on the cockpit slats. Today would be all right; I'd be there the whole time, and they'd have *Khalida* to lurk in for most of it, once she was back on the water.

'Lifejackets,' I told them. I rolled up the canopy over the little cabin entrance, and got them out. For once Kitten allowed me to put hers on with only a token-gesture squeak of protest. Gavin had let the straps out a little, I noticed, to accommodate her extra belly. 'And no strenuous climbing,' I added. 'You should be at home with your knitting.'

It was a perfect day for messing about with masts. The sea lay blue in front of us, a shining highway; the furthest shore, up at Brae, was fretted with cold mist, but the sun picked out geometric shadows on the banks of Linga, and brightened the front of Magnie's white house over on Muckle Roe. The cottage burn trickled in the stillness. Out past the stone pier, a shag suddenly popped to the surface, as if it'd been holding its breath too long underwater, bobbed there for a moment, dark-green back glistening, water dripping from its bill, then did its funny up-and-over dive back down. Only the chill in the air reminded me that it was still March. I drew a deep breath gratefully: clean, clear air, without a hint of teenage boy aftershave or generator diesel tang. It was good to be home.

It was quarter to ten when I parked the *Deuk* at the far side of the dinghy pontoon. The near side was clear, with Antony presumably out picking up his creels, but he'd likely be back during the day. The far side would be out of the way of pier shenanigans. I'd bring *Khalida* in behind her, handy for the cats to transfer if they wanted to. There was no sign of the crane yet, but Magnie's Fiat was parked above me, along with a black pickup and a police car, and there were voices coming from behind the *Day Dawn*. I tied the *Deuk* and went round to investigate.

Magnie and Ewan were there, and DS Peterson with them, along with one of her sidekicks, the gangly one. PC Macdonald. I nodded at them and turned towards Magnie and Ewan. Ewan's face was white, and his eyes were reddened under heavy lids. His mouth drooped, as if he was too tired to smile, but he managed a bleak nod in my direction and continued the conversation, speaking slowly as if every word had to be dredged up from deep water.

'I'll still go ahead with lifting her out, since the crane's here. A week or two drying out would do her no harm,' he said.

My ears pricked. If he'd even thought of leaving her in the water, then he must know what had caused *Day Dawn* to sink, and have already fixed it.

'And it'll be easier to work on the engine ashore.' He paused, as if he was thinking it through, then said, in that same drugged voice, 'The crane can lift it out. Onto a palette in the back of the pick-up.'

'It'll no' hurt her,' Magnie agreed. 'She can go back in when the rest do. Aye aye, Cass. All set?'

'As set as I'll ever be,' I agreed. Any interaction of cranes and boats made my heart sink, but at least this one was in the right direction, with my boat going seawards, and getting her mast back. I looked at Ewan. 'Do you ken what made her go down?'

'Yea,' he said. 'The hose was off one of the stopcocks in the heads.' His voice was almost indifferent. I thought of the simmering fury he'd shown yesterday, before he'd learned of Chloe's death, and grieved for him.

DS Peterson noticed it too. She gave him a sharp look. 'Well, I'll leave you all to get on with your boat-lifting. Good luck. I'll be speaking to you again, Mr Pearson.' She nodded generally to us all, and she and PC Macdonald headed back to their police car, and made it out of the drive just before the crane turned into it and clanked its way downwards towards us.

It all went remarkably smoothly. Having something to do seemed to do Ewan good, though every so often he'd pause, look out across the sea, lips working, then straighten with a deep breath and continue. *Khalida* went up into the air, I raced forward with a loaded brush of antifouling, slapped it on the four spaces where the cushioned supports had been and added a last slurp from the bottom of the tin on the underside of her keel bulb. The crane driver lowered her precisely into the water behind *Day Dawn*. Magnie wuppled her bow rope round one of the cleats, and I took the stern line a turn around a bollard and jumped aboard. Ah, she felt better with water under her, moving as a living thing should. I unhooked the slings and the driver pulled them upwards, dripping. 'Mast next?' he asked.

Magnie glanced at the superstructure of *Day Dawn*, with the mast jutting up above the pier railings. 'Will that be in the way?'

The driver shook his head. 'Let's get this one right out of the way, and then focus on the big job.'

That suited me fine. 'It's ready to go.'

Another couple of boat-owners had appeared to see if they could give a hand, so there were plenty of us around to carry the mast out from the mast shelving, and lay it on the pier above *Khalida*. I gave the wires a last check, Magnie put the strop around the mast and the driver twiddled his controls again. The mast rose into the air with all the wire stays swinging around it, like one of those fairground chair-o-plane rides. I jumped aboard, guided its foot into the plate on deck and shoved the bolt home, then everyone grabbed a stay and clevis pin and began attaching the stays to the deck. In less than ten minutes the mast was attached at all points. I drew a relieved breath and lifted a hand to the driver. 'All done.'

My engine started with no more than a token-gesture stall. Ewan manoeuvred the strop off, Magnie threw me my lines and I was free to take *Khalida* around to beside the *Deuk*. My heart was singing, singing, to feel my boat moving under me, and to look up and see the mast stretching skywards. I'd be sailing tomorrow. Over at the far side of the marina the grey blur of Cat stopped, raised his head to look, then turned and picked his way back along the shore, with the ginger blob of Kitten following him. By the time I'd got her backed in front of the *Deuk* they were waiting on the pontoon, and leapt aboard as soon as she was in place.

'Sailing again, boy,' I said, and Cat gave his soundless miaow, waved his plumed tail and headed below. I left him in charge and went back to help with *Day Dawn*. As she rose and came down to dangle above the cradle, there was a lot of adjusting of the huge bottlescrews that held it together, and rushing about to get more pieces of wood to go under her keel, but at last she was supported to everyone's satisfaction. Ewan gave a final nod, and the nose of the crane came down. The slings fell limp to the ground. Magnie came over with a ladder and Ewan climbed up it and detached the slings, then came back to ground level. 'Well,' he said, 'that's that. Thanks to you all.' He stood for a moment, looking at his boat, then suddenly the energy that had sustained him drained out of him. His shoulders slumped, and he swayed as he stood.

Magnie put a hand on his shoulder. 'She'll do now, boy. You get home to your mother, for she'll be needing you this day, and you ken you have a busy day tomorrow.'

Ewan nodded, and Magnie walked with him to the pick-up and saw him aboard. We got on with rolling up the slings, carefully not looking or commenting as he drove up out of the marina, the car wavering on the hill. Once he was out of sight, the group broke up, with the other owners heading to their boats, and the driver folding up the crane's nose and taking in the right-angled leg supports. I called 'Thanks' to him again, and he waved, backed the huge truck out as neatly as if he was reversing a Mini, and clanked off.

'All done,' Magnie said.

'Phew,' I agreed. 'Time for a cup of tea?'

'I would say.'

Cat was back on his usual perch on the forrard hatch, boss of all he surveyed. The Kitten was curled up on the sunny patch on the cockpit slats. I boiled the kettle and we sat in the cockpit, looking up at *Day Dawn* on the pier. 'So,' I said, 'was it an accident then?'

Magnie shook his head. 'Sabotage,' he said. 'We went below, Ewan and I, once she was out of the water. If that stopcock hose was attached the way the other one was, and I don't see why it wouldn't have been, then it wouldn't have worked loose, and it wasn't just loose, it was right off, and the two clips that held it in the bilge. No. Somebody loosed it, and opened the cock.' He thought about that for a moment. 'Somebody with a good bit of strength too. That hose had been heated to stretch it onto the cock. It wouldn't have come off easy.'

I looked at the bracket on the cabin roof where the radar should have been, and tried to phrase my thought carefully. 'It was lucky he'd taken his electrics out.'

Magnie gave me a shrewd look. 'The insurance isn't going to like that either. Na, na, he began rewiring her back in January, or at least, I dinna ken how far he's got wi' the rewiring, but he took all the instruments out and stripped the old wires out then. Besides . . . yea, I ken for most folk an insurance fiddle hardly counts, but Ewan wouldna do that.'

I thought about Ewan's long face and intense dark eyes and was inclined to agree. 'Did anyone else have it in for him? No family feuds down to the tenth generation?'

Magnie shook his head. 'Just the sooth man wi' the fancy fishing boat.' He rose. 'Well, where shall we start with getting this boat ready to sail?'

We got the rigging tightened and were just heading up to the shed when a little red car came down the drive. Magnie lifted his head. 'That's our Lizbet,' he said. 'I'd no' have expected her to be out and about the day.'

He raised a hand. The car slowed, turned and parked outside the clubhouse, and Lizbet got out.

The sparkle was gone. She wore jeans and a dark jumper that darkened the shadows under her eyes and drained the colour from her face, making her plainer than ever. I didn't think she'd slept that night. She glanced at me, then focused on Magnie. 'I need to speak to you. It's important.' Her mouth wavered, and she gripped her lips together. She looked around, and saw *Khalida* at the pier. 'Can we go on Cass's boat?' She looked at me now. 'You ken about it already. Well, part o' it.' Her hands lifted

81

to clutch at the air. 'I need advice. I need to ken what to do.' She looked back to Magnie, then to me again, and spoke with desperation. 'I've got the Book o' the Black Arts, and I dinna ken how to get rid o' it.'

We sat Lizbet down in *Khalida*'s cockpit. I offered tea, but she waved that away. 'I'm awash wi' tay. I'm had cup after cup this morning, trying to think.' Her eyes filled with tears. 'I ken I'm done wrong. I dug up the Book, and it killed Chloe.' Her eyes slid up the road to where Ewan had driven away, then returned to me. 'How's Ewan? Have you seen him since – since it happened?'

Magnie shifted across to sit beside her, and took one of her hands in his. 'Ewan's coping. He's shattered but he's coping.'

Her face crumpled. 'If he kent what I'd done he'd never forgive me,' she whispered. Her face was bleak with pain. Ewan had loved Chloe, but Lizbet, it was plain to see, loved Ewan.

Magnie patted her shoulder. 'Now, lass, you need to tell me it all from the beginning. How did you even ken about the Book, and where to find it?'

She sniffed and drew a hand over her eyes. 'It was me Nan. She took a breathess turn back, oh, five year ago, maybe, and I was the only one with her, and she told me this story. Well, she'd told me the story before, of her grandmother seeing the minister bury something in the old Cullivoe kirkyard, but what she hadn't told me was what it was. She said someone needed to ken, so that it wouldn't be disturbed again.' She gave a little wail and buried her face in her hands for a moment, then lifted it up again, eyes swimming with tears. 'And I let her down. She told me so that it wouldn't be disturbed, and I went and took it.'

'What in Heaven's name possessed you to do that?' Magnie asked.

She looked at me as she told the story of the audition, and what the producer had said, her voice soft and ashamed. 'And I

82

told Cass about it, on the beach, and she said something about a magic wand, and I suddenly thought . . . I mean, I didn't think it would really work, and I never ever meant to harm Chloe. I just wanted it to be me. So I went up to Yell that evening. I went home to pack a bag, and phoned my mum and went up to stay the night.' She looked at me. 'I grew up in Breckon, Cass, just across the field from the kirkyard. Brian, me brother, he was away at sea, but he had one of those metal-detectoring things, and I'd used it wi' him, so I kent how to work it.' Her eyes brightened momentarily, remembering. 'We found a coin fae 1813, and a Victorian brooch.' Then her face clouded over again. 'Nan said the Book was in a tin deed box, in a corner where nobody was buried. I reckoned that even if the box was half rusted away it should give enough of a signal. So I waited till everyone was asleep, and off I went.'

She paused, shuddering, and I imagined her making her way through the kirk gate and threading her way among the graves in the darkness, the metal detector flashing its red light before her.

'I didn't expect it to be that spooky,' she said. 'We played there all our childhood, hoosies in the old kirk, and hide and seek, and daring the Devil's grave, daft bairns' stuff. I never expected to be afraid, just because it was night. And you'd've thought it being moonlight would make it better, but it was worse, with the brightness catching the graves, and the dark shadows behind them. I felt as if eyes were watching me. It was like I was blundering about for hours until I found something that just might be it, and best of all it was on the far side of the old kirk from the houses, so I could show a light without anyone seeing it. The feeling was growing in me that I shouldn't touch it, and oh, God, how I wish now I'd listened, but right then I forced it down. It was only an old book. What trouble could it really cause? I set my phone by the site to see what I was doing, and dug until I heard the spade hit metal, then I cleared the hole out till I could see what it was.' She paused for a deep breath. 'It was a rusted tin box – no' as rusty as I'd expected. I pulled it out and put it in the bag I'd brought for it. I'd meant to fill the hole back in, but – ' Her voice wavered. 'It's really stupid, but I felt like all the forces of evil were gathering round me, and one voice in my head was yelling at me to put the thing back and bury it and never go near it again, but over it the snooty London voice was saying *Plain as a pudding.* I grabbed the bag and the rest of my gear, and ran for the car as if the furies were after me. I'd shoved my phone in my pocket, and my hands were full, so I kept stumbling over the graves, and I thought about the dead people I was walking over . . .' Her voice rose, and she stopped on a gasp. 'I knocked my shin on a stone. I only saw the blood when I took my jeans off. I drove home with my hands shaking on the wheel, and when I got into the house at last I collapsed on the bed, because my knees were trembling that much I couldn't stand. I just lay there, feeling the way my heart was thumping, and wanting to put the thing back. Then, once I'd recovered, well, I thought, I'd taken it now.'

The box was locked, but it was rusted enough that she could pull one side open with a hammer, and inside there was a book wrapped in cloth, with a Bible on top of it. She'd hesitated, part scared, part defiant, then opened it.

'I couldn't read the writing; it was like, all curlicues. I laid my hands on it, a hand on each side of it, and wished – ' Her voice quavered again and broke entirely. She was silent, swallowing, then she glanced at Magnie and me, a sideways, shamefaced look, and finished her confession. 'I wished to be famous. I imagined it, with my hands there on the book, a stage and lights and people cheering, and a record deal, and costumes, and appearing on TV, and my picture in all the papers, attending the NME awards, a sell-out tour.' Her voice rose. 'I didn't half-believe it would work, even then. Only in the middle of wishing my fingers tingled, as if they'd had an electric shock, and I snatched them back and shoved the book back into its box, and kicked it under the bed. It might be a load of nonsense, but the thing was going back into the kirkyard the first chance I got. Only I was that tired, and I had to get up for the ferry, and I slept in and didn't have time. I put it into the boot of my car and drove away from Breckon with it.' Her voice went dull. 'And at lunchtime I met up with Chloe and Tom, and we were celebrating, and then as we headed back to work – ' She stopped again, and swallowed, then finished in a heavy voice. 'Chloe died, as if she'd been struck down, and it was my fault.' She shuddered. 'It was like that horrible story we read at school, where this family got three wishes from a monkey's paw, and it killed their son, and when the wife asked for him back, then his corpse came.'

That story had made me feel sick too. 'Is the book still in your car?' I asked.

Lizbet nodded.

'Throw it in the sea,' I said.

'I daren't,' Lizbet said. She flushed scarlet. 'Suppose I got home and found it on the mantelpiece, like in the stories? Then I'd ken . . .'

She didn't finish but I knew what she was trying to say. Then she'd know it was real. She'd know that her taking the Book had given the Devil power to strike her friend dead.

'Put it back,' Magnie said urgently. 'Put it back where you found it, wi' the minister's Bible and his sixpence on the top, and never meddle wi' it more.'

'She can't,' I said. 'The police ken something was dug up from there.'

'Then bury it somewhere else, wi' the good book on top of it. Somewhere it'll no' be disturbed. Give the Devil his own again.'

Her face cleared. 'Yea,' she said. Her eyes grew intent, as if she was remembering. 'Yea, I ken the place for it. I'll do that.

85

Then I'll go to the kirk and pray as I've never prayed before that I'll be free o' it.'

She took a deep breath, and rose. 'Thanks to you both. You'll no' mention to anyone . . .?'

We shook our heads.

'I'll get rid o' it,' she said. 'It'll never be seen more.'

Chapter Eight

Lay dy wird apo dy knee
An shape him ere he spokken be.
(Lay your word upon your knee, and shape him before he spoken be.)
Weigh your words before you speak.

We got on well with *Khalida*; it was one of those days where every line ran smoothly, every shackle screwed in straight first time. After Lizbet had gone, Magnie and I re-threaded the electric wires back behind the cabin panelling and reattached the connections. We sorted out all the string up the mast, and got the deck furling lines back into their pulleys. We took the boom out of the loft and removed my old mainsail from it. Last and most exciting, we unwrapped the stiff, snow-white new jib and managed, with a bit of heaving, to haul it up its narrow slot in the metal foil. We spent a few minutes admiring its beautiful curve before I furled it away. I couldn't wait to try it out.

By then it was mid-afternoon. Magnie headed off home, and I was just walking back to the pontoon when a car drove round into the caravan park and stopped by one of the caravans. The park was filling up with caravan and motorhome owners staying over for Up Helly Aa, but I knew these folk, for they were regulars at Brae, the ones Magnie had pointed out as truly happy folk. Davie and Merran, from Mid Yell. I knew they weren't boaty people, but it might be worth asking them about Mid Yell marina.

Their little white dog leapt out of the car and rushed over to me, yapping, followed by Merran. 'Hello there, Cass,' she called. 'Never mind Scotty, he kens you really.'

'Aye aye, Scotty, stop that racket,' I said. I could see Cat's head appearing on board *Khalida*, whiskers bristling, and hoped he wouldn't feel he needed to come over and sort Scotty out. I went over to the car, and Scotty followed.

'Welcome back,' I said. 'Down for the Up Helly Aa?'

'Wouldn't miss it,' Davie said. 'Well, we were here at the weekend, but we went home for the middle of the week, and now we're back again. We have tickets for the club, of course.'

After the galley burning, the squads, the groups of guizers, went round a dozen local halls and clubs performing the short drama or dance they'd rehearsed, and the boating club was one of the venues.

'It'll be a good night.' I paused to end that conversation, then began, 'I was thinking I could ask you about Mid Yell marina. I'll be sailing up there over the weekend. I have my driving theory test on Monday.'

Davie nodded at Merran. 'Ah, I said to Merran as we came down the drive, that was a mast up, and I'd bet it was yours, if you were back from your ship.'

'And it's plain to see,' Merran said, inevitably, 'that you're been somewhere hot. You didna get that tan here.'

'Boston to Morocco,' I said, 'then down the west coast of Africa to Freetown.' I pulled a face, and lifted my face to the fresh Shetland air. 'Too hot for me. I'm glad to be back in the cool.'

Merran shook her head. 'Ah, me, I love the heat. We've booked the week after Easter in the Canary Islands, a big villa, so all the family can come too.'

'That'll be fine,' I said. 'You'll enjoy that.'

Davie got back to my question. 'I'm no' sure if there are visitor spaces in Mid Yell.'

'The phone number'll be in the marinas book, if there are,' I said. 'I was wondering more about the approach. I have a feeling the voe's bristling with lobster buoys, and I might be coming in before it's properly light.'

Merran pulled a face. 'You're fairly right there,' she said. 'There's a lot of them, all the way out to Bluemull Sound. It's a good area for lobsters.' She put Scotty down, and he ran off towards the pontoon, where Cat had come out of *Khalida* and was sitting on guard duty. Scotty tried a rush at him, Cat rose, swelled and hissed, and Scotty swerved, with an unconvincing imitation of a dog who suddenly realised he'd meant to go in another direction. Cat sat down again, and watched with disdain as he cocked his leg against *Day Dawn*'s cradle.

'Here!' Davie called him, then turned back to me. 'Ewan's got his boat out, then. He didn't mention he was taking her out when we spoke to him the other day. Ah, well, it's the time of year for it.'

I was hesitating over explaining the true state of affairs when a black 4x4 roared down the track, swerved into the first parking space and stopped in a scrunch of gravel. I recognised that style of driving, and raised a hand.

'My parents,' I explained. 'Have a good holiday.'

'Have fun with your boat,' Davie said, 'and see you later.'

Merran went off to collect Scotty, and Davie busied himself backing his car in beside their caravan. I strolled over to see what my parents were up to.

They were looking well. Maman had just finished a tour performing one of Rameau's more obscure operas in the Loire's most elegant castles, and Dad had joined her in Poitiers for spring there, running his various businesses by internet. Now they were back in Shetland for the summer, with the occasional excursion to whatever other venues Maman was booked for. Dad was dressed for the country in a dark jumper and jeans, like Pierce Brosnan posing for a yachting casuals catalogue; Maman looked as if she'd just stepped out of her image designer's salon in Paris, dark hair swept smoothly into a chignon at the back of her neck, eyes made up with a sweep of dark liner. *Je reviens* floated on the air. As a concession to the season, she'd swapped her full-skirted white woollen winter coat for a casually belted trenchcoat affair in cream silk. I hugged Dad, and kissed Maman on both cheeks. '*Salut, Maman*, hi, Dad. Did you spot my mast?'

'Sure, and we knew the first mast up would be yours,' Dad said. A lifetime spent elsewhere had barely dented his Dublin accent.

Maman slipped her arm through mine and replied in French. 'You're looking very well, my Cassandre. How was your voyage?'

'Busy,' I said. 'Teenagers everywhere, plugged into their devices all the time, even on watch.'

'Dreadful,' she said.

'But,' I said, 'I've been asked to take over as acting First Officer for Agnetha's maternity leave.' I translated for Dad's benefit. 'The First Officer's gone off to have her baby, and when I return I'll be in her place.'

'Cassandre, but that's marvellous.' Maman kissed my cheek. 'You must come over on Sunday, and we'll have a special French meal to celebrate.'

'First Officer?' Dad said. He put an arm around me. 'Well, that's something.' I could feel that he wasn't totally happy. 'What's Gavin saying to that?'

I could see where that would lead. 'I can't do Sunday,' I said quickly. 'I'll be sailing up to Yell, for my driving theory test. Next Sunday would be brilliant.'

Dad's still-dark brows drew together. He looked again at my *Khalida*, obviously being readied for a passage. Maman took a step to his side and took his arm. 'Next Sunday will suit us just as well, will it not, Dermot? We won't keep you just now, but we'll see you tomorrow, at the club.'

'Are you watching the burning?'

Maman pursed her lips and waved one perfectly manicured hand in a gesture of dismissal. 'Your father may. I shall wait inside the club – the wind disarranges one's hair, and the nights are still cold. Besides, I've seen it for thirty years, and one burning ship is very much like another. But we'll be at the club afterwards, for the music and the little plays. We'll see you there.'

I'd been too busy getting my boat back to think about actually going to it. 'I'm not sure if Gavin's got tickets for it. He hasn't mentioned it.'

'Magnie phoned specially on the day they went on sale,' Dad said, 'to tell me he'd kept us four for the boating club.'

I opened my mouth to protest that I'd be sailing on Saturday night, then caught Dad's eye and shut it again. Going out was what people who lived together did. If I'd been up late on Friday, I'd sleep sounder in the afternoon, ready to stay awake all Saturday night.

'That'll be good,' I said. 'We haven't danced together for ages.'

'We'll keep you places beside us,' Dad promised.

Scotty yapped from a safe distance as the cats came over to greet them. They both approved Maman as a source of interesting pre-cooking trimmings, and she and the Kitten were fellow stylists. Cat waved his tail, and gave his silent miaow; the Kitten gave a squeak, and stretched up against Maman's legs. Maman lifted her.

'*Salut*, Cat. *Salut, Chaton.*' She'd grown up on a farm; I saw her noting Kitten's rounder belly. She gave me a quick, interrogatory look and I nodded. 'Next month, apparently.'

I turned to grin at Dad. 'I need to get home to make Gavin's tea.' Maman's lips twitched as she put the Kitten down, but Dad took that at face value.

'That's more like it. Time you came home, instead of leaving the poor boy to look after himself all the time, and do his own lonely washing.'

'I might put a load of washing on too,' I conceded, though it would be my own rucksackful. Dad nodded in approval.

'We'll see you tomorrow,' Maman said again, and got Dad away before I said something undaughterly. I waved them off then coaxed the cats back on board the *Deuk* – Cat was reluctant to abandon his own boat for an obviously smaller model – and clipped them on to keep them there while I shifted *Khalida* to a space in the pontoons.

It was a bonny run home. The sun was playing peek-a-boo with the clouds, so that the hills turned from muted fawn, olive chocolate to dull khaki, and the sea changed with every alteration in the light, from airforce blue to yellow grey, then suddenly, as the sun came out, dazzling too brightly to look at, and with a warmth that reddened my cheeks. The sheep grazing on Linga were heavy with lamb, and as I came past the mussel rafts I spotted my first red-throated diver on the water, grey and graceful.

Our cottage basked in sunshine. The crocus by the path were showing their orange stamens, the hens were clucking contentedly under the trees that surrounded the garden, and the sparrows were cheeping like mad things among the bushes. The cats waited outside to harrass them and sunbathe on the doorstep. Up in the field, the ponies lifted their heads as I clicked the gate, considered me for a moment, then went back to grazing. I changed out of my sailing gear then put a pot of tatties on to boil. Yesterday's mince would be today's shepherd's pie.

The criss-crossed potato topping was just browning nicely under the grill when I heard Gavin's Land Rover and the thud of hooves. I stuck the plates under the pie, poured boiling water over frozen peas and went out to meet him. 'Welcome home.'

We hugged. He gave the ponies the police station leftovers,

then we turned to walk down the path together, hands linked. 'I can see you've had a good day,' he said. 'You've got that bounce of a woman who's been putting her boat back together. How's it going?'

'My new mainsail to do tomorrow. The jib looks amazing.'

'And all the stuff in the spare room to go on board.' He came into the kitchen and sniffed appreciatively. 'Mmmm. You have been busy.'

'Shepherd's pie with the left over mince.'

He sat down at the table with a long sigh that shed his working day. Kitten came out of her box and jumped onto his lap. He tickled her ears. 'This is wonderful.' His cheeks reddened. 'Coming home to have you here, I mean.'

'Tea made is even better,' I agreed. Dad would have been proud of me.

'A proper tea too. I've got sick of takeaways. I keep making resolutions about cooking and freezing at the weekend, but then it turns out to be a good fishing day, or I've picked up the wood to do something far more interesting around the house. I've cooked fish, but otherwise I don't think I've had a decent meal since your parents fled the gales of Shetland for the frosts of the Loire.'

'I've noticed the improvements.' I brought the shepherd's pie out of the oven, dished it out, added the peas and sat down.

'I'm planning to clear the shed at the weekend. It would make a great workspace, with room for a proper workbench. Now you're home for a whole eight weeks I can't leave half-finished carpentry all over the kitchen table. It's warm enough to work outside too.' He paused to consider. 'Of course, I may not be feeling at my brightest on Saturday, depending on how late we stay out on Friday. Still, shed-clearing's a fine thing to do with a hangover.'

I was glad I'd been pre-warned. 'It'll be good for you to see our local Up Helly Aa. We can dance together.'

93

We finished the pie and took our coffee through to the sitting room. Gavin settled himself back in his chair with a sigh. 'That's better.' He smiled across at me. 'Thanks for letting me relax before you ask what sort of day I've had.'

Lizbet's confession still rang in my ears. I didn't want to think about Chloe. 'Did you find anything out about Ewan's sunk boat?'

'One of the PCs had the fun task of watching eight hours of Delting Marina at night. Well, it wasn't a full eight hours, it's on a freeze-frame programme which cut it down to only two hours.'

'And?'

'At 02.37 the screen went black, as if someone had flung a cloth over it. At 03.16, the black was removed, leaving the PC with a grandstand view of the boat sinking. Frighteningly fast. You do have a liferaft aboard your *Khalida*, don't you?'

I nodded. 'It came with her. It's a year out of date for being serviced, though. Isn't there a camera at the front of the club that would catch the person walking down the drive?'

Gavin nodded. 'No sign of anyone on it. Our perp knew exactly where it was, and what its field of vision was, and walked to the other one down through a field.'

'But we knew it was likely a local anyway, so that doesn't get us any further.'

'It tells us that it was definitely sabotage. That's interesting in itself, don't you think? Why set up an apparent accident, then give the game away by blocking the camera?'

When he put it like that, it did sound odd. I tried to think about it from the perp's point of view. 'He couldn't have got onboard to do the sabotage without the camera recording him – that's what it's there for. You'd have film of him walking along the pontoon, or arriving in another boat. Maybe he hoped we'd think it had gone on the blink.'

'He'd have done better to disable it, in that case. Pull a wire out, as if it had worked loose, something like that.'

I tried to visualise the camera. It sat on one corner of the clubhouse, with the wiring coming out from inside. 'Maybe that was his plan, only he couldn't shift it, and cutting it would be just as much a give away.'

'Maybe. It's odd.' He hesitated. His voice darkened. 'We had the preliminary results on Chloe's death. The doctor phoned to check how reliable a witness you were. I put him on to Freya.'

'And she said?' I asked, in my blandest voice.

'She said that as far as she knew, you were spot-on with what you observed, though your conclusions might take a pinch of salt.'

I bowed in the direction of an imaginary DS Peterson. 'Thanks to you.'

'His preliminary finding was that she was dead by the time she got to the foot of the steps.' He paused, looking at me.

I nodded. 'There wasn't a flicker of a pulse. Nothing.'

'She hit her head coming down, and that was what killed her. That's straightforward enough. What he wanted to know was what made her fall like that, the way you described, just in a heap, with no effort made to save herself. He's sent off samples for examination, but his off-the-record guess, which I've promised not to hold him to, was that she'd taken a strong sleeping pill three-quarters of an hour to an hour before. She literally sleepwalked off the top step.'

Sleepwalked. Yes, that was how it had looked. 'So . . . somebody dropped a pill in her drink in the restaurant?' I felt a sudden surge of relief. Jesma couldn't have done that.

'The timing fits. The 999 call was registered at eleven minutes to two. They'd arrived at the restaurant an hour earlier, and the waiter brought them drinks straight away – it was lunchtime, busy, so he wanted them to get on with ordering.' He didn't need his notebook for the times and facts; they were neatly in order in his head. 'Chloe had a San Pellegrino, which she started drinking while they were talking about what to eat.'

95

'Good memory, your waiter.'

'Freya talked to him almost straight away. He remembered Chloe because of her looks, and because of her talking to the table next to her. He read the situation spot on: an old boyfriend with his new girlfriend, and Chloe keen to show the boyfriend how well she was doing without him. 'Very matey in a "see what you missed" sort of way,' he said. The girlfriend put a good face on it, but she wasn't best pleased at having their lunch hijacked by his past, in the shape of a dazzling blonde.'

'So she was nearest to them, the old boyfriend and new girl-friend, of the people at her table.'

Gavin nodded. 'And what's more, after she'd done the greeting and being matey, she left Antony to order for her while she went in to the ladies'. She hadn't finished her drink at that point.'

'DS Peterson was being very thorough, asking about food and drink before there was any idea that it might be involved.'

'Your description gave her ideas. Besides, when an investigation starts, you don't know what might be useful. You need to find out as much as you can. She was lucky the waiter was so observant.'

I tried to visualise the scene. 'Even while she was at the toilet, you'd think it'd be hard to reach over and drop a pill in someone else's drink without being seen.'

'Maybe, maybe not. If you palmed the pill ready – well, when would you do it?'

I tried to think like someone who had a pill in hand. 'While people are reading the menus, maybe, if you were sitting right beside the person whose drink you wanted to doctor.' I visualised myself doing it, and shook my head. 'No. When the food arrives. That's the obvious time. You could easily reach over and actually move someone else's drink pretending you were making room for the dishes.'

'My guess too.'

'Does that mean premeditation, meaning it was one of her own group?'

'Not necessarily.'

'But a sleeping tablet's an odd sort of thing to carry around. Wouldn't you keep it in your bathroom cabinet?'

Gavin smiled at me. 'Ah, Cass, you lead a conventional life. If you weren't sure whether you'd be sleeping at home or at your partner's, you'd carry your pills with you. You have to allow for the handbag habit too. Have you ever owned one?'

'They count as clutter aboard a ship,' I said. 'Besides, a handbag's an internationally recognised sign saying "Valuables inside" and I wouldn't risk carrying one in some of the ports I've been in. I have inner pockets, with a zip.'

'What does your mother keep in hers?'

'Maman? A clean, ironed white handkerchief, her spare lipstick, and car or house keys, if there isn't someone else to carry them for her.'

'No wallet?' Gavin said, interested.

'Just her credit card in a flat enamel box. She carried a purse with change when she and Dad were split up, but now she doesn't need to. He does the money stuff.'

'Maybe your mother was a bad example. How about Inga?'

I considered what I'd seen my friend Inga take out of her bulging brown leather bag. 'Purse. Keys are in her pocket. Complete kit for dealing with a small boy: wipes for sticky hands and face, pants in case of an accident, a wrapped biscuit for starvation emergencies. Leaflets for her current cause.'

'When I was a rookie PC,' Gavin said, 'I had to upend an arrested person's handbag in front of them, list the contents and get a signed receipt. You'd be astonished at what women carted around with them – including pills as old as the last time they cleared out the handbag.'

'So any of the group could just have had sleeping pills with them?'

He nodded. 'Freya's going to have fun tomorrow going round the doctors and asking if any of these folk are or ever have been on sleeping pills, or a parent they look after. Easy to take one pill from a bottle. The old flame's new girlfriend, Amy, is a nurse in the hospital. Chloe and Tom worked at the care home. You can get over-the-counter stuff too, which any of them could have bought. The forensic folk may be able to tell exactly what it was, but I reckon it must have been strong stuff to knock her out so hard that she didn't feel herself falling.'

'But why would someone feed her a sleeping pill anyway?' I said. 'Chloe was unlucky that she fell down the steps and hit her head. It was far more likely that she'd slump down in a corner and fall asleep there.'

'She doesn't work in Lerwick,' Gavin said. 'She works out here in Brae. She was heading for the Esplanade, where she'd left her car, to drive back here for the afternoon shift.'

I thought of the half-hour road between Lerwick and Brae, two hypnotic straight pieces with the twist of the Halfway House between them, and felt chilled.

'According to the helpful waiter, they took longer than usual over lunch, partly because of the chatting between the two tables.'

'So she should have been on her way sooner.'

He nodded, and echoed my thoughts. 'A long straight road with nothing to keep you awake. Murder that looked like a simple accident.'

III

Let ee deil ding anidder
(Let one devil strike another)
Don't become involved in other people's rows

Chapter Nine

Friday 17th March, Brae Up Helly Aa

Tide times, Brae:
LW 02.17 (0.65m);
HW 08.27 (2.03m);
LW 14.42 (0.42m);
HW 20.57 (1.96m)

Moonset 06.49; sunrise 07.13; moonrise 16.54;
sunset 19.11. Moon waxing gibbous.

Him at gets in a finger'll shön get in da hand.
(He that gets in a finger will soon get in a hand.)
Minor intrusions can soon become major interference.
(Give him an inch and he'll take an ell.)

I went across to Brae as soon as I'd waved Gavin off. Antony's flash fishing boat was back on the dinghy pontoon, but now the green ropes that had secured *Day Dawn* were gone I could easily lie at the inner side of it. I parked the *Deuk* there, shifted *Khalida* to behind her, then I set to work.

It was going to be a day of sunshine and showers, with slightly more wind than yesterday to wave the bushes above the club. The clouds scudded across the blue sky, white clouds gathering from behind the hills, darkening, shedding their load in a sudden April downpour that had the cats and me scurrying into the cabin, then clearing again, leaving the world sparkling clean for us to emerge back into. Cat stationed himself on the cabin roof, shaking his paws fastidiously; the Kitten curled up in the cockpit.

I'd have a grandstand view of the start of the Delting Up Helly Aa. The proper galley shed by the Brae Hall had needed serious repairs after a February gale took half the roof off, so the galley builders had moved to the big shed halfway up the clubhouse drive. I kept an eye upwards as I opened the box containing my beautiful new mainsail. The quality of it was worth the money: stiff, strong canvas, beautifully stitched. I'd bought a proper cover for it too, the sort that incorporated lazyjacks and a zip along the top, and now I realised that cover and mainsail had to go along the boom together. I wished we'd done this yesterday; four hands would have been better than two.

The first cars arrived as I was coaxing the slides along the slot in the metal boom. The Vikings that came out of them wore green kirtles and sheepskin cloaks; they were last year's Jarl Squad, the chief Vikings of the festival, acting as marshals for this year's procession. Magnie was in among them, looking impressive in breastplate and helmet; I waved, and got a brandish of his axe in reply. They formed a rough guard of honour lining each side of the drive. Next to arrive was the Lerwick Brass Band, and there was a squeaking of instruments as they got ready to play. The Viking lines straightened at the sound of a vehicle slowing, relaxed as it turned out to be an ordinary van, then bristled as they recognised it: the shiny-paint van with *Westside Shellfish Co. Ltd.* along the side. Antony Leighton.

He knew he was running the gauntlet. There was a little spurt of gravel from under his wheels as he revved up the engine to get away from between the two lines, and then a visible hesitation as he decided where to park. A shout and waved arm directed him left towards the parked boats on the hard; he turned defiantly right and backed the van in beside the bin store then got out and strode across the gravel to the end of the pontoon. Halfway along it he turned and snarled upwards, 'I didn't bloody sink his boat.'

The waiting squad couldn't have heard; it was said to relieve his feelings. He turned again, and saw me there. His cheeks reddened. He was silent for a moment, then he said, more quietly, 'I didn't sink it.'

He looked dreadful. His face was washed and his hair roughly combed into its funny bouncy tonsure, but his eyelids were swollen and his cheeks drawn. He jerked his chin over his shoulder at *Day Dawn*, sitting on the hard standing where *Khalida* had been. 'The police have taken the CCTV. Whoever it shows, if it was anyone, and not just an old boat sinking by itself, it won't be me. So they can put that in their pipes and smoke it.'

He gave a defiant nod upwards and turned on his heel, then paused, turned back and came slowly towards me. He said again, 'I really didn't sink it. Ewan's been a nuisance, followimg me round to check I'm keeping the rules, and photographing every bloody pot I sink, but for all his efforts, he's got nothing on me. I'm entitled to six hundred creels, and that's what I've set.' He paused, and looked straight at me. 'You were there when Chloe fell, weren't you? You did the first aid.'

I nodded. 'I'm sorry,' I said.

He gestured with his hands, as if he was pushing something away. 'It was an awful shock. I went straight to the hospital and waited, and I couldn't believe it when the doctor came and told me she'd passed.' He glanced down at the cockpit seat. 'Can I . . .?'

'Come aboard,' I said.

He swung over the guard rail and sat down. 'See, Chloe and I, we weren't serious. My wife and I are split up, but we're – ' He hunched one shoulder. 'We have two kids, and though we had our differences, one reason I came up here was to try and work them out.' He looked across at the shining water, and gave a wry grin. 'Though fishing for lobsters in Shetland is a far cry from doing deliveries by water on the Thames Estuary, which was the sum total of my boating experience.'

'It's all boats,' I said.

'Chloe was a good hand aboard a boat,' he said. 'She'd been going out with her dad or Ewan since she was a kid, she said. She was a lot of fun, smart as paint and pretty with it. Then on top of that, Ewan was being a pain in the arse, and I could see how much me taking out Chloe riled him, and it annoyed her too, that he was coming the heavy big cousin over who she went out with. But we weren't serious. We spoke about it, and she knew full well I was hoping to get Jesma back.'

He was putting this across well, leaning towards me, eyes wide with sincerity, and I'd have liked to believe him, but I remembered what DS Peterson had said. *Somehow, nobody was sorry enough.* I had no spyglass to read into other people's hearts, but I had that same sense. The reddened eyelids, the tousled hair, the air of not having slept last night, they were all a bit too theatrical. I didn't mean that they were fake; just that a night of intense mourning would get Chloe out of his system, and then he'd move on; back to Jesma or on to his next new thing. Maybe, as he was saying, Chloe hadn't been serious either, or maybe he hadn't been, but she had. Somehow, under the mourning, was an air of relief.

'For Ewan's boat,' I said, 'can't you prove an alibi?'

It threw him. He looked blank for a moment, then I saw it compute; he glanced across at the hard, where *Khalida* had been sitting when he'd had the argument with Ewan. I could feel him remembering what he'd said. *I think you'll find I have an alibi for last night.* Then he turned the full-wattage smile on me. 'How could I bring Chloe into it now?' He rose. 'Well, I'd need to be getting some creels raised. See you.'

He headed off to his boat. There were some thumps from inside, and it rocked against the pontoon. His engine started with a roar, calmed to a whisper while he cast off, and then roared again as he headed out of the marina. The wash of his passing splashed up the dinghy slip; the noise gradually dwindled into the distance.

I wasn't sure what to believe. If he was up here trying to win Jesma back, taking up with a spectacular blonde was a poor way to go about it; unless his affair with Chloe was dual-purpose, not just to annoy Ewan, but also to make Jesma jealous – or to pay her back for turning him down.

It also depended on how seriously Chloe'd taken him. I tried to sort out my own impressions from the day I'd seen them together, and couldn't tell. Yes, there'd been a hint of Ewan-annoying in the public kissing, but I'd thought she'd looked keen – keen enough to be an obstacle to getting Jesma back.

Lizbet would know how Chloe'd really felt. I wished I could ask her.

The crunching of vehicles signalled this year's Jarl Squad arriving: carloads of family and friends come to wish them well, followed by a bus. The lines straightened up and the swarm of folk from the cars came to stand behind them, phones at the ready. The band struck up 'From grand old Viking centuries Up Helly Aa has come', last year's Jarl led three cheers, and just at the right moment the sun came out to dazzle off their burnished breastplates and helmets. The new Jarl and his squad marched down from the road to the galley shed, helmets and shields gleaming, sky-blue cloaks swinging.

The Jarl looked like a Viking raider come straight from the past. The raven wings on his pointed helmet made him seven foot tall. He had a steel breastplate with a painted dragon on it, a maroon velvet tunic and black sheepskin leggings bound with maroon cord. He carried a circular shield on a wooden backing with the same dragon motif picked out in steel, and a ceremonial axe. Behind him, his squad were equally impressive, the men in tunics, and most of the women in long dresses with a circular band on their foreheads; one or two had joined the men as warriors. A quick count gave me forty-seven of them, along with the scattering of children dressed as miniature Vikings in the same maroon kirtles and sky-blue cloaks. Every relative who possibly could joined the Jarl for his big day. The ornate belt buckles and the silver dragons on the shields glinted in the camera flashes.

There was a lot of posing in front of the galley shed for the ranks of press. I was busy threading the fiddly sliders at the front of the mainsail into their slot on the mast and securing the boom before they could fall out again, but the cats watched with interest. When next I looked around they'd got the galley out of her shed. I paused to admire her. She was thirty feet long, with her sky-blue dragon head balanced by a tall curling tail. The jutting spikes of mane and tail fins were maroon, and her curved sides were maroon and white striped. The scarlet raven banner flew above the crow's nest and furled sail. She looked far too bonny to burn, even though I knew she wasn't a seagoing boat but a simulacrum, with only a flat plywood bottom below those elegant clinker sides.

The band struck up again, and the two squads hauled her down to the waterfront for more photos: galley without squad, squad in front of galley, groups of Viking children in the galley, squad members in the galley raising their axes, the Jarl in the galley alone, raising his axe and calling for 'Three cheers for the galley builders!' By now the caravan park was filled with local folk photographing like mad.

Once they'd done the squad photos, a tractor came down the drive and curved around to pick up the galley's trailer. The smaller children and very oldest Vikings surrounded the Jarl in the galley, the other Vikings formed ranks around her and the band started to play. The Jarl braced his feet and took a hold of the mast as his ship lurched forward, then lumbered upwards with its warriors

106

marching around it. They'd march to the Hall, where the galley would spend the day while the Vikings went off visiting: the area's three primary schools, ending with lunch in the Mossbank hall, then around the care centres. Gradually, the crowd dispersed. Cat decided the excitement was over, and headed off along the shore. The Kitten stayed put for a few minutes, then charged after him in a rush, pounced over him and raced ahead.

'Impressive,' a voice said from the pontoon. I looked up and saw a vaguely familiar young man stowing away a camera into its case.

'Very,' I agreed.

I was trying to place him when he said, 'You're Cass, aren't you?' His face twisted. 'You helped us the other day. The day before yesterday, when Chloe fell. Lizbet said who you were. I'm Tom. The guitarist from the band.'

'Oh, yea,' I said. 'I was talking to your dad just yesterday, about how well you'd done in the *You're the Stars!* thing.'

He stood tentatively on the pontoon, as if he wasn't used to walking on something that floated. He was on the tall side of average, with strong shoulders under his shrug-on dark jacket. The general look of him suggested he was about Lizbet's age, in his early twenties, but he had a strangely young face, pale-skinned, with a fringe of beard below, wispy hair that fell in a plume over his high forehead and round brown eyes that met mine with a lost expression.

I couldn't quiz Lizbet about Chloe, but Tom would know.

'I was just about to put the kettle on,' I said. 'Come aboard.'

He hesitated, looking at the bundled sail on the boom. 'I don't want to stop you working.'

'Actually, if you wouldn't mind, you'd be a great help,' I said. I gestured towards it. 'I need to put it into neat folds.'

He slung his camera case over his shoulder and clambered on, using the guard rails to cling on to instead of the wooden hand-rail, and looked vaguely at the end of the boom.

'If you pull it straight, as I fold this end,' I said, 'it'll be done in no time.'

He was remarkably unhandy, but we managed well enough between us to get it in rough folds, and I zipped the cover over it, paused for a moment to admire its smart blue, then headed for the kettle. Tom sat on the cockpit thwart and peered down below.

'She's not at all in her usual state,' I said, seeing his shadow darken the light from the companionway. 'The entire contents of her interior are in our spare room. I only got the mast up yesterday. Can you take your tea black, or would you prefer coffee?'

He went for coffee, and when I came back up with it he'd settled himself on the cockpit seat and was gazing into the water, eyes unfocused, as if he was glad to watch it and not have to think.

'Coffee,' I said. 'I have some KitKats, but they're a bit out of date.'

He gave a half-hearted smile. 'Bring them on. It's years since I had one.'

I produced them and he ate in silence. The sun was warm on our faces. I let him half-finish his coffee, then asked, 'How did you all come to be in the band together?'

He shook his head and smiled reminiscently into his mug. 'Me and Lizbet played together at the school, her on piano and me on the guitar. Most of the boys were listening to Linkin Park and most of the girls were trying to be Beyoncé, but we were into folk. Sufjan Stevens, Joanna Newsom, do you know her?' I shook my head. 'Augie March?'

I shook my head again, and gestured at the waves on the slip. 'That's my music.'

He thought about that for a moment, then nodded. 'Yeah. The two of us were out on a limb, but we were determined we were going to make music. Lizbet has a voice like, well, have you heard her?'

'At the boating club here, the regatta two years ago, maybe? You played out in front of the club. She was amazing.'

His eyes lit up. 'She is, isn't she? But folk on a night out don't want moody harmonics or poetry, they want "Take Me Home, Country Roads". So we went country. Lizbet could sell any song. I've seen grown men in tears at her "Coat of Many Colours". She'd slip one of her own songs in between the popular numbers, or one of mine. But even with Lizbet's talent it's not easy to break into the music business.'

'Or your talent,' I said. He looked sceptical, but I was remembering now. 'You did an amazing guitar solo.'

He made a face, but I could see he was pleased. "Stairway to Heaven" stuff. The punters'll take a bit of it, not too much. We could only do Shetland gigs while we were still at school, but then once we left we gave it a serious go. We did a tour in Scotland, a summer of pubs and clubs and festivals, the Lemon Tree in Aberdeen and folk pubs. It's a niche market, but the audience are keen. We did a bit of busking at the Edinburgh Fringe, and we had a lot of fun, but it wasn't enough to earn money, you know, not enough to go full-time, or to afford a proper demo to try around the record labels.' He pulled another long face. 'There aren't that many of them, and there are a lot of bands.' He made a frustrated gesture. 'In folk, there's no obvious structure. Country, there's a ladder in, but folk, you have to do your stuff and hope bands who heard you will mention you as worth inviting to festivals.' His face brightened. 'This year's Shetland Folk Festival, we're one of the support bands in the local hall gigs, so the other bands will hear us, and maybe . . .' He cut the hope off. 'Anyway, we did the summer, then we had to come back and take up our college places. Lizbet went for office stuff, she's in admin with the SIC. I went for care. I worked in the hospital for a bit, but the night shifts were chronic, and there was always someone off. Now I'm up at the centre there, being nice to dotty old ladies who think it's still World War Two.'

Reminded, he peered down into my cabin. 'Is your clock right?'

I nodded, and he relaxed. 'I'm due back at eleven. Anyway, we do gigs, and post stuff on YouTube, but it's all amateur recordings. To get anywhere, to get anyone even to look at us, even if other bands recommend us, we need a professional one. That's what we're both saving towards. I did ask about getting one of the local companies to film us, but . . .' He finished with a shrug that made it plain that even the length of a song was out of reach.

'When did Chloe join you?'

His round eyes clouded over. 'She'd always hung around a bit. She was Lizbet's best pal, so I had to take her as part of the package. She'd come in and try harmonies while we were rehearsing, but though she was keen to be in our band, she . . .' He paused, and I could see him wrestling with the tension between speaking the truth and not speaking ill of the dead. Truth won. 'She couldn't sing. Not well enough. And her singing with Lizbet, well, she just stood out like a sore thumb. So I was dead against having her, I reckoned she'd spoil our chances. Lizbet wasn't happy about that, but she saw my point of view. And then Chloe met this boy from Lerwick and fell in *lurve*, and we had peace for a bit. We got on with getting gigs – we were starting to make a regular amount, at least – and then suddenly the guy got fed up with Chloe, and dumped her.'

'Irvine?' I said. 'The guy you met up with in the restaurant?'

He nodded, then shot me a surprised glance. 'How did you know that?'

'He was with you when Chloe fell,' I said. It wasn't quite an answer, but Tom didn't pick me up on it. His face crumpled like a child about to cry.

'She just fell, like that, and then she was dead.' His voice was blank with disbelief. 'How could she just die, like that?'

'She hit her head,' I reminded him. 'Go on, about her and Irvine.'

He gave me a doubtful look, then continued, as if he needed to unburden himself. 'She fell apart when he ended it. Crying, and spending days in bed, and binge eating. Lizbet was right worried about her, and that's when she talked me into letting her come into the band. Talked Chloe into giving herself a makeover. The pair of them started going to the gym together, and Chloe went cycling in her lunchtimes and lost a fair bit of weight, though if you ask me she's too skinny now, and got her hair dyed. Went partying.' The corners of his mouth turned down. 'Hoping she'd meet him to show him what he'd thrown away. Anyway, we kept working with Chloe in tow and started a YouTube channel of our songs. Last Christmas we scraped together the money for a Christmas CD. *Christmas in the Country*, we called it. That was the title track, and, oh, the standards, "Beautiful Star of Bethlehem", "Pretty Paper", "Christmas in Dixie", that sort of thing.' He grinned. 'Grandma got run over by a reindeer.'

'What?' I said, startled.

'"Grandma Got Run Over By a Reindeer".' I heard it as a title this time. He sang a verse of it; indubitably country. 'Eight tracks, £9.99, and if I've made you want to hear the whole song, I'm afraid you're out of luck. We made five hundred and sold the lot. The start of our proper-video fund.'

'Well, that's great.'

'Then this Antony bloke came up, and Chloe went bald-headed for him.'

'Serious?'

He nodded emphatically. 'Yeah. Keen enough to make you sick. Antony this, and Antony that, and we're doing this on Saturday. Lizbet was worried about it, with him being married and all, but I was glad. It gave us peace for a bit. Well, she still came to practices and the gigs, but she wasn't pushing the way she had been. Until word filtered through about that damned heat for *You're the Stars!* He scowled at the water. 'Lizbet thought it was our big chance. I wasn't convinced – yeah, sure, it would get us to a wider audience, and that might make us the money we need, but we'd be doing the crowd-pleasers, the wrong stuff for a folk promoter, and that might knock our chances for what we really want to do.' He was silent for a moment, then spoke jerkily. 'On the folk circuit, what the audience want is good music. They loved Lizbet, they loved my guitar work, they loved our songs.'

He was silent for a moment, looking sideways at me, as if he wasn't sure he could trust me or not. 'Lizbet's naive,' he said abruptly. 'She would never think that Chloe would cut her out. I would. Chloe tried that on the minute we let her into the band.' His voice squeaked into sugary falsetto. '"Could I try a solo song, Tom?" "Could I sing that bit on my own?" Coming forward to share Lizbet's mic for the harmonies instead of staying at the back. Lizbet didn't see it, but I did.' He paused, then changed to Shetlandic. 'Little bears buik in a greedy man's eye. My dad aye said that when I wanted a second helping of something. Then that audition . . . Lizbet was too focused on singing to watch what Chloe was up to, schmoozing the producers. Well, it worked. Fuck, it worked. They asked her to sing one of the songs, and she gave it everything she'd got. Singing dreadful, presence turned up to eleven.'

I remembered Lizbet's heartbroken wail. *Being talented isn't enough. You've got to be pretty as well.*

He stood up, as if his anger couldn't be contained in stillness. I could feel it flowing from him. 'And I watched their faces and I knew, I just knew, that when that envelope came through the door it would have Chloe's name on it. Maybe she wouldn't get any more than ten minutes of fame, but she'd get that, and Lizbet and I would stay up here in our boring jobs and keep playing the pubs.'

112

'But,' I asked, 'wouldn't the TV people want you playing with Chloe?'

He shook his head vehemently. 'I wouldn't play for Chloe.' His eyes bored into mine. 'I don't care how much money I'd make. I'll say the same thing over and over to old ladies, I'll do extra shifts behind a bar or at the fish factory, anything else to make money, but I won't do that.' His expressive hands clutched the air. 'Music's what I live for, and Lizbet's a real singer. I'll play for her, but not for Chloe.' He was silent for a moment, then he spoke softly to the sun-dancing water. 'The new boyfriend was cooling off. I'd hoped she'd maybe bugger off with him, but I could see he wasn't as keen as he had been. He has a wife, and kids, and maybe he was thinking of a reconciliation. That would dump her back on Lizbet. On us. She wouldn't be dumped quietly either, we'd get all the histrionics again.'

Tom was giving Antony the motive I'd wondered about. If he really wanted Jesma back, public scenes with the young girl he'd thrown over wouldn't do him any good.

'Lizbet wasn't saying anything, but I knew she was dreading that. And at that lunch, the old boyfriend, Irvine, he wasn't interested, but he was, at the same time. Like being hypnotised by a snake. His girfriend was polite and calm, but if looks could kill . . .' He looked at the water for a moment, mouth working, then said vehemently, 'She was trouble. She was. And then she fell, when she was normally so agile, and you were there, down below . . .' He turned his head away from me and paused, swallowing, then came out with it. 'Do you think . . . did it look like . . . might someone have pushed her?'

There was a long silence, broken only by the waves shushing on the dinghy slip.

'No,' I said at last. DS Peterson would be asking about sleeping tablets soon enough. 'It all happened so quickly, and I couldn't really see, but I don't think anyone pushed her. She seemed just to stumble and fall.'

His hand came up as I spoke, almost as if he wanted to stop me saying it after all, then relaxed. 'An accident,' he said. He gave a long sigh, as if he was shedding a burden, and put his mug down. 'Thanks for the coffee. Have a good day.'

He turned and strode away.

Chapter Ten

Du'll wind someone a pirm yet.
(You'll wind someone a reel of cotton thread yet.)
You'll lead someone a dance.

By lunchtime *Khalida* was ready to go. It was a fine breeze for sailing home; the light airs of the morning had given way to a force 3 from the north, just strong enough to break the crests of the waves. I waited till a shower had passed, then zig-zagged down the voe in a series of broad reaches, with *Khalida* responding to every light puff, and the little *Deuk* bobbing behind.

My new sails were amazing. *Khalida* felt like a different boat – no, better than that, she felt like my own boat, but sailing the way she was meant to. Both sails set in a beautiful curve, she accelerated with the least puff of wind and she was turning on a sixpence. Cat sat in his usual corner in the cockpit, and Kitten snoozed in her basket below, while I went from one tack to the other, enjoying her, then sat with my feet up on the opposite seat, my familiar tiller snug in my hand, and the white sails stretched above me.

Even here, in my element, my thoughts went back to Chloe. *Might someone have pushed her?* She hadn't been pushed, yet Tom knew her and the situation, and that was the way his mind was going. He'd disliked her, that had been clear; Lizbet and he had been getting themselves into the pub circuit with the folk music that was their real love, and she'd muscled in, without the talent to earn her place in the band. She'd been trying to push herself forward, and he'd wanted to shove her back. He'd been succeeding, until the talent contest. He hadn't heard the producers talking, as Lizbet had, but he'd seen the writing on the wall. Pretty, sexy Chloe was in. She'd get the ten minutes of fame that might have changed his and Lizbet's lives, if the right people had heard them.

I paused my thinking to gybe the boat round, and found my thoughts turning too. Tom knew who I was. Whoever he'd asked about me, he'd have been told, somewhere in the conversation, that I was biding with that new inspector, you ken, the policeman that aye wears a kilt. I'd been down below when Chloe fell. If he'd been responsible for slipping her that sleeping pill, what better way of putting the police off the scent than by asking if I thought someone had pushed her? I thought about his round, guileless eyes, and felt it was a bit subtle, or a bit stupid. A clever person would keep quiet.

We'd reached Houbansetter, the sound between the hill where our cottage was and the island of Papa Little opposite; time to drop the sails and start the engine. I set speculation aside and concentrated on dodging lobster buoys, then cut the motor and let *Khalida* slide towards the *Deuk*'s pontoon. It would be easier for my next job, which was reconstituting the cabin.

I spent the rest of the afternoon barrowing cabin furnishings down to the pier and heaving them aboard. Each load made her look more like herself: the navy cloth cushions along one side of the cabin, the checked oilcloth ones in the forepeak, the heads curtain, my spare overalls on the hanging rail, my downie and pillow in my berth, the box of books back on the shelf. I took a bucket of soapy water and gave all the plates and cutlery a good wash, and finished by polishing the cabin wood with Pledge. Cat watched from the cockpit, sneezed at the spray, then came below and jumped up into my berth, purring. 'A real sail tomorrow night, boy,' I said. 'Off to Yell.'

In between loads I stuck the rest of the shepherd's pie in the oven, ready for when Gavin came home. By the time his lights shone over the hill, I'd had time to lay out my charts and check my waypoints. I greeted him with bright eyes and a spring in my step.

'I wish I could think all this enthusiasm was for me,' he said, returning my hug. 'You're lit up like a Christmas tree because you've got your boat back.' He glanced down at *Khalida* lying at the pontoon, mast stretching up towards the sky, sails neat inside their royal-blue cover. 'How were the new sails?'

'Amazing. She sailed like a dream. I can spend tomorrow fine-tuning, and then I'm all set.' I was about to ask how his day had been when I remembered that yesterday he'd thanked me for not asking until he'd wound down.

'And set for going dancing?'

I'd tried to think about it while I'd been working, but reconstituting my boat was more interesting, so I'd got distracted and forgotten all about it again. 'I will be once I'm dressed. What are you wanting to do about the procession?'

'Does something need done about it?'

'They start at the Hall and then walk all the way to the boating club. We could take the car to the club, walk along to the light-up and follow the procession back, or vice versa, leave the car at the Hall and go back to get it once the burning's over.'

'Are you particularly wanting to do the walking? How about just heading straight for the club and getting a good position for the burning?'

I'd had an active day, so I was happy to miss more walking. 'Sounds good.'

Gavin glanced at the clock. 'Leave here at quarter to seven, say? There'll be plenty of parking space at the club.'

'I just need to get my pretty dress on, and a warm jacket. I can do the make-up here, and touch up after the burning.' I dished the shepherd's pie up and sat down opposite him. 'It tends to create smuts. How about you?'

'Dress kilt from the start, with a big jacket over my black jacket. Magnie definitely saw it as an occasion.'

'I saw him on the pier, while they were getting the galley out. He looked great as a Viking. You'll see.'

The middle of Brae was bustling with people as we drove through: costumed people gradually forming themselves into two squashed lines by the Hall, and watchers in warm jackets milling around them. We found, when we arrived at the club, that we'd overestimated the amount of parking space, with half of the upper car park roped off for squad buses, and down by the marina similarly roped off for the squads marching in formation. Gavin squeezed the Land Rover between the boats on the hard standing and parked it nose homewards in a caravan space looking back towards Brae.

'Good thinking,' I said. 'A clear view of the procession walking along.' I glanced at the clock. 'Three minutes to go.'

The sun had set behind the Aith hills, but the sky was still light, and the crests of the waves flickered white in the moonlight. The wind tugged at the door as I got out of the car; I slammed it, and leaned against the rear door to watch. A white light soared skywards, followed by a crack: the maroon signalling the start of the procession. There was a brightness fizzing at the side of the Hall, then a plume of smoke lit flickering orange from below spread forwards to the road as the torches were lit. Another pause, then the head of the procession began to move and the smoke cloud became a fiery snake that reflected as a red-gold ribbon in the shifting water. I could just make out the dark shape of the galley near the front, blanking out as the procession went behind the houses, then reappearing once they came past Frankie's and into the open road. The torchlight flickered on the school, the leisure centre; now we could hear snatches of music from the band. The snake turned its head and became a mass of flaming light as the guizers began marching towards us, then disappeared again behind the curve of the headland, leaving only the orange-red cloud that billowed above them.

There was a shuffling behind us as the people there began to move into position for watching the burning. Gavin slipped his hand through my arm and we moved back towards the bin store. We'd just settled ourselves comfortably in the lee of the wooden fencing when the pillar of smoke flared above the entrance to the boating club drive, and we saw the first flaming torches, cubes of grey sacking held a metre above the guizers' heads on chunky sticks. The windward sides of them were black with the occasional red spark glowing, the leeward sides streamed half a metre of flame and sparks.

The river of fire came marching down the boating club drive in a wave of paraffin smell and heat, and flowed onto the cleared space in front of us. The band was playing the marching song, and the guizers sang with gusto, 'From grand old Viking centuries Up Helly Aa has come . . .' The torches lit up the guizers as they passed: the Viking squad in their maroon and blue, with the Jarl standing tall in his galley, then a motley assortment depending on the act each squad would later perform round the halls: a set of vaguely medieval-style warriors with long plaits at the front of their hair, a posse of black suits with incongruous yellow wellies and Fair Isle toorie caps; two men in pullovers with a couple of dogs, several schoolchildren and a Siamese cat; people in Superman costumes topped by a sheep's mask, and the inevitable busty blondes in fishnets, all wearing their beards to show they were macho really. There was a squad of people in chef's aprons and hats, and a man dressed in a slinky red dress, surrounded by people wearing councillor face masks who might be part of the same squad, or strayed in from another squad, the one with several people wearing wind turbines head dresses. In short, it was a pretty fair selection of Up Helly Aa costumes that formed up for the turning movement on the marina gravel, shifting and weaving in the flickering torchlight. Reflections flamed in the water and glinted off the metal and shiny fibre-glass of the boats behind them.

While the squads marched, the tractor manoeuvred the galley to the top of the slip and backed it almost to the water. The band waited at the pier, instruments ready. A motorboat came out from the pontoons and took a V of line from the galley's bows, ready to haul it out to deeper water once it was alight. The Jarl watched from his ship as his squad led the other guizers to surround her.

The band struck up, and a thousand voices took up the song: 'Waves the raven banner o'er us, as our Viking ship we sail . . .' The words got a bit uncertain in the second verse, but anyone with a shield had all the words of all three songs stuck to the back of it, and the rest of us had seen enough Up Helly Aas to be able to remember with them prompting us. When the song ended, the Jarl stood up straighter and waved his axe. 'Three cheers for the galley builders!'

The cheers echoed off the clubhouse wall and reverberated into the darkness beyond the blazing torches.

'Three cheers for our Marshals!'

The cheers echoed again. Another voice shouted out, 'Three cheers for our Guizer Jarl!' and the cheers answered him. The Jarl stood for a moment, looking around. He'd served ten years on the committee for this, his night. He took a deep breath, then raised his axe again, and yelled, 'Three cheers for Up Helly Aa.'

We all cheered with a will. A last look at his beautiful ship, then the Jarl climbed out of her. Above him, the bugle sounded. The first row of guizers came forward and threw their torches into the galley. The flying cudgels thumped into the bottom of the boat, and within seconds there was the crackling sound of burning wood. The further-back guizers pressed forward to get their torches thrown; the motorboat took up the tension on the bow rope. Now she was blazing fiercely, the wooden sticks of the torches adding to the fire, the flames licking along her gunwales and creeping up the back of her neck and the curve of her tail. A spark jumped upwards and suddenly her rolled sail was burning. The last torch went in, the motorboat braced itself and tugged, and slowly the boat began her only voyage. The dark water turned blood-red around her as she moved away into clearer water, where the wind would blow the sparks rising into the black sky away from the boats in the marina.

I stood with my shoulder against Gavin's and watched her burn. The sight raised an old memory: my beautiful longship, my first command, burning like this, out in the voe. I'd been fuzzy and groggy with smoke. Gavin had been there too, getting a doctor to look at my head. I slid my hand into his, and his fingers closed warm around mine.

Now her tail was a black silhouette in the flames, and the red tongues were licking up the back of her head. Her mast fell with a crash that shook her, and then the proud head tipped backwards and collapsed into her, the toothed mouth roaring defiance to the end. Around us, people were beginning to disperse: the watchers to their cars or to talk to friends in the squads, the costumed guizers clustering together. I heard snatches of talk: 'We'll see you at Voe, then.' 'We're no' on till fifth in Vidlin, we can easy get to the pub for a couple of pints first.' 'First on in Mossbank. We'd need to get a move on.' 'I canna mind what our bus was, was it one of Andrew's?' 'Are you seen Ertie? I'm lost track o' him.'

Gradually the space cleared, leaving only the dying flames in the middle of the black water. The motorboat came forward, unhooked its V of rope and came alongside the galley. A couple of men leaned over its side to reach under the raft the galley floated on and tip it upwards, letting the last timbers slither with a hiss into the sea. One raised a hand to the men onshore. The tractor began inching upwards, and the raft crept shorewards. The tractor hitched it on again and departed.

'Well,' Gavin said, 'shall we see if your parents have saved us seats indoors?'

It had to be fifteen years since I was last at the boating club on Up Helly Aa night, but nothing had changed. There was the band squished into a corner, and the kitchen hatch open for people to get soup, sandwiches and fancies, tea and coffee. Someone had lit a peat fire in the hearth under the *Swallow* nameplate, and the map on the floor had been cleared of tables for the squads to perform, and for dancing.

Maman and Dad had bagged comfortable seats in the corner by the fire. We'd just had time to exchange greetings and sit down when the band spokesman did his welcoming preamble, which ended with, 'And the squads are on the ball tonight. Put your hands together, ladies and gents, for squad number Six, The Great Brae Bake Off.'

We clapped, and the cook squad charged in. The boomer by the band gave a hiccup and blared into music, and the cooks went into a dance routine which included mixing up ingredients in a huge bowl and covering it with a cloth, which was whisked off to reveal a huge cake. There was a drum roll, and a Jarl look alike burst out of it, to cheers and laughter.

'I wasn't expecting that,' the band spokesman said. 'And our second big surprise of the night . . . the squad dance is a Boston two-step.'

He did a couple of chords of the dance which every guizer's feet could still do even after a night of drinking, and the cooks headed for their wives, husbands or neighbours sitting in the audience. Gavin and I looked at each other, and pulled a joint 'not enough people yet' face. 'Next one,' I said.

'Now, now, Cassie, that's not the spirit,' Dad said. 'A young couple like yourselves, you should be dancing the night away.'

'Next one,' Gavin said.

The next act was the jumpers over shirts and ties with two

dogs and a Siamese cat, which turned out to be *Blue Peter*, complete with a make-a-galley demonstration involving washing-up liquid bottles and a huge pair of lime-green bloomers for the sail. They chose the Boston two-step as their squad dance too, and then we got a St Bernard's Waltz as a filler dance while the next squad got themselves organised at the door.

'Good,' Gavin said. He'd been grabbed by a short-skirted, knee-socked schoolgirl who looked to be trying to find out what he wore under his kilt, while I'd been taken up by one of my fellow racing crew-members. He pulled me out onto the floor. 'We know this one. Now here's where it's a pity you don't have a handbag, you could have left it behind to keep our seats.'

'They'll keep themselves,' I said. 'You're in civilised Shetland here, boy.'

He smiled. 'You think I'd have suggested leaving your handbag unguarded anywhere south?'

We'd done only two rounds of the dance when the music stopped, and the band leader announced, 'Clear the floor, please, for squad number seven, squad number seven.'

We dropped back into our seats. Squad seven turned out to be the man/woman in red, and the councillors did a robot dance routine with her. She sank into a sad heap on the floor, then leapt up, flung off her head dress and cloak to reveal a toorie and Fair Isle jumper and cuddled up to the Chief Executive. I didn't get it.

'*Wandavision*,' Gavin said. 'TV. A superhero who fell in love with a synthezoid.'

Their squad dance was a Boston two-step as well.

'Come on, Cassie,' Dad said, and stood up, holding his hand out. Gavin, as duty bound, rose and held his to Maman, and we headed for the floor.

'A fine man, Gavin,' Dad said, after he'd twirled me round a couple of repeats of the dance. 'Just the fellow I'd have chosen for you, if we'd been in the kind of country where children listen to their parents' advice when they're choosing a man.'

'Not a sailor though,' I said provocatively.

'Ah, sure, you're not wanting a sailor. Fly-by-night, with a girl in every port, no, you want a good steady man.' He paused while we did the polka bit, then resumed. 'And a good church man too.'

I took several deep breaths as we did the in-and-out bit and changed the subject when we came together again. 'I was thinking about you as we were in West Africa. Didn't you do time there, in your oily days?'

It diverted him as nicely as I'd hoped. Six years ago he'd gone to advise on an installation that was being built in Nigeria, and talking about that diverted him until the final repeat of the dance. Not enough, though; as he twirled me an extra spin in the last chord, he said, 'Now you remember what I'm saying. He's a fine man, and the day I lead you down the aisle to him, Cassie, that'll be the proudest day of my life.'

I was trying to think of a rejoinder when luckily one of the *Blue Peter* presenters grabbed the mic to do the traditional leaving thank you. 'Three cheers for the hosts and hostesses of the . . .' He did an exaggerated blank look around the room, and asked the band loudly, 'Which hall are we in?' He got a cheer and a laugh for that; later, as the night wore on, people would be doing it for real. 'No, it's fine, I ken where we are. Three cheers for the hosts and hostesses o' the boating club, let's hear you!'

The squad marched out to the sound of the hornpipe, with a last return to retrieve the Siamese cat, who'd made herself at home draped over the bar.

There was a pause in the proceedings. Dad checked what we were all drinking and headed for the bar. I leaned back against the club's fancy red velvet chairback, and looked around. It was mostly the older folk and the youngest ones who were here, for anyone between twenty and forty was out in a squad, or living it up in the livelier conditions of one of the halls with a full five-piece dance band on the stage and an acre of space to do a quadrille in. I recognised most of the faces; though I couldn't have named every one, I could place them. There were several boat owners and points race folk, accompanied by their wives and grandchildren, all dressed in their best for Up Helly Aa, and a good few retired owners, in so far as a boat owner ever did retire, faces I remembered from my youth, come down from their all-electric one-storey houses to join the fun. To my surprise, Antony was hovering about on the fringes of the bar. I wouldn't have expected him here, so soon after Chloe's death, and given the ill-feeling over Ewan's boat, but then I realised that it was precisely that ill-feeling that had prompted him to come. He nursed his drink with a defiant black glower around at the tables of chattering, laughing folk, and turned his shoulder when the woman at the serving hatch tried to speak to him.

She looked at him in surprise, and I realised it was Jesma, dressed for a party with her blonde hair pulled up in a top-knot, straight strands dangling at each side. She was wearing make-up, coloured shadow, shiny lipstick and the blackest of mascara, and there was a velour and sequins top under her mauve check boating club pinnie. The surprise was overlaid with hurt at the abrupt rejection.

Antony seemed suddenly, belatedly, to recognise her, for he did a double-take and turned back again. His lips moved in an apology. He looked around the groups of children, and spotted his own among them, then turned back to Jesma, charming smile turned up to full wattage. She flinched; her face became wary, and her hands busied themselves with pouring out soup to offer to him.

He shook his head. Her face changed, coaxing; her eyes were worried. If I'd had to guess at what she was saying, it would be something in wife mode: 'When did you last eat properly? Go on, this is good and filling.' I didn't think either of them would mention Chloe, but her death lay between them.

Antony took the soup, and a bannock to go with it, and gestured over at two empty chairs at Davie and Merran's table. She hesitated, demurred, he persuaded, and at last she came out from behind the counter with a plate of bannocks and fancies in one hand and two cups of tea in the other. They went over to the table and sat down together. Jesma was obviously introducing Antony to Davie and Merran, and Davie replied with a gesture that said, 'Oh, yes, we've seen you in the marina', and in no time they were chatting away together, like any pair of married couples.

Gavin nudged me. 'Who're you watching?'

'The couple there, that just sat down.' I kept my voice to a murmur, and turned my eyes towards the band. 'Antony, the boyfriend of the girl who died, and his ex-wife. I wondered if it might be the wanderer returning home.'

Gavin flicked a glance at them, then joined me watching the band. 'Maybe. Or maybe they just want to let their kids see them being civilised, together.'

'Yes, they're here. I saw him picking them out.'

I'd just said that when two children, a boy and a girl, came over to join them, soup and fancies in hand. Davie and Merran laughed, and made room. Now they were any family having a night out together, and you could see from the children's faces how pleased they were. I glanced at my parents, together again after so many years apart, and knew how they felt. Maman turned her head and smiled at me. '*Bien fait*,' she murmured in French. 'Well done. I knew your father would be tactless. Never listen to him, make up your own mind.' Her face grew serious. 'But you know, your man is lonely without you. You need to think about that.' She held up one hand. 'No, I will say no more.'

The band had begun a Pride of Erin waltz. Opposite us,

Antony rose to lead Jesma onto the floor. She was protesting, but smiling too, and moved into his arms as if she'd always belonged there, light on her feet as a teenager. Dad came back from the bar and swept Maman up, and Gavin and I followed. We'd only completed one set when, instead of starting again, the band gave a chord and a drum roll. 'Please clear the floor for the next squad.'

Obediently we moved aside. The drummer rolled again.

'Ladies, gentlemen and sailors, let's give a welcome to the Jarl Squad!'

The accordian wheezed into life and they marched in singing the Up Helly A song, axes raised, cloaks swinging. Over at their table, Antony's arm was still round Jesma. He looked up. His eyes went straight to Ewan marching among them, and his face darkened again. Jesma put a hand on his arm, but he shook her off and took three steps towards the far door. That put him in full view of everyone; he hesitated for a moment, looking back at Jesma, then turned on his heel and shoved his way out. Under the sound of the song, the marching steps, I heard the door slam behind him.

Chapter Eleven

Mad folk is aye waur as mad kye.
(Angry people are always worse than angry cows.)
People, when angered, can create more havoc than animals.

The Jarl Squad was the only squad who didn't do an act: they sang all three songs, led several sets of three cheers, then went straight into their squad dance, which turned out to be the Canadian Barn Dance. Gavin's head went up as he recognised the tune.

'A good Shetland tradition?' he asked.

'Probably just wanting a change from a Boston two-step, but still simple enough to dance at your last hall, when you're dead beat and dead drunk. Or maybe the Jarl spends every summer in Canada.'

'Hi,' a breathless voice said in my ear. 'Can I take this chair?'

It was Lizbet, hand on the fifth chair at our table. She was wearing a stretchy gold sequinned dress that made the best of her curves. Her careful make-up made it hard to judge her colour, but her eyes were no longer swollen, and the smile she gave me was almost convincing.

'Go you,' I said.

She turned it around to the table next to us, sat down and leaned back to me. 'Having a good night?'

I nodded. 'And you?'

'Yea, it's fine to be out.' Her face lengthened. 'Sort of. But we had the tickets, and Tom reckoned we should come out and use them, rather than stay in brooding.'

'I'd've thought you'd be performing somewhere tonight.'

She shook her head. 'You need a dance band for tonight. But we're booked for here tomorrow night, for the Hop.'

Hop Night was the night after Up Helly Aa, where the parties continued in every available venue. It gave the guizers a chance to watch other squads and keep having fun in costume. I was glad I'd be sailing away from this stifling of other people, and chatter, and the relentless thump, thump of the band. 'That'll be fun,' I said. 'Look out of the window around half ten and you may see my sails in the distance. I'm off to Yell for my driving test.'

'Oh, the theory one? Good luck.'

'Speaking of Yell,' I said tentatively, 'did you put it back?'

Her earrings jangled as she nodded her head. 'I've put it where the Devil can stretch out his hand and take it, if he wants it. I've done with it.'

'Good,' I said.

Around us, couples were breaking up, the Jarl Squad members going over to talk to friends. Ewan came over to Lizbet, and she rose quickly and moved to the floor with him. I finished my juice then glanced back at them. Ewan was looking over her head at the darkening windows and his feet moved mechanically, as if his thoughts were miles away; Lizbet's cheeks were flushed, and there was a dreamy smile on her lips. I remembered her anxiety to know how he was, when she'd made her confession about the Book. It was a tangle: Ewan keen on Chloe, Lizbet keen on Ewan. Chloe keen on Antony. Antony back with Jesma, maybe . . .

I could do with another long glass of lemonade and orange. I glanced at the bar to see how crowded it was. Pretty chocca, mostly with Vikings made thirsty by the dance. Two of the men behind it were doing their octopus act of pouring pints, getting drams, taking money and handing out drinks and change simultaneously. The third bartender, Jeemie, the owner of the Starlight that I crewed for in the points races, was being buttonholed by a man standing at the end of the bar, a stranger, and a strange style of face to see here. Jeemie obviously thought so too, for he was talking to him in brief sentences, a guarded expression on his face. The man was short and plump with hair brushed back from his forehead in a style that had something American about it, and his skin was pink and soft in the bar lighting, with not a hint of the weathering that every other man showed, even in winter. He wore a crisply ironed blue and white striped shirt, open at the neck, a green velvet jacket and light-coloured trousers and brogues like Gavin's, the ones he only wore with his dress kilt. All in all, he looked completely out of place.

He must have sensed me staring, for he turned to glance in our direction. I shifted my gaze to the band, but kept puzzling. Maybe someone new who'd come up to work for the council? Some sort of auditor, or assessor? There was shrewdness in his narrow eyes. I nudged Gavin. 'There's an odd-looking bloke talking to Jeemie at the bar.'

Gavin flashed him a glance, then joined me in looking at the band, and continued the conversation in an ordinary tone, as if we were discussing the merits of the accordionist. 'Not a usual type up here, but they come by the dozen in the tourist-trade street of any Scottish town. At a guess, something to do with antiques, old prints, something like that. Antiquarian books, rather than just second-hand, or a specialist in wally dugs, or Burns portraits.'

I realised I hadn't told him about the Book o' the Black Arts. I lowered my voice. 'I think I ken what he's after. It's an old book of magic spells, written in white on black paper. That's what was dug up in the old kirkyard.'

Gavin's brows rose. 'Was it, indeed? Where did you hear that? Magnie?'

I nodded. 'And from the person who dug it up.'

I glanced back at the bar. The man at the bar seemed to have

130

asked a definite question. Jeemie was stalling, I could see that, could imagine the words, 'I doot I'm no' seen her here this night', when Jesma, passing with her still-full plate of fancies and emptied teacups, leaned into the conversation, nodding over her shoulder towards where Tom was sitting. The man thanked her, headed over and oozed himself into Lizbet's seat. Tom leaned forward apologetically, and was obviously explaining it was taken, and the stranger was replying with some sort of explanation when the dance ended, and Ewan brought Lizbet back to her seat. Tom reached for another chair, and she sat down, flushed and laughing.

The plump man leaned forward to talk to her, and the colour under the make-up drained away. She believed she'd got rid of the Book, and now this stranger was bringing it back. She brought one hand up to her chest, as if she couldn't breathe, then she shook her head vehemently. The plump man kept talking.

'No!' Lizbet said, so loudly that the talking stilled for a moment. 'I don't ken what you're on about!' she wailed. She shoved her chair back with a scrape and made her way blindly towards the door. It slammed shut behind her.

There was a long moment's silence, then the talk began again, with everyone carefully not looking at the dealer and Tom left alone at the table. Tom had risen in his seat as Lizbet had stood up, and as she ran out he'd stretched one hand after her as if he was trying to hold her back. Now he looked irresolutely at the door she'd exited by, took a step towards it then hesitated and slowly sat down again, looking worried.

The plump man leaned forward, talking persuasively. Tom shook his head, and the plump man notched up the persuasion. Tom shook his head again, and stood up. He spoke sharply enough for us to hear. 'If Lizbet says no, she means it.'

The plump man gestured with his hands: calm down, we'll say no more about it. Slowly, Tom sat down once more, with another glance doorwards. The plump man fished in his pocket, and produced a card, which he gave to Tom; then he too rose, and went back to the bar, leaving Tom turning the card over in his hands. He gave it a last look, shoved it in his pocket, and followed Lizbet out of the door.

'Interesting,' Gavin said. He lowered his voice to below the general chatter level. 'Was it Lizbet, then, who dug up the book he's after?'

I nodded. 'Dug it up, and put it back again. He can offer her all the money he likes, she won't give it to him.'

'Might her boyfriend persuade her?'

I shook my head. 'He's Tom, the guitarist in the band. She told Magnie and me about the Book yesterday. She was determined to get rid of it.'

There was a stir at the door, a chord from the band. 'Ladies and gentlemen, please welcome squad number six – Reservation Sheep Dogs!'

There was a blare of TV theme music, and the black-suited guizers were among us. In their dance routine some 'grew' paws, tails and put on a sheepdog mask, while others reversed their jackets to reveal a fleece, and sheep ears hood. The music ended with a crashing chord, the sheep did a double-take at the dogs, baaa'd in horror and charged round the room and out again with the dog flock following them. I didn't get that one either.

The squad dance was a Foula reel, and we whirled into it with enthusiasm. 'Three times?' Gavin asked, as we wove in and out of the couples for our second time.

I nodded. I didn't have enough breath left to speak; life aboard a tall ship was making me soft, in spite of regular mast-climbing. Still, I had seven weeks left. I could go for a good long sail every day. I was just contemplating places I could sail to and still be home for tea when the dance ended.

The table where Lizbet and Tom had been was still empty when we sat down again. I glanced uneasily at the door she'd left by. 'I wonder if I should go and see if she's okay?'

'She has her friend with her,' Gavin said.

'He doesn't know about the Book, though.'

'Unless she's telling him now. I think he'd ask what this was all about, don't you?'

I made a reluctant-agreement face.

'How about some soup?' he asked. 'Or d'you think they'll have saat flesh bannocks?'

'You're going native.'

'One of the community policemen brought them in for lunch one day. They were good.'

I was still full of lasagne, but the dancing had settled it enough to make room for a bannock with salted roast beef, and of course there would be fancies. 'I could manage a bannock,' I conceded, and we headed over to the kitchen hatch. Ewan was standing beside it, shield and axe returned to their bus for safe-keeping, fair head bare. He looked brighter than he had this morning, as if the excitement of the night was buoying him up. He greeted me with a cheerful 'Aye aye, Cass!'

'Aye aye,' I replied. 'Great suit.'

'The Jarl played for Delting all his footballing days. The galley couldn't be any other colour.'

'She was bonny. It seemed a waste to burn her.'

'Ah, she's all show. Built to be burned, not seaworthy.' He glanced towards the marina. 'I see you got your one safely out of the way.'

'She's down at the Ladie pontoon.'

'Aye aye. The sailing season starts once Up Helly Aa is by with.'

No, he wasn't brighter. He was saying all the right things, but his voice was mechanical, and his smile didn't make it to his eyes. It was like a performance by a robot. If it hadn't been Up Helly Aa he'd have been at home, mourning. Even as I looked at him, his eyes suddenly brimmed over. He rubbed them with one hand and forced himself to life again. 'And this'll be your man? I don't think we're met yet.' He held out a hand to Gavin.

'Ewan Pearson, owner o' the *Day Dawn*.' He nodded towards the window. 'The varnished one out on the hard.'

'Drying out,' Gavin said, sympathetically.

'Yea.' Ewan shrugged. 'Ah, well, the damage's no' as bad as it might have been. Her hull's fine, and I'm hoping the engine's taken no harm.' He glanced sideways at the door leading outside, then looked back at where Lizbet had been sitting, and bit his lip. His gaze came back to us and blurred again. He lifted his pint and prepared to move away. 'Have a fine night now.'

He wandered off through the jostle of another squad coming in: the ones with the medieval-style costumes. They were wearing rubber councillor masks and did a mock fight with crazy-shaped aluminium swords. The Convenor lost to one of the others, who chased him out and came back in brandishing a chopped-off head with scarlet cloth blood streaming from it. Their squad dance was a Polly Glide, which I hauled Gavin up for, abandoning my remaining bannock and fancy; my feet still remembered the steps, once I'd seen the first set, and his soon picked it up.

'Polly Glide?' he said, as we sat down again, laughing and breathless from the speed the band had set the third go. 'Or Palais, as in Glasgow?'

'Guid kens. But it's fun.'

We laughed our way back to our seats. The table beside us had two different folk sitting there now. I looked at Gavin. 'I'll just go down and check on Lizbet. She's maybe hiding in the Ladies'. I won't intrude.'

I went down the stairs. There was a trio of teenagers refurbishing their make-up at the bathroom mirror, but the cubicle doors were all open. I was just opening the door back into the Hall when there was a thud of sheepskin boots on the step, a clink of chain mail, and Ewan came past me and went out. 'Lizbet?' he called.

Maybe there was a chance for her after all. I caught the closing door before it banged and looked out. Tom and Lizbet were sitting on the bench where the Sport 14s were parked in the summer, in the shelter of the clubhouse. Tears glittered on Lizbet's cheeks, but there was a smile on her face as she looked up at Ewan, bending over her, caring enough to come and see she was all right. I wasn't needed here now.

I was backing into the Hall and easing the door shut when Ewan's head went up. He gave a roar like an angry bull and charged past me into the shadow at the side of the boating club. He yelled, 'What're you doing there, smooting about like the rat you are?' His hand grabbed someone's jacket and hauled him forwards.

It was Antony. He thrust Ewan's hand off him and retorted, 'You're a rat yourself, putting the blame for your sunk boat onto me!'

They'd come forward into the light shed from the club windows above. Both men's faces were twisted with anger. They glared at each other for a moment, then Ewan swung a punch which Antony parried. Lizbet cried out, then leapt up from the bench and ran forward to grab at Ewan's arm. He shook her off, swinging her back towards Tom. She stumbled, and Tom moved forward to catch her. Her face was white.

'Insured, was she?' Antony continued.

The taunt maddened Ewan. He gave a yell of fury and flung himself at Antony. The pair of them staggered around the square of light for a moment, grappling with each other, and then Antony gave a low punch which doubled Ewan over, and followed it up with a shove which overbalanced him. He fell sprawling onto the ground. Lizbet gave a cry, and struggled in Tom's hold. I swung my door open and ran out, reaching for Antony's raised arm with both hands. He shook me away with one fast wrench which made me stagger backwards into the clubhouse wall, and flung himself on top of Ewan. Just as he raised his arm to punch again there were shouts and a clatter of feet on the stairs behind me. A swarm of men rushed past me to surround them.

It took three of them to pull Antony up from Ewan and restrain him. They were all club folk, so there was no need to explain the situation. They surrounded him so that he couldn't see Ewan and took him upstairs in a phalanx. The others, Ewan's fellow Vikings, hauled Ewan up, dusted him down and took him up the gravel drive towards their bus.

I went over to Lizbet. 'Are you okay?'

She nodded. Surprisingly, she seemed less shaken by the incident than I felt; I supposed if you played pubs you got used to fights. 'I'll come back inside in a minute. Really, I'm fine.' She managed a smile. 'Thanks for coming out to look for me.' Her eyes shone for a moment as she glanced up to where Ewan was clambering into his bus. 'I'll see you up there in a minute.'

I climbed back up the stairs and went into the club. Antony was at the bar now. There was a dull red circle on his jaw from where Ewan had hit him, and he shook his head as if he was trying to take the sting of it away. His eyes were wicked with anger, but the men around him kept him talking as the Vikings began to gather on the dance floor.

'Trust you to be in the thick of it,' Gavin said as I sat down. 'Not hurt?'

The back of one arm stung where it had hit the wall. I shook my head.

The Jarl had taken the microphone. 'Three cheers for the hosts and hostesses of the boating club, let's be hearing you!'

The cheers were subdued.

'And three more for Up Helly Aa!' That was better. 'You all have a good night, now.'

They marched out. The men who'd been restraining Antony remained around him until the last cloak had swirled through the door, then moved away. Left alone at the bar, Antony downed his whisky, flung a tenner at Jeemie, then strode back out into the night.

Chapter Twelve

Saturday 18th March

Tide times, Brae:
LW 02.46 (0.57m);
HW 09.01 (2.12m);
LW 15.12 (0.35m);
HW 21.29 (2.01m)

Moonset 06.52; sunrise 07.10; moonrise 18.27;
sunset 19.14. Full moon.

When Lowrie's no' fishin' he's mending his net.
Said of a single-minded person, always with his goal in mind.

It was a bonny, bonny night. The sky was cloudless, and studded with stars; the bright silver of the full moon turned to gleaming pewter on the water. The hills had cast a shadow over *Khalida* at the pier, but by the time I came out into the channel my eyes had adjusted and the sea around me was bright as daylight. I gave Gavin a last wave, then motored clear of Houbansetter and hoisted the mainsail in Cole Deep. The wind was as good as the forecast had promised, force 3 gusting 4 from the north, so that I'd be close-hauled for most of the way, a good point of sail with my *Khalida*, then I'd be reaching across the top of Yell, and it would be behind me going into Yell Sound.

It was strange how you never saw how many folk lived in

Shetland till it was dark. This apparently quiet piece of country was filled with lights that reflected in the darkness at the sea's edge. Brae looked a little city, and even Muckle Roe, where there were more sheep than people, seemed to have house after house shining out into the night. I picked out Magnie's, and saw him standing silhouetted in the porch. A torch flashed: dot, dash, dash, dot. A pause, then he repeated it: P, the Blue Peter; this ship is ready to sail, or outward bound. I took my torch and repeated the message into the darkness, smiling. It might be cold, and I felt like Michelin man in full thermals and oilskins, but I was outward bound.

There was a long swell in the Røna. I fastened the main halyard securely and dodged the flapping mainsail to get back to the shelter of the cockpit. Cat was at his station on the cockpit bench in the lee of the cabin, paws braced; he knew all about the bouncing that went on until the boat was properly sailing. Kitten was curled up in my bunk. I'd worried that I should be leaving her behind, but Gavin had assured me again that she'd be fine, and Kitten herself had made it quite clear that if Cat was going, so was she. Cat had spent the afternoon on the cabin roof, Gavin told me, looking round with the air of once again being top cat in the harbour, while Kitten sunbathed on the shoreward side deck. The pair of them had watched my early-evening preparations with interest, bolted their dinner down in the kitchen, then headed for the boat and made themselves at home. When I came down to do last-minute stuff and get dressed for a long, cold night, their two heads greeted me from my berth. Cat stretched and came out on deck; Kitten yawned and stayed put, with only a token-gesture squeak when I put her lifejacket on.

I was passing Dad and Maman's house now. The big picture window out over the sea was partly blocked by a dark shape; Maman and Dad standing together, watching me sail into the night. I got my torch out and flashed again, and the window darkened, lit up, darkened, lit up in reply. The door opened. Faintly, from on shore, a siren's voice floated to me, the voice that could project right to the gods of the largest theatre without a microphone. I could even make out the words: '*Come away, fellow sailors, come away, come away.*' Maman was singing. Dad came to join her, and two arms waved. I raised my own arm, flashed my torch up into the sky, and sailed on. There was a lump in my throat. They didn't approve, they thought I should stay home with Gavin, but they still watched to wish me luck as I went past.

I was glad he was coming to join me.

The cold wind teased out tendrils of my hair and stung on my upper lip. I set my course straight down the middle of the Røna, between the two dark headlands that framed the shining seaway, wriggled my back down a little and put my feet up on the opposite seat. My tiller fitted snugly into my hand, my boat forged smoothly onwards, accelerating as she went down into the troughs, gliding up the crests. The waves slid away from her bow in fans of white water. I stroked Cat, and he gave his silent mew.

I'd left the cottage pontoon at 22.00, and for this voyage I reckoned I'd keep half-hourly log entries, mostly to keep track of where I was in the darkness, but also to keep myself awake. My chart was spread on the table below, with my log-book on top. Right now I could see exactly where I was. I hooked the chain over the button on *Khalida*'s tiller and left her to sail herself while I messed about in the red light from my port side shining through the cabin window. I took a pencil, marked us with a cross and the time, 22.30, confirmed the cross by taking sightings on the Vementry guns and the Roe light, just for the way of it, then made a mug of drinking chocolate and went back on deck.

The first part of the journey was across St Magnus Bay towards the cliffs of Eshaness, the projecting north-west corner of mainland Shetland. I saw the dark rim of cliffs stretching round the moonlit bay as soon as I came out of the Røna, and the white flash of the lighthouse, once every twelve seconds. I hauled jib and mainsail in, and *Khalida* tilted to the wind and surged forwards; the dark figures in the dim red light of the log rose to 4.2, 4.7 and levelled off at 5.7. Nice. Her new sails were making all the difference to how close to the wind she could point. There was a touch of west in the northerly, which would help me as I headed north-east towards the top of Yell. I'd been worried about how far out to sea I'd have to go now to get comfortably outside of the Uyea Baas and the Ramna Stacks on each side of the northern top of Mainland after I tacked back towards the land.

I sipped my chocolate and watched the shifting water. A double flash far ahead of us was the Ve Skerries, and to the north of it the sky was beginning to glow green with the effect of luminous paint dripped in a ragged arch of light: the Northern Lights. The green glowed and faded again; above me, there were white patches that I'd have taken for cloud if they hadn't brightened and dimmed. It was blissfully quiet, no electric hum of fridge or generator and absolutely no teenage giggles, just the ssssh and crunch of the waves under *Khalida*'s forefoot.

Over my aft shoulder, a light flickered close in to the cliffs. I turned my head to look. Darkness; then I saw it again, someone shining a light on the water, five hundred metres away. A dark blob bobbed briefly against a white hull: a fisherman hauling up creels near the red cliffs of Muckle Roe. I waited a moment, still watching, then reached for my spyglasses. I could just make out the shape of a boat against the darkness of the cliffs. Contrary to all regulations, she appeared to be unlit. Someone taking up creels in the dark, and on the Hop night, when there were bands and dances in venues all round Brae, with most of Brae busy enjoying themselves, and the Jarl Squad visiting each place. For tonight Ewan would be far too busy to worry about someone taking more lobsters than his licence allowed. The shape was too blurred to identify, but it looked to be the right size for Antony's boat. I watched as it nosed along the cliff, stopping with a brief flash of light, moving on again, until we were too far out to see it, and wondered if Ewan had been right about his illegal activities.

I was making good time. I went on into the Atlantic for another half-hour, checked my position against the Eshaness light, the Roe light and the Ve skerries, then tacked around. Now Muckle Ossa was visible as a black lump in the shifting sea, past the moonlit hills and the dark cliff where the light flashed. My plan was to go between it and the last corner of Eshaness, the Faither, and then up as close to the wind as I could. I was halfway to Eshaness now, and the Faither was the twenty-mile mark of the journey. I went below and buttered myself a bannock. Kitten was fast asleep in my bunk, the pink of her lifejacket gleaming in the darkness, and now Cat came down to join her. I unhooked him from his lead so that he could curl up in peace beside her, and sat down on the couch to eat my bannock, and give myself a rest from the wind. At midnight I wrote the new date and the tide times in the log:

Sunday 19th March
LW: west side 03.16 GMT (0.5m)
HW: Lerwick 07.34 (2.18m)
(slack tide in Bluemull Sound from 08.04)
LW: Mid Yell 14.19 (0.32m) (Lerwick minus 25 mins)
HW: Mid Yell 20.37 (2.02m)

Moonset 06.54; sunrise 07.07; moonrise 20.01;
sunset 19.16. Full moon.

I added our position, and a summary of conditions: *Port tack, full sail, clear bonny night. Eshaness light fine on s'board bow. Muckle Ossa visible.*

Muckle Ossa was a funny conical islet off Eshaness, the plug of a long-gone volcano flung out into the sea. We forged slowly towards it across the silver sea, under the stars, onwards and onwards, and gradually it grew in size, until by 02.30 I was slipping past it, nose pointed to the west of the Faither. The creel boat had made it here before me, going inshore under motor; I spotted him again just off Eshaness. At three, I was clear of Eshaness and headed towards the furthest headland I could see, Uyea, the west corner of the top of Shetland's mainland, a sloping line with a bristle of rocks on each corner. I blessed that touch of west in the north wind as I drew my course on the chart and projected it upwards; on this heading, I'd clear the Uyea Baas nicely.

It would have been a long hour, except that the whole sky suddenly lit up with a bonny, bonny display of the Mirrie Dancers, the aurora borealis, flickering green, rose, mauve around the horizon, paling only in the brightness of the moon in the south-east. I watched entranced as the bright shafts of light pulsed and faded, and only went below, yawning, to make a cup of coffee. When the Uyea Baas looked close on the water, breaking white below my sails, I sat on the lee side of the cockpit, tiller in hand, to watch them go. The top of Mainland was outlined against the silver water, with the Ramna Stacks like black witch's teeth jutting up; the Point of Fethaland light flashed its triple flash from the mainland to the right of them. 04.15. I took a last fix on the Eshaness light and another on the Point of Fethaland one, and marked my position on the chart, then confirmed it using the GPS.

I hadn't expected to see the first lightening of the sky so early. I'd come from the equator, where the sun suddenly blazed into a still-dark sky. Now I could see the hills of North Yell outlined against a paler sky, faintly tinged with amber. Soon it would be daylight, and I was glad of it, for Yell Sound was the entrance to the oil terminal of Sullom Voe, and from here on I needed to keep a serious lookout for tankers. They should be approaching the sound at slow steaming speed, 18 knots, unless they were in a hurry to catch a tidal stream, but that was fast enough for them to be on me in ten minutes. I began moving from side to side of my boat, checking all round. It wasn't yet light enough on the sea for me to spot ships, but a vessel larger than fifty metres should be showing two white lights, as well as assorted reds for tugs, or towing, or constrained by draught. In theory, of course, steam gave way to sail except in a restricted channel, but I wasn't going to argue that one with a tanker that took ten miles to stop and fifteen to turn.

I was also watching for the Bagi Stacks light on the other side of Yell Sound, marking the corner of Yell with four white flashes every twenty seconds. Once I reached that I was well past halfway. I stared under my sails into the darkness beyond the Ramna Stacks. There! Four flashes, well to the right of *Khalida*'s bow. We were nicely on course.

I'd had a good sleep in the afternoon, but I was starting to flag now. It took me another hour to draw level with the Ramna Stacks, with the light strengthening all the time, so that it was as near daylight as made no difference at sea. Now the sky behind Yell and Unst was glowing rose-gold, and the mainland behind me was lit with soft light. Just to keep my hand in, I did a running fix on the red sector of the Point of Fethaland light, then had another half-cup of coffee as I listened to the 05.00 forecast: *Fair Isle cyclonic, north-north-west, 3 to 4, occasionally 5, slight, fair, good.*

This was the most dangerous part of the voyage. Now I was past the Ramna Stacks I was crossing tanker highway on a long diagonal, with the grey bulk of Yell obscuring my view of anything arriving from the east. Looking down Yell Sound, I could see a bristling of lights around the terminal under the brighter orange flickering of the flare stacks; the street lights of Lerwick shone in the distance.

There was nothing coming out of the sound. Nothing behind me, coming from America. From the Ramna Stacks to the safety of the north of Yell was four miles. An hour to shelter. Cat came out of the cabin, yawning and tousled, disturbed by my moving about, and I clipped him on to his safety lead. Below, the Kitten was scrabbling in their litter tray. I checked the autopilot chain would come free easily, in case I needed to change course, and forged on. I was hearing an engine noise, but I couldn't quite make out whether it was ahead or somewhere behind me. Cat heard it too; he stopped washing and sat up straighter, whiskers bristling, turning his head as if he wasn't sure either. The sound became louder, and now it was definitely behind us: a motorboat on two wings of white wash, heading swiftly towards us. I reached below for my torch and shone it on my mainsail, flashed it towards him, then shone it on my sail again. The motorboat changed course to roar around me, leaving us bouncing in its wake, and sped on towards the corner of Yell. Cat crouched down as I got the boat back on course, and Kitten gave an indignant mew from below and appeared in the cabin doorway to see what was happening. I clipped her on too and looked around. Cat sat up and gave a little growl, looking up towards the direction the motorboat had gone in.

Its engine roar had masked another one. There was a tanker coming around the corner of Yell. The white lights lighting up its white superstructure made it look a mile high. Time to make all speed towards the shore. For a moment I wished I'd taken the precaution of having the engine idling for this section, but she'd get out of the way faster under sail. I slackened the mainsail and turned *Khalida*'s nose away from the wind, then let the jib out. She picked up speed smoothly: 5.5 knots, 6.2. There should be someone on watch in that monster control tower. I reached for my torch and shone it on my sails again. The tanker seemed to be coming steadily towards me, and then at last her nose moved from the stay I was checking it against. We were no longer on a collision course.

Her wash would be serious. I kept *Khalida* going as fast as she could towards the darkened shore. The tanker came level with us, blotting out the grey sea, the Fethaland light, the misted green hills of the mainland. It towered over us, a huge iron bulk. I could smell the diesel fumes, feel the wind of its passing, seeming frighteningly close although it was five hundred metres away. As it passed us I tacked around, so that *Khalida*'s nose was to its wake. The boom rattled, the sails flapped, as we jolted over its wash, up and down. Kitten mewed in protest and returned to my berth, trailing her lead behind her; Cat crouched, growling, claws gripping my wooden thwarts.

Engine time. That little detour had cost me my straight line up to the Bagi Stacks light; we'd need to motor up the side of Yell. My ancient Volvo Penta spluttered into life second turn and settled down to an even thumping. We'd still be going at 4 knots, so I wouldn't lose much time. I rolled the jib away and hauled the main in tight. It might catch some wind to speed us on our way.

There was the first faint hint of proper light over Yell now, a streak of palest creamy blue above the hills, the colour of the duck eggs stashed below the cooker; to the west, the penny moon was settling down towards the water. Two more tankers passed us going in and one going out, well clear of us, but making *Khalida* jolt over their wash. We made good time up the west side of Yell in spite of them, and by 06.45 we were at the corner and about to turn into safety.

The sun had risen now. A red-gold beam touched the wooden window frame and sidled into the cabin. The sky was grey with mist around the horizon, but the blue above promised a bonny spring day to come. The Bagi Stacks light was above us, and the north end of Yell stretched along to starboard. The whole far corner of Yell bristled with rocks, but if I kept in over thirty fathoms of water I'd be clear of them. Unst was clearly visible now, right to the slanted rocks of Muckle Flugga, topped by the white and ochre lighthouse tower.

I slacked off the mainsail and jib and let *Khalida* settle into her new course. Instantly it felt warmer, with the wind on her side, on my back, and her motion was steadier, rolling over the breakers. The log rose to 6 knots. The sun was shining straight in my eyes, so that I had to pull my hat brim down and squint from under it at the points of Atlantic-pounded rock reaching out into the sea. Their smoothness made them no less deadly to any ship unfortunate enough to end up on them. Shetland's worst sea disaster had been off this coast, a summer storm in 1881. Ten boats had been lost. Halfway down the voe, at Gloup, I could just see the dark shape of the memorial on its white plinth: a shawled woman with her child in one arm and the other hand shielding her eyes, gazing out to sea.

Breakfast time. I couldn't leave the helm for long, but I popped up and down from the cabin: food and fresh water for the cats, cornflakes and tea for me. While I was at it I reset the clocks. Spring forwards. Cat and the Kitten had a good feed, then sat out in the sun and washed their whiskers. The weathered headlands with the waves white at their feet slipped past, the gold curve of Breckon Beach, where Lizbet had grown up; where she'd dared the Devil. Nearly at Bluemull.

I washed and dried my bowl and put it away, then got my mooring ropes out and attached them to the cleats forrard and at the stern. Fenders at the ready on both sides; fenderboard. The grass parks of Lund and Flubersgerdie on Unst were bright in the early sun, the cliffs still mysterious with shadows. Last push now, but oh, I was so tired, and there was still another ten miles to go to Mid Yell, with all the awkward threading through pot buoys and around fish farms and mussel rafts that I remembered from my youth sailing days as being all round Mid Yell voe. Ten miles; two and a half hours.

A light twice flashed in the corner of my eye. I turned my head and waited, counting. Ten seconds. My heart lightened. Cullivoe, of course, only two miles down into the sound, less than an hour away, half an hour once I was into the sound, with a good clear entrance between red and green buoys, and a pier to lie beside. I'd been so focused on getting to Mid Yell that I'd forgotten the familiar port on the way. I could go into Cullivoe now, and carry on to Mid Yell this evening, at the next high water, once I was rested.

I set the engine going, went forrard, dropped the mainsail and zipped it into its cover, then turned *Khalida*'s nose into Bluemull Sound. The wind was on my back now, the breakers rolling ahead of us, with *Khalida* surging down the crests in a steady skoosh of foam, leaving a white wash from her bow. The far end of the sound was scattered with little islands, and the shore of Unst was dangerous with the rocks north of Lunda Wick, but I didn't need to worry about any of that. I slackened the jib off and headed to port of the broad Ness of Cullivoe. I couldn't see the entrance to the harbour, but the white rectangle of the ice plant was just visible above the lowest curve of the Ness. Half an hour, and I could sleep.

We were almost there when a fishing boat came snarling past Hoga Ness and through the narrows caused by the point, opening up his throttle as he came. I grabbed for the jib lines and rolled the sail away before his wash hit us. It was the same boat as the one that had passed us in the night, I was sure of it, and now it was light enough to see into the wheelhouse as it passed us. I waved, and the driver leaned back out of the wheelhouse to give us a cheery salute. Antony, looking pleased with himself, heading home after a profitable night's work.

We bounced to his wash then came around the point in good order. There were major works going on here. To the left of the rock wall enclosing the pier area was a second rock wall enclosing a new marina, empty as yet. On shore, a large bulldozer squatted in the middle of a quarry. A notice at the start of the works read 'Yell Industrial Estate'.

The pier area had several fishing boats moored along the wall, and I didn't want to double-park. There wasn't anybody at the long dock behind the pier, just a line of parked trucks, which perhaps meant something was happening there that I didn't know about. Well, somebody would tell me if I had to move. I chugged gently around the pier and manoeuvred up to the dock. It was lined with black rubber, so I slung the fender board over to keep *Khalida*'s white fenders clean and flung a stern rope around a handy cleat, then clambered ashore to secure the forrard one. I added a couple of springs for good measure, then unclipped the cats and eyed up the distance between my deck and the dock. They'd need a plank to get on and off the boat. I found a reasonably clean one and secured it as their own personal gangway from the cabin roof, then switched off the engine and headed below, shedding lifejacket, jacket, seaboots and waterproof trousers as I went, and drew the curtain against the sun. Sleep, sleep, sleep.

I sent Gavin a text saying I was at Cullivoe, not Mid Yell, switched my phone off, and slept.

IV

**Hit needs a muckle o' the Deil athin
you as can keep him ithoot you.**
(It requires a lot of the Devil within you to keep him outside you)
It requires a deal of inner toughness to keep on 'the straight and narrow'.

Chapter Thirteen

Needs most when da deevil drives.
(Needs must when the Devil drives).
If there's no alternative, there are times when you have to do
certain things, unpleasant though they be.

I was woken by a shadow on the cabin window, and the boat's lines creaking as someone climbed aboard. Gavin's voice called my name.

'Here,' I said, and raised my head to look at the ship's clock. Ten to one.

'I'd have let you sleep longer,' Gavin said apologetically, leaning in to kiss me, 'but Mass is at three, and I thought you'd want to eat.'

I tried to collect my scattered wits. 'Yes, please.'

Gavin dumped one carrier bag in the sink, the other on the cooker, and sat down on the couch. 'Shall I make you a cup of tea and let you wake up first?'

'I'm awake.' I rubbed my eyes. 'A cup of tea would be wonderful.' *Khalida* rocked as he went back into the cockpit to put the gas on, then returned to fill the kettle and set it on the stove. I blinked another couple of times and tried to remember whether Cullivoe had showers. I thought not. A basin wash would have to do. I wriggled myself out of my berth and squeezed past him into the heads, drawing the curtain behind me. 'I'll just wash.' I reached back out to half-fill my washing basin with water and set it on the heads floor. 'Won't be five minutes.'

As I washed and dried I heard him on the other side of the curtain, setting out mugs, getting the frying pan out, plates, cutlery. I reappeared, clean, with my towel wrapped around me. 'What are the cats up to?'

'Making friends with a fisherman on the main pier. Ertie Arthurson. He seemed to ken all about you.' He took a deep breath and went into quoting. 'He said he kent fine they were yours, he saw you come in this morning, and reckoned you'd have been up all night sailing from Brae, with that peerie boat, but it was a bonny night for it, and he dooted you'd have had a fine sail. Oh, and he gave us a hake for lunch and a couple of ling for the cats. Would you like it fried or grilled?'

That explained the frying pan, the carrier bag in the sink and the gentle waft of raw fish. I considered my stomach and decided that I could manage fish. I wasn't entirely sure what a hake was, but if Gavin said it would grill, then grill it would. 'Grilled, please, but in the frying pan rather than on the grill – it's less of a pain to clean. What's a hake anyway?'

'White fish, bigger flakes than a haddock, but nice flesh. I wanted to take you out for lunch, but with Mass at three that's not going to work.' He laid the two fillets in the pan, topped them with a knob of butter and set them under the grill. 'Bread?'

'Please.'

He produced a fresh loaf from his second carrier bag. 'Then I thought we could do dinner, but it's March.'

I was busy teasing out my hair, and it took a moment for that to sink in. 'Yell folk don't eat denner in March?'

'Population of Yell, just under a thousand. Cost of keeping a restaurant open, more than that population would justify, so everything mostly closes for winter.' He found the breadknife and began slicing. He added mournfully, 'The Old Haa's closed till April as well. I'm told the baking in the café there is spectacularly good.'

'It is,' I said. 'Nita's chocolate cake is to die for, and she does real squashed fly biscuits too.' I sighed. 'Ah well. Maybe we can come back in April.'

'But the Aywick Shop is open,' Gavin said, 'so we can get ingredients for dinner there. I want a look at the charity shop too.'

'You want to see Mary's,' I agreed. 'If Mary doesn't have it, you don't need it.'

I put rice in my flask for later, then went to retrieve the cats and thank Ertie Arthurson for the fish. I wasn't surprised he already knew all about me; he was likely one of Magnie's cousins. Even more handily, he turned out to be the person who organised berths.

'Yea, yea,' he said, 'you can easy lie against the pier there for a day or two. There's no boats due in, that I ken o', and if one comes I'll give you a shout and you could maybe back into the corner, to give them room. Just up for a visit, are you?'

I made an unenthusiastic face. 'My theory driving test, on Monday.'

'Ah, you'll do fine at it. A woman who can manage a boat'll have no difficulty with a car.' He paused to think about that. 'Mind you, there are more idiots on the road, and less sea room. Well, good luck. Is your man going to drive you down to it?'

I hadn't thought of that. My vague plan had been to sail on to Mid Yell, dodging the buoys I'd been warned about, but of course that left Gavin on shore, bringing the Land Rover, or if we went together, it left the Land Rover in Cullivoe. I could easily stay put in Cullivoe, two hours nearer home, and get him to drop me off on his way to the ferry tomorrow morning. I said that. 'He has to work tomorrow. He'll drop me off on his way. I can walk or hitch a lift back, have a good night's sleep and set off homewards on Tuesday.'

'Plenty of buses, lass, to bring you as far as Gutcher at least. Just ask them in Mid Yell, they'll tell you.' He shoved his cap back and scratched his head, thinking. 'The school bus, that goes from the school at five to four. It would likely have room for you, and it would bring you all the way. Otherwise it's the workers' bus, that's 18.35 at the Mid Yell junction, on the main road. You ken, just below Windhouse.'

'Shetland's most haunted,' I said. 'I ken it.'

'Ah, it's an unchancy place, Windhouse. I saw lights there myself just – now, when would it have been?' He straightened his cap. 'Two or three nights ago. Not long after dark, as I was coming in up the sound. A light like a torch moving about in the house, and dark figures moving around it.'

'Local teenagers daring each other?'

He snorted at that. 'Teenagers these days wouldn't have the nerve. Spending all their time on their phones. They can barely talk to each other, let alone go and talk to the Devil.'

I thought he was selling the younger generation short there.

'And then this morning again. Just after sunrise that would be. A light and a moving dark shadow in the house. I wouldn't go there after dark if you paid me. I'll leave the Devil to make himself home there, and never meddle more with him.'

I thought of Lizbet and the Book. 'I wouldn't meddle with him either,' I said. I gave him twenty pounds for two nights berthing, called the cats away from his catch and returned thoughtfully to *Khalida*. What had Lizbet said, on Friday night? *I've put it where the Devil can stretch out his hand and take it, if he wants it.*

If I was wanting to give the Devil back his own, I reckoned Windhouse would be a good place to start. You could bury it under a broken bit of flooring, or some tumble of masonry, replace what had been on top of the earth as it was, and nobody would know, unless they were looking for it.

'Hake's ready,' Gavin said. 'Have a seat, and let me dish it up, then you can tell me what you're looking so thoughtful about.'

I sat down. 'That book,' I said. 'The one the dealer was after. I think I know where it is.'

The brown hand dishing out the fish paused. 'Oh?'

'I think Lizbet buried it in Windhouse.'

He reacted as I had. 'Shetland's most haunted. The laird who sold his soul to the Devil, and bodies found under the floorboards.'

'Lizbet said, "*I've put it where the Devil can stretch out his hand and take it, if he wants it.*" Ertie saw lights up there two or three evenings ago, not long after dark.'

'Wednesday or Thursday. Thursday was the day after Chloe's death.'

I nodded. 'The day Lizbet spoke to Magnie and me about it. She must have driven straight up here after that.'

'And then told the dealer she knew nothing about it. I've found out a bit more about him.' He smiled. 'I phoned the owner of Leakey's, in Inverness, and described him. He sent me a few names I could look up online. Our visitor is Samuel J. Boult, originally from Kentucky, but settled in St Andrews, where he has an antiquarian bookshop with a particular interest in books on magic and the occult. Nothing dodgy about him, but your Book of the Black Arts would be right in his field, and worth a packet to the right buyer.'

I sighed. 'Lizbet wanted it to rot in the earth and never be seen more, and a good thing too, if you ask me.'

'Yes,' Gavin said. 'I've been meaning to ask that. Why on earth did she dig the thing up in the first place?'

'Ah,' I said. I was sorry he'd asked. Feeling as if I was betraying a confidence, I explained about the *You're the Stars!* heat and the snooty producer's comment. 'It was a daft thing for her to do, and she bitterly regrets it.'

'A book didn't kill Chloe,' Gavin said. He finished his fish and rose to put the plate in the basin. 'I'd like to go and see the old St Olav's Kirk after Mass. It's only a couple of miles up the road. That's the old graveyard for this area.'

'Where the book was dug up?'

He nodded. 'And your Lizbet grew up there, at Breckon, the

155

houses nearest to it. We could look at the Fishermen's Memorial too, while we're exploring.'

'The grey wife o' Gloup? I saw her as I passed. I'd like to see her closer.' I bit my lip, trying to tease out the uneasy feelings jumbled in my mind. I'd promised Magnie not to meddle with the Book of the Black Arts, but I feared that it was being meddled with. If it was buried in Windhouse, I'd gladly leave it be, and add an extra couple of stones to keep it there. 'I think I'd like to have a look at Windhouse first, d'you mind?'

'Not at all. Shetland's most haunted it is.'

We washed up the plates and then headed off down the short piece of road to Gutcher. The hills here still wore their autumn colours, sweeps of a lovely Titian auburn, but the burns ran between bright edges of new grass, and the sheep were busy cropping the roadsides. A pair of birds somersaulted in the air like circus acrobats.

Gavin said a soft word in Gaelic, then glanced at me. 'Peewits,' he translated. 'The first I've seen this year. Spring's coming.' He drove smoothly around the Z-bend and on towards Mid Yell.

'The light's coming back,' I agreed. I wriggled down into my seat with a sigh of contentment. 'And the whole summer's ahead to have fun in.'

Windhouse was visible from a long way off, the ruins of a once-imposing laird's house set on the top of the hill above the main road to the ferry. Gavin turned up into the gravel path leading past the lodge, past a huge new agricultural shed and almost to a house just behind. A couple of dogs barked at us from a wire run as Gavin parked the Land Rover off the road. We got out and looked upwards.

It was more of a ruin than I remembered. Fifteen years of Shetland weather had taken their toll. The roof was completely gone and the lower floor windows were dark holes in the damp-streaked walls. The gables were crowstepped, and the side wings topped by battlements whose notches stood out against the sky.

'It's a funny house to find in Shetland,' Gavin said. 'How old is it, d'you ken?'

I shook my head, and tried to catch the memory of what it had been like the one time I'd been inside. 'It's deteriorated a lot. I'm sure the roof was still on it, though in a pretty dodgy state. We went inside. The stairs were still there, and the upstairs floorboards. I remember the boys trying to get me to go up, because I was the lightest, but I wouldn't.' I wrinkled my nose and added, 'We still had races to sail, and I pointed out to them that I'd sail better without a broken ankle. I think there was a garden out behind. Well, not an actual garden, but you could see where it had been. I suppose it was the area within that outer wall.'

'And did you see any ghosts?'

'No. But we didn't stay long, not even with a group of us together.' I couldn't remember the layout of the house, just the damp chill of it in spite of the bonny summer's day outside, and the feeling that some of the shadows were moving. 'Dodie, you know, my classmate that works on the ferries, he was having fun telling us about a baby's skeleton found behind a nailed-up shutter, and another one, a workman, under the briggistane, and a tall man who was seen moving around the house.' I shuddered. 'And being the only girl in the group, I had to stick it out.'

We walked slowly towards it, and up three steps from the carriage drive onto the house path. The closer we got, the less I liked the look of it: the geometric remains of iron railings on the front wall, the rotting stones, the black doorway, the shadows behind the windows. The path ended in a flight of lichen-whitened steps onto a flattened terrace, and we paused to catch our breath. 'Hello,' Gavin said. 'Somebody's started repairing it. Well, stabilising it.'

Someone had reframed the door and two lower windows with white-painted wood, already looking the worse for wear.

157

One window was larger than the other, and had its upright, the other was an open square, giving the house a lopsided look, like a dog that lifts one side of its mouth in a snarl.

'Good luck to them,' I said. 'I wouldn't live here.'

Gavin turned around to look away from the house, turning a slow circle: north out over North-a-voe, east at the fawn and brown hill between us and Mid Yell, with the burn running in the foreground and Unst in the distance, and the hill falling away to the south, with only a glimpse of the head of Whale Firth. 'A good open prospect, and hardly another house in view. Just their fellow laird across there –' He nodded across at the large house on the way into Mid Yell.

'No sea,' I said, 'except for that sliver of Bluemull Sound past North-a-voe.' No doubt the laird kept an eye on his fishing boats coming and going. 'This must be the only place in Yell where you wouldn't see the sea.'

'Maybe the laird or his lady was so seasick that even the sight of it turned them green. It's a fine view of hills.'

'Views aren't everything. A roof's good too.'

'A cabin roof, for you,' Gavin said cheerfully. 'With sea all around.' He turned back to the house. 'The central bit is older, but I'd guess the fancy castle-style additions are late Victorian.' He swung himself neatly over the fence, whisking his kilt over the barbed wire with the ease of practice, and I followed. 'The family crest's survived well.'

The square carving between the door and the porch battlements showed a knight's casque with feathers sprouting from it, or possibly armorial leaves, and two shields below. 'Delusions of grandeur. I think they were Nevens, like the MP that used to own Busta.'

Gavin looked downwards. 'Best Victorian tiling there on the floor.'

I glanced and yes, the porch had red floor tiles with a border of surprisingly bright blue and white diamonds. Beyond them was a litter of slate shards and blocks of stone, and another doorway.

'Well, shall we go in?'

'I suppose we'd better,' I agreed gloomily. My promise to Magnie stuck in my throat. A check to make sure the Book was still where Lizbet had buried it, then a rapid exit.

We stepped into the chill that I remembered, as if the sun never penetrated inside. It was emptier than my memory, with only greened planks of wood that might have been the staircase collapsed in one corner. The upper flooring had fallen into rotting tumbles of plank higgledy-piggledy on and under the lumps of masonry, slate roof tiles and broken glass glinting among them. Nettles sprouted between the stones. There was no trace left of panelling or plaster; the only signs that this had been a house were the fireplaces. The mantel of the lower one jutted above the rubble on the floor and the other one was set incongruously in the middle of the gable, base just above the square joist holes for the timbers that had supported the vanished upper floor.

There was a rustling noise from somewhere above our heads, as though we'd disturbed some creature, yet it wasn't quite that either. I tried to focus on the sound. A crisp bag caught between stones, maybe, with the wind tugging at it. It had that hard-to-ignore quality of a fingernail run down a blackboard. If Lizbet really had come in here after dark to bury the Book, she was tougher than I'd given her credit for.

'Well,' Gavin said, looking around. 'We can either spend the rest of the day looking, or try intelligence.'

'Will intelligence be quicker?'

He turned to smile at me. 'Maybe . . . don't move for a minute.'

'I'm happy not to come further in,' I assured him.

He gave a flicker of a smile at that, then stood still, staring intently at the ground, before hunkering down, kilt pleats brushing the ground, and put one hand out to touch something. 'Plenty of older prints. The youth of Yell must spend their days daring each other to come in here. But there's been a visitor more recently, probably this morning, certainly within the last day.'

I craned over his shoulder. His forefinger outlined a shoe-mark in the mud. 'You can't always tell, but I'd guess at male from the size of the shoe and the depth of the print.' He'd once told me he'd spent his teenage summers helping his grandfather stalk deer. 'Let's just call him he. He went . . .' He stood up again. 'Now, this is interesting. He came in and walked across there, and stood still for long enough to make two nice prints.'

Now they'd been pointed out to me I could see the tracks: a tuft of grass still crushed, a slide-mark in the green algae on the rotting planks, a slate pushed forward to leave a paler shadow on the wood below, ending in two clear trainer prints in the earthy corner. Gavin went over and stood beside them. 'He stood and looked. Then he went into this extension bit.' He produced a small torch from his sporran and switched it on. 'Just far enough to see to the end. Maybe he had a torch too.'

'He did,' I said, suddenly remembering. 'That's what the fisherman said, that he saw a torch moving around, and a dark figure.' I felt a shudder down my spine at the idea. Above my head, the noise rustled.

'Aye. Then he came back.' He gave me a quick glance and put a warm hand on my shoulder as he returned to the doorway. 'Would you agree that all this stuff on the floor looks undisturbed?'

I nodded. The planks, the stones, the fragments of slate, were all well settled into the muddy earth.

Gavin headed into the other side. I retreated from the porch to the arched window and watched him from there. The rubble in this wing was worse, with stiff loops of roof felt and rectangles of rusted corrugated iron among the pieces of wood,

160

some still shaped as skirting board or cornice, all covered over with a layer of masonry crumbled to a fine ash. New red bricks had been shoved into the deteriorating walls, and the door at the back had what looked like the rusted remains of a Rayburn in it. The flue for a long-gone closed stove stuck out below the chimney. Gavin stepped among the rubble as neatly as one of the stags he'd stalked.

'Aha! Someone's had this plank up, and not quite replaced it in the same place. There are older footprints here too.'

I ventured over the sill and felt the chill down my spine again. 'Any sign of something having been buried?'

'No. It looks more like he lifted the plank and dropped it again. See if you can find any more that have been displaced. Here's another one.'

I joined him in looking, and we found half a dozen places where a plank or stone had been moved recently. There was no sign of digging under any of them.

Outside, the sun was bright, but even as it was sinking it didn't penetrate into any of these windows. Gavin switched his torch on again, and we moved into the last room. I stood outside the arched doorway and watched him. He moved around for a minute, then his head went up like a cat that's spotted a bird within reach. He played the torch on the floor, and I saw what he was seeing: earth scattered on several of the planks round about, on the tops of the planks, on blades of grass. Someone had been digging here.

Gavin hesitated for a moment, then took out his phone, and took several photos before moving in closer to where I could see even at this distance that planks had been shoved aside. There was a rotting door under them, and under that, as Gavin raised it, was a place where the hard-packed imprint of the door's panels was disturbed. The shifted earth had sunk down, as if something had been taken away. The patch was some fifty centimetres square.

'This is it,' Gavin said. 'Lizbet left the book for the Devil to take, if he wanted it, but someone in trainers got to it first.'

I thought of Antony passing us in Bluemull Sound, the sliver of bright water I could see from here. He'd been at Up Helly Aa, and heard the dealer offering for the book. He'd gone outside, when Tom had gone after Lizbet. Maybe he'd listened to them talking and found out where the book the dealer wanted had been hidden. He wouldn't have stolen it from Lizbet directly, but if the dealer was offering good money for it and if she didn't want it, well, why shouldn't he dig it up and take the dealer's offer? The fisherman had seen a light and a moving shadow this very morning, when it was still dark.

'As I was coming round,' I said, 'I saw Antony taking up creels, at the back of Muckle Roe, and then again at Eshaness. Then he shot past me in Yell Sound, and came down here. I don't know where he went after that, but as I was coming in, just on half nine, he came out past me, looking pleased with himself.'

'From the direction of Mid Yell?'

'Yes.'

Gavin nodded. 'I think we maybe need to have a word with Antony.'

Chapter Fourteen

He ran lang aroond da midden daek but did faa in at last.
(He ran around the refuse heap wall for a long time,
but fell into it in the end.)
Said of someone who took a lot of chances,
or was involved in wrongdoing, but was caught at last.

It was nearly quarter to three by the time Gavin turned the key in the Land Rover and lit up the dashboard clock. 'We'd better get a move on, or we'll be late for Mass.' He turned the big vehicle in one smooth movement and accelerated back the way we'd come. North-a-voe, Sellafirth, Gutcher. The church was on the outskirts of Cullivoe, with a parking space by the road. A glance below showed me *Khalida* snugly against the pier, with Cat sitting on the cabin roof, head turned our way. The Kitten was curled up beside him. Both fine.

The front door of the kirk faced the sea. It was an odd, Italianate chapel to find in these bare hills. It was white, with a squared tower at each side of the facade, the upward slope of the roof, and then a central tower with an arched window niche above the porch, and a higher little tower with the bell hanging in it. There was something like battlements on each level surface here as well. Maybe Yell had had a battlements fashion. Gavin echoed my thought: 'I wonder if it was the same architect as at Windhouse. That whole facade looks like a later addition, and about the same time.'

'I didn't know you were into architecture.'

'See, the joy of living together – you're finding out all sorts of things. I had three years on the beat in Edinburgh. I can spot neo-classical a mile off. And Victorian would-be baronial.'

'This is bonny, though,' I said. 'Graceful. D'you suppose Windhouse was like this in its day?'

'We should look on the internet for old photos of when it was inhabited.' He opened the door for me, and we walked straight into the smell of window polish and Pledge. The arched windows on each side spilled coloured sunlight which stretched across the wooden chairs and varnished floor to touch the pale green-blue wall opposite. A striped carpet led the eye forward down the aisle. The altar rails had been renewed with blond pine, and behind them, on a red carpet, was the communion table, and a matching pulpit with a curved staircase. There was a stained-glass window above, our Lord ascending into heaven, with his hands raised in blessing.

Father David was already there, setting out the chalice, paten and two candlesticks. He lifted his head as we came in, and nodded a greeting. We slipped into a pew at the front and knelt on the polished floor.

I found it hard to concentrate on pre-Mass prayer. My head was full of the chill, ruined house, and that square-dug place under the rotted door. I focused with an effort, then looked up with a start as Father rose to begin. It was the third Sunday of Lent, and the theme was repentence. Being furthest forward, it was us that Father looked at in that pause where we were all hoping someone else would step forward to do the readings. Gavin made a drama out of Moses and the burning bush, and music of the psalm, which left me with St Paul in uncompromising mood: the Israelites struck down in the desert as a warning to us not to desire evil things. The words shuddered in my mouth: if ever there was an evil thing, it was that book, on its travels again. The Gospel was the barren fig tree, and the gardener's plea to give it one more chance, and Father David gave us a good sermon on mercy.

We went up together for communion, and knelt shoulder to shoulder afterwards. As Father stood for the final blessing, Gavin turned his head and smiled at me, eyes warm. I slipped my hand into his, and left it there until after Father David had processed out.

'Well,' Father said, as we came out into the afternoon sunlight, 'I saw your Land Rover up at Windhouse. How did you like it?'

'Not at all,' I said.

'An interesting place,' Gavin said. 'Do you know the history of it?'

'The laird's house. The central part of it dates from 1707, then all the crenellations were added in 1885 – that's right, isn't it, Willie John?' He turned to appeal to the young man I'd noticed in the opposite pew.

The young man nodded. He had the look of a Yell Shetlander, strongly built and with reddish fair hair worn long and a beard, as if he too had been in a Jarl Squad recently. 'Willie John Goodlad,' he said, shaking hands with us. 'I do tourist guiding in the summer, and the visitors like spooky stories.'

I'd have betted he told them well too, with his dark eyes and expressive hands. 'But that old ruin it is now, it's hard to imagine what a bonny house it was once. The museum has photos from the twenties, with the house harled white, and the family in the doorway.' His eyes looked into the distance for a moment, seeing it, then came back to us, and went into guide mode. 'The present Windhouse was built on the site of a medieval church and graveyard, itself built within the foundations of a broch. A recent dig in the garden found skeletons dating back to the medieval period, but the ones inside the house are the most interesting.' He gave us a quick look to check he wasn't boring us. 'Stop me if I go on too long! Well, one of the ghosts is the Silk Lady, supposed to be a mistress of the laird, who met her death falling down the stair.'

'Amy Robsart,' Gavin said. 'Did she fall, or was she pushed?'

'Since she's haunting the place, I'd go for pushed, wouldn't you? She can't be seen now unless she's hovering in the air, for she used to be at the top of the staircase, walking in three circles then disappearing. She never speaks, but you hear her petticoats rustling.'

I thought of the noise I'd heard, and felt a cold shudder run down my spine. Willie gave me a quick look. 'You heard her?'

'Wind rustling a caught crisp bag,' I said firmly.

He smiled. 'Then there's the Tall Man, who walks along the terrace wearing a top hat. Now the interesting thing about him is that a skeleton was found during the 1885 remodelling: an unusually tall man, well over six feet tall. There was no sign of a coffin, and he wasn't far underground, so the speculation was that he was another murder victim.' He smiled at Father David. 'Like Moses, he had horns on his head.'

I gave him an incredulous look, and he laughed. 'Check your Bible. *And behold, he had horns on his head.*'

'No, he didn't, Willie John,' Father David said firmly. 'He had rays of light, from talking to God. You stick to the facts, now, and no misleading the police.'

'All the same,' Willie John persisted, 'you do sometimes get people who have a bony growth on the head, like horns, and that's what this man seemed to have. It's not in the official accounts, but it was my grandfather's grandfather who dug him up. 'Seven feet tall,' he told my Daa when he was a child, 'with his jaw gaping open as if he was like to bite you, and with horns on his head.' Of course the rumour ran round that they'd dug up the Devil. But it's likely that skeleton was from the medieval graveyard, so the tall man in the top hat remains a mystery. Then there was the baby nailed up behind a shutter,

166

likely some poor servant girl's hidden pregnancy – a servant girl ascending an invisible staircase is another of the ghosts. That was found by workmen in 1900, but it was only a skeleton, wrapped up in sheepskin, so dear knows how long it might have been there.'

'Being a workman at Windhouse sounds as dangerous an occupation as being a dog-walker,' Gavin said. We all gave him a startled look, and he added, apologetically, 'Most dead people are found by dog-walkers.'

There was a pause while we considered this, then Willie John went on. 'The third skeleton was under the doorstep. It's reckoned to date from the rebuilding of the house in the 1880s.' He gave Gavin's kilt an apologetic glance. 'There were a lot of Scots men up in Yell at the time. It was the time of the Clearances here, folk being moved off their land for sheep.'

Gavin nodded. 'We had that in the Highlands too.'

'These men were fencers, ditchers and the like, getting the parks ready for the sheep, and a rough lot they were said to be too. To celebrate the end of the work on Windhouse, the Nevens threw a party. Two of the workmen got into a fight, and one killed the other. The men decided to get rid of the body, so they took the back door off its hinges and buried the body under the large stone slab beneath it.'

'Without waking anyone?' I asked sceptically.

Willie John shook his head at me. 'Ah, you're just whistling to keep up your spirits. I expect the family was at one of their other houses while the work was going on. The body wasn't found till the thirties, in Jim Gordon's time. He got fed up of the draught under the door because the stone wasn't level, and got workmen to take the door off and turn the stone. When they raised it they found the body.' He turned towards the door. 'Anyway, you have a good time here in Yell, and I'll see you in Lerwick sometime.' He nodded to Father David, and headed off up the road.

'We'd need to get going too,' Gavin said, 'if we're to make Mary's before she closes.'

'Let's just check the cats,' I said.

'What, no kittens yet?' Gavin teased.

We drove down to the pier, and Gavin soothed the cats while I checked my ropes, then we headed back along the road to Windhouse. This time we turned into Mid Yell, a town the size of Brae spread upwards from the pier. I scoped the water with the eye of a sailor, and was glad I'd gone for berthing in Cullivoe; although it wasn't quite as bristling with the things as around Papa Little, Mid Yell voe had as good a collection of lobster buoys as Merran had said. We came past the council houses – one, I noticed, still displayed their window-sized Christmas decals of those gnomes with tall hats and a circle for a nose, thus maintaining Yell's reputation as the Land that Time Forgot. On the other side was the school I remembered, a sixties block, all window frames, and past it was the new one. There were three joined buildings of vertical planking, with a double row of black-framed windows and decorative red squares. It gave the impression of a Wild West double-decker train, with the tall red entrance as the coal bunker.

'I'm not sure I'm that keen on modern architecture,' I said, looking at it, 'though it's probably lovely inside.'

'It's like the Anderson one to look at,' Gavin said, 'best modern Wild West, and that's great when you go into it.'

He drove on through the grazing on the outskirts of the houses. Gradually the olive-fawn of rough grass gave way to the tussocked heather of the scattald, chocolate brown shot through with the old, gold grass. The Land Rover bumped over several cattle grids, through a gateway, past a house with a child's fort on stilts, and turned left to Mary's.

Mary's shop was in Aywick, and it was a complete one-shop shopping mall. Like a true country shop, it sold everything; if Mary didn't have it, folk all over Shetland said, you didn't need it. The bones of it was the original shop, extended by running shelving into adjoining sheds and byres to make a maze of a place with rooms for different goods leading into and through each other. The whole shop complex was encased in a large blue corrugated shell with extra storage space on one side, and the charity shop in the back rooms. Large white letters announced its official name, AYWICK SHOP, with a square placard saying 'Yell for Cancer Support Charity Shop' below. Opposite, behind the petrol pumps, someone had ploughed their tattie field; the earth looked like best-quality grated chocolate. Gavin parked below the cancer shop notice, and we went around into the shop.

Spring was definitely on its way. The porch was filled with the stuff gardeners were beginning to need, potato and onion sets, flower bulbs, and bags of compost and fertiliser, along with forks, hoes, spades and a range of implements I didn't even try to identify. Gavin paused to look. 'I could do with a decent-sized spade.'

'A Shetland spade,' I said. 'For dealing with wet, clatchy earth that weighs a ton. Isn't there one in the toolshed?'

'Oh, is that what it is? I thought it was a ladies' spade.' He put the one he'd been inspecting back, picked up a bag of dried cow manure and followed me into the shop.

It was an Aladdin's cave of a place, with Mary herself presiding over the till just inside the front door, and doorways leading off in all directions. I turned left to my favourite area, the hardware room with everything from anchors to model Zulus. Gavin found a basket and added a tube of superglue and a paintbrush to the fertiliser, then wandered off. When I regretfully decided that I already had all the sizes of spanners, and that spray-on wax would be awkward to apply to a boat on the water, I went off to search for him. He wasn't in either aisle of the fancy goods and presents room, admiring the vases, china ornaments, photograph albums or painting by numbers sets; nor in the next room with the socks and pants, trainers, colourful rubber boots, oilcloth in rolls and a whole wall of balls of wool; not contemplating the birthday cards and kitchen equipment; not eyeing up the lamps and china. I went back around racks of jerseys and blouses into the shop proper. He wasn't dipping into the Shetland books, nor choosing a bottle of whisky, nor getting meat from any of the three fridges, nor inspecting the contents of any of the four freezers, or the shelves of tins; not getting money from the Post Office counter in one corner, nor waiting in the line at the till. Opposite the till counter was a mouthwatering display of freshly baked bread from the Yell bakery, along with cakes, the German biscuits that I'd fed to Magnie, and hot cross buns. I picked up a four-pack of their wonderful cherry scones to encourage me tomorrow, then remembered it was Lent and put them back with regret. Yell cherry scones didn't often come my way.

When I was pretty sure I'd checked all the areas, with no sign of Gavin, I realised that of course he'd headed for the charity shop, which was squeezed into the former shop storerooms at the back. It had an official outside door as well as the unofficial one from Mary's, between the third fridge and the first shelf of tins. Naturally this was the one everyone used, as the charity shop was technically open only three afternoons a week, but the unofficial door meant you could have a quick scoit round even if it was closed, and pay Mary for your finds on the way out. I glanced over my shoulder before opening the door, and froze. At the far side of the shop, a man had just come in: a pinkly plump stranger in an immaculate blazer and white fedora hat with a black ribbon on it: the bookselling stranger from the Up Helly Aa, Samuel J. Boult, who specialised in occult books. I slipped back into the cover of a shelving unit and watched him. He looked around the shop with a pleased air, then strolled towards the book display, took out one book, examined the cover, then put it back, took out another and began to flip through it.

I could see his feet now. He was wearing a pair of shiningly new trainers whose orange soles were slightly dulled with what looked like dried earth.

He put the book back and turned towards the presents room. I watched his tailored back saunter down between the china and the games then dived for the door into the charity shop corridor, closed it gently behind me, and raced between the bookshelves on one side and stacks of boxes on the other to the outside door. I was way out of order, but while he was occupied with fancy goods I wanted a look at Samuel J. Boult's car. He didn't look like a stroll-over-the-hills type, and he wouldn't be gardening in those shoes, with their white uppers. I remembered the trainer prints Gavin had followed. Maybe I'd jumped to conclusions about Antony; perhaps his cheerful wave had been because of a good night's catch. Maybe he'd gone to Mid Yell for a couple of hours' sleep, or to deliver his lobsters to someone there. I wanted to see if there was any sign that Mr Occult Bookseller had been in Windhouse.

His car was easy to spot; he'd gone for Bolt's Car Hire, with the sticker on the rear window. He was parked two cars along from us. I tried to look like someone who'd forgotten her purse, walked quickly to the boot and tried it. I'd struck lucky; it opened. There was a travelling bag with its lid unzipped, a tumble of newspapers. I lifted them quickly: nothing but hoovered carpet beneath. I shook my head as if I was saying 'Where *did* I leave it?' to myself, closed the boot gently and went to the passenger door. A strong smell of pine air-freshener hit me as I opened it. There was a smaller bag with a bottle of water wedged in it in the footwell and an empty sandwich box on the seat. I gave a quick glance into the back seat. An overcoat was laid on the seats, and there was a pair of polished black shoes on the floor.

No sign of a spade, a tin box or an ancient book with curlicued writing. He was just a tourist on a day out, visiting the

171

North Isles while he was here in Shetland. All the same, I didn't like it, that he'd turned up so pat just five miles from Windhouse.

I closed the door quietly and went back into the charity shop corridor. There was music coming from behind the charity-shop door, a thin thread of woody sound. Someone was playing a tune like a Scottish pipe lament, but not on a pipe; it sounded more like some sort of recorder. The tune was coming out in starts, as if the player wasn't sure of the correct fingering. I was just about to peek around the door when there was an apologetic cough from the shop door, and a soft American drawl said, 'Beg your pardon, ma'am.'

I spun round as if I'd been jabbed with a pin, and found myself confronting Samuel J. Boult himself. He touched the white fedora with one hand. 'I didn't mean to startle you none, ma'am. I think you maybe saw me at the Delting Up Helly Aa. You're a friend of Lizbet's, aren't you? I saw you talking to her there.'

'I might have seen you,' I agreed cautiously.

He fished in his breast pocket, brought out a card-case and presented me his card with a little bow. *Samuel J. Boult* it read, in copperplate script. *Antiquary, Rare Books*, and an address in St Andrews, just as Gavin had said. 'I noticed you talking to Lizbet before I discovered who she was. I was pleased to see she had a friend who could give her good advice.'

I was torn between telling him exactly the advice I'd give Lizbet and stringing him along to see what he'd say. Curiosity won over bluntness. 'Well, I'd try to do that, of course,' I agreed.

He nodded enthusiastically, as if I'd made the world's most profound statement. 'You see, I knew I sure wasn't mistaken in you. I pride myself on being a good judge of character.' He took a step forward and leaned one elbow on the tower of book boxes against the wall. His aftershave smelt like the make-up department of a posh store. I managed not to wrinkle my nose. He continued, 'As you see, I'm a bookseller, and as you perhaps know, Lizbet's in possession of a book that's worth a lot of money. I'd be willing to give a commission to a friend who'd persuade her to realise that capital.' He gave my salt-stained black jacket a quick glance. 'Five per cent of the purchase price, say?'

Behind us, the tune was repeated more confidently, the notes coming clearly now, and I recognised it as one we'd sung in school, from the white book with the wren on the cover.

'That would depend on what the purchase price was,' I said. He didn't have the book then, if he was wanting me to talk Lizbet into producing it.

'Which in turn would depend on the book,' he said smoothly. 'Its condition and what exactly it is. If it's what it's reputed to be, the price could be very high indeed.'

I tried to look like someone who drove a hard bargain. 'Give me a figure.'

The beautifully manicured hands waved. 'At least several thousand, even in a damaged condition.'

I looked at his benevolent expression and multiplied that by ten. 'Tell me,' I said, 'what makes you think Lizbet has the book you're looking for? She told you she knew nothing about it.'

'So she did,' he murmured. His plump lips closed firmly. I could see I wasn't going to get anywhere with that. I turned his card over in my hands, then put it in my pocket.

'I'll think about it,' I said.

The tune stopped. There was a murmur of voices, then the door opened, and Gavin came out, with some sort of wooden tube in his hands. I saw Samuel J. Boult recognise him: the policeman in the kilt. He looked at him, at me, and put the two of us together.

'A legitimate business proposition,' he said to me. 'Think about it.' He touched his hat again and moved away swiftly, into the shop and between the shelves to the door.

'Well,' Gavin said. 'Did I scare him away before you'd finished?'

I shook my head. 'He was bribing me to talk Lizbet into giving him the Book.'

'I think we need to find out more precisely where she left it, and whether it's still there. I know it looked as if it had been dug up in Windhouse, but I'd like to know for sure. Meanwhile . . .' He went as scarlet as if I'd caught him taking bribes. He lifted the wooden instrument in his hands: a simple holed tube with brass circles at the joins. 'The charity shop has this for sale. D'you think you could stand it?'

'That was you playing?'

He nodded, cheeks still crimson.

'It sounded good.' I came out with the ultimate cliché. 'I didn't know you played the recorder.'

He shook his head, but his hands closed possessively around the wooden tube. 'I don't.' He gave a shy, sideways smile. 'There's a set of bagpipes in a box in the sit-ootery.'

I looked at him standing there in his kilt, his tweed jacket baggy in the pockets, and felt he'd outdone me in the matter of clichés. 'You've kept that very quiet.'

He grinned. 'It's impossible to keep a set of pipes quiet. Magnie assured me he'd enjoyed my playing from his briggistane, the morning after one still evening. I've just not got them out while you've been in the house.' He turned the instrument over in his hands. 'Then I saw this flute lying there, and wondered if I could get a tune out of it. It would be gentler on your ears.' He lifted it to sideways to his lips, curling them into a half-smile, and gave a long, pure note, then realised half the shop had turned round to look. 'Come in and listen.'

He drew me into the charity shop, and went into his lament again. He played it beautifully, and the wife behind the counter and I gave him a round of applause when he'd finished.

'"The Sang o' the Delting Lass",' the woman said. 'Did you

ken that's a Yell song? Well, it's no' about the Gloup disaster, it's about the Delting one, but it was written by a local wife, Mary Ellen Odie.' She nodded at the flute. 'It would have been a good one, that. It came from the old school as they were tidying out for the move into the new building, and it was likely bought for the old school when it was new, so that's no' yesterday. It'll be, oh, forty years old anyway. Probably when the oil money came.'

Gavin looked at me. 'What d'you say, Cass, can you live with it?'

'I think it sounds bonny.'

'There'll be scales,' he warned, 'and playing the same bit over and over as I learn a new tune.'

'I can go out for a sail until it's learned.' I took it from him, lifted it to my mouth and blew. Nothing happened, and nothing, and nothing. 'It's harder than it looks.'

'You need a lot of breath for the pipes. I'm in training.' He separated it into three parts, and laid them in its case. 'Will you take a cheque?'

'Oh, they'll give you money at the counter, when you get your errands.' She nodded at the basketful of stuff he'd acquired on his way round the shop.

'Let me just check out the jumpers,' I said. 'It's time I had a new gansey.'

'There's a beauty that would be your size,' the counter woman said. 'Helt new too. It came in only yesterday. The woman who knitted it said she'd spent so long over it that she never wanted to see it again. It got a prize at the East Yell Show.' She reached behind her and brought down a Norwegian-style jumper, navy, with the shoulder pattern in white and red. I tried it on, and felt it was mine straight away. It was a good weight of wool, and would fit several layers of thermals under it. £30 was a serious price for a charity shop, but not for a beautiful new hand-knitted prize-winning jumper.

Gavin nodded in admiration. 'Definitely.' He glanced up at

the clock. 'Creator Lord, is that the time? You'll be wanting to close up.'

We got as quickly through the check out as was possible in a country shop, where everyone was exchanging news as they handed items over, and racing back to the shelves for the items they suddenly realised they'd forgotten. Outside at last, we piled ourselves and our gains into the Land Rover.

'I didn't really want to learn the pipes,' Gavin said as he set the black case in the back seat-well. 'I wanted to try the fiddle, but we had my father's pipes in a box, so that settled that.'

'You could learn the fiddle now,' I said. 'It would be Shetland fiddle rather than Scottish, but there are plenty of teachers here. They even have an intensive residential school.'

'Maybe,' Gavin said. 'Once I've mastered this flute. Now.' He glanced at the sky. 'We only have light for one visit, I think. Shall we do the White Wife while we're here, then home for dinner, or go back, check the cats in passing, then go on to the old Kirk?'

I was about to vote for the old Kirk when his phone rang. He glanced at it and frowned. 'Hello, Freya, what's up?'

'I'm in Brae,' DS Peterson's voice replied, echoing oddly in the tin space. 'Antony Leighton's been murdered.'

Chapter Fifteen

A preen pricks love, but a needle shews it tagidder.
(A pin pricks love, but a needle sews it together.)
To keep a marriage together there is need for hard work and industry.

The information DS Peterson gave Gavin was minimal: there'd been a call to the house and the PC who'd attended had found Antony's body in the kitchen, looking as if there'd been a fight. All the necessary authorities had been contacted, and the forensics team from Aberdeen would arrive on the first flight they could get seats on.

'Good,' Gavin said. 'I'm still in Yell, but I'll be with you in the morning, and get an update then.'

'A fight,' I said.

Gavin turned his head to smile at me. 'I'm no' theorising until we have the data. Freya's in charge.' There was a shadow of regret in his voice. Being an inspector in a station meant he couldn't charge round viewing scenes of crime and interviewing suspects any more. I saw him make an effort to put it to the back of his mind. 'Well, what do you think? Old St Olav's Kirk?'

'I'd like to see it,' I agreed.

We were silent on the drive. The light was still bright, but the sun was starting to cast long shadows from telegraph poles, fence posts, sheep grazing on the tawny hillside. We turned off at Gutcher, came past the view across Bluemull Sound to the curve of Fetlar, past the Cullivoe kirk, with *Khalida* still lying placidly at the pier, past the valley beach that framed the cliffs of

Unst, through the white houses of Cullivoe proper and between the Cullivoe Hall and Henderson's shop.

'You didn't tell me there was a shop here as well,' Gavin remarked. 'It looks a good one too. Next time.'

Beyond the bus garage and the turn-off to the primary school we could see the Kirk Loch glinting gold in the dimming sun, and the graveyard beside it, with the walls of the old kirk in the centre. Gavin turned off towards it and came smoothly along the road, turned right at what seemed to be an upside-down tree trunk doing duty as a fence strainer, and parked beside a solar panel with battery attached, purpose unknown.

It was peaceful here. Two rabbits grazed in the park next to the graveyard; a flock of starlings rose, wheeled, and landed again a hundred yards further on. The loch seemed shallow on this side, with a pale green shadow under the water, a sandbank perhaps.

'What d'you reckon gives the loch that odd colour?' Gavin asked. 'You could see it on Google Earth too, right along this side.'

'We can go and look,' I said. 'Kirkyard first, though?'

'Kirkyard first,' Gavin agreed.

We walked alongside a little fenced garden with daffodils showing their first yellow, and through the gate. The new extension had a hearse-wide paving-slab road, but after that we were walking between older graves on soft turf. Just in front of the kirk was a grave like a table, on stone supports. The inscription was long gone from the top, but each leg was carved with a skull and a single bone. The slanted light darkened the eye sockets, giving them an eerie life.

'I like it,' Gavin said, pausing to look. 'There was none of this "try to live for ever" nonsense then. They were realistic about where they were headed.'

'*Dust thou art, and to dust thou shalt return*,' I quoted. 'Our annual Ash Wednesday reminder.' I thought of Antony and Chloe, each killed so suddenly, and fell silent.

Gavin glanced at me. 'Yes,' he agreed. 'Murder is different.'

Beyond the table grave, the old kirk walls rose to shoulder height on three sides, slightly higher on the north, grassed along that top, and a good metre thick. At the loch end, the altar end, were what looked like two fireplaces or low cupboards, and there was another in the west end, with an old bit of tombstone exactly the shape of a swaddled baby propped up inside it, a smudge of white lichen draped like a cloth around it. I looked at the alcoves and tried to envisage what they might have been. Pre-Reformation churches, I'd read, had a mock tomb of our Lord set up at Easter, with a plaster body of our Lord dead on Good Friday and Holy Saturday, and the Risen Lord on Sunday, but these were too small for tombs; perhaps saints' niches whose occupants had been destroyed? Except that saints wouldn't be at floor level. Maybe they'd simply been fireplaces, to keep the congregation warm on cold winter days. Three bushes grew against the north wall, one dead, the others with whippy bronze stems and the first green buds showing.

'Canmore,' Gavin said, and began tapping into his phone.

'You're getting a signal here?' I asked, curious.

'Just. St Olav's Kirk. Here you are.' He called up a drawing of a ruined building, far more substantial than this seemed, with a stone arch in the middle. 'This must be the west half remaining. We're standing in the middle of the aisle.'

'It looks a massive church,' I said. 'A monastry, maybe?'

'It just says fourteenth century . . . served the parish of North Yell until 1750 . . . accumulation of sand . . .' He flipped to a modern photo.

'The loch's that funny colour in these photos too. Maybe it is sand.'

'. . . became a burial place . . .'

'After 1750?'

Gavin nodded. I'd noticed the graves within the walls of the old kirk, and wondered if the folk had been Catholics resistant to the new religion, and wanting to be buried at least in the place of the old faith. Now I looked at the dates I could see they were too late. *The Rev. James Struther Douglas.* His qualifications, *MA MD* were partly hidden by lichen. *Minister of North Yell, 1877–1884. Died June 1884.* He'd died in harness, and if ever there was an odd person to be buried in an ancient Catholic church it was a Church of Scotland minister; but then it must have been a Church of Scotland church for a couple of centuries after the Reformation.

'Maybe they thought he'd exorcise the place,' Gavin commented. He turned to the one held up by a wooden support, like a kishie band across the forehead. *Captain William John Henderson of Gloup, 1801–1883. "A just man."*

He put his phone away, and we contemplated the graves in silence. It was a bonny place for the last sleep. The sun shimmered on the loch beyond the graveyard, and turned the winter-weathered heather on the hills to flax-gold.

'Wednesday or Thursday, wasn't it, that your fisherman saw lights at Windhouse?' Gavin said suddenly. 'And again this morning.'

I nodded.

'It would be worth having a word with him. Did you notice if he was still at the pier as we passed?'

'His boat was. I didn't notice him, but then I was looking at *Khalida.*'

'I'd like to ask him about it. It'd save Freya a trip to Yell.' I gave him a sceptical look and he grinned. 'I need to keep my interviewing hand in. Shall we have a gentle wander among the graves, go up to the Gloup memorial, then come back and think about dinner, and track him down after that?'

'Let's,' I agreed. We strolled gently over the turf. It was already studded with celandines, silvery-yellow against their shiny leaves. *Fraser,* I read on one grave, *Sinclair.* The kirk was only twenty yards from the wall, and the loch only an arm's length further. It was about the size of a football pitch. We rested our forearms on the wall and looked over. Even this close, it was hard to tell what made the discolouration of this side of the loch, and I was going to guess at silt, except that there wasn't an obvious burn here. Then I saw the creamy lichen that grew everywhere on the stones at the side of the loch. 'Is it the white stones causing the colour? Look, just there, where the water's clearer.' I indicated a whiter patch opposite the near corner of the graveyard where the stones seemed to be clear of the green colouring. 'Those look clean. Maybe this side dries up in summer, so the lichen gets a chance to grow, and make the colour.'

'Could be.' Gavin nodded over at the far side of the graveyard. 'And that rectangle of yellowed grass there is where Lizbet dug up the Book of the Black Arts.'

We walked over and stood looking down at the rectangle of yellowing grass stamped back over the hole.

'There must have been a tradition about it when they were bairns,' I said. 'She said she used to play here. Hoosies in the kirk, hide and seek among the graves, and daring the Devil.' I remembered the bitter pain in her voice. 'And the Devil killed her friend.'

'Human malice killed her friend. So she buried it again at Windhouse, and Antony dug it up from there.' Gavin frowned. 'I'm not sure that all hangs together. It must have been a frightening thing to do, digging it up in the dark. Would she have had the courage to face putting it back in Windhouse?'

I'd wondered that too. 'Maybe she felt she'd faced the worst, or was just so determined to get it back where it belonged that she steeled herself up to it.'

'Maybe.'

He bent down and lifted the yellowed turf. There was only earth underneath. He took a folded ruler from his sporran and prodded, then shook his head. 'She didn't put it back here, anyway.'

I took a deep breath of the grass-scented air. 'D'you suppose they buried the Windhouse baby and the workman and the horned man here?'

'More likely they're in a box in the museum store.'

It didn't feel right to me. 'So the poor baby never had a proper burial.'

'You can pray for its soul,' Gavin said seriously. 'Unless the mother did, nobody has.'

I had my own version of the Church's teaching on unbaptised babies to comfort me over my own little girl who'd never lived. A child who'd never lived and definitely never sinned might be gone now on earth, dissolved into the elements, but in God's eternal time she was already with him. I'd know her when at last we met.

The pain of loss for a child I'd never even seen swept over me again. I fixed my eyes on the shining waters of Kirk Loch and said abruptly, 'I was thinking of coming off the pill.'

Gavin's arms came around my waist. I felt his breath warm on my cheek. He was silent for a moment, then he said slowly, as if he was feeling his way, 'When we first met, once I got to know you, I was already thinking like that. I was hoping we might work, that we'd settle down in a cottage, and you'd be there, we'd have a brood of children and be happy.'

I felt stiff, as if my heart was freezing. He went on, in that same careful tone, 'But I didn't realise. I knew how much you loved the sea, but I didn't realise . . .' His chest tensed as he struggled for the words. He said a phrase in Gaelic, then translated it. 'You're my seal wife. The sea's a part of you. I've realised that more than ever these past three days. Seeing you preparing your boat, just bubbling with excitement. Longing to be out riding the breakers.'

He didn't say that I didn't bubble like that, long like that for him, but I heard a thrill of hurt in his voice, and felt a pang of the pain I'd caused without meaning to.

'I'd like to have a wife and children. I want to see my own bairns growing up around the loch, learning to handle a boat and round up the sheep. I want them to ken every otter, every fox and badger, just as I did. I had to leave for work, and maybe they will too, but maybe no', with the way technology's going, maybe they'll be able to work from home.' He leaned his cheek against my hair. 'But, *mo chridh*, that's an expensive lifestyle, more expensive than you're used to. You need a tough car in working order, and a lot of petrol, to travel to work, and I had the flat in Inverness too, and you need an all-weather boat with a good engine, to get the bairns to school. You need one partner with good pay.'

I'd paid my way in the cottage, then spent what was left over on new sails. I felt a pang of anger, followed by shame. I was taking Gavin for granted.

'I've been thinking about this, you see, these eight weeks on my own. Being a seawoman's grass widower isn't easy. I'm used to the single life, but I can't head for the farm at weekends the way I used to from Inverness, and hear how life is with my mother and Kenny. I've been busy around the house, and I've fished, and the cats are company. And I know you're pretty safe and perfectly happy.'

That stung again, but he didn't say it as a complaint.

'I miss you when I'm aboard,' I said defensively.

'I ken,' he said. 'And it's good having you home full-time when you are home. It's definitely not as bad as being a policeman's wife, where your man comes home late every day, and preoccupied and can't discuss what's worrying him, he just reaches for the whisky. The police divorce rate is appalling.'

I thought of sailors I'd known, and suspected we weren't much better.

'But a policeman is what I am.' I felt him shrug. His arms

183

loosened, as if he was preparing to let me go, and I felt a stab of fear so intense that his next words came through a mist. I was afraid he was trying to say that we weren't working, that there was another woman who would be there all the time.

'I love my job, I'm proud of what we achieve on the ground. I wish we had more resources out on the streets, being part of the people instead of only being called when there's trouble. But, Cass, I could give it up no more than you could give up the sea.' His arms came back around me, and I breathed again and leaned back against him, trembling with relief. 'I want very much to be a father in the evenings and at the weekends, and this job now would let me do that, but from eight to six every day they'd be yours, at least while they were small.' His head turned; he kissed my cheekbone. 'You'd have to reckon to that, my selkie lass.'

I understood what he was saying. It was no good me plunging into parenthood in the hope that it would all work itself out, that somehow I could have a child and still sail off over the horizon. *Wishing and wadding is poor househadding*, Magnie would say. There was more to housekeeping than saying 'I wish' or 'I would'. I knew liveaboards with babies, toddlers, teenagers, but in those boats both parents were sailors, and the boat was their home. Their children had a world-roaming education, made friends as they travelled, followed school syllabuses, but both parents were committed to the roving life. If I was to give in to this urge for a child that was tugging at me, I might manage day sails, maybe a weekend off as a family, but nothing more.

Also, as Gavin had reminded me, I'd be financially dependent on him. My job would be the work of his and my female ancestors: to keep the house, to cook the meals, wash the clothes, raise the children. I didn't despise it as a job; far from it. My schoolfriend Inga was a stay-at-home housewife to her fisherman husband, though in her case the stay-at-home was nominal, as she had a finger in a dozen pies, from the accounts of the hockey club to volunteering at Peerie Charlie's nursery. She'd raised two energetic, independent girls who'd go on to be the backbone of their communities, just as Inga was in Brae, and I had no doubt Peerie Charlie would be an equal success.

Gavin understood my silence. He nodded against my hair, and went into teasing mode. 'Besides, if you were to think about children, you'd also have to think about white dresses and the bridal march. You ken your dad. There's no way he'd be having his grandchildren born out of wedlock, what would the bishop say?'

I laughed, a little unsteadily. 'He'd be getting the shotgun out, wouldn't he?'

'Aye, and I ken fine who he'd be pointing it at.' His arms tightened, then he let me go, and pulled me round to face him. 'It would not be me, either.' He leaned forward, and we kissed. 'Now, shall we go and see Gloup before dinner?'

Chapter Sixteen

Makkin da day an da wye alaek.
(Making the day and the journey the same.)
Proceeding at a leisurely pace on a journey.

Once Gavin had turned the car we were facing Breckon. The stretch of golden sand was on the right of us, its water pale green before it shaded to dark blue, then grey. The drive to Gloup was enlivened by headgear used as strainer preservation lids: the first was by the substation, an outsize ex Up Helly Aa yellow head with a fluttering black moustache. After that came workmen's helmets, white, blue, yellow, and motorbike helmets, all fixed on with a nail through the top. The new grass was bright in the ditches.

At Gloup there was a sign to the Fishermen's Memorial, and a footpath to where the life-sized fisherman's wife stood staring out to sea, watching for her man's boat to come home through the waves. She was roughly hewn out of rock, with her child happed up in her shawl and one hand shading her eyes as she gazed seawards. Her face was carved more delicately, and you could read her anxiety as she strained to see through the spindrift. She stood on a grey marble plinth like a gravestone. The names written on it were gathered into boats. Gavin read the first one aloud. 'From Gloup, sixern *Ann Jessie*, Alexander Henry, Thomas Henry, William Williamson, Thomas Henry, Arthur Moar, Robert Williamson. A father and son and grandson, maybe, and the Williamsons another father and son.'

'Or a daughter's husband and son.' It was chilling looking at the black text on the flecked stone, set out like a book page. 'Ten boats, and six men lost from every one.' The place he came from was beside each man's name: Sandwick, Gutcher, Houlland, Mursetter, Colvister, Dalsetter, Gloup, Gloup, Gloup. It was the record of a community devastated and the industry that had given families an income to help them live off this infertile land smashed with the wrecked boats.

Gavin was reading a separate placard. 'Ten boats, fifty-eight men lost, and thirty-four widows and eighty-five children left to mourn them. Left in an acute state of poverty, I have no doubt. There was no widow's pension or state aid then. The women would have had to rally together to work the croft and feed their bairns as best they could.'

The hills here were green enough now, with sheep grazing the pastures that had been ploughed and re-seeded by tractors, but they would have been heather hills then, with women hauling seaweed in kishies on their backs to fertilise the patches they'd managed to dig, working in teams with their narrow spades.

I thought of Jesma. *Thirty-four widows and eighty-five children left in an acute state of poverty.* She'd called herself a grass widow, but she was a real widow now, and if she'd been struggling before, with Antony's help, her situation would be even more difficult without him. Presumably she'd inherit from Antony, but what would he have to leave? These fishermen's boats had been owned by the laird; his, I had no doubt, was owned by the bank. Jesma and the bairns would get nothing. They might even find themselves liable for his debts.

It was an uncomfortable thought. On its heels came another, that perhaps Jesma's wanting Antony back wasn't just for emotional reasons. Being a single parent was harder financially, harder practically. With two of you, you could juggle working times, so that you could manage childcare and still have two incomes. You had the expenses of only one house, not two; only one washing machine, hoover, car, to be repaired, only one set of plumbing to go wrong, and between you, one of you who might have the time to have a go at fixing it before calling out an expensive repair firm. With two of you, you had another person to be a backup for a stroppy teenager who moaned 'But all my friends are allowed . . .'

Jesma had had an interest in Chloe's death. She'd given the impression she thought Chloe and Antony were serious, and she knew her man, whatever he'd said to me about it being light-hearted. If it was serious, that would end any hopes Jesma had of a reconciliation. Chloe looked expensive too, what did they call it – 'high maintenance'? Antony would have less money to share with Jesma if he moved in with Chloe; Jesma'd said that herself, as we'd driven home from the foodbank. And she'd been there in Lerwick that day; in Boots, ten shops further on from the steps where Chloe had fallen. She worked in the care home; she could have access to sleeping pills. The drug cupboards would all be locked, of course, but if she was determined she could have got a sleeping pill somehow. I thought about how I'd do that. If you had a patient with dementia you could just not give them their sleeping pill, and say they'd had it, or substitute something else, aspirin or a vitamin pill of the same size, and say they were just misremembering if they said it was a different pill. Jesma could have done that. All she needed then was a chance to drop it into Chloe's drink.

DS Peterson's observant waiter hadn't mentioned a visit from an ex-wife. A woman who'd seen them in The Dowry window, and dropped in to check childcare arrangements with Antony, or ask if he could have a quick look at her car. It would take a lot of nerve to go in with a pill ready to drop in . . .

'Would a sleeping pill just dissolve, like that?' I asked abruptly.

Gavin looked up at the grey woman above us, her child in her arm, staring out to sea. 'Antony's widow?'

I nodded.

'The answer is that I don't know. I suppose some might. We've still not heard if that's what she took, or was given, and if so what exactly it was, but I did have a quick look online, and there are various over-the-counter sleep aids.'

'But even if it did,' I said, 'it wouldn't vanish just like that. It would be easier to put it in as a powder. Well, quicker, not necessarily easier. You'd have to have it ready in your hand and just pour it in. Even then, the powder would surely float on the surface for a bit.'

'You can get them as syrup as well. A little from a bottle would be as easy as pouring a powder.'

'I don't see how she could have done it,' I said. 'Even if she'd seen them through the window and gone in on some pretext, people would be looking at her. It would take a lot of nerve to doctor someone's drink in front of them all. Besides, DS Peterson's waiter didn't mention her going in there.'

Gavin glanced back at the widow, high on her plinth. 'She had a motive for getting Chloe out of the way, but from what I saw of them on Friday night, she wanted Antony back. She didn't want him dead.'

'I know he said to me he wasn't serious about Chloe,' I said slowly, thinking it through, 'but that doesn't have to be true. Maybe he was really keen on her. Maybe, even with Chloe dead, he still didn't want Jesma, and was just being nice on Friday to please the bairns, and for the look of things, but it gave her the wrong idea. She approached him, he turned her down flat and that made her angry enough to lash out at him.'

I didn't want to think it. I couldn't help seeing it as possible.

We drove back in silence. Ertie Arthurson was moving aboard his fishing boat as we came down the drive, and as we drew up he came onto the pier and greeted us.

'Well,' he said, 'what thought you to Windhouse?'

189

Naturally he'd seen the Land Rover parked there.

'Spooky,' I admitted. 'I wouldn't have cared to have gone in there on my own.'

He laughed out at that. 'Never fear o' you. A lass that can sail single-handed round the top o' Yell's no going to be put off her stride by a ruin o' a house.'

'You were saying that there'd been light in it, sir,' Gavin said. Ertie gave him a sharp glance. The 'sir' made it official.

'There's been a death in Brae,' Gavin said, as he hesitated over the answer, 'and the lights might be connected, if you could tell me about it.'

Mainland folk might joke about Yell being the Land that Time Forgot, with Christmas decorations still in the windows in March, but the bush telegraph worked just as well this far north. Ertie'd obviously heard all about the Brae man who'd been found dead in his own kitchen. He nodded. 'You think he mighta been up in Windhouse? Well, let me think.'

I gestured towards *Khalida*. 'Come aboard and have a cup o' tea.'

'I never say no to an offer o' a cuppa from a bonny wife,' he said gallantly, and followed me aboard.

The cats had heard our voices and were out on deck, ready to greet us. Gavin and Ertie installed themselves in the cockpit while I boiled the kettle and put down cat food. There was a bit of general chat about Ertie's boat and what kind of fish he went after while I chinked mugs around, but once we were all seated, Gavin fished his black notebook out of his sporran and got down to business. 'Those lights, sir.'

'There was a set last week. I'll need to have a think about what day it was, precisely. I was passing in the car, late, but not very late, more dusk than night, so that would make it maybe, oh, eight o'clock. Now what might I have been doing driving past at that time?' He shook his head, and added apologetically, 'You don't ken yet what it's like being retired, but I can tell you, you're

190

busier than ever, and every day is different, so it's hard to keep track.' He sat for a moment, frowning. 'There was one day I had to get a parcel from the ferry. No, that would have been earlier, for it came wi' the workers' bus. Half past six. And it wouldn't have been the day I was in town myself, for that would have been the same sort of time.' His face lightened suddenly. 'No, I ken. I had a spare bag of hens' meal that I took down to Joanie o' Scattlands, to start his ones off laying, and I sat and had a cup o' tay and yarned for a bit. Thursday, it was.'

Thursday, the day Lizbet had said to Magnie and me that she was going to get rid of the Book of the Black Arts. She could have come straight from her work to Yell, and been here by dusk.

'I came straight back along the main road,' Ertie continued, 'and when I came over the hill at the Herra turn-off I saw lights spilling out from the walls o' Windhoose. Well, I slowed down to get a look at what was going on. There was more than one person up there, for there were a couple o' torches shining. Ghost-hunters, I thought to myself, for we get a good few o' those, now Windhouse is being touted on this social media as Britain's most haunted house.' He snorted at that. 'Haunted, well, I won't say it isn't, but to read the articles you'd think there was a ghost in every corner of it. So, I thought to myself, ghost-hunters wi' a bristle o' daft equipment, and kept on driving. There were a couple of cars sitting there. The first one was by the lodge. That was a local plate, a peerie red car wi' a wife sitting in it, as if she was too feared to go up. The other one was further up the hill, where you parked.' He frowned and scratched his head. 'Yes. A biggish saloon, I didn't see the make. It was pale-coloured, fawn, maybe, or creamy-coloured, I don't think it was white, and it was a Star Rent-a-car one. I could see the writing on the door.'

'We can easily trace that,' Gavin said. 'And you saw lights this morning again?'

'One light,' Ertie said. 'I was down meeting the second ferry, that gets in at 8.35. We had a minister from the west side came up to preach this morning, and I said I could save her the ferry fare with her car by meeting her off the ferry, and then one of the other elders said he'd put her back to it, so that's what I was doing. 8.35, the ferry, and I didn't want to be late, because I'd not met the lady before, so I'd have been passing Windhouse, oh, maybe twenty past.'

'Eight twenty,' Gavin repeated, and jotted it down. It had been about nine, maybe just after, when Antony had passed me at the entrance to Cullivoe; time enough for him to get from Windhouse to his boat, and roar up the sound.

'It was just one light, staying still, not moving about. It was light by then, o' course, and a bonny morning too, but I could see it shining out of the right-hand side window, and every so often a shadow passed across it, as if someone was moving around.'

'Was there a car parked?'

I opened my mouth to say that Antony would have walked up from the marina, and closed it again.

Ertie pursed up his mouth, then shook his head. 'I was looking up at the hill, trying to make out if it was a light or just the sun shining on something, a broken bit of glass, maybe, and then a car came towards me, and I had to get my attention back on the road, and by that time I was past where a car would be, if there was one there. Maybe . . . I have an impression of a black pick-up, maybe, but I couldna swear to it, and o' course that coulda been Robbie that has the grazing there, checking on his lambs. He has a black pick-up.' He paused a moment, considering that. 'The light I saw might even a been him, if a yowe managed to get into the house and got stuck in some way.'

'I'll check with him.' Gavin waited, pencil poised. 'Robbie . . .?'

'Robbie Johnson, and he bides in Outrabister, just out o' Mid

Yell.' Ertie thought for a moment, then came up with the phone number. 'Mid Yell 136.' He rose, and nodded at our shopping bags. 'You're likely wanting your own tea, and the wife'll be ready wi' mine an all. Thanks to you for the cuppa, lass, and good luck wi' your test the morn.'

He clambered ashore, raised a hand and stomped off.

'It doesn't make sense,' I said, once he was out of earshot. 'Lizbet wouldn't have taken a group to Windhouse. The lights Ertie saw must just have been ghost-hunters after all. Yes!' I leaned forward. 'That's it. She got to Windhouse and found the ghost-hunters in possession. She has a peerie red car. That could have been Lizbet. She came off the ferry and drove to Windhouse, but then she saw the lights and decided to wait a bit and see if they'd go, so she could get on with burying the Book.'

'Maybe,' Gavin said. I could see he wasn't satisfied. He stood up. 'How about some dinner?'

We took our shopping bags below, and set to being domestic. Gavin had gone for that sailing-boat staple, a stir-fry with assorted vegetables and two packs of king prawns to throw in at the last moment. My flask rice was nicely done, and we ate a satisfying meal by the gold light of the cabin lantern, then sat side by side on the couch. The warmth of the cabin was reminding me that allowing for the changed hour I'd had only two hours' sleep. I stretched and yawned. 'I think I might need an early night.'

'D'you want me to test you on a few questions?'

'Only if you can be bothered.' I poured myself another cup of tea from the pot, to sharpen my wits. 'More tea?'

'Please.' He reached into his kitbag and pulled out his tablet. 'I downloaded a mock test. Ready?'

I'd been working on my driving theory during long night watches, so I was pretty confident I could pick out the 'right' answer from among the choices, but I often felt the answer I'd give, for example in the case of straying sheep (give them time to get off the road, looking particularly for lambs on the opposite side from their mothers who were liable to scurry across at the last moment), wasn't in the choices, and I wasn't sure that 'go slowly past' was the most helpful answer, but it seemed nearer right than 'sound your horn'. Then there was coming on a road accident.

'What injuries?' I protested. 'I need more information. Do they have broken legs? Possible concussion, so I need to keep them awake?'

'Unspecified injuries,' Gavin said patiently. 'Your choices are: keep them warm, feed them, give them something to drink or walk them.'

I made a face and conceded that keeping them warm, while inadequate if the ambulance was a ferry journey away, was better than the others.

We got through the questions quite quickly. 'End test?' Gavin asked. I nodded. He clicked a button, and nodded at the green 'Pass' banner. 'Don't look so smug. You only got one out of three for the motorway driving.'

'Lack of practice,' I retorted.

We went through what I should have said, and had a go at another motorway section. This time I got full marks. 'Good,' Gavin said. 'D'you want to try the hazard clips?'

I nodded, and took the tablet from him. This was easier, and once I'd clicked on stray pedestrians, junctions, hazard road signs and tractors from side roads, I scored a respectable 13.

'Bingo,' Gavin agreed. 'You'll do fine.' He stood, and stretched, and the cats instantly raised their heads. 'Shall we go for a walk before bedtime?'

It was a bonny night outside. Down to the south the sky was tinted orange with the flickering of the Sullom Voe terminal flare stack, and there was still the faintest hint of light in the west, but to the north and east the stars were clear points of blue-white light. We strolled gently up the drive towards the Italianate church. Kitten scampered ahead, then dived into the long grass at the side of the road to lurk and pounce out at Cat as he passed, then the pair of them went ahead in a mad charge.

'They've got into the habit of a bedtime stroll,' Gavin said. 'I usually go along the beach as far as the Quiensetter point, and they charge about after me.'

He paused to look out at the sky and said, rather too casually, 'When are you coming home again?'

'As soon as I can,' I said. His face brightened. 'If I can get a good sleep tonight and a doze in the afternoon, I can leave at midnight tomorrow night, and arrive at breakfast time. Well, late breakfast. I need to leave Cullivoe half an hour before high water, and then I'll have five hours of tide to sweep me along the top of Yell and Northmavine and down the side before it turns against me. Besides, this bonny weather's forecast to change. Slightly breezier tomorrow, and the clouds gathering overnight to make it cold, wet and nasty by later on Wednesday. Back to winter. I'd rather be home before then.'

It was strange being in the forepeak, a triangular bed in the boat's bow where our toes kept bumping together. Cat disapproved; there wasn't quite enough room for him to sleep on my side of the bed, as he did at the Ladie. He tried for a bit, then got up, growling softly to himself, and went back to my berth. The Kitten followed. The light slanting in from the pier illuminations showed the pair of them curling up together, Cat with one paw over the Kitten, just as Gavin had his arm over me. Just as I thought that, Gavin turned away from me. His breathing soon steadied to deep and regular, but I lay awake for a bit longer. The noises here were different from in my berth, with the water rippling around the bow, and there was slightly more motion.

The conversation from the kirkyard was circling in my head. It was all very well to talk of equality and a woman's career being as important as a man's, but we were the ones who had to carry and birth the children. My friend Agnetha was going to take as much of her year's maternity leave as possible after her child's birth. As a single parent she was also entitled to two years' benefits running on from her maternity leave, or she could transfer those benefits to another carer, like her mother, and still keep working. Agnetha lived and worked in Norway. I didn't know what the UK's benefits were, but I suspected that they were less generous, and anyway, it didn't matter. Gavin had spelled out the situation clearly, and knowing he was talking sense didn't make it easier to decide. If I wanted children, I would have to stay home.

It wasn't that decision that was keeping me awake, but Gavin. *Being a seawoman's grass widower isn't easy.* I was asking a lot of him. Maybe I was asking too much. He wanted a home, and a family, and maybe if I felt I couldn't give him those I should say so, loud and clear, and let him go home to the Highlands and make the sort of life he wanted with somebody else. Just the thought hurt so much that I could hardly bear it. I loved him. I loved the way he could read my mind, his sense of humour. I loved the neatness of his movements, his independence. I loved his passion for just-ice. When I was onboard *Sørlandet* the land world receded but he was always at the back of my mind, the home I would go to once my spell of duty was over.

I couldn't bear the idea of him not being there. I lay there and hurt at the thought while he slept beside me, and the sea whispered at my ear.

V

Better to meet the Deevil as meet the Minister.
Ministers were reputed to have a 'bad foot'
and unlucky to meet on a journey.

Chapter Seventeen

Monday 20th March

Tide times, Lerwick / Dover:
HW 08.23 (2.19m);
LW 15.21 (0.47m);
HW 21.51 (2.0m)

Moonset 06.56; sunrise 07.04; moonrise 21.38;
sunset 19.19. Moon waxing gibbous.

Da soo drems as shö wid.
(The sow dreams about what she wants.)
Wishful thinking. Said of someone who would like to
persuade events to occur to their own advantage.

We had an early start. Gavin had to get the 07.45 ferry to be in Lerwick for nine, so we were up at six and frying bacon and duck eggs for rolls by half past.

'What are you planning to do with yourself till your test?' he asked.

'Eleven fifteen,' I grumbled. 'I suppose it gives folk time to get over from Sandness. I'll go for a swim, have a cup of coffee, do some last-minute revision and go for a soothing walk if there's time left. I could inspect the marina, for future use.'

We ate our bacon rolls, brushed our teeth on deck, warned the cats to be good, and headed for the Land Rover. At 07.25,

Gavin dropped me off at the Mid Yell turning, and I walked briskly up the hill, around the bend and up again to look down at Yell's main town spread out below me.

It was a sizeable place, spreading out in a fan of roads from the pier. I had stopped by the old-old Mid Yell school, a cluster of long concrete huts now used for individual enterprise. The road I was on ran seawards, branching right to the former Hilltop bar, where we'd tried to buy an underage pint (we'd failed because the sneaky folk of Mid Yell had got an ex-teacher on the bar for regatta night, who could tell the age of teenagers to the second), and left to another cluster of houses and a low, red-roofed building that was probably either the care centre or the doctor's surgery. On the right was where I was headed: the old-new school, the new Yell Junior High School and the red-roofed leisure centre beside it. The main road continued down to run along the shore, with the shop and more houses on one side of the village's main pier. Up to the other side was the Mid Yell Hall and the imposing Lusseter House, the former manse. The minister had a good view over his parish.

I walked down towards the school. The old-new school, a mostly windows sixties block, was at the turn-off. It was obviously inhabited by more enterprising individuals. One large placard beside a buttercup-yellow bubble like a diver's sphere said *LJ's* in big letters, with *Diner & Pizzeria* below, and I was beginning to think hopefully of a nice, substantial lunch until I saw the notice on the door: *Sorry, we're closed for the winter season, but watch out for our Special Evenings!!!*

Ah well. There were still rolls, bacon and duck eggs aboard, as well as assorted tins, once I got back to *Khalida*.

I'd come to the car park and bus turning area. The new school was to the left of the leisure centre. Two wings were set slantwise to each other so that the wide entrance narrowed to the school porch and door, under a pillared overhang. Behind that was a higher rectangular piece, no doubt the taller roof of the assembly room, faced in irregular blocks of red, brown and fawn, with MID YELL JUNIOR HIGH in white letters.

Naturally there was no sign of life in the school yet, but the round windows in the front of the leisure centre looked ominously dark as well. I checked my watch. 07.40. The leisure centre in Brae opened at 07.30. A nice swim in warm water, a hot shower and hair wash and I'd be ready to face anything the DVSA decided to throw at me.

I was out of luck. The main centre didn't open till 09.00, a notice on the door informed me, and the pool wasn't available until 13.00.

I wasn't the only one balked of her swim. A young woman came up behind me, towel roll under her arm, and gave a disappointed 'Oh.' I turned, and her eyes widened in recognition. Her hand came up in a pointing gesture. She hesitated, then said, 'You're the woman who helped the lass who fell down the steps.'

Even as she was saying it, I placed her. She was the nurse who'd taken charge at the accident, the new girlfriend of Chloe's ex-boyfriend. I nodded. 'Cass Lynch.'

'Amy White.' She made a face at the Opening Hours notice. 'I can't believe they're still shut. The Lerwick one is open at seven. I thought I'd get in a nice swim before work.'

'I'm here for the driving test.' I shrugged. 'It's not till 11.15. A swim would have filled the time in nicely.'

'Come and get a coffee instead.' She gestured towards the other side of the main road. 'The regular practice nurse is on holiday,' she said. 'Two weeks with the family in Ibiza, getting some sun in after a long winter. I volunteered to be seconded from the Lerwick practice to cover these two weeks. It gives me a bit of a holiday in Yell.'

'Not as sunny as Ibiza,' I said.

She went straight into chat mode. 'Ah, but I still bide at

home, so this is a fortnight without my little sister trying to nick my phone so she can read my messages, and my mum trying to pump me about what patients I saw today, she never gives up, and when I try to say it's confidential she just says that anyone living opposite the health centre can see who goes out and in, so it can't be that private.' She rolled her eyes. 'Mothers. I only came up yesterday, which is why I hadn't figured the leisure centre hours out yet.' She motioned me forwards. 'Come and get a coffee.'

'Thanks,' I said, and fell into step beside her.

She chattered happily in her low-pitched, musical voice as we walked up the hill on what looked like a track out to a lonely crofthouse. Normally, she said, she lived in Gulberwick, just south of Lerwick, and there were plenty of buses to get into the town, and a taxi if she fancied a night out, or Irvine would run her of course, if they were doing something together, but her dad was one of the elders in the Muckle Kirk and he would be black affronted if his daughter was biding with a man without at least being engaged to him, so she just bade at home for ee now. She was twenty-two, and only a year out of her training in Aberdeen; she'd thought about staying down there, but she missed her family, and her best pal had gone off to a job in Inverness, at the Raigmore, and then this job had come up as practice nurse in Lerwick, and her mam had been that keen for her to take it, and well, she missed Shetland too.

I could get a proper look at her, walking along like this. The impression I'd had at the foot of those dark steps in Lerwick was of calm competence, and that remained, in spite of the non-stop chatter. She was bonny without being striking: smooth skin, a wide friendly smile, streaked blonde hair, long at the sides and caught back in a clasp, the fringe carefully straightened. A nice lass. I'd have betted she'd worked hard at her training, and probably came top of her class in some modules. She'd be good with bairns; they'd take one look and trust her.

Suddenly over the rise of the hill loomed the pantiled roof of a health centre. Amy led me across the cattle grid and around to the front. It was surprisingly big, a long, white building with a low roof and square windows set in pairs between the roof and the hip-height line of decorative red brick. There was a wide glass door with floor-to-ceiling-height windows beside it, showing cloth-covered institution armchairs and children's toys in the reception area. A half blue-plastic barrel held pink spring flowers.

'It's Yell and Fetlar,' Amy said, digging in her handbag for a bunch of keys. 'Hang on, while I sort the alarm.'

I waited outside while she pressed numbers into a keypad.

'Phew,' she said, holding the door open for me. 'That's always so fraught, with the light bleeping away while you type the numbers, and not being sure what awful noise will happen if you get it wrong, or how you'll switch it off before the police come roaring over the horizon.' She reconsidered that. 'Well, maybe no' roaring, exactly, given there's a drive from town to Toft and a ferry in between, but the neighbours would all be round, and I'd live on forever as that nurse who woke everyone up at the crack o' dawn wi' no' being able to work the burglar alarm. Tea or coffee? Have a seat.'

She disappeared into a room off the corridor, and I sat and looked around. It was the usual sort of country surgery, with one corridor leading towards Consulting Rooms 1 and 2 and Nurses' Room, and the other, where Amy had gone, leading to the reception office, the prescription window, glass closed, and further closed doors which I presumed were medicine stores. Mug/spoon chinking noises came from one of the open doors. Amy's voice floated through. 'Milk and sugar?'

'Just black coffee, thanks.'

'Good, because I think this milk is okay, it smells fine, but its sell-by date was yesterday. Still, there's no doctor in today, it's just me, so I'll finish it off and head for the shop in my lunch break.' She put the mugs down on the little table, and relaxed into one of the other chairs. 'I could have had an extra hour in bed.'

'I had to be up,' I said, and tried to be chatty myself. 'I sailed up overnight, Saturday night, and my partner drove up to join me, but he had to get to Lerwick for nine, so he dropped me off on his way past.'

Her eyes widened. 'You sailed on your own?'

I nodded. 'I could have taken the bus up for the test, but it was an excuse to get my mast back – in Brae they have to take them down over the winter.'

She nodded, thinking about that. 'That kinda explains . . . you were so quick, with the lass that fell. Used to taking command. I was expecting you to say you were a doctor.' Her lips tightened, and she swallowed. 'I've had folk dying on the wards, of course, but not very many. The first one was really upsetting, but the Staff Nurse said I wouldn't make a good nurse if I didn't mind. The trick was to focus on the work. But that lass.' She paused, then said her name at last. 'Chloe. It was so sudden. She'd been laughing and chatting in the restaurant, and then she just tripped like that, and she was dead.' She gave a shiver. 'The folk I've seen die, they were all older. She was the same age as me.'

'Did you ken her?' I asked gently.

Amy spread her hands. 'I kinda did and I kinda didn't. Well, I didn't, because she was at the Brae school, and I was Lerwick, and then while she was in the party scene in Lerwick, I was in Aberdeen, so I don't expect I'd have seen her. So I didn't actually ken her, but you see, Irvine, my boyfriend –' Her voice warmed at his name. 'He'd gone out with her, so I kent her from what he told me. She was his girlfriend before me, oh, well, there were a couple in between, but nothing serious. For serious, there was her, a bit after he left the school, while he was at the college, and then there was me. Is me. He split up with her about a year before we got together.'

I nodded, encouragingly, and tried to remember what Tom had said about Chloe and Irvine. *She fell apart when he ended it. Crying and spending days in bed. Stopped eating.* That was when Lizbet had talked him into letting her come in the band. And then Lizbet had persuaded Chloe to go to the gym and she'd dyed her hair. Tom's voice sounded in my head again. *Went partying. Hoping she'd meet him to show him what he'd thrown away.* Tom hadn't liked Chloe, that was clear. She was after Lizbet's place in the band. A glittery singer who would show her former boyfriend what he was missing. And then she'd met him in The Dowry.

Amy took a swig of her coffee and launched in. 'When we met, Irvine and me, well, it was at a Musicals Night at Jackie's — you know them?'

I shook my head. Her eyes brightened. 'Oh, they're so cool, you should go. It's up where the furniture shop used to be before they moved to next door to the Legion. Well, Jackie's turned it into a music place, with a peerie bar in one corner that does cakes too, and she does these Musicals Nights. She hires one professional singer and local folk get up and do numbers as well, in costume, and it's brilliant. There's a group of us get a table together. So this night, a year ago in November, there was this strange boy at the table with us, well, no' totally strange, for I minded him from the school, but I'd no seen him since, because I'd been away, and I was just too tired by the end of my week's shifts to go out clubbing.'

'Can you club in Lerwick?' I couldn't resist asking, as she paused for breath.

Amy laughed. 'Not quite like in Aberdeen. Anyway, Katey had brought him along, and he was sitting next to me and we got chatting. I checked with Katey if he was hers, and she said, no, he was all mine if I wanted him.' She blushed. 'And I did.

He looked me up in the phone book, and called to ask me out.' She rolled her eyes. 'And you can imagine, Mam asking fifty questions and wanting his complete pedigree, but luckily it turned out that she kent his mam, because they'd been in the annexe together. I'd been born at the same time as his wee brother. So he turned from "who's this?" to "you'll need to bring him round to tea", which was enough to put any boy off, so I staved that one off as long as I could.'

She paused to drink from her mug. 'Which was just as well, once he started telling me about Chloe.' Her eyes grew intent; her mouth pursed, as if she was trying to order the facts in her head. 'They met in Captain Flint's, when he was in his last year at the college – he's an engineer, he works to Jim's Garage. Over three years ago, that must've been, for we're been going out nearly a year and a half now, and he was without a girlfriend for a year, then he was with her for a year before that.'

Three years seemed a long time to bear a grudge. I nodded.

'Well, what Irvine said was that she did most of the running.' She pulled a face. 'Well, I ken, he would say that, but I think it's probably true. He's coming out o' his shell now, but he was quiet at the school, kinda serious way, so I could imagine him being flattered by this lass seeming to be keen on him. He said she'd phone him to say she'd got two tickets for the new James Bond, but her mate couldn't make it, or there was this party she fancied going to, but it was in Northmavine, and she didn't have transport, but maybe he'd like to come . . . that kinda thing. And then before he really realised it, suddenly they were an item, and she was sticking her arm through his in Captain Flint's, and talking about "we".'

'Unnerving.'

Amy nodded vigorously. 'It unnerved Irvine, all right. He said he felt trapped. He tried to start a conversation with her about it, but, well, he's not that good at speaking about emotions, and she turned the subject every time he tried. Then, one evening when he was round at hers, he was reading a car magazine and she was on the computer, and someone came to the door.' She flushed. 'Now this is really not like Irvine, I want you to ken that. It shows how he was feeling, that he'd do this. She was talking away at the door, and so he just stood up and went over to look in her computer, and for a moment he wasn't sure what he was seeing. She was on a party goods website, and there was a whole page of henny-night stuff. L-plates, pink furry handcuffs, "Bride" dressing gowns, the works. And she was still talking, so he opened her history, and there was site after site of wedding gear, dresses, cakes, jewellery, invitations, even poems to read during the ceremony. She never seemed to browse anything else. Well, he got back to his seat sharpish and opened his magazine again, and thought. It mighta been for someone else, like her best pal Lizbet, her that has the bonny voice. So Irvine asked, casual like, what her pal Lizbet was up to these days, and Chloe said that she was still singing, her and Tom, not a mention o' weddings. So he kent it wasna that, and this cold uneasy feeling began to spread over him. He made an excuse about a big job in the morning, and needing an early night. Then he made sure not to answer the phone for a couple of days, and then – now I ken this was awful of him, but he said he just didn't ken what else to do – then he texted her saying he felt they were getting too serious too soon, and he wanted a bit o' time to himself. Then he made sure that the next time he went to Captain Flint's he had another lass with him.' She spread her hands. 'I'm no excusing him. It musta been an awful shock for the poor lass. But he says that he didn't think she was keen on him, not really – not now he's been going with me. He said she was aye ambitious – no, that's not quite the word – she kinda wanted him to make the best of himself. She wanted him to wear a suit when his work was over, when he just wanted to relax in his old clothes in front of the telly, and she fussed about oil under his nails. She didn't love him as he was.'

'The waiter in The Dowry,' I said. 'He said that it looked like she was all over him, flirting and showing how bonny she was.'

'The Dowry! Irvine didn't recognise her at first. We were just starting our meal when they came in, and we glanced up, saw we didn't know them and glanced away again. Well, when I say didn't know them, I recognised Lizbet as the singer. And then this overdressed blonde lass with false eyelashes an inch long suddenly swooped on us cooing Irvine's name and saying how long it had been, and how fine it was to see him, and plumped herself down in the chair nearest to us at the next table, and monopolised him.' Her soft voice was harsh. It had been a humiliating experience for her, I guessed, having to sit by and not make a scene while Chloe flirted with her man in front of her. 'And Irvine said later that he didn't want to make a scene, and it was only for a short while, but I think he should have just said hello and turned his back on her. And I didn't want to have a dessert, but Irvine did, so that was how we came to be leaving at the same time as them.' The generous mouth pursed tight. 'And Chloe said she was feeling a bit drowsy, and draped herself all over him, pretending she needed his arm as support.' Her blue eyes came up, and caught mine. She made an impatient gesture. 'Oh, all right, it did annoy me. I kent he didn't want to make a scene, but since I was there to protect him, he rather enjoyed it too, being flattered by a dodgy blonde.' Her voice hardened. 'And somehow it came out that I was off to Yell for two weeks, so she was going on about how "We must meet up again properly while you've got your evenings free".' There was cruel mimicry in her voice. 'But I could see he wouldn't meet her. He wasn't going to get caught up in that again. And then we got to the steps, and she fell, and no wonder, with those ridiculous stilts of heels she was wearing, and somehow – somehow –'

Her face changed. One hand went up to her mouth, as if she wished she could take the words back. She was silent for a moment, then suddenly she leapt up. 'Goodness, is that the

208

time? The first patients'll be here any minute. I'm sorry to turn you out into the cold.'

'It's not that cold,' I assured her. 'I need to get down to the shop anyway. Can I bring you back a pint of milk?'

'Oh, no, that's fine of you, but I'll get there myself later, the walk will do me good. Good luck with your exam. I'm sure you'll be fine.'

'I hope so,' I said. 'Thanks for the coffee. See you!'

It was only twenty to nine, but she might have all sorts of things to do before her first patients arrived. All the same, there'd been an abruptness in the way she'd suddenly wanted me gone. She'd been speaking about how Chloe had grabbed on to Irvine's arm. *Chloe said she was feeling a bit drowsy, and draped herself all over him, pretending she needed his arm as support.* Nobody else had mentioned that. Had Amy suddenly realised that she'd just made it clear that Irvine, the person supporting her, was the one who could most easily have pushed her down those steps? More, if he really had been supporting her, it would have been difficult for anyone else to have pushed her without him feeling them doing it. I tried to remember what I'd seen from below. My impression had been that the men had stepped back to let Lizbet and Chloe go first. I didn't think she'd still been hanging on to him.

This was the road that led to the marina. I turned left and continued along it, thinking. Amy was a nurse. If she'd drugged Chloe, she should know that a drug would be detected in the body; that Chloe had fallen rather than been pushed. Did her worrying about having made it obvious Irvine was the person most able to have pushed her mean she was in the clear?

On top of that, though I liked her, it seemed to me that she and Chloe were sisters under the skin. She might not have ordered her henny-party tiara yet, but her family set-up sounded like white lace and satin bridesmaid dresses to me . . . except that she hadn't yet persuaded Irvine to give her an engagement ring, because otherwise she'd have called him her fiancé. *The girlfriend wasn't best pleased*, the waiter had said. *Nobody was sorry enough*, DS Peterson had said. *I felt this relief that they were ashamed of . . . She'd been a problem and now she was gone.* I had a sense of that too. She'd been denying too hard: *But I could see he wouldn't meet her. He wasn't going to get caught up in that again.* Well, maybe not, though he could easily have skipped his dessert as well and got out of there if he'd been that embarrassed, or pretended they were going the other way as they came out of The Dowry. Just because Amy wanted me to believe it didn't make it true.

Furthermore, though normally all she'd have had to do to hang on to her man was make sure she kept him busy enough in the evenings until he'd forgotten about meeting up with Chloe, somehow it had come out that she was going to be away for a fortnight. While she was in Yell, Chloe would have had a free hand with Irvine.

On top of that, although Amy didn't look in the least like someone who'd ever need sleeping pills for herself, she certainly had access to them both as prescription drugs and over the counter, and, at The Dowry, she'd access to Chloe's drink. She could have drugged her.

Chapter Eighteen

He trives best at never sees da laird's reek.
(He thrives best that never sees the smoke from the laird's chimneys.)
Too close proximity to the laird is not recommended.

The marina was tucked into a bay around the corner, with a sheltering rock wall around it. A single pontoon ran out from the pier, with thirty berths and room for a couple of visitors on the hammerhead. There was a commercial pier beside it, and a couple of agricultural sheds for mussels or salmon work. I had a vague memory of having been told that there was a John West canning factory in Yell.

It was only once I'd walked right down to the dark grey house with two old fishing boats leaning against each other that I realised I should have followed the Ravensgio sign for the marina. I went past the house to the shore and walked along the beach: past the piece of salmon metal walkway, past the little piece of concrete on the beach which, going by the tyre-tread marks, was where the marina boats came out, past the collection of fibreglass motorboats and onto the marina road. It was a neat little marina, similar to the one at Aith, with a single pontoon protected by a rock wall to seaward and another wave breaker at the open end. I could have fitted in there nicely, but I was glad I'd opted for Cullivoe, for there were two sizeable mussel farms as well as the lobster pots, and it wouldn't have been fun to sail into after a sleepless night. Besides, it would have taken two more hours to reach, so staying in Cullivoe had cut two hours off my returning time, eleven hours instead of thirteen.

I sat down on a handy rock and surveyed the boats. There were a good few empty berths, belonging to boats which had migrated home to their owner's driveway for the winter. The shoreward side was mostly small boats like our *Herald Deuk*, sixteen- and eighteen-foot motorboats with a small cuddy; the seaward side had more serious fishing boats, high-prowed and high-bridged, with orange spools for long lines above and gaps for hauling creels over the low stern. There were a couple of aluminium salmon boats at the end nearest the entrance.

I was just thinking about moving on when a man lugging a plastic fish box came out from one of the larger boats and headed up the gangplank towards me. I swung the gate open for him, and he stomped through.

'Thanks to you,' he said. The box was filled with seaweed. Something moved under it: blue-black lobsters with their claws taped with red electrician tape. The man set the box down and turned to look at me. 'You'll be Cass, I'm thinking. Magnie said to keep an eye open for you here, but I heard from Ertie that you'd gone into Cullivoe instead.' He held out his hand. 'Hakki Sinclair. Magnie and me, we sailed together for a good few years.'

We shook hands. His leathery palm would never have needed a sailmaker's glove to protect it.

'You'd have had a long journey of it. Nine, ten hours in a yacht?'

'More like eleven,' I agreed.

'It was a fine night. And you're biding for a day or two?'

I shook my head. 'The weather's forecast to turn. I'll get home this night.'

He thought about that, and came up with the same conclusion that I had. 'Yea, if you leave Cullivoe going on for midnight, you'll have the tide with you halfway home.' He took his cap off to wipe the sweat from his brow, replaced it and turned to look at me once more. 'And Ertie said you'd got your driving test today.'

There was no point in me trying to compete with the Retired Fishermen's Information Network. I nodded again. 'I think I'm all set.'

'No fear o' you.' He tapped his forehead. 'Touch wood. How are you getting back along the widow's road?'

I gave him a blank look, and he smiled, as if he was pleased to have caught a visitor out. 'The road north, that's the widow's road. You're likely heard o' the Gloup Disaster, when ten boats and fifty-eight men were lost?'

'We went to visit the memorial last night.'

'Aye. Well, the boats, you see, were owned by the laird. He supplied the boat, and took a third of the catch as rent, and another third went to maintaining the boat, and only the last third went to the men. Now the laird at Gloup when the boats were lost, he was a businessman with no heart at all.' He spat at the grey concrete path. 'Well, he's gone now, and his house with him. The boats had been his, and he'd have the price of them back from someone.' His bushy brows drew down over his eyes. 'You'll likely be able to guess who.'

I nodded. 'The women who'd already lost their men.'

'Lost their men and were left with children and old folk to support, and the crops to grow and harvest, and the sheep to shear, and the lambs to kill. And with no way of earning money either, for the laird used the tack system in his shop, that meant they could sell their knitting only to him, and for goods, not cash, unless they took a boat right to Lerwick, and any wife who did that would be on the wrong side of him, and likely to find herself evicted. So he told them, well, out of the goodness of his heart, he'd forego the price of the boat if they worked it off in making him a road.'

The casual cruelty of it silenced me. I thought of those poor women, grieving for their men and worried sick about how they'd bring up their bairns, being set to work to dig the broad ditch for the laird's road, then trek up and down from the beach with kishies of stones on their backs to fill it.

Hakki nodded at me. 'Those days are no' gone yet. The Cooncil may not pursue folk for rent, but the taxman has as harsh powers as any laird, and the big corporations are no better – look at those folk in the Post Office, thrown into prison over a faulty computer system.' He was getting into his stride now. 'Meanwhile these big internet companies dodge millions in tax, and the Post Office bosses, the ones that they all wrote to, to say the computers were playing up, get honours and new jobs at salaries of more per year than those folk saw in a lifetime.'

I nodded in agreement. Even in my lifetime I felt I'd seen the rich getting richer and more immune to the laws that governed the rest of us. Meanwhile, down at the poor end, folk like Jesma and all the others who'd called in at the foodbank on Wednesday were struggling to make ends meet.

'I just need to get these delivered,' Hakki said, 'then I was going up to me sister in Cullivoe for a drop o' soup and a bannock. I can easy pick you up at the leisure centre on my way past. It'll save you walking the widows' road.'

'That's very kind of you. Thanks.'

'When do you think you'll be finished?'

'Twelve thirty-five.' I thought about getting to my boat sooner and getting an afternoon's sleep. 'This is awful good o' you.'

'No bother, lass. I'll see you at the back o' half twelve outside the leisure centre.' He stood up, hefted up his box again and dumped it into the back of a pick-up parked at the end of the road. 'Can I give you a lift somewye?'

I shook my head. 'No, thanks. I've got time to kill.'

He raised a hand and drove off. I sauntered after him. His talk of widows and lairds, lost boats and corporations had put an unpleasant thought into my mind. Ewan had been determined to pursue Antony for the damage to his *Day Dawn*. I remembered Antony speaking to me on Up Helly Aa morning. He'd half-convinced me then that he was setting only his fair quota of creels, but no honest man would be out working in the dark, as he'd been on Saturday night, when the whole of Brae was at the Hop. That put him back in the frame for sinking *Day Dawn*. If the police found any evidence that it had been Antony who'd sunk her, to stop Ewan checking up on his fishing activities, then Ewan's insurance would follow that up. I couldn't imagine Ewan coming down on Jesma for the price of his boat, but the insurance people wouldn't care. If Jesma had inherited Antony's assets, or his debts, this one would be included in her burden.

Of course, I knew nothing about business. Maybe the boat had been a limited company, and its debts wouldn't touch Jesma, but I wasn't sure that would help her, because if Antony had sunk *Day Dawn*, that would be a personal debt. Someone in the Citizen's Advice Bureau would know, if they had all the facts.

I was striding along the road and mulling all that over when I heard a cheery voice say, 'Aye aye, Cass!'

I stopped and looked. It was Dodie, who'd been at school with me. His ambition then had been to be a ferryman on the Yell ferry, and as soon as he'd left school he'd applied, and got a job as junior under-deckhand. He'd been there ever since, with the occasional posting to the Unst or Papa Stour ferry, and he was completely contented. He was also just the man I wanted. 'Aye aye,' I replied.

He leaned against his car and prepared to speak. 'What're you up to in Yell?'

I made a face. 'Driving theory test. How're you doing?'

'Oh, I'm good. The tourists are starting to appear now, livens things up a bit.'

It was the opening I wanted. 'You didn't notice ones in a fawn Star rental, that came up on Thursday probably?'

'The ghost-hunters that went to Windhouse,' he said promptly. The ferrymen's spy system was every bit as good as the retired fishermen's, between folk on board and relatives ashore who could keep an eye out for where cars went. 'Yea, I mind them fine. They were booked on, so the office would have their registration, if your man wanted it.' He gave me a sharp glance. 'To do with the dead man in Brae, is it?'

I wasn't sure if it was. The tourists were ghost-hunting and knew nothing about the Book of the Black Arts. 'Not the tourists, though Gavin'll want to talk to them, but there was a local car too, a red one with a lass in it.'

'Lizbet,' he said promptly. 'Lizbet o' Upperbrak, came up to see her mum for the night, and went back first thing in the morning on Friday.' He gave me a sideways look. 'Her friend died in Lerwick on Wednesday.'

I nodded.

'She was still right upset about it. I said to her that I was vexed about it, and she had to wait a moment before she answered me. All stressed up, she was, but a night wi' her mam did her good. She looked like herself the next morning.'

She'd got rid of the Book, and it hadn't turned up on her mantelpiece. She thought it was gone for good.

'How about Sunday morning?'

'Sunday?' He thought about that. 'The very early ferry, that had just Joanie-Willie wi' a load of sheep, and a relief crewman for the Unst ferry. On a bicycle, he was. I didna get a right chance to speak wi' him, I was yarning wi' Joanie-Willie, but I wished him luck, cycling up the length o' Yell. There were more on the 08.15. Yea, two tourist cars, and a local black pick-up with a man in it.'

Ertie had seen a black pick-up parked below Windhouse on Sunday morning.

'Did you ken him?'

Dodie shook his head. 'He had a cap well pulled down over his eyes. I couldna tell you hair colour, or what he lookit like, and he was wearing a big bulky jacket that made him look broad-shouldered.'

'High voice, low?'

'Gruff. As if he had a cold, or been singing all night.'

Ewan had been singing all night; as they went round, the Jarl Squad sang their songs. 'Where was he from? Did he say enough for you to tell?'

'Brae or the north mainland,' Dodie said straight off. 'And he wasn't booked on, so the office won't have the registration.'

I hesitated over the next question. 'D'you ken Ewan Pearson, that has the *Day Dawn* in Brae?'

I could see he knew why I was asking. He nodded. 'I dinna ken him to speak to, but I think I'd ken him to see.' He thought for a moment, and shook his head. 'I dinna think the man in the pick-up was him. The big jacket made it hard to tell, but I think this was a slighter body.'

'When did the pick-up go back again?'

Dodie shook his head. 'Not on any ferry I was working on, but he coulda come back with the other one.' He took his phone from his pocket and had a quick conversation with one of his workmates, that ended with a 'Well, thanks to you' and a shaken head in disgust. 'These young boys, they pay no attention what's going on around them. "Oh," he says, "there might a been. I just didn't notice." What does he think he's there for?' He shook his head, and opened his car door. 'Cass, I'd need to head off, but I hope that's helpet you. Tell your man to phone me if he needs it official. Good luck wi' the test.'

'Thanks,' I said, and waved as he drove off at speed, towards his ferry.

The leisure centre was open now. I got a coffee from the vending machine and found a warm corner where I could drink another coffee and have a last flip through my theory book. I forced everything else out of my mind. I had a test to pass.

I felt a dinosaur as I waited in the foyer watching my fellow examinees arrive. There were seven of us, and the others looked like they'd got out of school for the test. We were gathered up in plenty of time and asked to sign in, then given lockers for our stuff and told to read the Test Rules before we were shown into the Community Room, which was laid out exam-style. I focused on my breathing and squared myself up to the allocated DVSA computer. The screen took us through how the test was answered and gave us a practice, then it was time to start.

It was all fine. Between common sense and searching my memory for the exact colours of motorway slipway lights, I got the fifty questions done in just over half an hour, which gave me plenty of time to go through the answers before going on to the hazard videos. Once that was done, I signed off and went up to the examiner with my driving licence. She nodded and pointed a finger to the door. I retrieved my backpack and went to the entrance desk, as per instructions. The lass there scanned my licence, the computer whirred to itself, then printed out a letter, face down. The lass checked the licence number again against the letter, then handed them both to me, smiling. 'Well done.'

I nodded my thanks, scanned it quickly, then stowed it in my bag. Pass.

There was no sign of Hakki yet, so I spent the waiting time sending off a triumphant text: *Passed! xxx* The answer pinged in straight away: *Of course you did. Now to look out for a car for you. Maybe a little runabout that'll go miles on a thimbleful of fuel? xxx xxx*

I smiled at that and retorted, *Will it have room for sails in the boot?*

Jim's Garage, where Amy's Irvine worked, sold second-hand cars.

Hakki's black pick-up pulled to a halt beside me just as I was musing on ways to find out what Irvine had really felt about

Chloe's reappearance in his life. Hakki leaned over and swung the door open. 'Well, how did you do?'

'Passed.' I climbed in and set my bag at my feet.

'No fear o' you,' Hakki said. 'Now, Annie, that's my sister, she said to be sure and ask you if you wanted to come up for some soup and bannocks. You're very welcome.'

'That's very kind.' I hesitated. 'I'll no' be able to stay long, though, for I'd need to sleep all afternoon if I'm setting off at midnight. I don't want to just eat and leave.'

'Na, na, lass, never worry about that, and as to this afternoon, well, Annie has her reading group, so she'll want to be off about ten to two.'

'Oh, in that case, yes, please.'

Being a native, he shaved three minutes off Gavin's time from Mid Yell, and drew up in front of a new-build kit house at the edge of Cullivoe. 'Annie and her late husband had a croft as well as the fishing,' he said, handing me out, 'and their son's keen on the animals as well, so when her man died, Annie handed the croft over to young Peter and built this house instead.'

It was a wooden bungalow, shipped over in kit form from Norway, assembled on site, and most beautifully warm inside. I copied Hakki in taking off my shoes, and felt the heat coming up from under the tiled floor. 'The tiles are recycled glass,' Hakki said, watching me wriggle my toes on it. 'Great stuff for insulation, glass, it stores heat. It's all insulated within an inch of its life, and there's a geothermal heat pump at the end of the garden and a wind turbine up the hill a piece. There's still a Rayburn but it's gas, and a closed stove in the sitting room.'

'I wasn't giving up my Rayburn,' his sister said, bustling through. 'But, oh, it's the fine to be free o the tyranny o' ash out, peats in and constant tending. Come in, Cass, I'm blyde to meet you. Magnie comes up every so often to yarn wi' Hakki, and he aye calls in on me and tells us what you're up to.'

He would. 'This is very kind of you,' I said. 'And Hakki said you have a reading group at two, so just you rise up and go when you need to, and I'll follow.'

'If that's fine with you, I can drop you off at the pier as I pass. The bathroom's just there, then come and sit down.'

The soup was best tattie soup, thick enough to stand a spoon up in, and the bannocks were fresh-baked, still cooling in their clean tea-towel. 'And our son that took over the croft is keen on kye, so we have our own butter too,' Annie said, handing me over a pat of the yellowest butter I'd ever seen. I balanced my Lenten conscience against the rudeness of a refusal, and spread it as sparingly as I could on the still-warm bannocks.

'And with your man being in the police, you'll have heard the news from Brae,' Annie said, once we were all settled.

'Only that a man had died,' I said cautiously.

It was enough to get all the latest news. Antony had rented a cottage along the Muckle Roe road that led to my house, and his nearest neighbour was a woman that I remembered as old in my childhood, and the most observant battleaxe that ever kept a spyglass on her windowsill. Inga and I steered well clear of her, for she was liable to get on the phone to our parents at the least little thing she felt we shouldn't be doing, usually to Inga's parents, as my dad was at work all day, and Maman insisted she didn't understand a word Baabie said to her.

'Well,' Annie said, 'Baabie kent his comings and goings, and she saw his boat coming in the voe and into the marina about half past ten, as she was getting ready for the kirk. Then, when she came home, there was a black pick-up sitting beside his fancy van outside the door. She kent he'd been out all night, so she thought he'd not be best pleased to be bothered, especially if it was Ewan's pick-up, for she kent fine there was bad blood between them. She thanked the folk who give her a lift, and went in to take her coat and hat off, and when she looked out again the pick-up was gone.'

'What sort of time was this now?' I asked.

'The service was at eleven, and then there was tea and biscuits and chat after it, so that would be, oh, past twelve. Say quarter past. After that she had her lunch, and watched *Songs of Praise*, then she went for her after-lunch nap and a read of her book, and when she got up again, she noticed the house was still dark.'

'It would still be light then,' I said. 'Four, five o'clock?'

'Four thirty-five. Light enough for most folk,' Annie agreed, 'but she thought that was odd, for normally he was a lights-blazer, with everything in the house blaring out all day, let alone when it was starting to get dark. His van was there and he wasn't much of a walker. On the other hand, he had been up all night, and he might just be sleeping that off. But when another car that it was too dim to see pulled up and then went away again, still with no lights going on inside, she began to be concerned, and in the end she went over. She opened the door and called out, and then when she switched on the light she found him lying there on the floor, and that gave her such a shock it's a wonder she didn't have a heart attack on the spot. Like there'd been a fight, she said, lying on his back with the front of his shirt all rumpled, and a pool of blood on the floor under his head, and his hand cold as ice. So she called the police, and that blonde Sergeant came with another lass with her. The younger lass stayed put, radioing for backup, and the blonde wife helped Baabie back to her house and made her a cup of tea, and called another neighbour to sit with her for a bit. Once the neighbour arrived then the police wife went back to the house, and by then there were half a dozen police cars sitting there, and blue flashing lights, and all sorts of comings and goings. Forensics like they have on CSI – but you'll ken all about that.'

I hastily disclaimed any knowledge of forensics. Annie looked disappointed, but rallied with her big news.

'But what Baabie told Magnie, and he told me, was that the house looked like there'd been a burglary. Kitchen drawers pulled out and not quite closed right, and Friday's paper lying on the floor, as if it had been thrown off a chair, and the shelf of recipe books higgledy-piggledy on the worktop.'

Books. Antony had dug up the Book of the Black Arts in Windhouse, and taken it back to Brae, all pleased with himself, but someone else had known it was there, and gone to take it; had killed him for it.

Chapter Nineteen

Hit's late ta cry 'Halt!' whin da skjoag is broken.
*(It's late to shout 'Stop!' when the iron ring assembly that holds
the nylon line and hooks of the fishing line is broken.)*
It's too late.

I got back to the boat just before two. I had an uneasy feeling
about the Book of the Black Arts being loose again, and felt I
should warn Lizbet about it. I didn't know her phone number,
though of course Magnie would, or her address at least, but she
worked to the SIC, Tom had said, so I could just phone their
switchboard and ask for her.

The lass on duty said, 'Lizbet? Yea, no bother,' and put me
through straight away. It seemed to ring on her desk, for she
picked it up on the second ring: 'Community Planning and
Development, can I help you?'

'Is that Lizbet?'

'Yea, who'm I speaking to?'

'It's Cass here, from Brae.' I didn't know how busy her office
was. 'Are you able to speak just now? I mean, are you on your
own?'

'Yea, Candy, the other lass in this office, she's on her lunch
break. She'll be back in five minutes though.'

'I'll keep it quick. I just wanted to let you ken that the Book's
been dug up.'

Her voice rose to a startled squeak. 'Dug up?'

'Yea. We were in Windhouse, and there were footprints and

223

loose earth around, and where it had been hidden under the door, well, there was only a dent in the earth where it had been.'

'But –' she said, then stopped and drew a long breath. When she spoke again, her voice was firmer. 'If someone else has got it, let them have it, whether they stick it behind a glass case or ill-wish their whole neighbourhood. I never want to see the thing again, or think about it either.' Her voice rose on the last words, and I reckoned that was as far as I could push her on that one.

'Fair enough,' I said. 'I just wanted to let you ken.'

I was about to say goodbye when she cut in. 'Cass, I was wondering – see, I had a visit from that blonde police officer. The one that makes you wonder how tidy your hair is. She was asking . . .' She paused. When she spoke again her voice was incredulous. 'She said that they'd had the forensics report back, and Chloe had been drugged. Some sort of sleeping pill.'

I wasn't sure what to say. Officially, of course, I didn't know this. 'A sleeping pill?' I echoed.

'That was why she stumbled going along the street, and hung on to Irvine's arm. She was literally sleepwalking. Someone – someone put a sleeping pill in her drink.' She hesitated, then added, in a lower voice, 'It wasn't me. Not the Book, I mean. It's just an old book, and finders keepers. It was someone who had it in for Chloe.'

It was too good an opening to waste. 'Lizbet, I was wondering, did you ken the folk that you met at The Dowry's that day? Irvine and Amy?'

'No. We were the Brae school, and they were Lerwick, so not really. Well, I'd likely have seen Amy at the netball or the hockey back in secondary, but no' to remember her. I kent Irvine, from him going out wi' Chloe, but no' very well either, because Tom and I were mostly at gigs, and Chloe was a club-ber, so I just met him in passing with her. I heard all about him, o' course. Chloe could talk o' nobody else while the fit lasted.'

'That's a funny way of putting it.'

Lizbet caught herself up. 'It's no' a very nice way o' putting it. I'm sorry. I just thought even then that she was dead keen on him but they were ill-suited and it was more that she was in love with love than with him.' She echoed Amy's words. 'She was all wedding dresses and a new house before she even knew him that well. And, yeah, he shouldna have dumped her the way he did, but I think he'd taken fright and wanted out. And Chloe went to pieces more than she needed to, and then once she started pulling herself together, that seemed aimed more at showing him than doing it for herself. So when we walked into The Dowry and they were there I wasn't best pleased, and when Chloe made a bee-line for Irvine I just felt there would be trouble. He and his new girlfriend were having a quiet meal together, and the last thing he needed was his old girlfriend turning up as a dazzling blonde. She was all, "Oh it's been ages" and "You're looking well, I like the new haircut" and "I hear you're the right-hand man at the garage these days", and I could see his girlfriend didn't like it at all.'

She thought a moment, called, 'I'm busy, be through soon,' to someone, and added, 'And then Antony's wife turning up didn't help either.'

I felt a cold shock. Antony's wife turning up?

Her voice had faltered as she said his name. 'The policeman wife didn't say, but it was the first thing I heard at work this morning. He's dead too. Him and Chloe. And I wondered, the two of them together, maybe . . .' She stopped and then came out with it. 'I wondered if his wife might have something to do with it.'

'Jesma?'

'Is that what she's called? Yeah, she came in, oh, just after we'd arrived, to talk to Antony. She'd spotted us through the window, she said, and she just wanted to check when Antony might be free at the weekend to take the kids.' She gave a half-laugh. 'Well, maybe, but I thought myself she was queering

Chloe's pitch, reminding him he had a wife and kids. She came in straight after we'd ordered, and stood between them, though his other side was nearer the door she came in. And I think Antony was fed up with Chloe having been all over Irvine, because he was matey with her, and invited her to join us for the meal, and Chloe flounced off to the toilet, and the wife, Jesma, sat down in her seat.'

In prime position for doctoring her drink. I was certain nobody had mentioned this. The observant waiter must have been sorting out their order, and Jesma hadn't been with them when Chloe fell. 'But she didn't join you for the meal?'

'No. She just sat down for a moment and they talked times. He was to have them all day Saturday, and put them back after they'd had their tea, then again on Sunday after they got back from their football and swimming. Then she left.'

I was processing this. 'What did Chloe say to that, when she came back to the table?'

'Focused harder on Irvine, I think – but I was kinda fed up of her. Her faffing around over "Darling, what a surprise to see you" had made us a bit late, and I had to get along to the Peerie Shop before I came back here, so I got on with eating my burger, and talked to Tom a bit, and ignored them all.'

'If someone put a sleeping pill in Chloe's drink,' I said, 'who d'you think it was?'

There was so long a silence that I thought we'd got cut off. Then she said slowly, 'Sleeping pills are a wife kinda thing, aren't they? I don't see Irvine going to a doctor and saying he couldn't sleep, and he didn't look like someone with sleep problems. His girlfriend didn't look the sleeping-pills type either. Clear eyes and a bonny complexion, and not a care in the world. Whereas Antony's wife –' She stopped, then continued. 'She had dark circles under her eyes, and she looked tired to death. I remember thinking it was a bad idea for her to sit where Chloe had been, unless she was going for making him feel guilty about how much work he was dumping her with, looking after the kids on her own. She was older than us too, more like your age? So she might be more likely to go to the doctor for sleeping pills.'

'She was in my class at school,' I agreed.

There was a shocked silence. 'I didn't realise you kent her. Look, I really have to go. I'll likely see you around at Brae. Bye.' She laid the phone down in a hurry.

She'd made it obvious who her suspicions were focused on. Jesma, to get rid of her younger, prettier rival; to get her husband back.

Nobody had spoken about Jesma being there at The Dowry. I needed to tell Gavin. I glanced at the clock. He'd be at work now. I made a face and called him. 'How's it going?'

'Busy.'

'I won't speak, then. Anyway I got all the gen from the folk I had lunch with, the sister of another of Magnie's cronies. She knows Baabie, the woman who discovered the body. She said the house looked like it had been searched. Books particularly.'

'Maybe,' Gavin said cautiously, as if he was being overheard. 'Are you going to sleep now? Call me when you set off, will you?'

'I will,' I agreed. 'Just one thing . . . I spoke to Lizbet on the phone ee now, and she said that Jesma had been there at The Dowry. She dropped in to talk about the kids over the weekend and sat in Chloe's seat while she was at the toilet.'

'Oh?' Gavin said. 'No, that's not been mentioned. I'll pass it on to Freya. She's spoken to Jesma already. She had to break the news.'

I couldn't ask how she'd taken it. 'Speak to you later,' I said, and rang off.

The moon had already risen when my alarm sounded at half past ten. I dressed warmly and spent the next hour getting ready to go: a flask of hot water wedged in the sink, along with the tub of bannocks Annie had given me for the journey and a couple of bacon and egg rolls wrapped in tinfoil and buried under my pillow for later. Cat watched with interest as I got everything stowed for sea, then he and the Kitten retreated into my berth while I went up on deck to take the cover off the mainsail and get it prepared for hoisting once we were round the corner. It wasn't, they made it clear, a night for cats to be on deck. The wind was still from the north, but with a touch of easterly in it now, and colder with the extra strength. For the first stage, getting out of Bluemull Sound, I'd be motoring into it.

I left as early as I dared, pulling the lines aboard and chugging away from the pier at quarter past eleven, but when I got to the end of the headland I saw I'd been too precipitate, for the tide racing up was fighting the tide coming down in a series of overfalls, jostling standing waves with sharp white peaks. I backed *Khalida* up, and we lay ahull in the shelter of the entrance until they'd subsided enough for me to edge her nose out. We bumped over the last of them and headed north.

Gavin would be in bed by now, but I'd said I'd ring. I put a reef in the mainsail but rolled the full jib out, and set the autopilot to steer towards my first waypoint, just off Gloup Holm, then got my phone out. He answered on the second ring. '*Halo leat.* Are you on your way?'

'Just heading towards the top of Yell. The signal may cut out at any moment.'

'It's very quiet here without you and the cats.'

'We'll be with you tomorrow. Just quickly, I met up with Dodie, who works on the Yell ferry. The rented car at Windhouse on Thursday was tourists, and the booking office has their registration, the red one was Lizbet, and there was a black pickup on Sunday morning, driver unknown.' I glanced at the signal. Still good. 'How's your day been?'

'Busy. We got the post-mortem results for Chloe, and we're definitely treating it as a suspicious death. She had an excess of melatonin in her bloodstream – it's the active ingredient of various common over-the-counter medications. Frequent flyers buy it for jet lag. The medical version of it's called Circadin, and it's also given to insomniac people with various disorders, and the over fifty-fives. The forensics professor wants to run more tests, but so long as I don't quote him, he's pretty sure that's what it was.'

'Jet-lag medication.' I'd never even heard of it; jet lag didn't affect people travelling by sailing ship. 'Does it come in liquid or pills?'

'Both. On sale everywhere in Lerwick, and the officer I sent round the chemists said a good few people had bought it recently, with the Easter holidays coming up, people not wanting to waste any time of their sunshine break with jet lag. The one in Boots recognised Jesma's and Lizbet's photos, but didn't think either of them had bought that kind of thing, and she was sure Chloe hadn't.' He sighed. 'Never easy, is it?'

'I didn't know you could get jet-lag pills. So the people who have access to medication, like Amy and Jesma, that's not really relevant.'

'Only that if they were intending to use strong sleeping pills for harm, they could get them without risking their faces being recognised by a chemist. Freya's re-interviewed most of them – she didn't manage to get Amy, of course, nor Antony, obviously – and nobody remembered seeing anyone interfere with Chloe's glass, or put anything in their own glass.'

'Then swap the glasses, you mean? What were they all drinking?'

'As far as Lizbet and Tom could remember, what they usually did. Lizbet had orange juice because she felt a cold coming on, Tom, Chloe and Antony had lemon San Pellegrino. Irvine said he and Amy both had sparkling water. The till receipt agrees.'

'Lizbet couldn't have swapped her glass for Chloe's, but the others would look fairly interchangeable.' I thought about that.

'Is there much difference in taste between the lemon stuff and sparkling water?'

'Enough to notice, I'd have thought.'

'The taste of the food might mask it.'

Gavin looked dubious. 'Maybe. Lizbet and Amy were the ones who would have found it hardest to do it. Lizbet was diagonally across from Chloe on a rectangular table, and Amy was on the opposite side of their table, so her reaching across would have been obvious. Tom was opposite Chloe, and Antony beside her, with Jesma between them for that short conversation – she was mentioned in the second interview, once Freya focused on the meal. Neither Lizbet nor Tom knew her name, but they knew who she must be.'

'Fighting back, Lizbet reckoned. Reminding Antony about his bairns.'

'Irvine vaguely noticed her, but he was bemused by Chloe. He was on Chloe's other side, but he was at another table, so he'd have had to reach across, and of course Amy was watching him like a hawk.' He paused. 'Freya asked them about jet-lag knock-out drops. Lizbet and Tom both said they'd never heard of them, but neither of them have travelled further than a festival in the north of England. Antony's done a bit of jetting around. He said he'd heard of them but never tried them. Amy and Irvine went on a holiday to New York, and Amy tried them, so Irvine knew about them from that.'

He was beginning to sound as if he was talking to me underwater. 'You're starting to break up. Just quickly, how about Antony?'

'He fell . . . pushed and hit his head . . . worktop.' We were going to lose the signal at any minute. '. . . pathologist . . . unconscious straight away . . . ambulance . . . saved.'

The phone went dead. I glared at it. So much for modern communications. I checked my heading and tried to fill in the blanks. *He fell or was pushed and hit his head on the worktop. The pathologist said he was unconscious straight away, but if someone had called an ambulance he could have been saved.*

Chloe. Antony.

It was a long night. I'd written a list of the timings coming up and reversed them, and as *Khalida* forged on through the cold night, sliding over the backs of the waves, I ticked them off one by one: 11.15 at the end of Bluemull Sound. First bacon and egg roll. 02.00 at the Bagi Stacks, and changing course towards my second waypoint, off Eshaness, six hours away. The cats remained below, curled up; I kept myself awake by moving about, keeping the log, doing a bit of cleaning. I passed the Ramna Stacks at 03.45 (second bacon and egg roll, still faintly warm), and the Uyea Baas at 04.30; there was the first flush of light in the sky behind us as we passed the Faither at 05.45, and it was almost full daylight to see the holes in Muckle Ossa at 06.15. I was on the homeward stretch now, a direct line across St Magnus Bay with the wind behind us and the mainsail full out, which felt like dawdling but was warmer than the wind blowing on my cheeks. The clipped penny of moon to the west paled as the light strengthened. By 08.00 I was almost at Vementry. Cat appeared on deck, yawning and looking around as if he knew we were almost home. I fed the pair of them and took my helm back in my hand. I wasn't going to leave *Khalida* at the Ladie pier with the wind that was expected. I'd take her to her own berth in Brae, and trust Magnie to make it right about my illegal mast.

I stowed the sails outside the marina, then putted into my space. There was no sign of anyone about. I tied *Khalida* up, closed the washboards as a 'Do not disturb' sign, crawled into my bunk and slept.

Chapter Twenty

Tuesday 21st March

Tide times, Brae
LW 01.12 (0.46m);
HW 07.03 (2.16m);
LW 12.50 (0.39m);
HW 18.41 (1.96m)

Moonset 06.59; sunrise 07.01; moonrise 23.20;
sunset 19.21. Moon waxing gibbous.

Hit's aesy ta see he's stöd i da Waster.
(It's easy to see that he's stood out in a westerly gale.)
It is easy to see he has come through hardships and stress.

I slept solidly for three hours and woke at lunchtime. I found
a still-in-date tin of meatballs, and ate them sitting in the
cockpit, then decided that since I had time to kill before the
end of Gavin's day I'd go along and get the latest news from
Inga.

Inga had been my best friend since our schooldays. We'd
shared transport to mother and toddlers, nursery, primary
school, secondary. I'd gone to Maman in France aged fifteen,
run away on a tall ship and sailed the world; she'd married her
first boyfriend and now lived opposite Brae School. Her two
daughters, Vaila and Dawn, were both in secondary, and Peerie

Charlie was four, and in the nursery, giving Inga even more time to get involved in local organisations.

Their house was Charlie's family home, an eighties build in the centre of Brae, below Brae Garage, where Inga had had a Saturday job, and with a big picture window looking out over the water. Charlie's late father used to watch the regattas from there, once he wasn't able to be out on the water himself. There'd always be one buoy of the race which was below the house, so we'd hear him shouting encouragement as we rounded it, and later, in the club, he'd give us a tack-by-tack account of what we should have done. Charlie was a fisherman, with shares in one of the isles' pelagic boats, and his own whitefish boat for when he wasn't at sea on the big one.

I was almost at the house when I realised Inga had visitors: there was a car standing in front of the door beside Inga's little red runabout and Charlie's pick-up. It looked very like the car Jesma had run me home in. I was hesitating, feeling awkward, when there was a shout of 'Cass!' from the wooden fort in the garden (built from scratch out of pallets by Inga's Charlie in one of his sheds, and hastily assembled in the garden during the night before Christmas). Peerie Charlie scrambled down the ladder and came running towards me, blond curls flying. I picked him up and swung him round. 'You're getting heavier.'

'I'm growing. I'm the tallest boy in the nursery.'

'Isn't it nursery time now? I hope you're not skiving off.'

He gave me a withering look. 'I'm a morning nursery boy. Are you coming to play in my fort?'

'Ten minutes,' I agreed, and was instantly marshalled into being the crew of Pirate Captain Peerie Charlie, terror of the seven seas, repelling dangerous mauraders from the Black Skeleton Army. We'd fought them off and were making our captives walk the plank when the house door opened and Inga came out.

'You're winding him up again.'

'He's winding me up,' I said, rather breathlessly, for it had been a serious fight against heavy odds, with a lot of desperate swordplay and several deaths, all by me, as I was playing the skeleton army for him to vanquish as well as his trusty crew to cheer when he won.

'Kettle's on.' Inga gave Charlie a look. 'There'll be millionaire's shortbread for pirate captains with clean hands.'

'Millionaire's shortbread!' Charlie leapt groundwards, and headed for the house with a whoop of glee. I followed more sedately. As if doling out KitKats to everyone else wasn't bad enough, having to refuse Inga's millionaire's shortbread was a Lenten penance all on its own.

I had been right; it was Jesma's car. She was sitting at Inga's table with a roog of papers in front of her. As I came in she rose and moved to the couch.

I sat down opposite her, looked straight at her and forced the words to come. 'I heard your news. I'm sorry.'

There was no need to say *How are you doing?* I could see it had hit her hard. *Weel tells the hair what the hert has to bear*, Magnie would say. Her face was reddened, her eyelids puffy, and her hands trembled as she sat down and laid them in her lap. Her voice was hoarse. 'Thanks, Cass. I don't think I believe it yet. The police came and told me, the day before yesterday, when they found him, and it just sounded so unlikely. Then your man came and talked to me, yesterday, and I had to go and do a formal identification.' Her voice shook; her eyes filled with tears. 'He didn't look like Antony. So still . . . Antony was always full of life.'

'How are the bairns doing?'

She shook her head, and the tears spilled over. 'I kept them home yesterday, but they're at school today. I thought they'd be better with their pals . . .'

'And so they will,' Inga said firmly. She pressed a mug of tea into Jesma's hands. 'They'll have their everyday routine to divert them a little. They may not do much actual work but they'll have their pals around them to support them.'

234

Jesma drank some of the tea and set the mug down, then picked it up again, cradling it as if she was cold. Her head tilted in a listening position as Inga gave me the third degree about where I'd been off to over the weekend, but her eyes were blank, as if she'd switched off and retreated to a world of her own.

Inga noticed that too, and brought her smoothly into the conversation. 'Do you have family on Yell, Jesma, or am I remembering wrong?'

Jesma started, looked round at us and set her mug down. 'Yea, but oh, four generations back. Me great-great-granny came from Yell, after the Gloup disaster, to bide wi' her sister, who'd married a Brae man.' Her face clouded. 'She lost both her man and her eldest son. I should be grateful . . .' Her head turned towards the front door, towards the school where her children were. She gave a long sigh, then visibly pulled herself together, sitting up straight and taking another drink of her tea. 'Did I see millionaire's shortbread on the go?'

'Here.' Inga passed her the plate. 'Take two bits. The Easter eggs are in the shops, so it's Cass's no-chocolate time of year. She was aye awkward.'

I didn't bother to rise to that.

Jesma took one, and gestured towards the papers on the table. 'Income Support forms. I asked Inga to give me a hand sorting them out.' She shrugged. 'But maybe I'll no' need them after all. Or maybe I'll need them more. Goodness knows what Antony'll have left me. Riches or debts. He was a great one for getting rich quick.' She looked at me, then at Inga. 'You're lucky, the pair of you. Your men have steady incomes, and they're contented. Antony always wanted more, and he never understood . . .' Her eyes filled with tears again. She said passionately, 'He could never see that there's no get rich quick. He'd have all these schemes, all this enthusiasm, and when we met I believed in them, I believed in him, but he was just a dreamer. To make dreams come true you need more than vision and energy. You need to be willing to put in the solid work behind them.' She sniffed and drew her hand across her eyes. 'I thought that he'd settle down once the bairns were born, but they made him worse than ever. I just wanted a nice house, and decent clothes for them. I wanted them to be well fed, and happy at school. He wanted the moon.' She shook her head. 'It's all different in England, you have no idea how different. Up here, the folk we were at school wi', well, just look at us all. Just from our class, there's Brian Georgeson became a university professor at Cambridge, and Richard Leask's the CEO of a Norwegian oil firm.'

'Kerry,' Inga said. 'She's a hot-shot lawyer in London.'

'Norman,' I said. 'International fiddle player.'

'Yeah.' Jesma's eyes were brighter now. 'And the ones who stayed home, well, Peter started up that farm shop and café, and Rhona's a staff nurse at the hospital.'

'Davie and Megan are both teachers,' Inga said. 'Brae and Mid Yell.'

'And Dodie got a job on the Yell ferry,' I said. We all smiled, remembering his determination in school whenever future ambition was mentioned.

'But why no'?' Jesma said. 'He's happy. It's what he always wanted to do and he's happy doing it. Isn't that the most important thing? He greets the passengers with a cheery smile and chats as he takes their money, and he goes home feeling he's had a good day. Why should he be shoved into some supposedly more prestigious job where, okay, he might earn more, but he wouldn't be happy?'

We nodded in agreement. 'The ferry pay's probably quite good,' I added. 'It's a skilled job.'

'And here in Shetland,' Jesma said, 'folk get the chance of a good education, and they can take it where they like. There's a hole to fit every shape of peg, and nobody thinks the worse of you if you don't want to fly high.' She sighed. 'It's not like that in England. You have to get on. You have to push your kids, start them reading at home at three, and extra tutoring at five, and shift houses to get them into the best nursery you can, and then get them into a private school as soon as you can afford it. I hated it. That was part of why we split up. I wanted to bring them home here. I wanted them to enjoy their schooling the way we did, instead of being pressurised with tests all the time. I wanted them to be twenty in a class, the way we were, instead of thirty in a class and two hundred in a year group, and to be able to go and run outside without needing to be watched.' She smiled. 'D'you mind all the things we used to get up to? It's a wonder we weren't drowned, or lost in a bog, or frozen to death, but somehow we all survived it. We had a lot of fun as bairns, charging around in a group. But Antony wouldn't see it, he wanted them to go to a private school, and spend a fortune on tennis lessons and music lessons and extra coaching for this and that. He said he'd get the money somehow, and then we quarrelled, and split up for a bit, and then, well, he had this girlfriend, and I saw red and came home.'

Her face sobered again. 'And he came after me. He didn't want to lose his kids.' She gave a wry smile. 'I hoped he didn't want to lose me either. And he got the boat and he seemed to be doing well. For once he was working at it.' She glanced around as if she was afraid the taxman would hear. 'He was able to give me money, cash in hand, to pay the rent, or to put towards electricity. I was even thinking . . . because I still loved him, you see.'

She stopped there, rose abruptly and headed for the toilet. We left the words echoing in the silence. Inga rose to gather up the mugs and I sat looking out at the water, across at the marina where my mast rose up above the rock wall. *I still loved him.* I didn't, couldn't believe that Jesma had killed Antony. All she'd wanted was happiness, for them, for the bairns. I sympathised with that. If I had children, that's what I'd want for them. Like

Jesma, I'd want them to have the country upbringing we'd had, where they ran free on the beaches and climbed the hills in a cheerful, muddy gang, and played pirates in the garden. I'd want them to grow up to do a job they loved, not caring about getting rich, so long as they had enough for necessities.

Gavin was offering me happiness, if I could give up the sea for it.

My gaze went back to the papers on the table. Income support. Jesma didn't have enough for necessities, even with Antony's handouts. There was a lined pad with Inga's writing on it, columns of figures and working-out of outgoings against income. Even upside down I could see how discouraging the figures were, though Jesma didn't want a glitzy lifestyle, or designer dresses, or to spend money on the latest device. She wanted a warm house with a waterproof roof. She wanted to be able to put decent food on the table, proper Shetland food, mince and tatties, or roast lamb, and she wanted to afford a whole lamb from the Marts for her freezer, not to spend ridiculous amounts on buying a roast at a time. I'd learned through the years that you could save a lot if you could afford to bulk-buy, which I never could. She wanted her bairns to have decent clothes and shoes, not the cheapest possible which fell apart after five wearings, and to go to any clubs they wanted to, and on the school ski trip. She didn't want them to be child prodigies or world-beating athletes or famous scientists; she wanted them to be safe, and secure, and happy.

The toilet flushed, the washbasin tap ran. Jesma blew her nose and came out. She'd splashed some water on her face, and her mouth was set in a determined line. 'Inga, I can't keep you all afternoon. I don't know what's going to happen next, but I want to put those forms in, because whatever does happen, it'll take them several weeks if not months to decide, and we can't live on air in the meantime.'

She sat herself down at the table.

'I'll leave you to it,' I said, and rose. 'I've a whole leave, Inga, so we'll catch up again sometime.'

'Fine that,' Inga agreed. I raised one hand in a wave, murmured 'See you' at Jesma, and headed off.

I was almost at the end of the garden when Ewan came walking down the road and turned into their drive. He was dressed for mourning visiting, in a dark suit and polished black shoes, and a black cap instead of his usual toorie. When he saw me he halted and took the cap off. His hair had been flattened down with water.

'Aye aye,' I said. I looked at his drawn face. 'I'm sorry about Chloe.'

He gave me a bleak look, and nodded. 'Yea. I canna believe . . . she was aye that full o' life.' He looked over my shoulder at the water and gave a sudden spurt of words. 'She was like you. She loved being out on the water. She came out wi' me on the skiff as soon as we were old enough to be trusted out together. She could handle a boat like she'd been born aboard one. We'd go out after twartree pilticks for the cat, or mackerel to barbecue. And nothing frightened her. I mind one day the wind blew up, and I was a bit faered, because I was supposed to be looking after her, but she just laughed at the waves, with her hair blowing all round her face, and dug her oar in deeper.' He looked at me again. 'Like you, out in your peerie boat in all weathers. If she'd set her heart on something she was determined about it. She wasn't going to let anything stop her.'

He gave a long sigh, then looked over at Jesma's car. 'I was going to call on Jesma, then I saw her car here. I wanted to tell her that *Day Dawn*'s taken no real harm from being sunk.' The cap in his hands twisted awkwardly. 'I was planning to replace the engine anyway, and the electrics were safely out. The salvage bill's no' going to be that big, so I'll pay that myself. I mean, it'll no' be an insurance job. I just wanted to let her ken that.'

What he was trying to say, although he was making it sound nothing at all, was that he'd rather pay some two thousand to Ocean Kinetics and another five for a new engine than have the insurance company come down on Jesma. I looked at him standing there, red with embarrassment at offering a kindness, and thought how very Shetland this was. I was proud to belong here.

'And as well,' he said, talking more easily now, 'there's a net bag of best-quality lobsters hanging under the dinghy pontoon.' Antony's lobsters, from Saturday night. He hesitated. The flaming hatred he'd shown before was gone. His mouth turned down. 'You dinna think how short life is. I was so mad wi' him, taking up wi' Chloe when he had a wife of his own, and I grudged Chloe her fun, going out clubbing, and now they're both gone.'

He was silent for a moment, before he straightened up and spoke clearly again. 'These lobsters, they're Jesma's late man's catch from that night he went out. The Hop night. I thought there might be something, since he'd been out, so I had a look, and there they were. There was nobody about, so I just moved them to by my boat. I was thinking I could maybe sell them for her, and nobody official needing to ken, just cash in hand. Hotels, now, they're aye glad of a lobster or two.'

Lobsters were luxury goods that would fetch a good price. Not only was he relieving Jesma of anxiety over the *Day Dawn*, he was offering her cash money too.

'I think she'll be glad of that,' I said.

'I'll go in then,' he said. He squared his shoulders, and went on down the drive.

I thought about Ewan's generosity as I walked back along the road. My sceptical self wondered if it was suspicious; guilt money. He had a black pick-up. He could have seen Antony coming into the marina and gone up to his house on Sunday to tackle him about *Day Dawn* sinking. The fight they'd started at the Up Helly Aa could have reignited, ending with Antony's death.

I could imagine that, but Ewan wouldn't have killed Chloe, his brave, determined little cousin who'd laughed when the waves got up, and dug her oars in deeper. Never. Unless in some twisted way he was killing, cleansing the woman he thought she'd become, taking up with a married man.

I frowned, and changed direction across the field to the beach, sat down on a rock and contemplated the waves, washing up the pebble shore and trickling back. The sound, the rhythm, was soothing.

I hadn't got to grips with Chloe yet, the main person in all this story. I tried to clear my head and assemble what I knew about her. As a child, she'd been Ewan's fearless little cousin who'd come out in the boat with him. Their mothers were close sisters, and Antony had spoken about her going out with her dad, but I didn't know anything else about her family background. Then I had a gap, because Tom's memories of her as a nuisance who'd wormed her way into the band had to date from when they were all sixteen. He lived here, and Chloe too, but Lizbet had grown up in Yell, so she wouldn't have come to the Brae school until she was in S5. She and Chloe must have palled up then.

I thought about that. Maybe Chloe's friends from through secondary had all left school after their Standard Grades, or maybe she'd been a bit of a loner, that little tomboy who'd loved boats. I knew about that. After Maman had gone back to France to sing I'd thrown myself into sailing. Inga had found another best pal, and I'd sailed even harder to shove the loneliness away. In S5, Chloe had found Lizbet and clung to her. She hadn't been a blonde bombshell then. The makeover had come after the break-up. I tried to imagine what she might have looked like before. A bit like Lizbet, maybe: chunky, mousy-haired, ordinary, with a hunger inside to matter to somebody. Then she'd found a boy she liked, Irvine. She'd thought she'd found her happy-ever-after ending and began dreaming of white dresses, except that he took fright and dumped her.

She fell apart when it ended, Tom had said. Lizbet had been there for her, helped her pull herself together and persuaded Tom to let her into the band. Chloe made herself over and wanted a chance to be somebody in this new sphere: '*Can I sing this song, Tom?*' Lizbet would have let her, but Tom held out against her.

Then Antony had come along, and she'd gone overboard for him. I thought about that, and wasn't convinced. She'd talked about him all the time, Tom had said, and I'd seen that big show of slushiness on the pontoon, but if she'd really felt they were a serious couple, she'd have stayed focused on that, returned to her need to matter to somebody. Maybe she'd thought at first it might work out, but realised that Antony wanted Jesma and the bairns more than he wanted her.

Then *You're the Stars!* came up, and she switched back to her chance to be somebody. Lizbet and Tom cared about the music more than the fame. For Chloe the music was only the route: *singing dreadful, presence turned up to eleven*. She schmoozed the producers, and it worked. I imagined her coming out of the audition glowing with triumph, and insisting they all had lunch in Lerwick to celebrate. She'd been high as a kite in The Dowry, showing off for Irvine's benefit, ignoring Antony and Jesma, when she came in. She was a gorgeous blonde who was going to appear on the telly. How could Irvine resist her now? Especially if this interloper girlfriend was going away for a fortnight, giving her a free run. Maybe she genuinely still loved him, maybe she wanted to whistle him back so that she could dump him as he'd dumped her. I couldn't answer that. Whichever, her triumph angered someone enough to put that drug in her drink. She clung on to Irvine's arm all the way along the street, then fell to her death.

If I'd got this scenario right, it exonerated Jesma. Yes, she'd turned Antony down in anger, and maybe he'd taken up with Chloe to make her jealous, or, more likely, I thought cynically, because a blonde bombshell was too good an offer to resist, but he and Jesma had been married for years. They knew each other. He hadn't taken her rejection as final. I'd seen that at Up Helly Aa, where he'd persuaded her to dance with him. She was unquestionably devastated by his death.

Furthermore, there was no reason for Jesma to have searched Antony's house. She didn't know about the Book of the Black Arts – unless Antony had told her about it, when they'd been chatting so amicably at Up Helly Aa. I frowned, and paused to lean against the fence, looking out over the water. No, that wouldn't work. I hadn't thought this through. I was certain Lizbet wouldn't have talked about the Book to anyone, not after Chloe's death. The only way Antony could have learned about it was during that night. He'd been there when the dealer bloke was trying to smarm it out of her. He could have put two and two together, and made four . . . but then, how would he know where to find it? I tried to revisualise the evening in my mind. The bloke trying to be persuasive, and Lizbet saying she didn't know what he was talking about, and storming out. The bloke had tried to persuade Tom, and Tom had taken his card, but shaken his head. *If Lizbet says no, she means it.* Then he'd gone out after Lizbet. After that the Jarl Squad had come in, and Antony had left, to avoid Ewan, and the next I'd seen of him was down on the hard standing, fighting Ewan with Lizbet and Tom watching.

No. I'd got it mixed up. Antony had been sitting with Jesma, right enough, but the Jarl Squad had come in before the dealer bloke had talked to Lizbet, because she'd been dancing with Ewan just before. Antony had been outside during all that conversation.

I tried to put myself in Antony's place. He'd calmed down, he was talking to Jesma and the bairns, then Ewan had come in, reminding him he was being blamed for sinking the *Day Dawn*. He was still angry about that, and he went out to keep out of the way of trouble. He was standing outside the club, looking at the moon and breathing deeply, when Lizbet came out, visibly upset. He might have talked to her, but presumably he didn't really know her, except as Chloe's friend. He'd be more likely to move deeper into the shadows and leave her be. That was where he'd been when Ewan had spotted him. Then Tom came after Lizbet. He'd have asked what on earth this was all about – what was this valuable book this dealer thought she had? I remembered what she'd said to me: *I've put it where the Devil can stretch out his hand and take it, if he wants it. I've done with it.* Maybe she'd mentioned Windhouse, probably not, but Tom might have said something like 'In Yell?', or mentioned her driving up to Yell the day before, or maybe just knowing she was from Yell, if Chloe had mentioned that to Antony, was enough to make Windhouse the obvious place to start, and as soon as possible, before she thought better of the dealer's offer.

Another piece of the jigsaw clicked into place in my head. The next night had been Hop Night. Antony had taken advantage of it to get his creels in without Ewan watching him, because Ewan would have been with the Jarl Squad all night, going round the dances. But Lizbet was also busy; she and Tom were on stage here at the boating club. Antony could pick up his lobsters then go on to Mid Yell and retrieve the Book from Windhouse, and still be home by mid-morning, with nobody any wiser.

That just left one question: who else knew about the Book, to kill him and search for it? Magnie had known about it too. He'd warned me against it. I pushed myself off the fence and took out my phone. Once we'd gone through my two journeys (he already knew I'd passed the test), I asked him straight out, 'Magnie, how did you ken about the Book of the Black Arts?'

'It's a well-kent story,' he said. 'There's something about it in the archives. Well, the Book was well kent, but likely no' about the minister burying it. I kent that because o' my grandmother, she'd have been a cousin once removed to Lizbet's great-grandmother. The full story was kent through the family, though no' the exact spot where the Book was buried. But we'd none o' us have thought of meddling with it.'

I'd learned today that Jesma had Yell ancestors. She too could have known about the Book of the Black Arts. She could have guessed the kind of price the smooth bookseller was offering for it, money that would heat her house and mend her car, give her and the bairns financial security that didn't depend on Antony's get-rich-quick schemes. I shook my head at that one. She genuinely wanted Antony back, I was sure of that.

Perhaps it was the other way round: maybe, instead of wanting the Book, she most definitely didn't want it. Maybe Antony had shown it to her, and she'd told him to put it back right now, and never meddle with it more, no matter how much it was worth. He'd refused, and she'd tried to grab it from him, and he'd slipped and fallen, hit his head on the worktop. She'd panicked and run for it –

No. Jesma would never have left Antony to die. She'd have picked him up, put a wet cloth on his head, called the ambulance, had a blazing row with him over it, been reconciled or not. They were too close for her to have left him injured.

Whoever had killed Antony, I didn't believe it was Jesma.

I rose and started back towards the marina. I'd just got to the main road when a dark-clad figure cycled past me, raising one hand. Ewan had got his errand over quickly. He looked diminished in his dark suit, without the neon ferry-crew jacket I was used to.

The thought, the cycle, sparked something in my mind; something someone had said. I tried to catch at the train of thought. A bicycle. Looking less bulky . . . jacket.

It came back: talking to Dodie yesterday morning in Yell. I heard his voice: . . . *a relief crewman for the Unst ferry. On a bicycle, he was. I didna get a right chance to speak wi' him, I was yarning wi' Joanie-Willie, but I wished him luck, cycling up the length o' Yell.* If he'd known who it was, he'd have named him – and given the way ferry crews were assigned as they needed someone, he'd know most of them. He'd taken this man as a relief crewman because of his jacket.

Ewan could have hesitated at the boating-club door, just as I had, and heard the last of Tom and Lizbet's conversation about the Book. Maybe he wasn't as well-off as he looked. A bicycle and a foot passenger left fewer traces than a car. He could have taken the pick-up as far as the ferry terminal, with the bike in the back, and gone aboard, cycled to Windhouse, got the Book and headed back the same way.

My fingers were itching to phone Dodie and run this past him, but I knew I couldn't. Leading the witness, DS Peterson would call it. I needed to tell this to Gavin too.

VI

The deil is aye kind to his ain.
(The Devil is always kind to his own.)
Some folk have unexplained good fortune in circumstances
where the opposite seemed probable, i.e. the Devil's own luck.

Chapter Twenty-one

Dir a hantle ta wite whin onything misförs.
There's usually more than one person to blame when things go wrong.

I hesitated as I passed the Co-op, then went in. It had to be my turn to cook again, and though my general style of cooking depended on how much gas it used, I did know how to do a steak pie. I got the ingredients and some greens to have with it, added some fish for the cats and headed back to the boat, swinging my carrier bag cheerfully. Gavin and I had a whole seven weeks before I was due back on *Sørlandet*. I could try living the life that having children would give me. I'd cook nice meals, and we'd spend evenings together. I could re-explore my own territory here and enjoy my *Khalida* sailing like a dream. Even though last night had been a long, cold slog it had been good being alone at sea. I could take a trip out to Foula, or I could sail right round Shetland for the fun of it, if Gavin would join me wherever I ended up each night.

I paused at the foot of the boating club's gravel drive. There was a police car and a van parked along at the far pontoon gate. Antony's flash boat had been moved from the dinghy pontoon to a marina berth. A solitary police officer stood beside it, and it was rocking as if someone had just gone aboard. Searching it, I supposed. Looking for the missing Book? Cat was in guard position on *Khalida*'s cockpit roof, three boats along, with the Kitten curled up beside him. Both heads were up, watching the goings-on with interest.

Davie and Merran, the caravan folk, were back, sitting on deckchairs in front of their caravan, sheltered from the wind. I greeted them, and paused to chat. 'Now then, fine day in the lee.'

'It is that,' Merran agreed. Her eyes shifted to the officer on the pontoon. 'This is a dreadful thing, this. Found murdered in his own kitchen, they're saying.'

'We saw you come in this morning,' Davie said. 'How did it go? Have a seat and tell us all the news.' He got up from his chair and set it out for me, then reached into the caravan and got another for himself.

'Well,' I said, 'I passed my test, that's the main thing. And I had a great sail up. I went into Cullivoe in the end, and lay up at the pier there.' It was hard to chat naturally when we were all watching Antony's boat. DS Peterson appeared from below, followed by her sidekick, Shona, and paused to talk to the officer waiting on the pontoon.

'And your man got up to join you?'

I nodded. 'We were hoping to go out for a meal, but apparently everything was closed for the winter season.'

'Yea, yea,' Merran agreed, 'there's just not the custom.' Her eyes followed DS Peterson, nodding emphatically at the officer. 'But if you'd hit on an LJ's theme night, you'd a enjoyed that. They hold them maybe once or twice a month in the winter, and they're very popular. They do a curry night, or pizza, or traditional BBQ with sweet potato wedges, and it's all good.'

On the pontoon, DS Peterson cast a look at my boat, held out a hand to Cat, then turned to look around, as if she was expecting to see me somewhere. I lifted a hand, and she nodded and headed along the pontoon towards me. I watched gloomily as she came through the gate and along the curved road. Shona followed her.

'Hello, Cass,' she said. 'We're just trying to establish Antony Leighton's movements on Sunday.' I sensed rather than saw

Davie and Merran exchange a look at that, and felt a tenseness in the air. 'Gavin said you'd seen him.'

She'd said Sunday. There was no need to go into details about lobsters from Saturday night; let Jesma have those. 'He passed me on his way to Yell, just as I was going across Yell Sound. He came roaring up from behind me. That was, oh, about ten past five on Sunday morning. I'd listened to the forecast not long before. Then, just about nine, as I was going into Cullivoe, he met me, coming out of Bluemull Sound again.'

She made a note of it. 'He arrived here just after eleven. But he wasn't in Cullivoe?'

I shook my head. 'He came from further down Bluemull Sound.' I tried to remember my impressions at the time. 'I thought he might be coming from Mid Yell. I can't swear to that, but the noise seemed to come from that direction, rather than from Unst or Fetlar. Isn't there a fancy chart-plotter aboard, with his exact route and the times?'

'We'll be investigating that,' DS Peterson said primly, which I took to mean she didn't know how to work it. 'It's always good to have corroboration. Ten past five in Yell Sound, coming out of Bluemull past Cullivoe at nine. And it was definitely Antony Leighton aboard?'

'It was his boat,' I said cautiously. 'It was too dark to see him in Yell Sound, but I'm pretty certain it was his boat, and it was definitely him as I was going into Cullivoe. He was pleased with himself too,' I added. 'He gave me that kind of jaunty wave that means you're feeling on top of the world.' I glanced across at the boat, and the uniformed officer standing in front of it. 'Are you thinking you might find anything in particular aboard?'

'Just routine, madam,' she replied, best police-officer style. 'Thanks for the information.'

She and Shona headed off, leaving me uncrushed. Davie and Merran exchanged glances again, and there was a long silence, then Merran shifted and took a deep breath. 'She'll likely want to know what he was doing in Mid Yell.' She and Davie exchanged another long look. I couldn't read what they were saying to each other, but in the end they both nodded.

'If we tell you, you can pass it on,' Davie said. 'He'd come up to Mid Yell to look for us.'

I stared at him. He nodded and repeated it. 'Antony was visiting us.'

He leaned forward in his deckchair, forearms on his knees. 'See, we kent nothing about the sunk boat. It was last Monday, in the night, wasn't it? Well, that was the day we went off early to do a big shop in Lerwick, then went home. We had a holiday on the Monday, but I had to get back for my work on Tuesday, and Merran had her spinning session in the afternoon.'

'We're not boaty folk,' Merran added apologetically. 'We were busy getting shopping bags, and bags o' clothes to wash, and getting Scotty into his car harness and into the boot. We got into the car and drove off without so much as a glance at the marina.'

'So,' Davie said, 'we kent nothing about it, and then when we came back on Thursday for the Up Helly Aa, well, the boat was sitting out on the hard.' He tilted his chin towards the *Day Dawn*. 'Just with all the other ones, why would we think anything about it? They come out and in all the time.'

I nodded, and waited for him to go on.

'The first we heard about it was at the Up Helly Aa,' Merran said. 'Someone mentioned that Ewan's boat had sunk.' Her cheery face reddened. 'And we thought it might be an insurance job, and we didn't want to be involved. We decided we'd just keep quiet, as if I'd never woken in the night, and go home on Saturday, as we'd planned, and say nothing to anyone.'

I jerked upright, and the dog lifted its head and growled at me. 'You saw something in the night?'

Merran nodded, but continued telling her story backside foremost. 'We'd enjoyed the procession and the Friday evening, but we're no' as young as we were, so that was plenty. We didn't stay for the Hop night. We went back home on Saturday, and then, on Sunday morning, first thing, while we were making the toast, there was this knock at the door. A kind of apologetic knock, as if the person didn't want to bother us, but hoped we'd be awake.'

'We answered it,' Davie said, 'and it was him that's away, he was standing there. I kinda vaguely kent his face from us coming here, and we'd been sitting at the table wi' him and his wife on Friday night. I thought he'd got the wrong door, but then he asked if we were the folk who stayed in the caravan at the Brae marina, and if he could come in and speak about something important.'

'So we asked him in,' Merran said, 'and he explained what he'd come about – about the sunk boat, and how he was being blamed for it, and how the CCTV that he was expecting to clear him had been put out of action. He asked if by any chance we'd seen anything that night.'

'And it so happened that we had,' Davie said. I wondered if Gavin and I would do this sort of double act in forty years' time, telling one story between us.

Merran nodded. 'Scotty was growling at something, in the night.' We all looked at the white dog in the shade under her chair, and he thumped his tail, recognising his name. 'Maybe half past two, three o'clock, I didn't look at the time, but that's what it felt like. About then. Well, he does growl from time to time in the night. He growls at dreams, and every now and then your grey cat passes by, and he growls at him.'

I had no doubt that Cat would growl back; he had strong views on dogs in his marina.

'So as we'd seen you about I thought it might be that, and told him to shoosh, but then I thought it might be the moon shining in on his bed that was annoying him. There was the net curtain, but the moonlight was still coming through, plain as plain. So I got up to draw the proper curtain, and that's when I saw someone walking along the pontoon.'

The breath stuck in my throat. 'Could you see who it was?'

Merran shook her head. 'We ken some o' the Brae folk, but there are so many boats that we don't ken all the owners. It was the nearest pontoon, the one the boat was sunk at.'

'You need to tell this to the police,' I said. I gestured towards where DS Peterson's car had gone. I remembered the routine she went through when interviewing a suspect. 'You shouldn't be telling me any more, in case it puts false memories into your mind. You should tell DS Peterson.'

'You're biding with the policeman in the kilt,' Davie said. 'If we tell you, you can tell him.'

'They'll want to speak to you.'

'Well, they can come and speak,' Merran said, 'but it'll do them no good, for I won't have them badgering me into seeing more than I did. I saw a man walking along the pontoon in the dead o' night. He was wearing some kind o' a bulky jacket, I think it was a parka, for I've a notion I saw the streetlights glint on the fur round the hood, and a toorie cap, and he walked like a Shetlander.' She looked at me defiantly. 'And it's no good you asking me to describe what I mean by that, for I canna, but he walked like someone that kent he was in his own place, setting his feet square upon the ground. No' like a soothmoother, striding here and there, always in a hurry.'

I wondered how DS Peterson would take to being told that Merran knew it wasn't Antony because the person she saw didn't have a soothmoother walk.

'So,' Merran said, 'I thought to myself, it's just Ewan taking his boat out, we do ken Ewan, for he's ages with my Greta, he was at the school with her. I just took it to be him, because, well, who would think of someone sinking someone else's boat in the middle of the night? Fishermen come and go at all sorts of odd hours, to catch the tide. So I canna swear to who it was, but I can swear to who it wasn't, and I'm certain sure it wasn't the man who's away.'

She paused for breath and Davie took over. 'So we said this to him, and he asked if she'd sign a paper for him, saying what she'd seen. Well, we weren't keen to make trouble, but then he said trouble was being made, and Ewan was accusing him of having sunk his boat, and he'd expected the CCTV to clear him, but the police had told him it had been put out of action, so there was nothing to say it wasn't him, unless we'd speak up for him. We still weren't keen, so he promised he'd no' use it unless the police actually accused him, and we agreed to that. So Merran made her statement, and wrote it up on the computer, and signed it. He thanked us, and folded it up, and off he went to his boat, and ten minutes later we saw him heading off out of the marina.'

'He stowed it away?' *The house looked like there'd been a burglary*, Annie had said. My speculation blew away like the air it was. Antony hadn't been after the Book o' the Black Arts; he'd likely never even heard of it. He'd gone out of the club to avoid Ewan, that was all; but before that he'd been talking to Merran and Davie, and learned that they'd been here the night the *Day Dawn* was sunk. If he hadn't done it, then either it was an accident, and nobody had, or Ewan had. He couldn't ask them if they'd seen anything in the middle of a busy boating club, with Ewan's friends all around, but he'd flung the accusation of it being an insurance job at Ewan in their fight. Then, as soon as he could, he'd gone up to Mid Yell.

He hadn't got the Book. He'd got a paper saying that he hadn't sunk Ewan's boat; that it had been sunk by a Shetland man in a parka and toorie.

I realised Merran and Davie were looking at me, as if they were expecting me to answer them. 'I'm sorry,' I said. 'I was thinking. Can you say that again?'

'He put it in his pocket,' Davie repeated. 'He was wearing

one of these sailor oilskins wi' a velcro pocket in the chest o' the trousers, and he put the paper in there and velcroed it shut.'

'So you'll tell your man,' Merran said. 'They'll find the bit of paper as they search, so they'll ken about it, but you tell him straight that I can't identify the man I saw.'

'I'll tell him,' I agreed.

The wind was rising, rattling my rigging and tugging strands loose from my plait. I tightened *Khalida*'s halyards up, thinking. *He put it in his pocket . . . a velcro pocket in the chest o' the trousers . . .* At least I could tell Gavin where to look.

Had Ewan really sunk his own boat? *An insurance job*, Davie and Merran had thought. Certainly the boat's owner would be the best person to sink her, knowing where the stopcocks were, and how they were closed, but I remembered all the work he'd put into the *Day Dawn* when he first got her, taking the hull back to the wood and revarnishing it, and had difficulty believing it. I made myself a cup of coffee and sat in the shelter of the cabin, looking over at her, and set aside the owner's pride in his boat. It had all been very dramatic, but as he'd said himself, not two hours ago, she hadn't taken any real harm. The electric wiring would be done for, but he'd been planning to replace that anyway, and I'd seen for myself, as she'd lain at the pier below me, that all the portable stuff had been taken out for the winter, just as I'd emptied my *Khalida* — except that I was going to be away for much of the winter, and my mast was down, whereas he was going to be about and using his boat. Why would he empty it out?

I remembered his roar of fury as Antony had accused him of sinking her for the insurance, and the way he'd launched himself at him, cutting the words off in his throat.

The offer to Jesma made more sense now. If Ewan had sunk the *Day Dawn* for the insurance, the money either to refit her out completely or to buy a newer boat, the insurance firm coming down on Antony wouldn't have worried him. Serve him right for taking his girl. Them coming down on Jesma, that was a different matter. He wouldn't want her having to pay up for something he'd done himself.

There was a cold feeling at my heart. I liked Ewan. I didn't believe he'd have harmed Chloe, and he hadn't been there at The Dowry to give her a sleeping pill. I didn't want to see him as a murderer, but Davie and Merran had just given him an even better motive than fury over his sunk boat: a threat of prosecution for attempted insurance fraud. Antony could have phoned him to gloat that he'd got him now, in spite of his promise; Davie and Merran might even have warned him that Antony had visited them, after they'd watched him head out from Mid Yell into Bluemull Sound. *He's ages with our Greta, he was at the school with her.* They could easily have phoned him. He could have gone round in his black pick-up to wait for Antony to come home, have confronted him, struck out . . . and then searched for the paper. I'd homed in on the mention of books being tumbled about because I was thinking of the Book of the Black Arts, but in a book or between two books was the obvious place to hide, to find, a paper.

In the front pouch of his oilskin trousers . . . Of course maybe he hadn't taken Merran's statement to the house. Maybe he'd left it aboard. I thought about that too. I wouldn't leave anything as fragile as a piece of paper in my oilskin trousers. They were waterproof in theory, of course, and mostly in practice too, but it would take just one wave to drench you and that would be your paper done for. I'd take it out and put it somewhere secure in the cabin.

Nobody had mentioned there having been a search aboard the boat. If Ewan had found nothing in the house and gone to search the boat, there would be signs of that. DS Peterson seemed only to have had a quick look; she'd be waiting for forensics, likely. It would be interesting to get a scoit aboard.

Chapter Twenty-two

Him at winna whin he may sanna whin he wid.
*(He that won't when he has the chance won't be
able to when he wants.)*
Take your opportunities when they come or they might not return.

Unfortunately, Antony's flash boat was guarded. I turned my head to look at the bored police officer standing on the pontoon. He looked like a newbie sent up from south; the flaming red hair was a giveaway. I went below to boil the kettle.

I took him a mug of tea and one of the needed-used KitKats. 'Cold work standing about.'

He shrugged, but didn't refuse the tea. 'We're dressed for it,' he said, in an accent that was pure Glasgow.

'I'm Cass,' I said. 'That's my boat.' I was about to say 'I live aboard' when I remembered that I didn't any more, not really.

'I ken who you are,' he said. *The Inspector's girlfriend* hovered in the air.

'I was just wondering,' I said, in my most diffident voice. His face went wary. He looked as if he was thinking he should hand the mug back. 'I heard that the house had obviously been searched. I was just wondering if anyone had looked at this boat to see if it had been searched too. Someone who's used to boats, I mean.'

'You, you mean,' he said bluntly, but he unwrapped the KitKat and ate it while he thought.

I did, but I could see he'd need coaxing. I'd got good at persuading teenage boys to do things. 'Or you,' I said. 'If I showed you what to look for, then you could point it out to DS Peterson, when she comes back. No need to mention me.'

He liked that idea. His face brightened; he took a gulp of the tea, and nodded.

'And I wouldn't need to go into the cabin,' I said. 'So there wouldn't be a problem with forensics, or my DNA.' I spread my hands. 'I can't promise, of course, but I think I'd be able to tell from the cockpit if someone had been in the boat since Antony moored it up.'

He took another gulp of tea, thinking. 'Just from the cockpit?'

'I can give it a go.'

This time he finished the tea, dropped the KitKat wrapper into the mug and handed it back. 'Well, there'd be no harm in looking.' He gave me a distrustful look. 'And talk me through what you're thinking, so I can say it for myself. The nearest I'd been to boats before I came up here was the Govan ferry to the transport museum.'

'Okay,' I said. 'Well, come and have a look at mine first.' I motioned him aboard *Khalida*. He came reluctantly, casting a backward glance over his charge and up the pontoon, to make sure nobody was waiting at the marina gate ready to sneak in. 'Have a look around. What d'you notice?'

'It's like a house,' he said. 'A playhouse, made of wood.'

I let that pass.

He leaned into the companionway, looking. 'A cooker, and plates, and the table, and the cushions, and books on the shelves.'

I nodded encouragingly.

'It's very tidy. Clever, the way everything's put away. The ledge in front of the books, and the little cubby-holes that the plates fit into, and the metal thing to hold the kettle on the cooker. But it's tidy even on top of that.' He leaned further in, looking around the corner into my berth and the port storage space. 'Everything's in a tote box, and even the table's clear, except for the chart and the book. And stuff is jammed with other stuff, like the

259

books have the first-aid box holding them, and the tote boxes are the size for the space, so they can't shift around.'

I nodded again. 'That's exactly what I wanted you to see.'

His expression didn't change, but his shoulders broadened.

'Boats tilt,' I explained. 'Sometimes, under sail, this boat goes so far over that the waves wash the windows on the down side.'

He imagined it. 'And everything stays put?'

'Yeah. It really does.' I turned to look at Antony's boat. 'And that boat you're guarding came home from Yell in two hours yesterday morning. It's not a sailing boat, so it wouldn't have tilted so far, but it would've bounced over waves. Now Antony, that's the guy who owned it, he'd have secured everything for sea, tidied it like this, with everything wedged, before he set out from Yell. He went back to his house not long after he arrived back, so if it's not as tidy as this, then someone's been aboard.'

He got that. 'Well, let's have a look.'

We crossed the pontoon to Antony's boat. 'We had to go on it to shift it from where it was,' he said, 'so my prints'll be on these door things anyway.' He opened the hatch up and set the little cabin doors back so we could see inside. Cat naturally swarmed straight inside, whiskers bristling warily and the Kitten followed him.

We stayed outside and looked. It was a standard motorboat layout, with an upper deck for the steering wheel and instrument dashboard, a couple of seats for passengers, and more accommodation below.

'Those books,' I said, nodding towards the shelf at the driver's left shoulder. 'They're too spaced out. Someone's been looking through them. And there's one lying on the seat.'

It was a small, black-bound book with a plain front and faded gold letters on the spine.

'He might have wanted to check it as he went. Check on where rocks were, that kind of thing.'

I leaned forward, straining my eyes to make out the title. '*Principles of Navigation*. No. If he'd wanted to check his passage in a book, rather than relying on that chart plotter, the TV screen in the middle there, he'd have used that A4-size white-spined one with the ring binding. It's the local guide.'

'So that book was taken out to make space to search.' He looked wistfully forwards at the stairs down to the main cabin. 'You definitely can't go down there.'

'The cushions here too,' I said. 'On that seat. There's storage underneath them, and you can see the forrard cushion is not quite exactly in the wooden rim it sits in. If it had been like that when he came back from Yell, it'd have gone on the floor.'

'Maybe he needed something from under it when he arrived home.'

'Or was putting something away. Yes, maybe. But it's second nature to stow things properly, and boat cushions are a neat fit.'

He gave it a long look, nodding, then his eyes went back to those tempting stairs. 'I'll just look from the steps.'

He went forward, down two steps and stopped. 'Aye. You're on the right track. It's the same here. I wouldn't have noticed if you hadn't shown me. The cushions have definitely been lifted, and there's, like, books on the table, you wouldn't have left them there.' He turned and came back up, gestured me onto the pontoon, and took his police radio from its holder.

'No need to mention me,' I said, and retreated to *Khalida*. 'I'm not here.'

He did it very well: 'It's PC Stewart here, ma'am. I was thinking about the house being searched, and I've had a look at the boat, without touching anything. I was thinking that some-one's been in there as well. It's very slight indications, but there are things that wouldn't be how it would have been left for the voyage back from Yell. Misplaced cushions, and a book he wouldn't have needed left lying on a seat.'

Ewan wasn't to know where Antony had hidden Davie and

Merran's piece of paper. It could have been put in a book for safety, or hidden in a locker.

I needed to tell Gavin about it.

I'd tidied *Khalida* away and was waiting in the cockpit when Gavin's Land Rover came down the gravel drive and along to the pontoon. He got out, waved, and reached into the back seat for the Kitten's basket. I clipped Cat's lead on, collected my stuff and headed along the pontoon. We kissed, and he took one of my bags from me. 'You made good time home.'

'A good brisk wind. Cold, though.' I lifted Cat into the car and squeezed in after him. Kitten squeaked in disgust as Gavin put her in her basket. 'For your own safety,' I told her. 'You need to look after yourself.'

I sat quiet as Gavin reversed back along the marina road and backed into the space beside the caravan, then said, once we were moving forward, 'I've several things to tell you.'

He glanced at me. 'Oh?'

I did my best to explain it all: Jesma's financial difficulties, and Ewan waiving the insurance money (I didn't mention lobsters, in case Gavin had to do something official about them), and the cyclist on the ferry. I explained my thinking about Antony knowing or not knowing about the Book of the Black Arts, and finally Davie and Merran's twist to the tale.

Gavin listened, and nodded as I finished. 'So Antony had a paper clearing him of sinking Ewan's boat, and you're thinking that Ewan sank the boat himself, found out that Antony might have proof of that, and Ewan killed Antony so that he wouldn't be accused of insurance fraud?'

'I'm thinking it,' I said, 'but I don't believe it. Oh, sure, people do sink their boats for the money, but he'd worked on that boat.' It would sound stupid, but I said it all the same. 'He loved it. He was proud of the good job he'd made of it. He wouldn't do it for the money.'

'But,' Gavin said, 'he might do it for love.' His eyes were on the road but I could see his thoughts were gathering. 'He loved Chloe, and she'd taken up with a married man who was a waster, in Ewan's view. Would he sacrifice his boat to make it look as if Antony'd sunk her? Chloe was his cousin and his childhood friend. He'd have expected her to stick with him against Antony, if it looked as if Antony had done that.'

I caught my breath. 'That's just what he said. He did! I'd forgotten. When Magnie and I were working on *Khalida*, and Chloe and Ewan had a row on the pontoon. He actually said that to her: *Now you see what this waster's capable o' — sinking my boat because he kens I'm on to him.* And then he said something to Antony, after she'd gone, about him having a wife and bairns.'

'And the odd way the camera was interfered with. A serious saboteur would have made sure it looked like an accident that it cut out. He was trying too hard to make it look like sabotage.'

I thought about it. 'And after the boat came up, after Chloe's death, he regretted it. I'm sure he did. The day before he'd been breathing fire and slaughter in Antony's direction, but the next day he didn't care any more.'

'Insurance companies don't like fraud. Antony threatening to expose him is a better motive than the chance of getting a fancy price for an old book that's rumoured to have been dug up.'

'But he wouldn't have killed Chloe,' I said. 'If he did sink his own boat, he wanted to split her and Antony up. He'd never have harmed her.'

'No,' Gavin agreed. He indicated and turned onto the Voe road. 'And his motive for killing Antony depends on him knowing that Antony had the paper. We've listed all the calls to and from Antony's phone and there's none to Ewan. Unless they spoke in the marina, he didn't know.'

'Antony'd come straight in with the paper still on him. If they'd talked in the marina, why would they go to the house?'

'Davie and Merran in the caravan might have warned him.'

'They say they didn't. They just didn't want to be mixed up in any of it.'

He drove in silence for a moment, then said, 'The Book of the Black Arts is still a possible motive. I've spoken to Samuel J. Boult, the bookseller. He went back south on yesterday night's boat, and denies all knowledge of the book's whereabouts. He said he'd heard a rumour about it in the occult books fraternity – we're trying to follow that up, but it's likely enough.'

'Magnie guessed straight away that was what had been dug up in the old kirkyard,' I said. 'I phoned him. He said Yell folk knew the story of the Book, though not where it was, and it's mentioned in papers in the archives. If he knew, other folk would too.'

'Boult said he offered Lizbet a good price for it, but she insisted she knew nothing about it. He couldn't deny that, because he knew I knew he'd tried to bribe you. We'll keep an eye open, in case it turns up for sale, because somebody dug something up recently in Windhouse, but if he had it, and passes it straight on to a collector, it may never be heard of more.'

'It wasn't in his car, nor a digging implement.'

'No,' Gavin agreed. 'There could be ways round that – that he'd dumped the spade and put the Book in his case – but I'm inclined to rule him out. I think he was genuinely trying to get you in on it, which means he hadn't got it.'

'Did you investigate the cars Ertie saw at Windhouse?'

'Freya talked to Lizbet. She went up on Thursday after work, and back down first thing on Friday morning. Visiting her mum, she insisted. She jumped like a startled pony when Freya mentioned the Book, but she just kept saying she'd never heard of it. "I don't know what you're talking about," over and over, like a stuck record.'

'How about the other car that was at Windhouse on the Thursday? The Star Rent-a-car one?'

'Oh, yes. It took a bit of chasing around but it turned out to be two couples in their late twenties who're keen on ghost-hunting. From Edinburgh, and they were doing a tour of all the most haunted places they could find, with a ton of equipment. Their last stop was Windhouse. An Edinburgh officer interviewed them on Monday morning. They insisted they hadn't dug anything up, but he wasn't sure he believed them. They had a metal detector standing among walking poles in the hall, and what Shetlanders would call "bits of bruck" on their mantelpiece. A door handle, and a hinge, and an old lock. Souvenir hunters, he reckoned.'

'But they were at Windhouse before Lizbet. She was waiting for them to go so that she could bury the Book.'

'Maybe. I'm still not sure she'd have braved Windhouse after dark, alone, and they said they arrived at dusk and stayed there till it was properly dark, for atmosphere. Their YouTube videos certainly show it as dark, though that could just be in contrast to their torches.'

'Then there was the black pick-up on Sunday morning. That's sinister, now we know Antony didn't dig up the Book.'

'It definitely wasn't Robbie Johnson checking his lambs. We had no bother finding that out. He wasn't there. All the ewes in that park had birthed a week back, and the lambs were doing fine. So far no luck with the unknown man on the 08.15 ferry.'

'Ewan has a black pick-up,' I said. 'But Lizbet would never have told him about the Book, and I can't see why he'd want it anyway. How about alibis for Antony's death? Do you know when it was?'

Gavin shook his head. 'The best forensics is willing to say is that it's between ten thirty, when his boat came into the marina, as spotted by Magnie, and four thirty, when the body was found. Freya thought he wasn't recently dead then. I'm suspicious of the black pick-up that arrived after quarter to eleven, when Baabie left for church, and was gone by twelve fifteen.'

'A black pick-up again. There are so many about.'

265

'Baabie took it to be Ewan, but that could be because she knew there was ill-feeling between them.'

'I'd have thought she'd have known his registration.'

Gavin went into quoting mode. '"My sight's as good as ever it was, but I was too busy thanking the folk who'd given me a lift and finding my door key to look particularly, and then when I lifted my spyglasses he was already gone."'

'Alibis?'

Gavin sighed. 'It was the morning after Hop Night.'

'Ah,' I said. 'Everyone in bed nursing a hangover?'

'A lot of them were, or say they were. Ewan. The Jarl Squad were out all night, so it's perfectly plausible that he went to bed and slept. However, they were at the boating club last night second thing, just after nine o'clock. He says he didn't, but he could have seen Antony going out in his boat.'

He had seen him; that's how he'd known about the lobsters. Gavin gave me a sharp look. I shook my head. 'Not relevant, but take that with a pinch of salt.'

'Ewan's house overlooks the voe, so he could have seen him coming back. He might have gone to confront Antony at his house, where they'd be private, rather than in the marina, and then when he didn't find the paper on him, or in the house, gone to search the boat too. I can't find anyone who saw him, but it was the morning after the Hop. There weren't many folk about, and as for noticing one black pick-up among the dozens that drive around Shetland, not a hope.'

'But that still leaves the question of how he knew Antony had the paper, and he wouldn't have killed Chloe.'

'Think of all those ballads that have a man killing a woman rather than see her with another man,' Gavin said. '"Banks of the Ohio" and all that. Men that kill their children rather than let their wife have them. Ewan could cause her death and still be genuinely devastated by it.'

'He wasn't at The Dowry, to slip a pill into her drink.'

'No. Freya and I have tried to come up with a scenario where he'd given her a pill to take that lunchtime, and totally failed. Besides, why should she make a secret of that?' He shook his head. 'No. I can see him killing her, but not like that.'

I nodded.

'Jesma.' He stopped. I waited. 'Jesma was at her house, with the children, until Sabina went off to swimming at the leisure centre, and Garry went off to football in Scalloway with three of his pals. They were both back by half past twelve, and Antony was supposed to come and pick them up at one, to take them out for lunch and keep them for the afternoon and night, then put them to school in the morning. When he didn't come she phoned him, and left a message – we listened to it. She didn't sound best pleased.' The corners of his mouth turned down. 'She made chips for lunch instead, and sent the bairns off to the playpark, and went round to read him the riot act.'

'The car that Baabie saw just after two.'

'Yes. She said she hammered on the door, and he wasn't in, so she went back home.'

'She didn't go in and look?'

'She says she didn't. When Freya asked why not, she said things were awkward between them, and she couldn't invade his privacy like that. She didn't even try the door. She knocked, he didn't answer, she went back home.'

'It could be true.'

'It could. Who else? Lizbet and Tom were playing at the boating club on Saturday night, and they both said they were sleeping it off. Lizbet was alone in the flat she'd shared with Chloe, and Tom's folk were asleep till nearly denner time too. Either of them could have gone round to Antony's house during the morning. Amy was at church with her folk in the morning, then she went to the Co-op to get stuff she needed for Yell. She went straight there from the kirk, which finished at twelve, and her till receipt was timed as 13.37.'

'An hour and a half shopping?'

'She said she went into Peacock's too, and tried on jumpers, and thought about a new swimsuit.' I gave him an incredulous look. 'Well, some people do enjoy pottering around shops.'

'She could do Lerwick to Brae in half an hour.'

'Yes, she'd just have time to drive up, kill Antony, drive back and do her shopping. Tight, but possible. Irvine lives on his own in Lerwick. He says he lazed about and did stuff around the house – hoovered, washed the dishes, put a washing on. He didn't have his computer on. His own car's a dark blue Estate, but Jim's has a black pick-up for sale right now, and he has keys for the garage.'

'But,' I said, 'I know motive isn't needed for a jury, but why would any of those four kill Antony?'

'That hoary old chestnut, he saw someone putting something in Chloe's drink. As for the house search, the person wore gloves. That doesn't mean it was necessarily premeditated. For one thing, it's still cold enough to want them on, if you walked somewhere. Also, when we asked Jesma specifically, she said Antony always wore gloves to do the dishes and kept a pair of Marigolds by the sink. They weren't there. Equally, his death looks accidental too. A hard shove, he fell backwards, hit his head on the worktop at just the wrong angle, and that killed him.' He sighed. 'As far as I'm concerned, the field's still wide open.'

Chapter Twenty-three

Wednesday 22nd March

Tide times, Brae:
LW 01.58 (0.49m);
HW 07.45 (2.07m);
LW 13.31 (0.5m);
HW 19.20 (1.88m)

Sunrise 06.58; moonset 07.04;
sunset 19.23. Moon waxing gibbous.

Du canna draw a straw afore my nose an tell me it was a dokken.
(You can't draw a straw before my nose and tell me it was a docken.)
You can't fool me.

Winter returned in the night. We woke up to a rattle of hail-stones on the skylight and when I looked out there was a knobbling of white on the ground and frosting over the hen-house roof. The sea was back to winter cobalt, the hills dusted with icing sugar. Behind Brae, the cone of Ronas Hill was pure white. The ponies were huddled under the shelter of the trees, and when I went out to give them their breakfast I noticed they had little balls of snow around their furred ankles, and frost on their backs. They didn't seem bothered, especially with food on offer. I left them tearing mouthfuls of hay from the net and checked on the hens; reluctant to come out, if mash would be provided in their warm straw bed. I obliged. Cat came out with me, tail fluffed, but the Kitten stayed on the doorstep, shaking her front paws disdainfully.

'I thought I'd come into town with you today, for the morning, anyway,' I said over breakfast porridge.

Gavin glanced up. 'Oh?'

'I thought I'd go in and look at cars. Just to get an idea of the likely o' them, and prices.'

'Don't forget to allow for repair costs too.'

'I can fix my boat engine. I was hoping a car wouldn't be too different.'

'Your boat engine isn't run by a computer.'

'And cars are?'

Gavin nodded gloomily. 'All of them these days, meaning you need a garage with a computer able to talk to your make of car to fix the slightest thing. That's why I keep my Land Rover going. I ken it's old-fashioned, but I can fix it myself if need be. So the less any car you look at costs, the more you have to factor in for spending on it.' He looked at the clock. 'I need to leave in fifteen minutes.'

I piled the dishes in the sink with some water, flung on warm clothes for being stuck in Lerwick till the bus home and walking the four miles from Voe, added my scarlet sailing jacket with warmest hat and gloves stuck in the pocket and was ready in twelve. Cat looked up hopefully at the jacket. 'Sorry, boy,' I said. 'Not today.'

He walked up to the car with us all the same, and sat on a fence post to watch us go.

'So,' I said, once we were bumping up our track, 'what do I want to look at, or look out for?'

He turned his head to smile at me. 'You're serious?'

I nodded. 'I prefer going about in boats, but this land life, you do need a car.'

He thought about that for a moment, then nodded. 'Okay.

You want under 70,000 miles on the clock, and under ten years old, unless it's a really low mileage because it belonged to someone who used it only for Lerwick on Saturdays and kirk on Sunday. Ten thousand a year is average. Anything that costs less than double your new sails isn't worth it.'

I looked at him in horror. 'Seriously?'

'Seriously. I've been keeping an eye on the garages, just in case a useful small runabout turned up, to save fuel in the summer. The possibles all start at the £6,000 mark.'

'Practically the cost of a yacht.'

Gavin slowed for the gate. 'Thinking better of it? Shall I drop you off now?'

I ignored that, and got out to open the gate, then hopped back in again. 'I have a couple of boat bits to get as well.'

'Which garages are you wanting to visit?'

'The one at the top of the hill, on the way in, for starters, and then I can walk down from there.'

'Jim's, of course,' Gavin said. He gave me a sideways glance, teasing. 'Of course you'll maybe not get to speak to any of the mechanics.'

'The thought never passed my mind,' I said virtuously. 'Though if I was interested in something, I'd need to ask about its service history, that kind of thing.'

Gavin's mouth twitched. 'I'd love to hear that conversation.'

'I can talk gaskets and pistons with the best of them,' I assured him. 'Besides, hadn't you noticed, men love blinding women with car science? All I'll need to do is ask. Maybe even get a trial drive in it, if they'd be happy taking me out with L-plates on.'

'You mean, if they bring out the right mechanic. But how will you know?'

'Most garages have overalls with the person's name on.'

'I suppose you can't come to any harm in a busy garage surrounded by people,' Gavin said. His eyes turned serious. 'You might do some harm, though, and to my ship.'

'I won't,' I said. 'Promise. No questions, no prodding. I just want a look at him. I want to see where I'd put him on a ship.'

'You can't read a man by a look at his face.'

'No,' I agreed. 'But I've heard Amy's side of the story and it didn't quite ring true.'

'I wish it had been a better day,' Gavin said. 'You'd have taken your boat out and ignored the investigation.'

'I'd still have thought about it, though,' I said. 'I saw Chloe fall.'

Gavin nodded. 'I ken.' He shrugged, then smiled. 'And it'll serve you right if you get a solid half-hour of gaskets and pistons from someone else wearing Irvine's overall. What are you thinking for getting home?'

'Lunchtime bus and walk.' His face was still too grave. I slid my hand down his arm. 'I won't meddle. Really. I promise.' I produced my notebook from my pocket. 'See, a notebook to write down possible cars. I need to allow for the cost of driving lessons too.'

'If you'll let me use it while you're at sea, I'll go halfers on the cost.'

'Deal.'

I spent the rest of the drive in considering my finances. I'd joined *Sørlandet* in April, and had saved most of my pay from then until October, when we'd started renting the Ladie. Now my expenses were higher, living in a house with electricity and coal bills, but even after the cost of my beautiful new sails, I had a healthier bank balance than I'd had for many years. I could look seriously at half-cars.

He dropped me off at the first garage at the top of the hill, and I spent half an hour strolling among their used cars, getting a feel for what was on offer, even though these were well above my price range.

Jim's Garage was next down, and looked much more promising. They had three cars in the £7,000+ range which, if Gavin would share the cost of it, it wouldn't quite clean me out. I'd have time to save more if I was going to leave *Sørlandet*.

The thought jolted me. Leave my beautiful ship, even if she was overrun with teenagers; leave my command? Yet somewhere deep down I was thinking about buying a car so that I could treat the Ladie as home, could get out even on a cold, windy winter's day when only a fool would take a boat down to the shop at Aith. I was thinking like a land person.

I wasn't ready to decide yet, I retorted. I noted the make and model of the one with the lowest mileage and headed into the garage building. The office was pleasingly warm, and I'd struck gold, Lynch's luck, for the mechanic behind the counter was dark, a bit older than Chloe and Lizbet, and wearing a rather grimy boiler suit with IRVINE above the breast pocket.

He didn't quite look a man two women would be vying for, especially not the showy Chloe. He had a pleasant enough face with an outdoor complexion, glossy black hair and dark eyes under flyaway brows. He looked up as the bell jangled, and gave me a slightly forced smile. His face was drawn and there were dragged lines about his eyes, as if he'd slept badly. I went forward to the counter. 'I was looking at the used cars there – the blue Ford Fiesta. I want a small runabout that'll go for miles on a tank of petrol, and give me as little bother as possible.' I smiled at him. 'Only I've never driven a Fiesta, and I wanted to have a look inside it, see how much space there is.'

He reached behind him for the keys and came forward from behind the counter with a speed that suggested he was glad to have something to do. 'More as you'd think,' he assured me, and proceeded to give a very thorough demonstration. He was too tongue-tied to talk me through it, but he took care to show me how far back and forward the front seat could go to make space in the seat well or behind, and how much room there was in the boot with the back seat down. I was impressed; I reckoned it would take most of the contents of *Khalida*'s cabin, if they were neatly packed. There'd definitely be room for all my sailing gear, if I wanted to head up to Brae to take *Khalida* out.

Gavin had been right, though. It was impossible to read a man by the look on his face. I thought I saw unhappiness there, and regret.

'How about the mechanics? Service history?' I did a quick mental division. 'Forty-two thousand miles, that's low, surely, less as five thousand a year.' I strolled round it, noticing the glossy metallic blue, and the undented mudguards. 'It looks in good condition too.'

'It is,' he said. He gave the top of the roof an affectionate pat, as if it was a horse, and suddenly became chatty. 'I'm kent this car fae it was new. It was bought from us and I'm done the service for it every year since. It belonged to a wife in Nesting that wanted it as a second car, for doing her own shopping without having to drag the man into town, or getting to the WI, or for her haircut or whatever, and that was all she used it for, but her man retired back in the summer, and they decided that they didna need two cars any more.' He gave me a shy, sideways smile. 'I ken, I'm sounding like a used-car salesman, "one careful lady owner". She kept the car like she kept her house. I was in there once, when she left the lights of the car on in the garage – she kept it in a garage – and I'm telling you, not the most particular trowie wife would have found a speck of dust to complain of. I was faered to step apon the kitchen floor.' Now he was talking easily, he looked at me properly. He frowned, and then I saw recognition dawning. His face went bleak. 'I mind you now,' he said. 'You were there, you helped, when Chloe fell down those steps.'

I nodded.

'You told me to call the ambulance, and what to say.' He swallowed. 'Did you hear that she died?'

'Aye,' I said. 'The policewoman came to call on me too.'

Irvine turned his face away for a moment, towards the grey

sea stretching north towards the Brothers, Whalsay, the Skerries. I saw the muscles in his throat move. 'Someone had done it
on purpose. She said that. The second time she came. Chloe fell
because she'd been drugged. The police wife asked about The
Dowry, and if I'd seen anyone tampering with her drink.' He
looked back at me. 'I can't believe anyone would do that. I didna
see anyone, but then, I was looking at Chloe. She was looking
that bonny.'

I'd promised Gavin I wouldn't meddle, wouldn't prod. It
took an effort to keep silent; but Irvine wanted to talk to someone who'd been involved at least.

'She was an old friend o' mine,' he said. He gave that shy smile
again, and reddened. 'Well, my first proper girlfriend, actually,
after I left the school. We were courting for a while. She was a
lot of fun, aye up for a spree. We used to do, oh, all the things
teenagers do, the pictures, and Captain Flint's, and I mind we
went together to the Cross at New Year, to hear the boats hoot
the bells in.' He shrugged. 'I'm no' that good at socialising, but
wi' Chloe I'd be joining in whatever.' He smiled, reminiscently,
and repeated, 'It was a lock o' fun. I'd no seen her, oh, since we
split up. She was looking well, and right bonny.' His face stilled.
'I canna believe she's gone. We were going to meet up this week
sometime, go for a drink.' *But I could see he wouldn't meet her,* Amy
had said. *He wasn't going to get caught up in that again.*

Irvine's brown eyes blurred with tears. He said heavily, 'And
instead I'll be going to her funeral.'

I nodded.

'And I hope they catch the person that did it,' he said, with
sudden force. He looked across the car roof at me. 'I was thinking about it, after the police wife went. The only time . . . well,
there was the wife who came and sat in her place for a bit, she
coulda done it, but otherwise −' He paused, then came up with
the same idea as I'd had. 'Otherwise, it would have been when
the waiter came wi' the food. The wife had gone by then, but

275

everyone was leaning in clearing their glasses so he could get the plates down.' His jaw hardened. 'And I told the police wife, the only person who couldn't have done it was Amy. We weren't involved in the food coming, we'd finished our main course, and we were at a separate table, with me on Chloe's side and Amy across from me. There was no way she could have reached across without me seeing her, and she didn't.'

His hand clenched on the top of the car, and then straightened again. He took a deep breath and said in a normal voice, 'Well, can I tempt you to a test drive?'

I might hop happily into the car of a strange fisherman in Yell on the strength of him knowing Magnie, but I wasn't driving anywhere with Irvine. I shook my head. 'I can't. Well, I mean, I can drive, I've been driving for years, but I haven't actually sat my test yet. I wouldn't want to try town driving in a car that's no' mine.' I didn't want him to think I was a time-waster. 'But I will bring my partner to see it, because he's going halfers with me on it. Now the snow's gone he wants something that guzzles less diesel than his Land Rover.'

We both looked around at the rim of white at the edges of the road, and sprinkling the grass. 'Nearly gone,' I amended. 'Spring's on its way.'

The idea of a fuel-saver made sense to him. His brow cleared. 'Tell him to come soon. This one won't be long in the forecourt.'

'I'll tell him now,' I said. I hauled my phone out of my pocket, and sent a text: *Really nice Fiesta in Jim's 9 yrs 42000 miles could you have a look at it xxx*

The reply pinged back straight away. *Really seriously? You want to buy a car xxx*

I temporised on that one. *Enough to be worth looking. If you do too. If you're not too busy xxx*

Your car. I'll just borrow xxx

The land life was closing in on me. I wasn't sure what to

reply. I felt panic rise in my throat, and turned quickly to Irvine. 'Thanks for being so patient wi' me.'

'You're welcome. I'd be blyde to see it get a good home.' He smiled. 'Another careful lady owner.'

I said goodbye and walked off, thinking; thinking about cars, about commitment; thinking about Irvine. Where would I put him on board ship? Down in the engine room, was my answer, talking gaskets and pistons with my engine-nerd friend Anders. Down there, he'd be quick and practical in an emergency. Up among the trainees, I wasn't so sure. A ship emergency, sure, but I thought he'd be weak in an emotional emergency. He'd panicked with Chloe being too keen and made a mess of dumping her. He had been going to meet her while Amy was away, even though anyone could have told him it was a bad idea.

I didn't think he'd have put a sleeping potion in her drink, but I was less sure now about Amy – and if Irvine had been sitting beside Chloe, with Antony on her other side, then Antony had been in the right place to see her do it, and Amy had spent a suspiciously long time shopping at around the time of Antony's death.

Chapter Twenty-four

Friday 24th March

Tide times, Brae:
LW 06.46 (0.66m);
HW 13.14 (1.82m);
LW 19.20 (0.81m);
HW 01.33 (1.73m)

Moonrise 02.48; sunrise 05.50; moonset 07.34; sunset 18.30. Moon waning gibbous – last quarter.

Da stillest water breeds da warst wirm.
(The stillest water breeds the worst worm.)
Appearances are deceptive (All that glitters is not gold).

I'd taken the *Deuk* up to Brae, to bring *Khalida* back. We'd had two days of a blattering north wind bringing a haze of snow down the voe and depositing it on the barely flowering currants and first daffodils. The ponies had stayed put in their corner, munching hay; the hens had fluffed up their feathers in their house and refused to try the garden for exercise. Now it had blown itself out we were promised a week of spring weather, with light, chilly breezes, and maybe even some sunshine. I was just unzipping my flash new mainsail cover when I heard a voice at the pontoon gate. I looked up and saw Tom there. He called my name again, and waved as he saw me turn.

I went along the pontoon to let him in.

'Are you busy?' he said, diffidently. 'I mean, I'm not inter-rupting anything, or stopping you going anywhere?'

'No, it's fine,' I said. 'I'm just taking the boat back to the Ladie. Tea, coffee?'

He went for coffee and scrambled aboard, sat down in the cockpit and unwound the scarf from around his neck. That air of anxiety I'd noticed before was stronger now, with a new crease between his brows, and a tightness at the corners of his mouth. His black toorie was pushed back on his head, and a couple of strands of his brown hair fell forward onto his fore-head. His round eyes met mine as I handed him the mug, looking up at me like a child who trusted his teacher.

'I'm worried about something,' he said. 'About these mur-ders.'

I nodded encouragingly. He set his mug down on the cockpit seat and dug both hands into his pockets. 'I'm afraid –' His head jerked up and he sat up straighter. *What was that?*

He was staring at the mouth of the marina. I stood up to look, but didn't see anything. 'It was a fin, huge, but going backwards,' he said. 'Right at the mouth of the marina. I mean, really huge, as tall as a person, and it was the wrong way round.'

'Ah,' I said, enlightened. 'It would be one of the orcas.'

'Orca?' He looked even more worried. 'Like, a killer whale? The ones that pick seals off beaches?' He cast a glance around him, and didn't seem reassured by the pontoon arm and bulk of Antony's boat to landward of us and Magnie's to seaward. 'It won't come in here, will it?'

'I've never heard of them coming into a marina,' I said. It wasn't the time to tell him about the trouble yachts were having in the Bay of Biscay with a particular pod of orcas who'd taken to attacking the rudders of smaller boats. 'Relax, and tell me what's worrying you. I'll help if I can.'

He picked up his mug again, but kept his eyes on the marina's rocky entrance. 'It's going to sound awful.' His eyes slid to mine, briefly, then focused on the water again. 'I'm afraid that the police suspect Lizbet killed Chloe.'

'Lizbet?' I echoed. 'But Chloe was her pal.'

'I ken. But see, I was thinking about that. Like, the blonde policewoman said she'd been given that sleeping pill at The Dowry. Well, you'd think that the person who gave it to her expected her to be killed driving back to Brae, but I don't see it like that. Not necessarily. It's not like she was down south, on a motorway surrounded by mad drivers going at eighty, where straying off your lane would cause a pile-up. If she'd felt sleepy on the road to Brae she'd just have gone slower, and if she'd swerved off the road she might go into a ditch or a fence but she wouldn't be much hurt. She always wore her seatbelt too. At worst she'd get a bump on the head, or a broken wrist. Nothing much . . .' He stopped, and swallowed. 'Just enough, maybe, to stop her taking Lizbet's place on *You're the Stars!*'

I felt cold. It was horribly plausible. Chloe's fall down the steps of Campbell's Closs and the way she'd hit her head had been sheer bad luck. If she'd made it to her car and set off, if she'd started feeling sleepy at the wheel, she'd have opened the window. She'd have slowed down. Once she'd got out of Lerwick it was a long, straight country road with two sides, very little traffic at that time of day, and a verge on each side. She was far more likely to slide sideways onto a fence. If she was very unlucky with a ditch she might overturn the car, but even from that, if she'd had her seatbelt on, she could easily have walked out unhurt.

My throat felt tight. I didn't want it to be Lizbet.

'And Lizbet was that upset at her death,' Tom said. 'Well, of course I'd have expected her to be, but it felt like something more.'

'Murder's always a shock,' I said. 'And she had no motive to kill Antony.'

Tom spread his hands. 'But that was an accident too, from what they're saying. What I heard was that he'd been pushed, and he'd stumbled back and hit his head right on the edge of the worktop, and that had killed him.'

I shook my head. 'But why? Why would Lizbet attack Antony? And how could she? He wouldn't just shove over like that.'

'If he wasn't expecting it, he would,' Tom said. 'I've seen that often enough in pubs. A sharp, hard push from someone he didn't think was a threat. She's strong, Lizbet. She goes to the gym, remember. And have you ever picked up an amp? We prefer acoustic, but for outdoors or noisy pubs you have to be miked up, so she has her own mike, that makes the most of her voice, and an amp to go with it.' He made a shape with his hands, a metre high and nearly that broad. 'That size, and it's heavy.'

'Why, though? Why would she attack Antony?'

Tom's face was grim. 'That book. That Devil's book she dug up. She was mad to do it in the first place, but after Chloe died she was determined to get rid of it. She went up to Yell and buried it in Windhouse, and then Antony went and dug it up again.'

I opened my mouth to say he hadn't, and then realised that was definitely not information to be shared. I substituted, 'But how would she ken he'd done that?'

'We saw him.' Tom leaned across to me, his eyes earnest. 'We saw him heading out, while we were playing at the club on Hop Night. I thought he'd just be doing his creels, but he didn't come back. Lizbet kept watching for him coming back, in between sets, but he never did. Then she turned to me and said, 'He was listening.' And I didn't ken what she meant at first, but then she reminded me that he'd been there while I was calming her down about that dealer who wanted to buy the book. The dealer speaking to her at Up Helly Aa, that was the first I'd heard o' it. She told me the story when I followed her outside, about her digging it up, and how she'd taken it back to Windhouse for the Devil to take, if he wanted it. "I bet he's gone to dig it up," she said. "He heard us speaking and how much that man was offering for it, and he's gone to take it." So . . .' He trailed to a halt, swallowed and continued. 'Maybe she watched for him coming back, and went round to his house when she saw him go there, and told him he'd to put it back, and he laughed at her, and she shoved him, and then he fell, and she ran.' He took a deep breath. 'Listen, I ken I've a cheek asking this, but . . . do you know what the police are thinking? Do they suspect her?'

'I really don't know,' I said. 'Genuinely, I don't. This kind o' thing –' I spread my hands to indicate all this mess. 'It's no' something to talk about out of work. But do you think she might have done it?'

He stood up abruptly, shaking his head, then stilled, and looked me straight in the face again. 'I don't ken. I was hoping you'd say it was all nonsense. I don't think it was Lizbet, but I can't be sure.' He lifted his empty mug and passed it back to me. 'Thanks for the coffee. I'll need to be going now.' He shoved his hands back in his pockets, as if he was checking that nothing had fallen out as he was sitting, then took them out and clambered over the guard wire. Halfway over, he paused. 'You won't say . . . what I've been saying?'

'No,' I promised.

'Thanks, Cass.' He gave a half-wave and headed back along the pontoon, out of the gate, walking briskly round the marina gravel, up the drive and out of sight.

I stowed the two mugs below. My head hurt. I didn't want to believe it was Lizbet who'd killed Chloe. *At worst she'd get a bump on the head, or a broken wrist.* And if she'd thought Antony had taken the book, she would have wanted him to put it back. It hung together, but I didn't want to think about it.

I went back to getting ready to sail. Extra jacket; lifejacket. The wind had shifted from north to south, so I'd be closehauled

282

all the way, but the sail to Yell had shown how beautifully my *Khalida* would go into the wind with her new sails. Sail cover. I could hoist the mainsail in the berth with this wind and back out under sail, then turn between the two pontoons and sail out. I hoped the orca Tom had spotted had gone, along with his mates. There were a couple of pods circling Shetland just now, eagerly followed by the Facebook group, and while I enjoyed the spectacle of them from the deck of *Sørlandet*, I didn't really want to meet up with them in *Khalida*. The bull of one pod was as long as she was, with a six-foot fin, and teeth that could do serious damage. I wondered for a moment about shutting the cats into the cabin, and decided I'd be better safe than sorry. They wouldn't try to take Cat off the deck, but if they rocked the boat unexpectedly they might catch him off balance. The Kitten was below already; I lifted Cat and put him with her, then shut the washboards and cabin hatch. Just in time I remembered the cat-flap, and locked that. There was an indignant growl from within. 'If we don't see them, boy,' I promised. 'If we don't see them I'll let you out again.'

I was going to moor her at the Ladie pontoon again. That would be fine. She'd lie at that. There was no need to use the pier. I didn't need the fender board or extra ropes. For a moment I couldn't think what I needed to do next, then I remembered. Sailing out, that was what I was going to do. I hoisted my crackling white mainsail and admired it for a moment, then untied all the mooring ropes and held the sail back against the wind. We slipped slowly backwards until we were free of the berth, with enough momentum to make a neat turn. The wind was dead behind us as we turned towards the marina entrance, then side-on as we came up between the two rocky walls. I reached for the jib sheet and unrolled it. *Rope on the winch.* I found myself repeating the words in my head as if I was giving instructions. *Two turns around, because we're going to be close-hauled. As soon as we're clear of the marina mouth, take all the ground we can get.*

I hauled the jib in tight, followed with the mainsail and set *Khalida*'s nose as close to the wind as it would go. The Sparl. We wouldn't make it, with leeway, but good enough.

Orcas. There was no sign of them, but they could still be about. I wouldn't let Cat out yet. Devil fish. My thoughts were freewheeling. Devil fish, devil book. Lizbet's devil book. Playing in the old kirk graveyard, digging up the book and daring the Devil. No, I had that wrong. Hoosies in the kirk, hide and seek among the graves, daring the Devil. Not the Devil's book.

I jerked my head upright. My brain cleared and my thoughts steadied. Facts I'd known seemed to come together like jigsaw pieces. *Daring the Devil.* Lizbet hadn't known about the Book of the Black Arts being buried in the graveyard until her Nan told her, during a bad turn. Two or three years back, when she'd been in her late teens. Daring the Devil had been when she was a bairn, playing in the kirkyard. There had been some other devil buried there.

I knew what, too. I'd asked Gavin myself, *Do you suppose they buried the Windhouse baby and the workman and the horned man here?* If ever there was a devil's skeleton, that was one, the horned man, seven foot tall, with the jaws open as if he wanted to bite you. For a flash I saw him in front of my eyes, teeth snarling, looming towards me like the angels of death at the end of the first *Indiana Jones.* 'Likely in a box in the museum,' Gavin had replied, but we hadn't had a Shetland museum then. No. They'd been buried in the graveyard, and Lizbet and her friends had known about him being there. They'd had some sort of bairns' ritual for defying the Devil, where he'd been buried. Her words made sense now: *I've put it where the Devil can stretch out his hand and take it, if he wants it.*

The jib flapped as *Khalida* veered off course, and filled again as I corrected her. The sky was darkening with a cloudy mist: rain, perhaps. I could go another five minutes on this tack.

I kept thinking. My brain felt odd, fogged and working fast

at the same time, connections making themselves. Lizbet and the Devil in the graveyard; but she'd been surprised when I said the Book had been dug up. She'd buried it a long arm's length from his grave. I repeated the words she'd used out loud. 'Stretch out his hand, if he wants it. Take it, if he wants it.' But she wanted it destroyed. It had come out of its grave undamaged after being buried for over a century. Burying it was no good. *I've put it where the Devil can stretch out his hand . . .* She wouldn't have said that if she'd burned it, or ripped it apart. 'Paper,' I said. 'Water.' The Kirk Loch was right there. I remembered seeing the whiter patch in the water a long arm's stretch from the far corner of the kirkyard, where the stones shone clear of silt, as if they'd been disturbed. As if someone had lifted them and put a book underneath them. Lizbet had put the Book under the flat white stones of the loch and left it to dissolve in the water. Never to be brought out again.

Khalida brought her nose up into the wind again. 'Never,' I said to her. I must have rigged the mast wrong. Forestay too loose. I'd look at it once we got home.

We could tack now. I pushed the helm too quickly and was caught scrabbling at jib sheets among flapping sails. 'Peace now,' I said. I freed the jib, and hauled it in on the other side. 'Better.'

Below in the cabin, Cat growled. I'd caught him off balance with that tack. Then I glanced over the side and saw the orcas had arrived.

This close they were something from a nightmare. Fin backwards, Tom had said, and that was the impression the bull gave, with upright edge leading, the slanted edge backward; the cows had the dolphin sickle. It was the bull who was alongside *Khalida*, and his fin in the water was as tall as I was, casting a dark shadow over my face that seemed to come closer and waver away again. The smooth black skin was polished as funeral shoes, with the water running from it as the head surfaced. He gave me a quick, wicked look from the dark eye under the white oval, then cruised alongside, seeming to expand and contract as the waves lapped at him. Beyond him, two others surfaced and cruised with us. I turned my head to look on the other side, beneath the mainsail. There was one there too, close enough to touch with *Khalida* slanted over like this so that the water was only a foot below her side. Close enough to reach up to me and grab, if he had a mind. The flimsy grab rail wire strung from hollow metal staunchions wouldn't stop a creature that size.

The light felt all wrong. It was brightening and darkening again, and the creatures around me seemed to be getting bigger. The jib flapped and I looked at it stupidly for a moment or two before correcting my course. I'd need to tack soon anyway, the shore was getting close, but I wanted these devil fish to go away before I turned among them, in case it annoyed them. Maybe they thought *Khalida* was some kind of white whale, with a sail taller than theirs. Did orcas attack a whale? I'd a feeling that they might, if it was injured. Attack seals. Attack cats. No, I'd shut Cat in the cabin. Attack me. I had to tack soon. The depth sounder showed 6.7 . . . 6.5 . . . 6.3. Sloping beach beneath me. 4.5. These creatures went right onto the beach to snatch seals. I'd seen it in wildlife videos.

'I've got to turn,' I said loudly, to the nearest one. 'Tacking now.'

I undid the jib and pushed the helm over. The flapping sails seemed to startle him. He flipped his tail and went under me. I hoped my keel turning wouldn't hit him. Annoy him. He was too big to annoy.

I fumbled the lee jib sheet in and got *Khalida* settled on the other tack. Now we were heading towards Weathersta. The wind was as on the nose as it could be. 'Zig and zag,' I said, indicating with one hand, 'and zig, Weathersta, zag, Magnie's house, zig, Linga, zag, Muckle Roe. Zig, Houbansetter. A lot of tacking.' My brain felt like it was trying to fight through sludge.

Underneath the surface thoughts another one was hammering *get home quick. Start the engine. Get home as fast as you can.* 'Start the engine,' I agreed. The dark cloud hovering in the Røna was shaped like the Devil, with horns and a tail. The Devil, come for his book. 'I don't have it,' I told him. *Start the engine.* I turned the key, and there was only a snick, then I remembered the starter battery, and switched it on. This time it started. That fierce voice in my head told me to roll the jib away, and I obeyed, because I was too tired to argue, and set *Khalida*'s nose for home.

Water, the fierce voice said. I didn't know I sounded so determined. *Wash your face. Wake yourself up.* The Devil cloud darkened and leaned towards me, and the tall fin came up beside me again. Good to have him where I could see him. I leaned over the lee side and scooped up water, splashed it over me. *Again.* Should have taken my gloves off first. The second splash cleared my wits for a second.

Tom. I remembered him putting his hands in his pockets as he rose, as if he was checking he hadn't dropped anything. What had he got in his pockets? Then, with absolute certainty, what had he put in my coffee? He'd pointed to the marina mouth, and I'd stood up to look, back towards him. I'd felt *Khalida* shift as he'd moved. When I'd turned back to him, he was withdrawing the hand nearest my mug from his pocket, as if he'd just put something back in there. A little container . . .

Without stopping to think about it, I leaned over the lee side and retched. Nothing. I took the end of my plait and shoved it into my throat, and this time my whole breakfast came up, and the coffee with it. There was a bottle of water in the cockpit. I drank as much as I could. The bull orca seemed to be laughing at me.

On Up Helly Aa morning Tom had told me about Chloe trying to cut Lizbet out, but he'd said Lizbet didn't notice. He didn't know she'd overheard the producers talking about her and Chloe. He didn't know she knew, for her motive to harm

Chloe that he was trying to sell me. He'd said Lizbet had buried the book in Windhouse, but she hadn't. Antony hadn't dug it up. My thoughts were whirling with the flashing lights in the sky. Tom had drugged me. His excuse for coming to talk to me was spinning a yarn blaming Lizbet, but to really get himself off the hook he had to get Lizbet out of the way and let her take the blame. I needed to tell Gavin to check on Lizbet. I just needed to press one button. Didn't need to remember his number.

It took two hands to get my phone out of my pocket, and the lights on it were swaying too. One button. For a moment I thought he wasn't going to answer and a blind panic swept through me, then at last the rings stopped and I heard his voice, sounding totally normal, as if the sky wasn't changing colour, and there wasn't a monster beside me. 'Cass?'

'Gavin,' I said. My voice sounded in slow motion. 'You need to check on Lizbet.'

'Where are you, Cass?'

I lifted my head to look around and tried to gather my thoughts. The hill beside me was opening and shutting like a Spanish fan. 'Linga. Going home. Engine. Check on Lizbet. Going home as fast as I can. Orcas. May not let me land. Devil too.'

'*Cass*,' Gavin said. His voice was as firm as the voice in my head, and it broke through the fog.

'Tom,' I said. 'Drugged my coffee. Going home.'

'When you get there,' Gavin said, 'don't sleep. Okay? Get off the boat and start walking. Don't go into the house. Walk and walk, and when you get to the end of our road, turn towards Aith.'

'Walk,' I agreed. 'Turn towards Aith. You check on Lizbet.'

'Where are you now?'

'Still Linga.' For a moment I couldn't remember the points of the compass. 'Nearly home.' I gathered my wits together. 'You check Lizbet. I'll walk, if the orcas will let me. Cat's shut in.'

The water I'd drunk had had time to get down. 'Need to be sick again.' I snicked the phone off and went back to the lee side. One of the smaller orcas was only ten metres away, watching me. *Ignore it*, the voice in my head said. *Be sick.*

I wasn't sure whether that second dose of vomiting made me feel worse or better, but every grain less of whatever Tom had poisoned me with had to be good. You could fight sleeping pills. I wanted coffee but I couldn't get into the cabin without letting Cat out. I finished the water, and leaned over for cupped handfuls of seawater to splash over my face. The Devil cloud swayed above Papa Little, as if it was laughing.

It must have only been ten minutes more to Houbansetter, but it felt like forever. The bull orca paced me all the way, the shadow of his tall fin slicing my cockpit in half; once he yawned, showing two half-ovals of curved teeth. The others came and went like mirages at the corner of my vision, a fin jutting up then sliding under the water. I tried to fix my gaze on the Ladie pier, to steer a straight course towards it. Going home. That was the important thing. Get home before I slept. *Fight it.* I splashed my face again. Lobster buoys. Go round them. Waves from starboard, go to port. I was so tired . . . *fight it.*

My phone rang. It was Gavin. There was a car engine in the background, and a siren. 'How're you doing?'

'Going home. Point o' Houbansetter. Two hundred metres. Tie up and walk.'

'Walk,' he agreed. 'However sleepy you are, walk. Keep talking to me. Where are the orcas?'

'On starboard. The bull. The others . . . all over. Following me. Do they eat whales?'

'*Khalida*'s not a whale.'

'They eat rudders. The Bay of Biscay.'

'Spanish orcas,' Gavin said. 'Shetland ones don't eat rudders.'

I managed a laugh at that. 'Tell him. A hundred metres. Need to go. Concentrate.'

I laid the phone down again. As if at a signal, the bull dived, the great fin curving downwards, disappearing, rising again further away. The fin and dark back veered away from me, and the others converged towards it. For a moment I had them all in one sight, then they dived, leaving only empty water, rose again in a group of dark fins, heading away still, dived again. I hoped they were gone. The bare water felt ominous, as if they might suddenly rise all around me, toothed mouths open like something from *Jaws*, might leap at the last moment into the boat.

The pontoon was only thirty metres now. I cut *Khalida*'s engine to neutral. Her momentum would take her the rest of the way. Loose the mainsail. I felt too unsteady to go up onto the cockpit roof to drop it here at sea. Once I was tied up. She glided in smoothly. I was so intent on watching her reach it that I forgot I needed to steer her, and made a bungled turn, a half-circle which had her bumping the pontoon nose on and getting stalled there, stern sticking out, wind filling the main and holding her that way. Wouldn't do. I made a loop of rope and threw it to catch the sticking-out tube at the end of the pontoon. It took me three goes to lassoo it. Pull. Her stern went in, her nose came out, the mainsail flapped. I hauled the rope tight and secured it. Bow rope. I made my way forwards, testing each step as if I was at sea in a gale. Secure the rope to the bow. Round the pontoon handrail. Back to the bow. Midships line. Spring. I fumbled each rope on and drew it tight. Secure. Sleep. *No, not sleep yet.*

My head was clearing, though it still spun as I clambered up onto the cabin roof, holding the swaying boom to keep my balance. My hands knew the movements to fold the sail as it fell. 'Zip,' I told myself. 'Other end.' I held on to the boom to the end of the cabin roof, then had to go back to where the stays were, for a handhold down. 'Zip.' I swayed as I stood on the cockpit seat, and for a moment I was suspended backwards over the water, then the boom swung across, and I followed it, my left hand feeling for the long zip pull. I found it, and hauled. It ran sweetly, smoothly along the top of the folded mainsail. Secure. Front part later.

The black fins had gone. I let Cat and the Kitten out, and took their lifejackets off. I took my own lifejacket off. *Walk*, the voice in my head reminded me. Not into the house, not even for coffee. Walk. Walk and turn towards Aith when I got to the road. I was so weary. I just wanted to go into my berth and sleep, a little rest, but the voice in my head was determined. *Walk*. I sat down to take my seaboots off, and found my eyelids closing, my back swaying towards the cockpit side. I was about to succumb when the phone rang. I picked it up and jabbed at the button. Gavin's face swayed in the screen. 'Cass?'

'Still me,' I agreed. 'I'll have to walk in my seaboots. Can't sit down. I'll just sleep.'

'Walk in your seaboots,' Gavin agreed. 'Is *Khalida* tied up?'

I nodded. My head felt too heavy.

'Cass?'

Khalida was swaying just as the hills had. 'Tied. Bow, spring, midship, stern. Tied.'

'Is your cabin shut?'

'No.' I laid the phone aside again. 'Washboards.' They were hard to fit in their groove. 'Cabin hatch.' I pulled it towards me. 'All shut.'

Cat and the Kitten had bounded ahead. I followed them. 'Walk,' I said to the phone in my hand.

'Yes, walk,' Gavin agreed. 'Recite me some poetry.' The siren still wailed in his background.

'We're all going to the zoo tomorrow. Tomorrow . . .' I remembered bending over Chloe in Campbell's Closs, and searched for another poem. Easter was coming. 'Love bade me welcome, yet my soul drew back.' I lost the thread and repeated it. 'My soul drew back.'

'Guilty of dirt and sin,' Gavin prompted.

'Something . . . Love sweetly asked, If I lacked anything. Walk.' I couldn't keep walking, I was too tired. I had to keep walking. 'A guest I answered fitted to be here.'

'Ah, my dear, Love answered, you are she.' His voice was like honey.

My legs were tired. I stumbled on: up the gravel track and past the house. The ponies snorted at me as I came past, and walked on their side of the fence with me as I staggered up the drive behind. Up. I wanted to lie down on the verge of soft grass. 'I the unworthy . . . The ponies are staring at me.'

In the phone, Gavin laughed. 'I can't remember any more. Try another one. If you can keep your head . . .'

Sailors had their own version of that one. 'When all about you, are losing theirs and blaming it on you.' Keep walking. The top of the hill. 'If you can trust yourself when your helm doubts you . . .' Going down was easier. Step after step after step. 'I'm at the gate now. Make allowance for his doubting too.' I could see where the loop was but when I tried to put my hands on it they were to the side, and they seemed to be transparent. I could see the blood in them, red going down to my fingertips and blue coming back. *Tom drugged you*, the fierce voice said in my head. *Pull yourself together.* The fence at the side of the gate was swing-a-leg-over height. I swung, overbalanced and ended up on the ground, and it was so comfortable, the grass tickling my cheek. *Get up*, the voice insisted. *Up.* My fogged brain knew the voice was right. 'Cass?' Gavin said in my ear. '*Cass?*'

There was a ringing noise in the distance, over where the hills were still shivering under the Devil cloud. A blue light flashed. Pretty. I watched it with interest as my legs forced me up. My hand grabbed the fence wire. Like a Christmas light. *Walk.* I let go of the fence and staggered forwards. So sleepy. Each step seemed to take a minute. It was like tacking, I thought muzzily, a bit one way, then a bit the other, and you ended up forwards. I looked around me for the orcas, but they'd gone, and

I remembered I'd left them behind in the voe. 'Water,' I said. 'Orcas swim. Land. Keep walking.'

The ringing was getting louder, splitting the dark sky. The Devil cloud dissolved in the noise. The hills shrank back. The police car stopped beside me, and Gavin got out.

'Hi, Cass,' he said, and held out a bottle of clouded liquid. 'Drink this.'

VII

The deil goes awa' when he finds the door
steekit against him (Scots proverb)
The Devil goes away when he finds the door locked against him.

Chapter Twenty-five

Better to wael your haand oot o a wolf's mouth as rive him out.
(Better to ease your hand out of a wolf's mouth than to tear it out.)
When in a dangerous situation the best results are
achieved through acting calmly and quietly.

I lay awake in the hospital ward and ached with homesick-
ness. I wanted to be in our bedroom at the Ladie, with Gavin
sleeping beside me, back turned, so that I could snuggle up
around him and lay my cheek against his back, and Cat on my
other side, curled up on my pillow. I longed for the silence of
the country, and darkness shot with stars in the square of
window.

Instead, I was stretched uncomfortably on my back on a
pneumatic bed fitted with a sweat-inducing rubber sheet, and
attached to a machine by a series of wires which were taped on
my chest. Orange street-lighting oozed around the drawn cur-
tains, and in the dim green light of the emergency signs the
hospital ward was as full of noises as a tall ship, but unfamiliar
noises, tickings and tricklings, a machine wheezing in the far
corner, the measured tread of two nurses in the corridor, soft
voices at the reception.

They hadn't let me sleep earlier, and now that I was alone at
last I'd passed the sleepy stage and was awake again. Since the
doctor in charge didn't know what drug Tom had given me, I
was 'under observation', which meant the wires and a nurse
checking my pulse, blood pressure and temperature every hour,

right through the night until morning, when I hoped I'd be allowed to go home.

Lizbet was home already, discharged without being taken in. Tom had visited her just before he'd come to me, but she was certain he hadn't slipped anything into her coffee, or doctored anything else in the house, and there were no signs of her being drugged. 'He wasn't in the kitchen,' she assured me, when she came up to the ward to see how I was, before the police took her up to her folk in Breckon for safe-keeping. 'He sat on the sofa for a bit, and then we ran through some songs, and then he went. He didn't seem anything out of the ordinary.' She paused and gave me a sideways glance. 'I can't believe Tom would have done all this. I really can't. Are you sure you didn't just eat something that disagreed with you?'

'Positive,' I said.

'But you didn't actually see him putting anything in your coffee.'

'No.'

'Why would he want to drug you anyway?'

I wanted to know the answer to that too. 'What did you talk about, while he was sitting?' I asked.

'Our sets for the Folk Festival. What songs, in what order, and what we'd do as a big-finish encore that would get people clapping along. Then we tried out various combinations, to see what sounded best.'

Focused. 'He didn't speak about Chloe, or Antony?'

She shook her head. 'We didn't want to think about it. He did try to talk about the Book again, where I'd put it. I repeated what I'd told him that night at Up Helly Aa, after that old-books man talked to me, that it was where nobody would find it.'

'In the loch,' I said. 'Under the white stones, where the horned man could reach it if he wanted it.'

She stared at me as if I was a witch. 'How did you ken that?'

'Guessed,' I said. 'You mentioned daring the Devil in the

298

graveyard when you were a bairn, and there were folk in Wind-house when you got there.'

'I did think of putting it in Windhouse,' she said, 'under the rubble, but it seemed too obvious a place, and folk are always going there. It'd get found sooner or later. I'd have had to dig it deep, and it would still be obvious something had been bur-ied. Then when I got there I stopped for a moment, wondering, but there were tourists with torches, and Mam was expecting me off the ferry, and I wasn't going back to Windhouse after dark. The horned man was a much better idea. I stopped at the kirkyard on the way home. I reached as far as I could into the loch, shifted some stones and dug up the sand to make a hollow, and put it in. I put the stones back on top and added a few extra, and left it there for the water to destroy.'

'But you didn't tell Tom that?'

She shook her head hard. 'I wouldn't. He did ask if it was Windhouse, and I kinda snapped at him that I wasn't going to tell him. He didn't ask any more after that. I didn't care how much it was worth, or what we could do with the money. I ken someone killed Chloe, though I don't believe it was Tom, but I think the Book kinda caused it all, and I wanted it to stay in the loch and dissolve and do no more harm.'

'Me too.' I hoped the police wouldn't have to produce it as evidence. 'Was that all he asked?'

'He did ask if anyone else knew about it. I said I'd told you and Magnie, and that was all.'

I was silent for a moment, thinking about that.

'You're making a mistake,' Lizbet said firmly, and rose. 'Tom's not like that. I ken him.' She paused, and added, 'I hope you feel better soon,' then raised a hand and left the ward. *Naive*, Tom had called her. Loyal. She wasn't going to believe her friend Tom was a killer.

Now, in the hospital night, I lay and thought. Tom. DS Peterson had been on her way to bring him in for further questioning when he'd come to drug me. Gavin had once said he thought about the how, and that led him to the who, and Tom had had the easiest how. He'd been at Chloe's end of the table, facing her. He was the one who could most easily have doctored her drink as he helpfully moved it out of the waiter's way when the food arrived. He knew he was going to meet her for lunch, as Jesma, Amy and Irvine didn't.

Only once he'd thought of how did Gavin consider the why, because motive wasn't per se evidence. I didn't need to worry about convincing a jury, but I thought I knew why Tom might want to kill Chloe: his belief in his talent, his ambition to make a career in music.

When he'd been speaking of Lizbet, he'd been thinking of himself. The sleeping potion had been a gamble, to get Chloe out of the way; to get the exposure of *You're the Stars!* for him and Lizbet. He'd disliked Chloe. He hadn't wanted her in the band. He'd given her the jet-lag potion before she drove home to Brae, not caring whether she was slightly hurt or killed, so long as she didn't get in the way of him and Lizbet appearing on TV. *That might make us some money*, he'd said. The money they'd wanted to make the kind of music video producers would look at. He might have been right in dismissing the fame as any use to them, because it would be the wrong sort of music, but I thought now that had been partly smokescreen. If they'd got into the national heats they might have been able to do their own music in the final rounds. Even if they didn't, their talent would have been recognised, their names known. Producers would have been interested.

For all his pooh-poohing, he'd wanted that gig as much as Chloe and Lizbet had.

He'd been speaking of himself about Antony too, except that he'd twisted the reason. He'd said Lizbet had wanted the book back to make sure it did no more harm. Tom had wanted the Book because it was valuable, worth the kind of money that

300

would let them make that video. Lizbet wouldn't tell him exactly where she'd put it, but he knew she'd gone up to Yell.

He was going to have got a lift home with Chloe, he'd said afterwards, though I presumed he'd have thought of an urgent errand in town and said he'd get the bus when it came to it. That meant that he didn't have a car. His dad did. I remembered the line of black pick-ups as workers were clearing the slip for Up Helly Aa. He'd borrowed his dad's black pick-up on Sunday morning and headed for Yell to search for the book Lizbet had hidden. He knew her well enough to follow the way her mind worked. Give it back to the Devil, and where did the Devil bide in Yell but in Windhouse? He didn't know about the bunch of ghost-hunters in the Star Rent-a-car; he'd gone there and seen the way some planks had been displaced, and the space where someone had been digging there already. Then he'd remembered seeing Antony heading out the night before – Antony, who'd been outside as he'd been talking to Lizbet at Up Helly Aa. Maybe he'd looked out across that sliver of Bluemull Sound visible from Windhouse and seen Antony's flash fishing boat heading homewards. He'd have thought, as we had, that Antony had got there first and found the book. He'd got the next ferry back and headed to his house to confront him.

Antony would have denied it, of course, and Tom wouldn't have believed him. Antony had stolen his book. He looked gangly but, as he'd said of Lizbet, he was used to carrying a heavy amp. He had the strength to push Antony hard enough to make him overbalance. He hadn't cared whether Chloe was slightly injured or dead, and he hadn't cared about Antony either. If Lizbet had done that, she'd have called for help. Tom searched for the book, and when he didn't find it in the house, he went down to the boat. It was books that had been disturbed, and the one I'd seen lying on the cushion had been the most old-fashioned on the shelf, the only one that might have been what he was looking for.

If Lizbet kept quiet about the Book, Tom had no motive for killing Antony – but she'd told me, and I was the policeman's girlfriend. That must have made Tom decide that he needed to get rid of me. A longshot, like with Chloe, drugging me before I sailed my boat home.

While Gavin had come for me yesterday, another squad had gone to get Lizbet. DS Peterson hadn't found Tom. He'd been practising with Lizbet, his mother said, then he'd taken his dad's pick-up in the middle of the afternoon, and he wasn't home yet. He'd be back later. DS Peterson had posted a squad car to look out for him, but he hadn't returned, and the lass at Northlink was pretty certain he'd not gone on the ferry; he'd not pre-booked, and there'd been no last-minute passengers who hadn't shown a photo ID. The pick-up had been found parked opposite the library in Lerwick.

That was why I had a bored police officer snoozing in the armchair that had been placed at this end of the ward, between two windows. There was another officer down at the main reception, just in case, though, as Gavin had said, this place had a dozen exits and entrances, with corridors leading between them. In theory, at this time of night only the main reception door that led directly to A&E was open.

I glanced across at my officer's chair, and realised I must have dozed off after all, for it was empty. Maybe he'd gone to stretch his legs to keep himself awake, or to watch TV in the room whose door gave a good view of the ward reception. I eased myself up to a sitting position and looked around. There were quiet footsteps coming from the corridor, but they turned off into the smaller ward next door. I leaned back again. I was feeling perfectly all right. Maybe next time the nurse came to check my 'vital signs' she'd let me take the wires off.

All was obviously well next door; the soft footsteps came towards this ward, halted in the doorway and advanced again. The curtain of the next-door bed blocked my view. The person was doing the usual ward round, pausing by each bed. I watched the corner of the curtain, and he came into view: a young man in a green overall going softly to each bed, checking the name above it. He had a tray with a plastic beaker of water on it, and one of those little pill cups. His face was hidden under a surgical mask.

That wasn't right. I'd been here only a day, but I'd never seen even a doctor masked like that, let alone a green-shirt, who were the tea-givers and ward-cleaners, and the green-shirts definitely didn't give out 'meds'.

He had his back to me, walking slowly along the far side of the ward, looking for the right name. I recognised the shape of him, the uncoordinated walk, and remembered: *I worked in the hospital for a bit.* He'd known his way around: the signing-in system, where the overalls were kept. He knew the hospital routines. He knew that if a patient was touched on the shoulder in the night and given pills to swallow, they'd do it without questions.

It was Tom, come to look for me. He must have waited and watched as I'd sailed home, and seen that I'd made it, in spite of his best efforts. No doubt we'd made Radio Shetland. *A woman from the Brae area was taken in to the Gilbert Bain Hospital in a suspected poisoning incident.* I kept watching him from the corner of my eye as I eased the wires off my chest and let them slither down the side of the bed, then slid my legs down between my bed and next-door's curtain. It wasn't easy to move on these beds without them creaking. Inch by inch I went floorwards, as he moved along the beds opposite. My heart was thudding so loud I was surprised he couldn't hear it.

My feet found the floor at last. I stood and dropped quickly to the ground, under the curtain. The woman in the bed was fast asleep, mouth slightly open. I didn't want to wake her with an alarm in the night, but I couldn't get past her bed to the door without shoogling the bed or making it obvious someone was moving behind the curtain.

I dropped down and slid under her bed. There was a discreditable amount of dust in the middle, where it was too much bother to hoover, and a piece of plaster-backing, as well as the mechanics of the bed, which was lower than I'd expected from the upper height of it. I wormed silently under it, and came out on the other side. Nearly at the door now.

A glance through the curtain crack showed me that Tom had reached the last bed, the one opposite mine. He turned slowly and began walking towards mine, the plastic tray held before him. I let him get closer, to where he couldn't see this side of the curtain, then slipped out between the curtain and the wall and leapt for the door, bare feet silent on the warm linoleum.

Now I was in the corridor. There were doors all the way along: the smaller ward, the bathroom, the toilet and shower, the sluice room, before it opened out to the ward reception on one side and the TV room on the other. There was nobody at reception, just a computer screen shining into the dimness, and no sign of my police officer in the day room. I felt like a target in plain sight.

Wherever my officer had gone, there was another one at reception. I slid behind the desk and tried to make sense of the list on the phone. Usually it was zero. I stretched out my hand to it, then realised that if Tom came out as I was speaking, I'd be cornered behind the desk.

Where was everyone? In the men's ward at the other end, maybe, or called to a sudden emergency, while I played hide and seek with a murderer.

There were footsteps in the corridor from the direction of the ward I'd been in. I had to go now, downstairs, as quickly as I could. I bolted for the door, not caring about noise and hurled myself at the flight of steps, one hand out to grab the bannister. The footsteps behind me speeded up. I had to reach help, he had to catch me before I reached it, and he had the advantage of me in knowing the fastest way to the main door. I ran down the steps at a dangerous speed, bare feet slipping on the treads, hearing him gaining on me, and hesitated for a second in the square at the bottom before I saw the exit arrow.

It was a second too long. A hand grabbed at the back of my t-shirt. I wrenched myself free and darted through the door, shoving it closed against him behind me. There was another set of doors only ten metres further. I leapt for them and saw a corridor stretching out in front of me, too long a corridor. With his longer legs he'd be on me before I'd got halfway.

I wasn't going to make the mistake of looking behind. I could sense his hand at my back again. I grabbed the side of the door and slammed it against him as hard as I could.

It took him off balance. He went down with a satisfying thud, giving me the start I needed. The end of the corridor, with its big EXIT sign, was in plain sight. The main reception, where the other police officer was stationed, was just round the corner. I sprinted along the corridor and as I reached the bend my officer and the reception one came charging out from the other side in full alert mode. I side-stepped them just in time and pointed back to Tom, picking himself up from the floor.

They advanced on him with a speed and heaviness that was a joy to watch. He was handcuffed in seconds, and my officer held on to him while the other one got on the police radio.

I wanted to stay and hear what excuse he'd think up, but I suddenly realised that I was standing there in a baggy t-shirt, with dust down my front and my hair curling wildy round my face. I left them to it and retreated to bed.

Chapter Twenty-six

Monday 27th March

Tide times, Brae:
LW 04.16 (1.02m);
HW 10.15 (1.58m);
LW 15.58 (1.4m);
HW 21.27 (1.46m)

Sunrise 05.41; moonrise 06.40; moonset 12.15;
sunset 18.39. Moon waning crescent.

Better da peerie coll at waarms you as
da muckle ane at burns you.
Better the small coal that warms you as the big one that burns you.

It was three days later. The last gold rays of the sun burnished the water and shone in the sit-ootery windows, highlighting a discreditable veneer of salt from the winter gales. I'd get out there with a bucket tomorrow. The couch below them was bright with a multicoloured crochet cover. The Kitten slept in one corner of it, with Cat on watch beside her, and me at the other end. Gavin and DS Peterson sat in the easy chairs one each side of the table and gloomed at each other.

'Lawyered up,' DS Peterson said. She put on a lawyer voice. 'Have you any proof that my client drugged Chloe's drink? Have you proved he's ever bought a jet-lag pill or liquid?'

'No,' Gavin agreed, 'we haven't.' He glanced across at me, doing my best to be innocently inconspicuous. 'All we can reasonably do him for is an attempt to attack Cass in the hospital, and as he had the presence of mind to dispose of whatever he was going to feed her before he ran after her, and didn't manage to lay hands on her anyway, all we have is a suspicious set of circumstances and an unharmed policeman's girlfriend who alleges she was given some sort of hallucinogenic drug, which was mostly vomited up before she got there, so they couldn't identify it. We can't do him for that.'

'Police harrassment,' DS Peterson said. 'Personal vindictiveness because it's your girlfriend.'

They both fell silent for a moment.

'Here's what we've got,' DS Peterson said at last. 'Under questioning, Irvine thinks he might, just might, have noticed Tom moving Chloe's glass as he cleared the table when the waiter arrived with the food. Amy didn't notice, nor Lizbet. Any decent prosecution counsel would demolish that, and keep pointing out that Tom had told everyone he was going back to Brae in Chloe's car. "Would my client have said that, m'lud, if he was planning for her to have a driving accident on the way home?" There's no sign of him having bought jet-lag medication and he's never been abroad, though his parents had a trip to New York three years ago for their silver wedding anniversary, and his mother thinks she might have bought some, because she didn't want to waste any of their time there with jet lag, but she can't just mind, it was a while ago, and she thinks she likely threw what was left out. It's certainly not in the house now. Lizbet agrees that she told Cass the producers liked Chloe, but she's definite that she never told Tom that.'

'He could have worked it out himself from their reactions,' Gavin said.

DS Peterson sighed. 'No jury'll ever believe it as a motive.' She put on the lawyer voice again. ' "She was a lousy singer, and she sang the wrong kind of songs, m'lud." End of case for Chloe. Even less for Antony. Tom might have threatened him to hand over the Book of the Black Arts, and struck out at him when Antony said he hadn't a clue what Tom was talking about, but we can't prove it. Lizbet admitted in a flood of tears that she'd dug up an old book, but insisted that she never told Tom where she'd got rid of it. Then when we mentioned the Kirk Loch there were more tears. That down-loosing last week stirred up all the algae over the stones and added an extra foot of water, so we can't see where she put it. Angus tried in the most likely spots, and that mass of sludgy paper was probably it, though I don't think it would have destroyed that easily.'

It was the Kirk Loch, I thought. The water in it had run over consecrated ground. She gave me a sharp look. 'I ken you have a soft spot for youngsters, Cass, but she's as bad as he is. She was determined enough to dig up that book at dead of night and ill-wish her friend, whatever she says about "just wanting it to be her". What did she think the Devil was going to do, wave a sparkly wand like a good fairy and wish everyone happy ever after?'

She was surprisingly vehement. I wondered if she had an Evangelical background.

'The whole point of it was malevolence,' she continued. 'She should never have touched the thing. And if he gets off the pair of them will take that TV show, if they get it, and probably dedicate their performance to their talented friend, Chloe.' She gave a disgusted snort and turned back to Gavin. 'Not a print in the house,' she said bitterly. 'Not one. The door jamb had been wiped. There might, just might, be a smudged print they can lift from the front of Antony's shirt, the stiffer bit at the throat. One smudged print. Tom says he was home in bed, his parents are sure they'd have heard him go out. Nothing in the boat either, except glove-smudges.'

'We needed one decent print,' Gavin said. 'One print where

it shouldn't have been. Enough to tie all these suspicious circumstances together.' He sighed and drank the rest of his coffee. 'I don't blame the Fiscal. He couldn't have done anything else. No evidence, no case.'

'Maybe . . .' I said, and stopped as they both turned towards me. Gavin's face was resigned; DS Peterson's expression said she was desperate enough to consider suggestions even from me. I cleared my throat and began again. 'Tom wasn't used to boats. He was awful unhandy aboard. Clambered on using all the wrong handholds. And if you're not sure, you'd want to be able to grip properly, with your bare hands, quite apart from it being really conspicuous walking along the pontoon wearing Marigolds, even on the morning after the Hop when there shouldn't be anyone about to see you. You wouldn't put them on until you were safely in the cockpit. Do you know if your forensics folk printed the whole outside of the boat, even the unexpected places, like along the rubbing strake, or even under that moulded bit that sticks out, or the staunchions that hold the guard wires? He could have grabbed any of those.' I ended with a shrug. 'Worth a look anyway.'

Slowly, their faces changed. 'He did the obvious places,' DS Peterson said. 'I'm sure he didn't do the whole side of the boat.'

'Prints live for ages on hard surfaces,' Gavin said. 'And fibreglass takes bonny prints. It's worth a try. Juries love fingerprints that show someone was where they had no reason ever to be. Especially if it's similar to a smudged one on a dead man's shirt.' He smiled at me. 'Thanks, Cass.'

Wednesday 12th April

Tides of no relevance to a woman acting as cat midwife.

Spring came suddenly in the first week of April, washing over the hills in soft green and bursting into daffodils at every

309

roadside. The hens came out of their house again and clucked contentedly round the garden. The ponies left their sheltered corner and took notions to suddenly stop grazing and charge around their park together, bucking exuberantly. I spent the time being domestic, trying out what I could cook with an oven and turning the sit-ootery into a dining area, ready for Dad and Maman coming over for Easter. I'd taken *Khalida* out to Vementry, the Hams o' Roe and Papa Stour; I'd had four driving lessons in town without crashing the instructor's car, and I'd put in for a cancellation test, if it came before 6th May. I'd inspected the garden, removed obvious weeds and couch-grass and dug over the vegetable patch, with supervision over the fence from both ponies and the active assistance of several hens and both cats. I'd almost got used to sleeping on land.

Forensics had re-dusted Antony's boat, and found prints that had enough points of resemblance with Tom's to get the Fiscal rethinking the case, including a beautiful whole-hand print where he'd steadied himself on the outside of the cabin. He was now in custody.

I'd done some serious thinking. I'd sailed out into St Magnus Bay and hove to, so that the boat edged gently forwards, sails balanced against each other, waves washing gently on her side, and sat back with my feet up on the opposite seat and thought. I'd thought about ambition, and whether I really genuinely enjoyed the responsibility of a tall ship with twenty crew and seventy trainees; about wanting to have it all, about what I already had and could have.

Our local tall ship, the *Swan*, was looking for a new skipper. She was a converted former fishing boat a third of the size of *Sørlandet*, with only two masts and no tiers of white sails, but she spent her summer taking groups of twelve trainees around Shetland and to Scotland and Norway, and each year she went further afield with the Tall Ships Race. I was pretty sure the current mate would get the skipper's post, but that left a mate's berth vacant. She only sailed from May to September, so I'd be home all winter, and around more in the summer. I'd written to express interest, and heard nothing, until the letter came offering me an interview.

That had been three days ago. I'd been ridiculously nervous. I'd gone dressed in my best *Sørlandet* shore-going uniform of navy shirt, navy trousers, hair smoothed into a plait. It felt like a venture thrown up into the lap of the gods, a penny tossed. If I got it, I'd be home with Gavin. If I didn't, I'd keep sailing the oceans. I wasn't sure what to wish for, though I suspected that, like a penny tossed, I'd only know which way I'd really wanted when it fell.

I did my best. I knew I had the qualifications, the experience. Given they already had a good woman, they might want a man in second place. I heard my voice shake at first, but it steadied as they asked me questions I could answer, and by the end of the interview I was leaning forward to give them my ideas of where the *Swan* could go and how I'd take her there. The interviewers were smiling and nodding, and in imagining what I could do with her, I was feeling myself part of *Swan*'s crew already.

Then the one on the panel who'd sat quiet throughout had leaned forward and asked how soon I could take up the post. 'Not till the 4th of July,' I'd had to say. I saw their faces change. That was almost halfway through the season. I looked straight at them and told the truth. 'I'm Acting First Officer aboard *Sørlandet* for the current First Officer's maternity leave. I'm due back aboard for my eight weeks on the 9th of May, and I can't expect them to find another replacement just like that. If they did, I could come sooner.' I knew it was the wrong answer, but I couldn't leave *Sørlandet* in the lurch, even if it meant this job would go to an equally good candidate who could come now.

They'd thanked me, and I'd left. I hadn't heard anything since. I should have heard by now, I thought, and felt a pang of disappointment so sharp that it startled me. This was the way

I'd wanted the coin to fall: this peaceful, comfortable life with the domestic routine we'd settled into: breakfast together, the day apart, meet again at dinner, evening together. Most days I made our meal, since I was home, but on Fridays and Saturdays he did, and on Sunday we went to my parents'. Dad bloomed like seaweed in a flood tide to see his wayward daughter so domesticated.

'It's only skin-deep,' Gavin said cheerfully. His wooden flute was beginning to sound good, and his bagpipes resounded over the hills on dry days. We went for evening walks along the shore at dusk, with both cats following, though as the Kitten had got rounder the walks had got shorter. Now she was a little football on paws, and she'd been restless for two days, which Gavin reckoned was a sign. She'd taken to investigating dark corners in a nesting sort of way. We'd got several boxes from the shop, put towels in them and had left them around the house for her to try, but naturally she was having none of them. Her favourite place was the Aladdin basket in the bedroom, where we put clothes for washing; she had a clever way of stretching up it, pushing her nose under the rim of the lid and oozing in. We'd see the apricot tail-tip waving above the tilted lid, and then it would close behind her, and the only thing to tell us she was in there was the contented purring echoing from inside. It looked an awkward place for kittens to me, but if she was determined, then so be it.

All the same, I hoped she'd save them for an evening, when Gavin was there. I'd consulted the internet, and there was quite a lot about cats wanting privacy, and to leave them alone until it was all over, but it'd be good to have an experienced hand to keep out of the way with; and besides, she was Gavin's special cat, just as Cat was mine. The weekend would have been better still, even if it was Easter, but judging by her belly she wouldn't wait that long. It was a good sailing day, but I didn't want to risk leaving her.

I was hanging up a load of washing on the pulley above the Rayburn when she came to get me. She miaowed twice, a demanding wail ten times louder than her usual squeak, took two steps towards the stairs, turned back to me and yowled again. *Now*, she was quite clearly saying. I flung the t-shirt I was hanging over the rail and headed after her. She climbed the stairs slowly, checking that I was still behind her, and made straight for her basket. I lifted the lid for her and knelt down beside it. She clambered in, crouched in the bottom for a moment, stiffening, then lay on her side. She was obviously having contractions now, breathing with her mouth open. I gave her belly a tentative stroke. '*Push,*' I said.

Suddenly a dark bundle slid out of her, glistening wet, and enclosed in a greyish membrane. I wondered if I should be doing something, but the Kitten was straight there, licking it off and getting her baby dried.

It was a tiny, tiny creature. I'd never been present at a birth – Maman had been dead against pets – and I hadn't expected it to look so complete. You could have fitted four of it on my spread hand, and it had a funny flattened face and sewn-shut eyes, but it had fingernail-tiny white paws with miniature claws, and a fluffy coat, the same tortoiseshell colour as the Kitten, which I thought made it a girl, but darker, with more black among the ginger, and a white muzzle and bib. Once her baby was washed to the Kitten's satisfaction, she curled up around it and purred proudly as it felt its blind way to a teat and began sucking.

'You're very clever,' I told her. 'It's a beautiful ketling.'

The website I'd looked up reckoned a litter of kittens could take from four hours to all day to be born, giving the mother time to rest in between. I fetched my phone and book, put a cushion on the floor and stationed myself in readiness. Let Gavin know first. I sent a text: *First ketling born all well*. I made sure the flash was turned off and added a photo. *Think it's a girl*.

313

He phoned back straight away, face excited. 'You caught me in my tea break. Is everything okay?'

'All good,' I assured him. 'She insisted I needed to be there. She just pushed and it came out.' I turned the phone so he could see into the basket. 'It's so tiny – should it be that small?'

'Smaller the better,' his voice assured me. I turned him round again. 'Particularly from the mother's point of view, and especially when she's as small as the Kitten. Any sign of more?'

'Not yet. It's sucking away, and she's purring like mad.'

'Keep me updated. I must go. See you later.'

I switched off and picked up my book. It was a Hornblower, full of seamanly derring-do, and it had held me enthralled last night, but I couldn't concentrate now. There was purring and sucking coming from the basket, and the occasional indignant squeak as Kitten washed too hard. Feed the mother, the website had said, and of course she wouldn't want to leave her baby alone. I spent the next ten minutes organising food, water, cat milk and a litter tray, with a pause to check that no more kittens were arriving between forays downstairs. Nothing. The Kitten came out, had some food and a good drink, used the litter tray and went back in. I picked Hornblower up and had managed to remember what I'd read last when my phone pinged again. It was a text from Gavin: *The only female saints for today are Acutina, Teresa of the Andes and Vissia of Fermo xxx*

I imagined standing at the door calling, 'Acutina! Vissia!' and shook my head. *Doesn't trip off the tongue. No male saints we could adapt? xxx*

The answer came back quickly. *Pope Julius I. Julie, Julia, Julianne in English or French.*

I tried them with a soft French J. Julia. Yes, I liked that. I was just about to say so when my phone pinged again. *I ken you're not used to giving cats actual names, but I put my foot down at Kittenette xxx*

So do I, I texted back. *I like Julia said in French.*

314

No sign of more?

Not as yet.

I sat by the basket for the rest of the morning, with excursions downstairs to hang up the rest of the washing and take some mince out of the freezer, and there was still no sign of any more. One hour, two, three. I nipped down to make a sandwich for lunch, and brought it up. Cat came up to inspect, stretching up the basket to peer over the rim. 'Now you appear, once it's over,' I said to him. The Kitten stretched up to sniff his whiskers, then lay down again, one paw over little Julia, but more as if she was enjoying cuddling her than in a defensive way.

Gavin gave a quick call in his lunch hour. 'No more?'

'No.' I turned him to let him see. 'Mother and baby doing well. Cat came up to look, then settled on the bed.'

'Obviously plotting the first train set and football training already. I looked up the cat birth website, and it reckoned a small cat might have only one kitten. I think they'd have come by now if there were going to be any more.'

'She seems fine. Not as if one's stuck or anything. She's had food and milk and water and used the litter tray, and now she's washing the ketling again.'

'She'll be fine,' Gavin said.

He went off to have his lunch, and I finished my sandwich and fetched an apple as pudding, then joined Cat on the bed. I'd just opened Hornblower when my phone rang. I grabbed it. 'Cass, hello?'

'Hello, Cass,' a vaguely familiar voice said. 'It's Peter here, from the *Swan* Trust. I'm sorry it's taken a while to get back to you. We had several very able candidates, and it was a job to decide between them.' My heart plummeted. As I'd thought, I hadn't got it. 'As you'd probably expected,' Peter went on, 'the skipper's post went to Kathleen, our current mate, but we're delighted to offer you the mate's post.'

For a moment I couldn't breathe. Although I'd hoped for it,

315

tried for it, suddenly it was too soon, and I had a panicky impulse to say I'd changed my mind. *Sørlandet*'s white sails and the wide ocean wavered across my eyes. I closed my eyes and steadied my breathing. If I wanted Gavin, if I wanted this peaceful life with the hills green around me and the cats at my feet, I needed to do this.

'Thank you,' I said. 'I'm delighted to accept.'

In the basket, the Kitten and little kitten purred.

Acknowledgements

Thank you to Steven Wilson for coming up with the idea of a regulating order to annoy other fishermen, and Robbie Anderson for explaining more about it.

Thank you to my flute teachers, Neil Morris, Linda Peterson and Pauleen Wiseman, for getting me to the stage of playing harder tunes badly . . . and to the Aywick Charity Shop, for the wooden flute. Life in Yell moves so fast an author can't keep up; the shop has now moved from Mary's to the Gutcher Ferry Terminal (the former Wind Dog Café), opening hours Thursday and Saturday afternoons, and as far as I could tell by pressing my nose against the window, the stock looks just as interesting.

Thank you to Angus Johnston of Shetland Archives, who helped me track down the various skeletons buried in and around Windhouse, particularly the 'tall man' found in 1887, and to Jill Blackadder, who told me the story of Tammy Willie from Cullivoe, who dug up the skeleton of a seven-foot-tall man with horns − I'm not sure if this is an echo of the Windhouse story, so I put the two together.

I had a lot of fun visiting Yell to check my memories of all the places Cass gets to in this visit. Thank you to Vaila and Roger Randle for a lovely catch-up, and for the scones, which kept me going all day. I have one apology to Yell folk: on the mainland here the church/manse/kirkyard combination is usual, and so I wrote my opening, with Lizbet's gran's gran seeing the Book o' the Black Arts being buried, before I looked at the map and realised that there wasn't any manse overlooking the kirkyard at Cullivoe, or, indeed, anywhere in Yell, as far as I can see. I was too pleased with the opening to waste it . . . but as far as I can find out, the main manse in Yell was Lusseter House, in Mid Yell, far too far from the kirkyard for strange goings-on at night to be seen even with a spyglass.

The ketling birth scene is based on experience; none of my female cats would ever have dreamed of having kittens without me there. The original of the Kitten insisted on having her sole kitten in the laundry basket, just as described, and my dear, supportive husband Philip insisted on moving the basket to his side of the bed so that he could check the baby's breathing in the night.

Thank you, as always, to my wonderful agent, Teresa Chris, whose support and advice is always much appreciated; thank you to the amazing team at Headline: Celine, Bea, Emily and Toby, who made this a much better book than I'd achieve on my own.

A Note on Shetlan

Shetland has its own very distinctive language, *Shetlan* or *Shetlandic*, which derives from old Norse and old Scots. In *Death on a Shetland Longship*, Magnie's first words to Cass are:

'Cass, well, for the love of mercy. Norroway, at this season? Yea, yea, we'll find you a berth. Where are you?'

Written in west-side Shetlan (each district is slightly different), it would have looked like this:

'Cass, weel, fir da love o mercy. Norroway, at dis saeson? Yea, yea, we'll fin dee a bert. Quaur is du?'

Th becomes a *d* sound in *dis* (this), *da* (the), *dee* and *du* (originally thee and thou, now you), *wh* becomes *qu* (*quaur*, where), the vowel sounds are altered (well to *weel*, season to *saeson*, find to *fin*), the verbs are slightly different (quaur is du?) and the whole looks unintelligible to most folk from outwith Shetland, and *twartree* (a few) within it too.

So, rather than writing in the way my characters would speak, I've tried to catch the rhythm and some of the distinctive usages of Shetlan while keeping it intelligible to *soothmoothers*, or people who've come in by boat through the South Mouth of Bressay Sound into Lerwick, and by extension, anyone living south of Fair Isle.

There are also many Shetlan words that my characters would naturally use, and here, to help you, are *some o dem*. No Shetland person would ever use the Scots *wee*; to them, something small

319

would be *peerie*, or, if it was very small, *peerie mootie*. They'd *caa* sheep in a *park*, that is, herd them up in a field – *moorit* sheep, coloured black, brown, fawn. They'd take a *skiff* (a small rowing boat) out along the *banks* (cliffs) or on the *voe* (sea inlet), with the *tirricks* (Arctic terns) crying above them, and the *selkies* (seals) watching. Hungry folk are *black fanted* (because they've forgotten their *faerdie maet*, the snack that would have kept them going) and upset folk *greet* (cry). An older housewife like Magnie's mother, Jessie, would have her *makkin* (knitting) *belt* buckled around her waist, and her *reestit* (smoke-dried) *mutton* hanging above the Rayburn. And finally . . . my favourite Shetland verb, which I've at last managed to work into this novel: *to kettle*. As in: *Wir cat's just kettled. Four ketlings, twa strippet and twa black and quite.* I'll leave you to work that one out on your own . . . or, of course, you could consult Joanie Graham's *Shetland Dictionary*, if your local bookshop hasn't *just selt* their last copy *dastreen*.

The diminutives Magnie (Magnus), Gibbie (Gilbert) and Charlie may also seem strange to non-Shetland ears. In a traditional country family (I can't speak for *toonie* Lerwick habits) the oldest son would often be called after his father or grandfather, and be distinguished from that father and grandfather and perhaps a cousin or two as well, by his own version of their shared name. Or, of course, by a *Peerie* in front of it, which would stick for life, like the *eart kyent* (well-known) guitarist Peerie Willie Johnson, who recently celebrated his 80th birthday. There was also a patronymic system, which meant that a Peter's four sons, Peter, Andrew, John and Matthew, would all have the surname Peterson, and so would his son Peter's children. Andrew's children, however, would have the surname Anderson, John's would be Johnson, and Matthew's would be Matthewson. The Scots ministers stamped this out in the nineteenth century, but in one district you can have a lot of *folk* with the same surname, and so they're distinguished by their house name: *Magnie o' Strom, Peter o' da Knowe*.

Glossary

For those who like to look up unfamiliar words as they go, here's a glossary of Scots and Shetlan words.

aa: all
an aa: as well
aabody: everybody
aawye: everywhere
ahint: behind
ain: own
amang: among
anyroad: anyway
ashet: large serving dish
auld: old
auld clootie: A Shetland name for the Devil, of Scots origin
aye: always
bairn: child
ball (verb): throw out
banks: sea cliffs, or peatbanks, the slice of moor where peats are cast
bannock: flat triangular scone
birl, birling: paired spinning round in a dance
blinkie: torch
blootered: very drunk
blyde: pleased

boanie: pretty, good looking
breeks: trousers
brigstanes: flagged stones at the door of a crofthouse
bruck: rubbish
caa: round up
canna: can't
clarted: thickly covered
closs: a narrow lane between tenement houses
cludgie: toilet
cowp: capsize
cratur: creature
crofthouse: the long, low traditional house set in its own land
daander: to travel uncertainly or in a leisurely fashion
darrow: a hand fishing line
dastreen: yesterday evening
de-crofted: land that has been taken out of agricultural use, e.g. for a house site
dee: you; *du* is also you, depending on the grammar of the sentence – they're equivalent to thee and thou. Like French, you would only use dee or du to one friend; several people, or an adult if you're a younger person, would be you
denner: midday meal
deuk: duck
deukey-hole: pond for ducks
didna: didn't
dinna: don't
dip dee doon: sit yourself down
dis: this
doesna: doesn't
doon: down
drewie lines: a type of seaweed made of long strands
du kens: you know
dyck, dyke: a wall, generally drystane, i.e. built without cement

eart: direction, *the eart o wind*

eela: fishing, generally these days a competition

ee now: right now

everywye: everywhere

faersome: frightening

faither, usually faider: father

fanted: hungry, often *black fanted,* absolutely starving

folk: people

frae: from

gansey: a knitted jumper

gant: to yawn

geen: gone

gluff: fright

greff: the area in front of a peat bank

gret: cried

guid: good

guid kens: God knows

guizers: People in fancy dress, either for Up Helly Aa or visiting round houses at Halloween or New Year.

hadna: hadn't

hae: have

harled: exterior plaster using small stones

heid: head

hoosie: little house, usually for bairns

howk: to search among: I *howked* ida box o auld claes

isna: isn't

keek: peep at

ken, kent: know, knew

kirk: church

kirkyard: graveyard

kishie: wicker basket carried on the back, supported by a *kishie baand* around the forehead

knowe: hillock

lem: china

Lerook: Lerwick

likit: liked

lintie: skylark

lipper: a cheeky or harum-scarum child, generally affectionate

mad: annoyed

mair: more

makkin belt: a knitting belt with a padded oval, perforated for holding the 'wires' or knitting needles

mam: mum

mareel: sea phosphorescence, caused by plankton, which makes every wave break in a curl of gold sparks

meids: shore features to line up against each other to pinpoint a spot on the water

midder: mother

mind: remember

moorit: coloured brown or black, usually used of sheep

mooritoog: earwig

muckle: big – as in Muckle Roe, the big red island. Vikings were very literal in their names, and almost all Shetland names come from the Norse

muckle biscuit: large water biscuit, for putting cheese on

myrd: a good number and variety – a *myrd* o peerie things

na: no, or more emphatically, *nall*

needna: needn't

Norroway: the old Shetland pronunciation of Norway

o': of

oot: out

ower: over

park: fenced field

peat: brick-like lump of dried peat earth, used as fuel

peerie: small

peerie biscuit: small sweet biscuit

peeriebreeks: affectionate name for a small thing, person or animal

piltick: a sea fish common in Shetland waters

pinnie: apron

postie: postman

quen: when

redding up: tidying

redd up kin: get in touch with family – for example, a five-generations New Zealander might come to meet Shetland cousins still staying in the house his or her forebears had left

reestit mutton: wind-dried shanks of mutton

riggit: dressed, sometimes with the sense dressed up

roadymen: men working on the roads

roog: a pile of peats

rummle: untidy scattering

Santy: Santa Claus

scaddy man's heids: sea urchins

scattald: common grazing land

scuppered: put paid to, done for

selkie: seal, or seal person who came ashore at night, cast his/her skin and became human

Setturday: Saturday

shalder: oystercatcher

sho: she

shoulda: should have

shouldna: shouldn't have

SIBC: Shetland Islands Broadcasting Company, the independent radio station

skafe: squint

skerry: a rock in the sea

smoorikins: kisses

snicked: move a switch that makes a clicking noise

snyirked: made a squeaking or rattling noise

solan: gannet

somewye: somewhere

sooking up: sucking up
soothified: behaving like someone from outwith Shetland
spew: be sick
spewings: piles of sick
splatched: walked in a splashy way with wet feet, or in water
steekit mist: thick mist
sun-gaits: with the sun – it's bad luck to go against the sun, particularly walking around a church
swack: smart, fine
swee: to sting (of injury)
tak: take
tatties: potatoes
tay: tea, or meal eaten in the evening
tink: think
tirricks: Arctic terns
trows: trolls
tushker: L-shaped spade for cutting peat
twa: two
twartree: a small number, several
tulley: pocket knife
unken: unknown
vee-lined: lined with wood planking
vexed: sorry or sympathetic – 'I was that vexed to hear that.'
voe: sea inlet
voehead: the landwards end of a sea inlet
waander: wander
waar: seaweed
wasna: wasn't
wha's: who is
whatna: what
whit: what
whitteret: weasel
wi: with
wife: woman, not necessarily married

wir: we've – in Shetlan grammar, *we are* is sometimes *we have*
wir: our
wouldna: would not
yaird: enclosed area around or near the crofthouse
yoal: a traditional clinker-built six-oared rowing boat